LET THE CHIPS FALL
WHERE THEY MAY

COURTNEY BEEMAN

BUILT TO LAST PUBLISHING LLC

Paisley

"I really didn't want it to go this way." I said to him. "This is all yo fault. All you had to do was keep buyin' me what I wanted then I wouldnt have to take this from you."

I held the gun to Jermaine's head. "Put all the money in the bag. Now!" I yelled at him.

"Paisley, you dont need the gun." Jermaine whined. "You can have all the money. I'm not gon' do anything to you."

He started shaking. I had been dating Jermaine for about a month or so. He was so gorgeous. But once he started buyin' me stuff, he just wanted to control me. He wanted to know my every move. And demanded that I stop workin' at the strip club. The same strip club we met at. He knew the kind of life I led. I don't know what made him think it was gon change just 'cuz we was hangin' out.

I had to get away from him. And I needed his money to do it. Once I didn't want to do what he told me to, he tried to cut me off. Wouldn't buy me anything anymore. The nigga barely kept food in the house when I came over.

"Shut up." I yelled. "Just put it in the bag so I can get the hell outta here."

"Why are you doin' this?" He whined as he started to put the money in the bag. "I thought we had somethin', Paisley."

1

"Jermaine, I gotta do what I gotta do." I said. "You just holdin' me back. Now hurry up." I snapped.

He slowed down putting the money in the bag and tried to jump up and take the gun out of my hand. I slapped him in the face with the gun. This nigga was trippin'. All he had to do was give me the money and I wouldn't'a had to slap his ass. He fell on the floor. I put the rest of the money in the bag and ran out of the house.

Nicholas

I was startin' my sophomore year off right. Moved off campus. Ended freshman year with a 3.7 GPA. Football season and basketball season both went good. Still hadn't figured out what to major in but I was leaning more towards business than anything. I knew I had a lot of options, but I really just wanted to narrow it down to the main thing I was interested in. I was good at operatin' me and Malcolm's business back at home, so I thought I could do somethin' with those skills, legally.

"What's goin' on busy woman?" I asked Jada as I answered her Face Time call.

"Hey you." She smiled. "What you up to?"

"Nothin' straightenin' up before Cassidy get here." I said. "You finally got a minute, huh?"

"Ha." She laughed. "Shut up. It's just been so much goin' on here."

"I know what you mean." I said. "I'm surprised I'm getting some time to myself right now. But I am glad to see you. It's been too long."

"I'm sorry." She said. "I promise I'll make it up to you."

"Only way you gon' do that is by comin' to our homecoming." I said.

"Are you comin' to mine?" She asked.

"I told you we gotta game that day." I said. "I can't make that happen. But if you don't gotta game the day of ours I really want you to come."

"I do too." She said. "Laya been beggin' me."

"Hold on, I ain't beggin'." I said. "This really ain't a request, either."

"So, you makin' demands now?" She laughed.

"Call it what you want." I said. "Just get yo ass here for homecomin'. You already missed the first game."

"And you missed mine." She said. "I gotta competition next weekend out there. I would appreciate it if you could make it."

"Gotta game Saturday." I said. "What day is it?"

"Sunday." She said.

"Aw yea I'll be there." I smiled. "Malcolm and Laya goin'?"

"Yep." She smiled.

"Cool." I said.

"And Cassidy is invited too." She smiled. "Is she there yet? I'ma tell her myself."

"Naw she ain't here yet." I said. "But I think she got somethin' to do next Sunday so I don't know if she gon' make it."

"Em hum." She smirked. "So how yo classes goin' so far?"

"Not too bad." I said. "Nothin' I can't handle. Your's still too easy?"

"Yes." She whined. "I registered for some stuff I thought was gon' be challenging and I was so wrong. I don't know what I'm supposed to do."

"Shoulda just came here with us." I said.

"Shut up." She said. "It's really a good school though. I don't know why everything just seem so easy to me."

"Cuz that ain't where you need to be." I said.

"Yea whatever." She said. "I'm getting ready to pull up at the house. I think Carter home. So, I'll probably talk to you tomorrow."

"Am I callin' you, or you callin' me?" I asked. "I ain't tryna get you in trouble." I laughed.

"Boy shut up." She laughed. "Just call me after practice. I should be done around the same time as you."

"Yea alright." I laughed.

"Good night, Nicholas." She smiled and blew me a kiss.

"Night beautiful." I said before I hung up.

As soon as I put my phone on the charger Cassidy walked in.

"You kinda late." I said to her as she came in with an attitude.

"Didn't wana interrupt yo phone date with Ms. Jada." Cassidy snapped.

"What?" I asked. "You was out there listenin'? Why you ain't just come in?"

"Seemed like you was in the middle of somethin'." She said.

"You know I talk to Jada everyday on Face Time." I said. "We agreed to that with her goin' to a different school."

"Why is it so important for you to see yo ex girlfriend everyday?" She asked.

"She my best friend." I said. "I don't know why you actin' like you ain't know that."

"Sometimes it's just overwhelming, Nicholas." She said. "It's a lot to deal with. You don't see me keepin' in touch with my 'ex.'"

"Y'all had a different situation." I said.

"Not really." She said. "We had drama, and y'all had drama. Both our situations got violent."

"Where are you goin' with this?" I asked. "What's the problem?"

"I just don't know if I'm okay with this anymore." She said.

"Okay with what?" I asked. "Me bein' friends with Jada? Cuz that ain't gon' change."

"Well I guess I just gotta get over it then." She said.

"Baby, it ain't nothin' goin' on between me and Jada." I said. "You don't have nothin' to worry about. You trust me, don't you?"

"I guess." She cracked a smile.

"What you mean you guess?" I laughed at her.

"Alright I do." She said. "Don't have me out here lookin' stupid, Nicholas."

"Baby you look amazing." I smiled at her.

She laughed at me and rolled her eyes.

Lisa (Trevor's Mother)

"Got some mail today, Joe." I said to Joseph as he walked in the house. I handed him the envelopes and went into the kitchen.

"What the hell?" Joe yelled.

I walked back into the living room to see him reading a letter, lookin' like he was ready to fight.

"What happened?" I asked him as I walked over to him.

"This girl talkin' bout I owe back child support." He said. "I been givin' her money since that baby was born."

"That baby is your daughter." I corrected him. "Stop talkin' about her like she ain't yours."

"I didn't mean it like that." He said. "You know I been givin' her money every month. And what she need extra money now for anyway? She way over 18. Why do I still have to support her?"

"Somethin' ain't right about this." I said. "First she tell you she don't want nothin' to do with you. Then ask you for money. You give her money every month since she was born, and now she want more money. Somebody havin' some financial issues or somethin'."

"I gotta fight this." He said. "It's no way I'm gon' pay all this money when I been givin' her money for 21 years."

"That's exactly why I told you to keep receipts of when you gave her money." I said.

"What was I supposed to do?" He asked. "Write up a receipt for our own version of child support?"

"You should have." I said. "For times like these. Now you have no proof that you've been contributing."

"I had the money transferred from my account to hers every first of the month." He said. "It's in my bank statements and I know it's in hers."

"That might work." I said. "But first, we need to get a lawyer. Cuz this ain't goin' away easily."

"I can't believe this shit." He said as he sat on the couch.

"You can't stress about it." I said tryin' to comfort him. "We gon' get it all figured out."

"You really gon' help me with this?" He asked as he looked up at me. "You know I ain't mean to put you in this situation."

"I know." I said as I sat down next to him. "We got past that years ago, Joe. I'm not mad anymore. These are just the repercussions we gotta deal with. I mean I know it's from yo problems, but if I chose to stay with you after that mess, then I gotta deal with it too."

"Thank you, baby." He kissed me.

"You welcome." I said as I lay my head on his chest.

Laya

"So, what's been goin' on there?" Jada asked me as I talked to her on the phone.

"Not much." I said. "Just cheering and school for right now."

"Did you find out about that internship you applied for?" She asked.

"Not yet." I said. "I should know somethin' in the next month. So, are you comin' for the weekend, or just the competition Sunday?"

"I mean I could come for the weekend." She said. "But I don't have nowhere to stay."

"Girl shut up you know you can stay at my place." I said.

"Yea but I don't wana make Malcolm uncomfortable." She said.

"Uncomfortable with what?" I asked. "We all friends. Come Friday and you stayin' with me. I don't care what you got to say about it."

"Are you sure, Laya?" She asked. "I can just catch up with y'all Sunday after the competition."

"Yes, I'm sure." I said. "What you fightin' for? Is it somethin' you ain't tellin' me?"

"No." She said. "I don't know. I just don't wana be feelin' weird around everybody."

"You mean Nicholas and Cassidy." I corrected her. "It ain't nothin' for you to worry about. She goin' home this weekend anyway. So, it's just gon' be the four of us. Like the good ol' days."

"Oooh." She laughed. "And what is that supposed to mean?"

"Nothin'." I laughed. "I love Cassidy for real. But lately she just been real whiny about Nicholas talkin' to you on Face Time. She's really bothered by it."

"He told you that?" She asked.

"No, she did." I said. "Every time they have an issue, she come to me. And it's always about you."

"What?" She asked. "I didn't know it was a big issue. She was cool with us bein' friends in high school."

"That's 'cuz she thought she knew what was goin' on." I said.

"She do know." She said. "It ain't nothin'. We just really good friends. That's it. Why is that so hard for everybody to believe?"

"I'm not the one you need to convince." I said. "I already know y'all in love. Now what I don't know is why y'all still doin' this lil' silly dance. What is the hold up?"

"Laya, you know I'm engaged." She laughed.

"To the wrong guy." I said. "I mean don't get me wrong, Carter is great and all, but he ain't Nicholas. You posed to be with Nicholas and you know it."

"Is that right?" She laughed.

"You know what? I'm tired of you not takin' me seriously. I'm for real Jada." I said.

"I hear you crybaby." She said. "Let's just talk about this later. Carter just pulled up and I ain't tryna have him listenin' to my conversation."

"Alright." I said. "Make sure you call me back. Tonight."

"I will girl." She said. "Bye." We both hung up.

Nina

I was layin' on the couch in the living room when Music Note came in from outside.

"Hey girl." Music Note said to me as she kissed my cheek. She sat down at the end of the couch. "What you watchin'?"

"Nothin'." I laughed at her. "Tryna see what's on TV. Where you comin' from?"

"Across the street at Kelly's house." She said. "I told you I was goin' over there after school."

"What you mean you told me?" I asked her.

"I asked Daddy when he dropped me off this mornin'." She said. "He ain't tell you?"

"He did." I said. "What y'all was doin'?"

"Nothin'." She said. "I was tryna teach her how to braid."

"Who taught you how to braid?" I asked her.

"Myself." She said. "I told you I could braid. I don't know why nobody believe me."

"I ain't seen you braid nobody hair." I laughed at her.

"Just to show y'all I'ma do my own hair tonight before I go to bed." She said.

"Ha." I laughed. "Okay. I would love to see this. Do me a favor and go get those pills off my nightstand for me."

"What's wrong?" She asked.

"Nothin'." I said as I started to cough. "I just need to take my medicine."

11

"You never told me what the medicine was for." She said. "Are you sick?"

"I'm fine baby." I said. "I just need to take a pill."

"Alright." She said.

She got up and went to my room. A few minutes later she came back and handed me the pill bottle. I picked up my towel and wiped my mouth.

"Mommy why are you coughin' up blood?" She asked me as I wiped my mouth.

"I'm not." I said. "I just bit my tongue."

"You sure?" She asked as she looked at me suspiciously.

"Yes." I tried to laugh it off. "Pour me some water so I can take this and get a nap in before yo dad get home."

"I'm callin' daddy'." She said as she got up.

She went in the kitchen and brought me back a cup of water. She took the house phone and went in her room. The last thing I needed was her tellin' Trevor about this. All he was gon' do was make me go back to the hospital and that was out of the question. If I could just get some rest, I knew I would be fine.

Jada

I was at the airport waiting on my ride. Laya was always late so I ain't know when she was gon' show up. Nicholas said he was gon ride to the airport with her and Malcolm to pick me up but I ain't know if he was able to. As I walked outside the airport I saw bumblebee pull up.

"Oh my God I can't believe you came." I yelled to Nicholas as I hugged him. I didn't realize how much I missed him until I saw him again.
"Told you I would." He laughed and kissed me on my cheek.
"You look so good." I smiled at him as I held my arms around his neck.
"Thanks." He smiled. "But you look better."
"Aw thanks." I couldn't believe I was blushin'.

Nicholas got more and more handsome by the day. It was crazy for me to be away from him this long. I was so glad to be back around him.

"Come on let's go meet Malcolm and Laya." He said as he grabbed my hand and led me to the car.
"What happened to her pickin' me up?" I asked him.
"I don't know." He said. "I think she just wanted to set us up."
"That girl is crazy. So, what's the plan for tonight?" I asked. "Why Cassidy ain't come?"
"She went home this weekend." He said. "Where you stayin'?"
"With Laya and Malcolm." I said to him as he put my bag in his trunk.

"I think you'll have more fun stayin' with me." He smiled at me as we got in the car.

"What?" I laughed at him. "You really trippin'. You know I ain't stayin' at yo house. In Cassidy's bed."

"First off, it's my house." He said. "And my bed. She went home for the weekend. I don't see what the problem is."

"Alright." I laughed at him. "If Cassidy agree to it, then I'll do it."

"What do she have to agree with?" I asked. "She don't pay none of my bills. I say who stay there and who don't."

"Nicholas I'm stayin' with Laya." I said. "I don't think Carter would be comfortable with that."

"Oh, so that's what the real problem is." He said. "Yo man ain't cool with it."

"Would you be if it was you?" I asked him.

"We ain't talkin' bout me." He corrected me. "Just think about it. We getting ready to go get somethin' to eat and probably go to a party tonight. By time we get back in it's gon' be late. With no time for nothin' else but sleep. You can have the bed and I'll take the couch."

"That ain't even necessary." I smiled at him. "We'll talk about it later." I grabbed his right hand as he held the wheel with his left one.

"Don't think I'ma forget about it." He looked at me.

"Shut up." I couldn't stop laughin' at him.

Jamal

My lil' June Bug had just turned 2. He was getting so big. Walkin' and runnin' all over the place. Talkin' non-stop. I couldn't believe how fast he was growin' up. Seemed like a grown man to me. I was headed home to see what he was up to when I got a call from an unknown number.

"Hello." I answered.

"Hi is this Jamal?" A woman asked.

"Yea." I said. "And this is?"

"My name is Valerie." She said. "I was actually tryin' to get in touch with your father. Is he around?"

"No, he's not." I said. "Can I give him a message?"

"Just tell him that Valerie Tucker needs to get in touch with him as soon as possible." She said.

"What is this about?" I asked. "Maybe it's somethin' I can help you with."

"Oh no it's a personal matter." She said. "Just do me a favor and pass on the message sooner than later."

"Alright I will." I said before I hung up.

For a minute I thought about what this woman could want with my dad. I mean it coulda just been a simple bill collector, but I felt like she woulda said somethin' about a debt. I wasn't bouta keep guessin' so I just called my dad.

"What's up, man." My dad said as he answered my call.

"What you up to old man?" I asked him.

"Nothin' much just sittin' here talkin' to yo mama." He said. "What's goin' on? Where my grandson at?"

"He at the house I'm headed there now." I said. "Dad you know somebody named Valerie Tucker?"

The phone went silent. For a minute, I felt like he didn't hear me ask him anything.

"Did you hear me?" I asked him to make sure he heard me.

"Yea I'm just tryna think if I know that name." He said.

What? Was he serious? Either he knew her or he didn't. From all the hesitation, I assumed he did know her, but he didn't want me to know that he knew her.

"Um I don't think I know anybody with that name, son." He said after another awkward pause.

"You sure?" I asked. "It took you a long time to answer. Seem like if you didn't know her, you woulda said that as soon as I asked."

"I just told you I don't know a Valerie, Jamal." He said.

"Well she called me lookin' for you." I said.

"Really?" He asked. "Did she say what she wanted?"

"Why it matter if you don't know her?" I asked.

"It don't matter." He said. "I just thought I could figure out where I knew her from if she gave a reason for why she called."

"Naw no reason." I said. "She just said for you to call her as soon as possible. And she seemed really persistent about it. Told me to get the message to you sooner than later."

"Oh okay." He said.

"Dad." I said.

"Huh?" He asked.

"Who is she?" I asked him.

"Jamal, I don't know who this woman is." He lied. "Probably just a bill collector or somethin'."

"She didn't say anything about a company she was with." I said.

"Well I really don't know what to tell you." He said. "But thanks for lettin' me know. Stop worryin' about me so much."

"I ain't worried I just don't want you to be lyin' to me." I said. "You want us to be honest with you, you gotta do the same thing."

"I am, Jamal." He said. "Look, just go home and take care of my grandson. I'll call you back later on."

"Alright." I said. "Bye dad."

"Bye Jamal." He said before we both hung up.

He was hidin' somethin'. I didn't know if I had the patience to find out what it was. This time, I felt like I should just sit back and let it come out on its own. I ain't feel like doin' no extra work tryna catch him up in a lie.

17

My dad was squeaky clean. Or at least that's what he made us believe. Anything he ever did wrong, we would never know about.

Guess he felt like if he made any mistake, we wouldn't look up to him. Honestly, we admired him. And we still would've admired him, in spite of his mistakes. He just never gave us the chance too.

Nicholas

"So, did you enjoy yourself tonight?" I asked Jada as we left the club.

"I did." She smiled.

"You decide where you gon' stay?" I smiled at her.

"Yes." She laughed. "Nicholas, I gotta stay with Laya. I just can't do that to Cassidy. We are kinda friends."

"What?" I asked. "You ain't doin' nothin' to her. You know ain't nothin' gon' happen. You engaged and I'm with somebody. I just missed you. I ain't tryna spend another minute without you while I got you here. That's it. I swear."

"You mean it?" She smiled at me.

"I'm for real." I gave her the serious look.

"And you sleepin' on the couch, right?" She asked.

"If you want me too." I smiled.

"Don't play with me." She laughed. "I am too drunk for these games."

"Drunk and high." I laughed at her. "Just like I like 'em."

"You terrible." She said as we turned down my street.

"Did you let Laya know you stayin' over here?" I asked.

"Yea I just texted her." She said.

"They probably talkin' shit about us over there." I said.

"I know they are." She said. "Oh well. Anyway, what we doin' tomorrow?"

"You know we gotta game at 7." I said.

"Aw yay I get to see y'all play." She squealed. "And Laya cheerin'. I'm so excited."

"Shut up." I said. "We all gotta be at the field at 5:30. So I'll probably just ride with them and have you drive my car up there."

"Alright that's cool with me." She said as we pulled up to my place. We walked in and I turned on the lights.

"This is actually nice, Nicholas." She said surprised.

"What you mean?" I asked. "You thought it wasn't gon' be?"

"I ain't mean it like that." She laughed. "I just meant you actually cleaned up for me?"

"You know I wasn't gon' have you come on one of my junky days." I laughed as she sat on the couch.

I went back to the room and got an extra blanket out of the closet. I walked back out to the livin' room and sat on the couch. I started to take off my pants and I felt her starin' at me.

"See somethin' you like?" I smiled at her.

"Shut up." She said as she lay back.

"I told you to sleep in the room." I said as I took off my pants and my shirt.

"Huh?" She asked like she didn't hear nothin' I just said.

"Girl I'm bouta go to sleep. Unless you wana stay out here with me." I smiled at her.

"Ha." She laughed. "I dont think so."

She got up and walked back to the bedroom. I followed her. She got in the bed and looked up at me.

"Can I help you?" She yawned.

"I just wanted to say good night." I said as I sat on the bed.

"Good night handsome." She smiled and blew me a kiss.

"Good night gorgeous." I leaned in to kiss her on her forehead but she sat up and kissed my lips.

I knew I shoulda stopped it but I ain't want to. I hadn't been this close to Jada in so long and I missed it. A few minutes of kissin' and touchin' went by. She stopped and stared at me like she wanted to say somethin' but couldn't.

"I'm sorry." She finally said.

"It's cool." I smiled. "Get some sleep." I started to get up.

"Can you stay?" She asked. "I don't wana do nothin'. I just want you to lay with me."

"Alright." I laughed at her and got in the bed. "Go to sleep."

I put my arm around her waist and pulled her close to me. Her body felt so warm. Everything about layin' with her felt right. I ain't never want her to leave.

Paisley

I was workin' the graveyard shift tonight at The Spot. Magic was mad at me cuz I left early a few days ago. I had some other business to tend to and I just couldn't be late. Normally 11 at night to 6 in the morning was cool on the weekend, but not on a Tuesday night. Only the old geezers came in on Tuesday. If they was the old ballers, I could handle that, but not the geezers. They came in with about 50 dollars in they pocket for the whole night. What in the hell did they think I was gon' do with that? I couldn't pay none of my bills with $50.

Not to mention Magic had all the little white girls in here on Tuesday night too. Them girls wasn't no competition for me, but when it came to the geezers, they loved them hoes. I had to pull my best moves to get ten dollars outta them. That shit pissed me off. Any other day of the week I ain't have to work for shit. The money came to me like I was a magnet.

Magic hadn't worked me on a Tuesday in almost a year. I told him that was the only night I wouldnt be available. He hated when we left early from a shift. Said it was unprofessional. How ironic? Professionalism in a strip club? He really tried to run this place like it was a 9-5. I'll give em that. If anything got outta hand he shut it down before any violence broke out. So, in a way, I felt safe at Magic's club. The other places I worked before I damn near had to fend for my life every night. I never thought I could find a place to do the work I do, and still feel protected. Until I came to The Spot.

"Hey Peaches." Jenny said to me as I walked in the locker room. "What you doin' in here tonight?"

"Magic mad at me cuz I left early the other night." I said. Peaches was my stage name.

"I hate when he do shit like that." She said. "This yo only off night and he gon' make you come in."

"You know how he is." I said. "I don't even have the energy to complain this time."

"Aw what's wrong, boo?" She asked.

"Nothin'." I said. "I just got a lot goin' on at home. I'll be alright. Don't worry about me."

"Everything gon' work out for you girl." She said. "Especially when you got fine men comin' in here lookin' for you all the time."

"What?" I asked. "Who came in here lookin' for me?"

"That gorgeous Jermaine." She smiled. "I don't know why you runnin' from him."

"I ain't runnin' from him, Jenny." I said. "But if he come in here again, just tell 'em I don't work here no more."

"I already did." She smiled at me. "I got yo back, girl. You know that."

"Yea I do." I smiled. "Thanks girl."

She walked out of the locker room and went out to get on stage. I sat in the back at my table and stared in the mirror. Sometimes I hated what I saw. I never wanted to work in no strip club. I wanted to own my own jewelry store. I loved jewelry. And I loved designin'. it. That's the only reason I would take money from the guys I slept with.

I wasn't lookin' for no commitment. I just needed somebody to help me get my first store. After that, I would turn it into a huge success. But the guys I dated would never just give me the money without somethin' in return.

Workin at The Spot paid all my bills and more. So, the stolen money was actually all for a good cause. I never let anybody get in the way of what I was out to get. I couldn't waste my time fallin' in love with somebody. Once I let myself get attached to someone, I couldn't hurt them. Which is why I had to keep my walls up with the guys I dated. I didn't date for companionship. I dated for financial growth.

After my shift was over I left the club and headed home. As I got into the elevator I noticed a fine chocolate man walking towards me.

"Can you hold the door, please?" I heard him say as I pushed the close door button.

I was extremely tired and didn't feel like entertaining anyone. Yes, he was fine, but I wasn't in the mood to start a new move. I held the door out of the kindness of my heart. I inhaled his scent as he got on. He smelled delicious.

"Thanks." He smiled at me as I closed the door after he came in. "Early start today?"

"Late end." I corrected him. "What about you? What's got you up so early?"

"Money." He answered. "What else?"

"I know what you mean." I said.

"You look like you had a hell of night." He smiled. "Overnight bag with ya thong hangin' out." He looked at my bag.

"Shut up." I laughed at him. I looked down at my bag to make sure my thong wasn't hangin' out. I knew he was playin' but I just had to double check. "Well have a good day." I said as we got to the 7th floor.

"Wait." He said as I started to get off the elevator. "I didn't get ya name."

"You never asked." I said as I walked away.

When I looked back at him, he smiled at me. I got to my door and he waved as I went in. I laughed to myself. It was too damn easy to control these men. They loved the thrill of the chase.

Nina

"So, I'll email you the files now, Larry." I said as I talked to my boss on the phone.

"Okay, thanks Nina." He said. "Have a good weekend."

"You too." I said before I hung up the phone. I sent him the files he asked for, and then my buzzer went off on my phone.

"Mrs. Johnson, it's someone here to see you." My assistant said over the speaker.

"I'm not expecting anyone." I said. "Do you know who it is?"

"I don't." She said. "She just asked to see you."

"I'll come out there." I said.

I got up from my seat, walked to my door and opened it. As I walked out, the woman waiting at my assistant's desk, looked at me, and left out of the office.

"Did she say what her name was?" I asked her as I walked up to the desk.

"Nope." She said. "Just said she needed to see you."

"Thanks." I said. "Let me know if she comes back again."

I headed across the hall to Trevor's office. He was on a call so I just snuck in quietly.

"Alright thanks." He said. "I look forward to hearin' from you." He ended the call.

"What's up babe?" He asked me as I sat on his desk.

"Did you see that woman that just came to my office?" I asked him.

"Naw I been on this call I ain't even notice you had somebody over there." He said. "What happened?"

"She said she needed to see me." I said. "Wouldn't tell Sherry her name. Then when I came out to see who it was, she saw me and left. I ain't never seen her in my life. But when she saw me, she looked like she was scared of somethin'."

"What you mean?" He asked.

"I don't know she just look like she was runnin' away from somethin'." I said.

"That don't make sense." He said. "Especially if she came to see you."

"I know right." I agreed. "I just feel weird about it now. Like I wana just let it go, but what was that really about?"

"I have no idea, baby." He said.

"You sure you don't know her?" I asked.

"I didn't see her to tell you if I know her or not." He said.

"What the hell that's sposed to mean?" I asked.

"Exactly what I said." He said. "I wasn't payin' attention to who was out there. So, I don't know if I know her or not. Maybe if you find out a name, I could tell you somethin'."

"She didn't give a name." I said.

"Right." He said. "So just leave it alone for now. I'm sure she'll pop back up again sooner than later. Maybe this time she'll stick around to tell you what she's here for."

"But what if she don't come back?" I asked.

"Then it wasn't important." He said.

I left his office without responding. I couldn't shake this weird feelin' I got since that girl ran outta here. I ain't know what was goin' on. I ain't know who she could possibly be. I ain't have no long-lost people that would just pop up in my life. Only connection I could think of was Trevor. I knew someway, somehow, he had somethin' to do with this. Besides the Benjamin situation, every piece of drama had somethin' to do with him.

I loved that man with everything in me, but he sure did have a lot of baggage comin' back to haunt him. And everything in me, told me this woman showed up because of somethin' to do with Trevor. I knew he wasn't involved with her. I trusted him with my life. He would never do that to me. So, what the hell else could it be?

My mind was all over the place tryna answer my own questions. I hated it when he left me to my own assumptions. Most dangerous shit anyone could ever do to me.

Nicholas

"I ain't tryna let you go." I said to Jada as I held her in front of the airport.

The weekend went too fast. I ain't know how I was just gon' let her leave again.

"Nicholas, you know I gotta go back to school." She said as she looked up at me. "Cassidy gon' be back in a lil' bit anyway."

"So." I said. "That don't mean I want you to leave."

"Don't be like that." She said. "We need to make this as simple as possible."

"How you expect me to do that?" I asked. "We been apart too damn long. You know that just as much as I do."

"I know." She agreed. "But what do you want me to do? My whole life is in Florida."

"When did he become yo whole life?" I asked her as I let her go.

"Nicholas, it ain't like that." She said as she pulled me back into her.

"Guess you made yo choice." I said.

"I never said I was choosin'." She said. "We can't do this everytime we see each other. I wana see you as much as possible, but how can I if you make it so hard for me to leave you?"

"What I'm supposed to just not give a fuck?" I asked. "You want me to act like I don't care about not seein' you for who knows how long? Is that how you feel about me?"

"You know that ain't true." She said as she took her phone out of her pocket. Carter was callin' her.

"Ain't you gon' answer that?" I asked as I looked at her phone.

"No." She said as she ignored his phone call. "Look I promise soon as I get home and get a minute to myself I'ma Face Time you. We can talk about whatever you wana talk about, but I just gotta make this flight."

"Alright." I hugged her again. "I love you. Be careful." I kissed her cheek.

"I love you too." She said as she slowly let me go.

I watched her walk into the airport and out of my life. Again. I got back in the car and headed to the house. When I pulled up I noticed Cassidy's car in the parking lot. She wasn't supposed to be back until later. I got out the car and walked into the house.

"Hi baby." Cassidy jumped on me and wrapped her legs around my waist.

"What's up baby?" I smiled at her as I held her. "What you doin' back so early?"

"I wanted to surprise you." She said. "Where you comin' from?"

"Just went to get somethin' to eat." I lied.

"I don't see no food." She said.

"Ate it in the car." I lied again. "So, how was it? You have fun?"

"Yea." She said. "My mom's party was great. I wish you coulda came. Everybody was lookin' for you."

"I know I wanted to come but I couldn't miss the game." I said. "I'm glad you had fun though."

"Me too." She smiled as we sat down on the couch.

"What's for dinner?" I asked as I smiled at her.

"Nicholas, I just walked in the door and you askin' me to cook?" She asked.

"I missed yo cookin'." I smiled.

"That's it?" She asked. "What about me? So, you just usin' me for my cookin'?"

"Naw." I laughed at her. "Girl shut up you know I missed you. I'm just kinda hungry."

"I thought you said you just ate." She said.

"Yea but that was just a lil' burger." I lied. "Ain't really fill me up like yo homecookin' do. I'm in the mood for some fried chicken, fried corn, and mashed potatoes. What you think?"

"That's a lotta work." She said.

"Good thing it's early." I kissed her. "Good time to start so you can get it over with."

"Don't rush me, Nicholas." She said. "So, what you do this weekend?" She looked around.

"Nothin' much." I said. "Went to that party Friday. Game Saturday. And I studied this morning a lil' bit."

"On yo own?" She asked. "Now that's a surprise. You musta really been bored to just study when you ain't have to."

"I was." I lied. "I just been waitin' on you to get back."

She gave me that look like she ain't believe me.

"Now you makin' me think somethin' ain't right." She said. "You tryin' too hard."

"I ain't tryin' nothin'." I said. "Wana watch a movie?" I turned on the TV.

"Now you changin' the subject?" She asked in her high-pitched voice.

"Aw naw what did you do this weekend that I need to know about?"

"Nothin'." I lied again. "Why you keep questionin' me about this weekend?"

"I only asked you once before this." She said. "You actin' real suspicious, Nicholas. But it's cool, 'cuz whatever happened this weekend gon' come out. Sooner than later. Believe that."

"Why are you so crazy?" I laughed at her.

"I'm not." She said. "You keep changin' the subject. I know it's a reason for that too. You actin' nervous. For what?"

"Ain't nobody nervous." I said. "I'm happy to see you. You know I been missin' you."

"Em hum, yea right." She said as she shook her head at me.

I ain't know how to get out of the hole I just dug myself into. I wasn't in the mood to argue with her so I definitely wasn't tellin' her about Jada bein' here this weekend. I decided to keep that information to myself, and make sure that Malcolm and Laya didn't say anything about it either. The only problem there would be makin' sure Jada didn't say anything.

I mean Cassidy and Jada didn't talk on a regular basis. We were all high school friends. So, when we all got together, they did talk to each other. It was no way I could tell Jada to keep that from her. I guess it was gon' come out eventually. Oh well. I'll cross that bridge when I get to it.

Laya

"So, Nicholas texted me sayin' not to say anything to Cassidy about Jada bein' here." I told Malcolm as we drove home from school.

"Ha." He laughed. "I know he told me the same thing."

"I mean did he really think we was gon' tell her." I laughed.

"Naw I think he just wanted to make sure we knew that he ain't want her to know." He laughed again.

"I love Cassidy, but they need to quit playin' around and just get back together." I said.

"What about Carter?" He asked. "I thought you liked him."

"I do." I said. "He is a really great guy. But Jada is meant to be with Nicholas. That's all it is to it. They just fightin' it for some reason."

"Guess they happier with other people." He said.

"You really believe that?" I asked.

"They seem happy." He said. "You always tryna make things go yo way. You can't control other people relationships."

"I'm not babe." I said. "I just want them to get back together and stop wastin' all this time bein' apart. They gon' regret it in the end."

"Shut up." He laughed. "Stop worryin' about them so much. Focus on us."

"What you mean?" I asked. "I'm always focused on us. I can't want my friends to be happy together?"

"I think you just usin' this as somethin' to distract you from what you got goin' on." He said as he looked at me.

"I don't have nothin' goin' on, Malcolm." I said.

"Have you talked to yo uncle?" He asked. "They still ain't heard from yo mama?"

"Nope." I said quietly. "I'm not worried about it. She'll show up eventually. She always does. She just want somebody to look for her and I'm not fallin' for it this time."

"You really believe that?" He asked. "She been gone for 6 months. Even the guy she moved in with ain't seen her. Where would she be?"

"I don't know." I snapped. "I don't know nothin' about where she hang out at. I don't know about the niggas she be with. You askin' the wrong one."

"What you yellin' at me for?" He asked. "I'm just tryna help you out. You seem like you ain't even concerned about her bein' gone."

"I'm not." I said. "Cuz this ain't the first time she disappeared, and I'm sure it won't be the last."

"That's crazy." He said. "I mean I know she done did this a few times before, but you said yoself she ain't never been gone this long. What if somethin' did happen to her? Then what you gon' do?"

"Same thing I been doin'." I said. "Takin' care of myself. Only good thing my mother ever done for me was bring me into this world. That's all I have to be thankful for from her. I don't have the relationship you and yo mom have. You know that. I don't know why you surprised that this ain't botherin' me."

"I'm surprised that you can actually sit here and constantly deny that you worried about her." He said. "Especially to me. I know you, Laya. Ever since you found out you been slackin' on yo school work, late for class, not wantin' to leave the house, entertainin' yoself with other people's problems. It's obvious that somethin' is irritatin' you. You think I don't pay attention to you."

I didn't know how to respond. I knew he paid attention to me, but I didn't think he would notice how different I been feelin'. I knew I was in denial about carin' if my mom was okay or not. But I wasn't gonna admit it. I wasn't ready to. If I did, that meant I actually still cared about her. And if I still cared about her, that meant I wasn't over the shit she did to me.

I had been over her and her bull shit for so long, nothin' she did surprised me. Nothin' she did bothered me. She was no longer my concern. Now I couldn't even get through my daily routine without thinkin' about her. Worrying if she was okay or not. Her disappearance was starting to consume me. And I didn't know how to handle it. I felt like I was drowning in her bull shit.

"I dont wana talk about it anymore, Malcolm." I finally said.

"That's what you on?" He asked.

"Can we just drop it please?" I asked.

"Yea if you can focus on you and not worry about everybody else." He said. "If you can do that, and get back on track with school, then I'll leave it alone. If not, I ain't droppin' shit."

"I do what the hell I wana do." I said. "I ain't bouta let you control me. If I wana help my friends get they shit together, I can do that. I'm grown as hell."

"So, if you wana fuck up yo scholarship, 'cuz you worried about some shit that's outta yo control, I'm supposed to just let you?" He asked. "How I look? I'm yo man, and I'm just gon' let you fuck up yo life?"

"It ain't like that, babe." I said quietly. "I'm not messin' up nothin'. I'ma get it together."

"Just admit that you worried about her and we can go from there." He said. "If you wana look for her, you know I'll help you. But you ain't gon' get nowhere actin' like you dont give a damn when it's obvious that you do."

"Okay." I said. "I am worried."

"You should be." He said. "I'ma make a few calls when we get to the house and see if anybody seen her. We'll take it from there. You just go home and catch up on the work you been missin'."

"All these demands." I laughed at him.

"Stop trippin'." He smiled. "You know I run shit."

"Ha." I had to laugh at him. "Yea okay. Whatever you say Malcolm."

"I know." He laughed.

Sometimes I could not stand this man. But then other times, I couldn't stand bein' without him. He always had my best interest though. So, I knew I couldn't ask for more.

Trevor

"So, what's been goin' on with you man?" I asked Jamal as we walked into the gym.

"Shit." He said. "Just work and June Bug for real."

"I know what you mean." I said. "Me and Nina been at the office like crazy lately. We been getting so many new clients all at once and it's only us two there to really run everything."

"I mean at least that's bringin' y'all more money." He said.

"Right." I said. "I been feelin' bad for Music Note though. We wasn't gone this much with Nicholas. Nina be bringing her to the office as much as she can. But don't no kid wana sit in the office all day long."

"Hell naw." He laughed. "She'll be good. Y'all just gotta make sure she understand what's goin' on."

"I know." I said.

"I forgot to tell you some lady called me lookin' for Dad the other day." He said.

"What?" I asked. "What lady?"

"I don't know." He said. "Said her name was Valerie. You know a Valerie?"

"Naw." I said. "Did he say he knew her?"

"Claim he didn't." He said. "But I know he lyin'."

"How you know?" I asked.

"I just know." He said. "He was actin' weird about it."

"Well what did she say she wanted with him?" I asked.

"She didn't." He said. "Just told me to have him call her asap."

"Did she give you a number to give him?" I asked.

"Nope." He said. "Which means, she know he already got her number. He think we stupid. It's somethin' goin' on. I don't know why they act like we ain't gon' find out."

"They think just 'cuz we ain't at home no more we dont need to know what's goin' on." I said. "I don't know where they got that shit from."

"Me either." He said. "But whatever it is, he need to get his shit together."

"Yea." I said. "That's probably the lady who came to the office."

"What lady?" He asked.

"Some lady came to the office lookin' for Nina." I said. "Then when she came out to see who it was, the lady left."

"What?" He asked. "That dont make no sense."

"Don't none of this shit make sense." I said. "A random lady lookin' for Dad. And another random lady lookin' for Nina. I don't know what's goin' on with all this bull shit."

"You think Mom would tell us?" He asked.

"Hell naw." I said. "I mean if he did her wrong, you would think she would be the first to let us know. But she ain't goin' against him for nothin'."

"Whatever it is, we still need to know." He said. "Whether they want us to or not."

"It ain't that easy." I said. "If the Valerie lady ain't tellin' you what you wana know, I dont know how we gon' find out what's goin' on."

"For right now, all we can really do is sit back and wait for it to all come out." He said. "They can't keep it a secret forever."

Paisley

I was opening my door to go get my mail when I noticed a bouquet of roses on the floor in front of my door. Immediately I smiled. I had no idea who left them, but it was a beautiful much needed surprise. I picked them up and took out the card to read it.

> *Thought you might need somethin' to get your day started off right. Don't know your name but I can't stop thinkin' about you. I really wana see you again.*
> *313-555-1234   Money Makin' Elevator Guy*

I was blushin' so hard my cheeks hurt. He was such a sweet guy. Whoever he was. And I will admit he was handsome. I just wasn't up for another project right now. That's all men had become to me lately. Projects. Another job. And I didn't have the time or patience for that. The Spot kept me workin' around the clock. What in the world would I do with another shift?

I already liked his charm which meant I couldn't hurt him. So, there was no use for him in my life. Unless I detached myself. I thought about it for a while as I walked down to the mailboxes. I took my mail out of my box and headed back to my apartment. As soon as I got back inside, my phone rung.

"Hello." I answered without realizin' who it was.

"Where you been?" He asked. "You ain't been answerin' none of my calls. I done came by yo place too many times for you to not be there."
"I told you before I ain't want shit to do with you." I snapped on him.
"Paisley I'm sorry I lied to you." He said.

I met him 3 years ago at The Spot. He told me he was single. No kids. Living alone. The only part that was somewhat true about that was he had his own place. Last year, after actually opening myself up to this man, I found out he was married with three kids. He had been with his wife for years. They started havin' kids in high school. I felt so stupid for believing all the lies he told me for two whole years.

One day I saw him at the mall with his wife and kids. They really looked happy. Which amazed me because as soon as I confronted him about it that night he said he was so miserable with her.

"I am too." I agreed with him. "But that don't change the facts. Don't you have somewhere you gotta be right now? Some kids you need to pick up or somethin'?"

I could've easily taken advantage of him. Used him for what he had. But once I fell for him that was impossible. I wanted to pull one of my stunts on him after I found out the truth, but I still loved him. I still loved him to this day. But I could never be with him again.

"Stop with the bull shit, Paisley." He said. "I'm out the house now. I filed for divorce. I don't want her. You know I want you."

"It's a little too late for that now." I said. "Had you done that before you lied to me about her, then maybe we could work somethin' out. But you chose not too."

"I know I handled the situation wrong." He said. "But I'm tryna make it right. You gotta give me a chance."

"No, I don't." I said. "I gave you a chance when I let you in. I'm not gon' keep havin' this conversation with you. It's over. Don't call my phone no more." I hung up the phone.

I was so over him callin' me constantly. Every time I got a new number he magically got it. I knew he was comin' to the house I just didn't answer the door. Luckily my car was in the garage so he couldn't see if I was home or not. I had no intentions of ever seeing him again. As far as I was concerned, he was dead to me.

Jada

Carter had been on my ass for a while. Ever since I came back from goin' to visit my friends at Howard, he just seemed like he was always upset. About nothing.

I had just got out of class. I walked outside the building and looked for him. He said he wanted to meet me after class. We rode in his car the days we had class around the same time, but for some reason he wasn't outside when I got out. I waited for ten minutes before I called him.

"Hey." I said as he answered the phone. "Did you forget about me?"
"No." He said.
"Okay so, where are you?" I asked. "I been outta class."
"I'll be there in a minute." He said. "I had somethin' to take care of."
"You coulda said that before we left the house and I woulda just drove my car." I said. "Are you gon' be long, 'cuz I can just go get some work done in the library."
"I ain't gon' be long." He said. "Just stay there. You don't get no service in the library no way."
"So, I'm just supposed to sit out here waitin' for you?" I asked. "You can't even tell me how long you gon' be?"
"Jada, I'm pullin' up now." He said.

I hung up the phone as he pulled up.

I got in the car without even speakin' to him. I ain't know what his problem was, but I really wasn't in the mood to figure it out.

"You ain't got shit to say?" He asked as we left campus.

"Nope." I said quietly.

"What is yo problem?" He asked.

"I don't have one." I said. "Wana tell me what yours is?"

"I'm good." He said. "I don't know why you trippin' about me bein' a few minutes late."

"It ain't even about that." I said. "I told you this mornin' I would drive my own car in case one of us was runnin' late. I'm sure you knew ahead of time you had to do whatever it was that was so important. You coulda just let me know and I wouldn't'a had to wait at all."

"Why you so impatient?" He asked. "Did it really kill you to wait 15 minutes for me to get there?"

"You coulda at least let me know you was gon' be late, Carter." I said. "That's all I'm sayin'. You been really inconsiderate lately."

"Oh, I'm bein' inconsiderate?" He snapped. "I ain't say shit when you conveniently ignored all my Face Time calls when you went to Howard. How ironic is that? You get around yo ex and I can't see you? Got somethin' to say about that?"

"I already told you I ain't have no service when you called." I said. "When I finally found some I called you back but you wanted to be childish and ignore my calls."

"If I ain't answer, I was busy." He said.

"So don't you think it's the same thing for me." I said. "I wouldn't just ignore yo call if I could answer it. You know me better than that."

"I don't know, Jada." He said. "I feel like it's somethin' goin' on with you and Nicholas."

"What?" I asked. "Stop trippin'. You know he my best friend."

"I ain't with that best friend shit." He said. "I think y'all need to stop that shit."

"Stop what?" I asked. "He's always gonna be my best friend. And I'ma always be his. That's one thing that's never gonna change. I told you that when me and you got together and you ain't have a problem with it then."

"It's just getting to be too much now." He said.

"So that's really what it is?" I asked. "Bout time you admitted what the real issue was."

"Yea whatever." He said.

"What exactly is too much for you Carter?" I asked. "I already split up from my friends to be with you. I'm doin' everything I can to show you this where I wana be and you still question my loyalty? What the hell do you want me to do?"

"You know I ain't ask you to come out here." He said. "You made that decision on yo own."

"Fuck that!" I snapped. "You know damn well you influenced this decision. Accept it. It is what it is. I followed my man. I ain't the first woman to do it, and I'm damn sure not the last. That ain't the problem here. I have never made you question me in all these years we been together. Why would you even think it's somethin' goin' on with me and him?"

"Y'all too close." He said. "And I ain't comfortable with it no more. I know you still sneakin' to FaceTime him after I asked you not too."

"What?" I asked. "I didn't agree not to FaceTime him anymore."

"You just decided to do it when I ain't around." He said.

"I'm not sneakin'." I said. "I just ain't wana keep hearin' yo mouth about it. We can make our own decisions. I promised Nicholas when we left that we would FaceTime each other every day. Because of you I sometimes have to break that promise, which is messed up 'cuz he would never do that to me. Regardless of how Cassidy feel about it, he keeps his promises to me."

"And I don't?" He asked as we pulled up at the house.

"I never said that." I said. "But I'm not gon' start bein' a bad friend to him, just because you all of a sudden uncomfortable with a friendship that started way before you even came in the picture. We have way too much history for me to just be a stranger to him."

"Wow." He said surprised. "At least you finally said it."

"Said what?" I asked.

"You not over him." He said.

"Here you go with this shit again." I said as I got out the car. "Carter, get over that shit now. I'm not havin' this conversation again."

He stayed in the car and started it back up.

"Where are you goin'?" I asked him as I walked around to the driver side.

"Out." He said before he pulled off.

This nigga was really trippin'. I don't know what he thought this was, but I wasn't havin' this shit. I went in the house and fixed me somethin' to eat. I thought about callin' or textin' him, but I changed my mind. As soon as I went to lay down he texted me.

Sorry I was trippin' babe. I'll be home soon.

I read the message but didn't reply. I had nothin' to say to him. I rolled over and turned on the TV. As soon as I put my phone on the charger, Nicholas was callin' me on FaceTime. I knew it had to be important 'cuz ever since I told him Carter had a problem with us FaceTiming, he had been waitin' on me to call him.

"Hi." I smiled at him as I answered his call.

"What's up?" He asked. "What you doin' in the bed this early?"

"I'm just tired." I said. "What you up to?"

"Shit just got home from practice." He said. "You ain't have practice today?"

"Naw." I said. "You look tired. You ain't been sleepin'?"

"Not for real." He said. "Cassidy mad about somethin' everyday."

"I'm in the same boat." I said. "Carter just left here with an attitude. Then gon' try to text me and apologize. I ain't tryna hear it. He been trippin' since I got back."

"Cassidy been on the same shit since she been back." I said. "I just be goin' to sleep before she call to say she comin' over. Hopin she don't come if I don't answer."

"Ha." I laughed at him. "Is that workin'?"

"Sometimes it actually do." He laughed. "You can't even get away with that cuz y'all live together."

"I know right." I smiled. "It's cool though. He'll get over it."

"Right." He said. "I know she will too. But she piss me off, sayin' she over somethin' then bring it back up the next time she mad. Clearly she ain't over it if she gotta keep throwin' it in my face."

"Aw naw Carter don't do that." I said. "Once he say he over it, I don't hear it again."

"You lucky." He said. "I wish I had it that easy."

"Ha." I laughed. "Whatever you say. So, how's everything else goin'?"

"Everything good for real." He said. "Grades still lookin' nice. Ball still keepin' me sane. What about you?"

"I'm fine." I said quietly.

"You don't look fine." He said as he looked at me. "You look like you wana talk about somethin'."

"I really don't." I said. "I appreciate your concern though."

"Shut up and tell me what yo problem is girl." He said.

"He just been trippin' about us bein' friends." I said. "And that shit really pissin' me off. We been friends all this time and I don't know what make him think that's bouta change."

"You know I ain't tryna mess y'all shit up." He said.

"I know." I said. "This ain't yo fault. For whatever reason, he got some insecurities all of a sudden. I don't know what it is, but I really don't have the patience for it anymore."

"So, what you sayin'?" He asked. "I know you ain't leavin' that nigga."

"Should I?" I asked. "Am I trippin'? Or should I just let this shit slide."

"If it's the first time he brought it up, I say let it slide." He said. "But if he constantly whinin' about it in the future, then that's up to you whether you wana keep hearin' the same shit or not. Cassidy started that shit a while ago, and that was the only thing I got her to shut up about."

"What did you say to her?" I asked.

"I just told her shit wasn't gon' change." He said. "Told her me and you was always gon' be friends, and that was it. Wasn't shit she could do to change it. When you put it to 'em like they have no control over us bein' friends or not, only thing they can do is accept it, or move on to somebody else. You must be makin' him feel like he can control somethin'. He seem like he just mad he ain't getting his way like he used to."

"But how do I make him accept that he ain't getting his way this time?" I asked.

"'You can't make him do anything." He said. "If he wana stay with you he has to accept it, but if he don't then you let him go. It's that simple. If a nigga can't accept the friends you had before him, then you don't need to be with 'em no way."

"Of course, you would say that." I laughed at him.

53

"I'm for real, Jada." He said. "I felt the same way about Cassidy. But she accepted it. If she didn't, we wouldn't still be together. But either way is cool with me. Had I told her I would stop bein' friends with you, I woulda been lyin' to her. And me and you too cool to be sneakin' around to be friends. I wasn't bouta do that to you, or her."

"You make it sound so easy." I said quietly.

"It is." He said. "If you really know what you want. Maybe you just ain't figured out what that is."

"I know what I want, Nicholas." I said.

"Well this shouldn't be that hard then." He said. "Just tell 'em like I told Cassidy. If it's meant to be, he gon' accept it and drop it. Then you won't even have to worry about this shit no more. But if it ain't, you gotta be prepared for the aftermath. If he decide he don't wana accept it, then you gotta take that. Don't go back on yo word. Stick to what you say. Cuz if you go back on it once, you gon' be doin' that the rest of y'all relationship."

"I know I ain't tryna do that." I said. "I meant what I said when I told him I wasn't givin' you up. He knows that. So now the decision is up to him."

"Exactly." He smiled. "So, you feel better now?"

"A little." I smiled at him. "Thanks Nicholas."

"No problem, baby." He smiled again.

Nina

I was out with Stacey doin' some grocery shoppin' when I saw the woman who popped up at my office. She didn't even notice me but I knew it was her.

"That's her right there." I said to Stacey as I showed her the woman.

"She's cute." Stacey smiled. "Who is she?"

"I don't know." I said. "She ran out of my office before I could even speak to her."

"You wana go over there and ask her?" She asked me.

"Naw let's just wait and see if she come over here." I said. "If she don't then we'll go over there."

"Alright." She said.

"So, what's goin' on with June Bug?" I asked. "Did y'all find him a good preschool yet?"

"Yea Jamal found two we posed to go check out this week." She said.

"I'm so mad they closed the one Music Note went too." I said. "You know I loved that place."

"Me too." She said. "I just knew June Bug was gon' go there."

"Right." I said. "Girl you gon' lose yo mind the first day you take him in there. I was a mess when I took Nicholas."

"Girl you was a mess when you had to let that boy go away to school." She laughed.

"Whatever." I said. "That's my best friend. You know that."

"You terrible." She said. "How yo dad been dealin' with 'em bein gone?"

"Girl my daddy been at every game." I laughed. "He see Nicholas more than I do."

"I can believe that." She laughed. "But that's good for him to have a support system. I'm so proud of him."

"Me too." I smiled. "I was so worried that he wouldn't be able to get away. I just felt like he was gon' get caught up in whatever him and Malcolm was doin'. I'm so glad they got away from here. They ain't need none of that drama."

"I know." She said. "Even though they had some issues, they did what they had to do to get away from here and make everybody proud."

"Em hum." I agreed. "Did you hear about Vanessa? You know she been missin' for a while now."

"Yea I heard." She said. "She ain't never been gone this long though. What you think happened?"

"One of them niggas she be with probably done beat her up so bad she just ran away." I said. "That's what happened last time when she was in the hospital. The same man that put her in the hospital, picked her up from there and took her back home."

"That don't make no sense." She said.

"I know how she feel though." I said. "You just feel like you can't get away from him. And most of the time, you can't unless you get rid of em. I'll never judge anybody for stayin' through that crazy shit. They just put so much fear into you, you don't even wana leave, when you know you should."

"Damn." She said. "I ain't never think about it like that."

"It's hard to imagine it, if you ain't never lived it." I said. "It's one of those things you really can't say what you would do, until you was in that situation."

"That's what make it so hard." She said. "Before you get into it, you say you would never stay with nobody like that, but then when it happen, you don't know what to do. I ain't sayin' never to nothin', 'cuz shit always change once it finally happen to you."

"Damn straight." I said. "I just feel bad for her. She been chasin' niggas her whole life. And Laya missin' out on a relationship with her mother."

"Em hum." She said. "I talked to Michelle the other day. She said she try to be there for her as much as she can. Laya been like a daughter to her for so long, so that's the closest relationship to a mother she probably gon' ever have."

"Right." I agreed. As soon as I started to walk towards the check out, the woman approached me.

"Excuse me." The woman said. "Are you Nina Johnson?"

"Yes I am." I answered. "Are you the woman that came to my office and disappeared?"

"I am." She said.

"What can I help you with?" I asked.

"I just always wanted to meet you." She said. "I've been readin' about you in magazines. About how you helped yo company become number one in the market. All the work you've done with the community. I'm a freelance writer, and I wanted to do a piece on you. I guess when I saw you the other day I got a little nervous. I didn't know how I would react to meeting you, but I guess it was a little overwhelming."

I hesitated before I answered her. I felt like somethin' was a little suspicious about this situation. I didn't believe her. But I decided to play along, just to see where this thing was really goin'.

"Well thank you so much." I faked a smile. "I'm actually super busy around this time though. If I get a few minutes in between my meetings Wednesday, we could probably talk then."

"Thank you so much." She smiled. "That would really help."

"Aw you're welcome." I said. "Why don't you call the office Wednesday morning, and let Sherry know I'm squeezing you in and she'll give you a time to come in."

"Alright." She said.

"What did you say your name was?" I asked.

"Tracy." She said. "Tracy Brown."

"Okay well I'll see you soon Tracy." I smiled as I gave her my card.

"Thanks again, Ms. Johnson." She smiled as she walked away.

"You believe her?" Stacey asked me once Tracy was gone.

"Hell naw." I said. "But I am gon' play along to find out what she really want. I just know it got somethin' to do with Trevor. I don't have nothin' comin' back to haunt me, so it gotta be from him."

"You got a point there." She agreed. "What you think it could be though?"

"I have no idea." I said. "I really can't even think of a reason she would be approaching me. I know he ain't cheated. That's not a question. So what else could she really want from us?"

"That's somethin' y'all need to find out before it's too late." She said. "Y'all dont need no more drama. After all the shit that been thrown yo way, I'm surprised y'all still hangin' in there."

"Girl me too!" I laughed at her as we walked to the check out counter.

Kane

"Tasha, I told you I ain't tryna talk about this no more." I said to her.

"I don't understand how you can just up and leave yo family every night, Kane." She yelled at me.

"I don't leave my family every night." I corrected her. "I moved out so I go back to my place. That's what happen when you move away. I ain't bouta be stayin' over there and confusin' the boys. Shit just ain't workin' for us no more. It ain't been workin' for a while. And you know that."

"That don't mean we can't try to make things work." She said.

"That's what we been doin' this whole time." I said. "And ain't shit changed. Look Tasha, we been together since high school. I love you. I'ma always love you. But I just can't be with you no more."

"Really?" She asked. "After all these years, Kane?"

"See this the shit I be talkin' bout." I snapped. "Here you go with the 'all these years' speech. And I'm done hearin' that."

"Wow." She said quietly as she stared at me. "After everything I've taken from you. The non-stop cheatin'. All the lies. The embarrassment of you havin' a kid with somebody else. You really just gon' walk away from us? From me?"

"I don't have a choice, Tasha." I said. "If I stay, all the bull shit gon' continue. It ain't even about me wantin' to be with other women, 'cuz that ain't it. Only reason I cheated on you is 'cuz you was stressin' me out. If shit was smooth, I wouldn't have to go nowhere else to relieve my stress. I just need to be with somebody, who wana be with me, as much as I wana

61

be with them. You don't wana be with me no more. You just don't wana be lonely. And you too worried about what other people think. You ain't wanted to be here since the first time I cheated. I see that shit in the way you look at me everyday. The way you talk to me. Shit ain't been the same, Tasha. All these years I been waitin' for it to get back right, and it just ain't."

"I can't believe this shit." She said. "*You* leavin' *me* after all the shit I took from you. I shoulda been the one to leave."

"But you didn't." I said. "And maybe that's the reason we can't be how we used to. You just couldn't get over it. Thought you could but it's obvious you been carryin' this shit with you all this time. I can't live the rest of my life like this. I'm sorry for hurtin' you. I really am. I been stayin' here all this time to make up for hurtin' you. But now I gotta get away from this for myself. It's somebody else turn to be with you. Just take this as a situation we can both learn from."

"It ain't shit I need to learn." She snapped. "I stayed by yo side through all the hoes. All the lies. And you gon' tell me I need to learn from this. Get the fuck outta here with that bull shit. Only thing I got from this is to leave the next nigga that cheat on me. Don't stay around and wait for them to leave you."

"Well then you learned somethin'." I said to her. "I gotta get ready for work. I think you should leave."

"Unbelievable." She said quietly.

She got up off my couch and walked out of my apartment slamming the door shut behind her.

Tasha was my high school sweetheart. And yea I was wrong for cheatin' on her. But I wasn't wrong for wantin' to let her go. I had to. The relationship became a job after I started cheatin'. And that was before we even got married. I didn't have to cheat. I just turned to other women when she was getting on my nerves.

I knew it wasn't right, but I ain't know how else to express my frustration. All I knew now was, the next woman I got with, I couldn't do the same thing to her. I wanted it to work with her. Now I knew that cheatin' would only cause me to lose her or destroy her. And neither one, was good for me.

Trevor

"So, what's been goin' on man?" I asked Nicholas. "Ain't heard from you in a while."

"I just talked to you a few days ago, Dad." He said to me over the phone.

"Yea whatever." I said. "Ain't you posed to be at practice?"

"Headed there now." He said. "I was just callin' to check on everybody."

"Well we all doin' good." I said. "You talked to yo sister?"

"Nope." I said. "Every time I try to talk to her she say she gotta do somethin'."

"She just miss you." I said. "Seem like it's getting a lil' harder on her now."

"I know." He said. "Why she just won't talk to me about it? She used to talk to me about everything before I left."

"Yea well she's mad that you left." I said. "I mean she want you to do great things with yo life, but that don't mean she don't want you around. Maybe you could try to squeeze in a weekend trip with her or somethin'. You come here, or she go there. Y'all need to do somethin' to get things back right."

"I wana do somethin'." He said. "But it's just really hard with games every weekend, and practice when it ain't no games. It's damn near impossible for me to get away from here."

"I know what you mean." I said. "It was the same way when I was in school. You just gotta find the time, to make the time. You know she's important to you. Maybe you just need to show her that she still is."

"Yea." He said. "I get what you sayin'. Maybe she can come down to one of the games with Granddad or somethin'."

"That would be good for her." I agreed. "So how everything goin' with Cassidy? She still tryna move in with you?"

"Little by little." He laughed. "I be havin' to tell her to take her stuff home sometimes. That sound really bad, but I just ain't ready to have no female in my space permanently. I just got my own spot. I don't see what's wrong with me livin' by myself for a year."

"It ain't nothin' wrong with it, son." I said. "But you know how women are. They wana be right up under you all the time. Now I don't know why she ain't over that phase since y'all been together so long, but she should be over it soon."

"I think she just wana be around all the time so I can't talk to Jada." He said.

"Now that's crazy." I said. "You can't talk to Jada around her?"

"I mean I can." He said. "But it ain't the same 'cuz Cassidy be all up in my face tryna do stuff to get me off the phone. She just make it impossible for me to have a decent conversation when I'm around her. And don't let me be on Face Time with her. It's really gon' be a problem then."

"So you still do it?" I asked.

"Yea." He said. "I don't get to see Jada everyday like I used to. That's how we get to see each other, so that shouldn't be a problem. I told Cassidy none of that was gon' change just 'cuz she whine about it. So she stopped whinin' about it, now she just try to be around all the time."

"Now I know she ain't trippin' like that." I said. "Cassidy ain't never been like that."

"I know." He agreed. "She really just got bad after she came back from home the last time. It's like she just had a feelin' that somethin' was goin' on here when she was gone."

"Was it?" I asked. "I know Jada was there that weekend."

"Nothin' happened." He said. "We just hung out. With Malcolm and Laya too."

"She stayed with Laya?" I asked.

"She was supposed to." He hesitated.

"But what?" I asked. "What happened?"

"She stayed with me." He said.

"What?" I asked. "Why?"

"Cuz I wanted her too." He said. "What's the problem?"

"Ain't none." I said. "Unless Cassidy and Carter know about it."

"Cassidy don't pay no bills in this house." He said. "She don't need to know everything that go on in it. As far as Carter goes, I ain't concerned about him. That ain't my problem."

"You don't pay no bills in Cassidy dorm room, but you wana know everything that go on there, right." I said.

"Don't nothin' go on there she always over here." He said.

"But what about when she ain't there?" I asked. "You feel like you have the right to know what's goin' on in her room, don't you?"

"Hell yea." He said.

"My point exactly." I said. "You can't have yo ex stay with you for a weekend when yo girlfriend away. I know y'all best friends and all but I'll be damned if yo mama stay with a nigga she call her best friend. I don't care if he sleep on the couch or not. It ain't happenin'. She know better. I'm surprised Jada don't. If she posed to be engaged, she gon' have to act like it."

"It ain't her fault." He said. "I talked her into it. But nothin' happened, Dad. I swear."

"So why you ain't tell Cassidy?" I asked.

"Cuz she don't need to know." He said. "All she gon' do is blow it outta proportion."

"You don't think she should be mad?" I asked him. "You would be mad if she had a guy stayin' in her room."

"That ain't the point." He said.

"So, what is the point, Nicholas?" I asked him. "What's the point in stringin' this girl along, when you know you wana be with Jada?"

"What you getting so mad for?" He tried to change the subject.

"I been here before." I said. "I messed up and cheated on my high school girlfriend. She forgave me. We were supposed to go to school together in Texas but a few days before we planned to leave, she left me and went to school in New York. Eventually I moved on when I came here. But I never stopped wantin' her. I found somebody else. She was the best thing for me. And I messed that up by still wantin' my first. I ain't never seen nobody as hurt as she was when she found out that I still loved Ashley. That I still wanted Ashley. That I was actually still waitin' for Ashley. Until she got engaged. I felt like I had to settle for Carmen. Carmen wasn't havin' it. She left me. And honestly, that was the best thing for the both of us. It was a lesson learned for me, and a way for her to be able to find somebody she deserved. But nobody should go through that. Especially not somebody you say you love."

"I do love her." He said. "And I ain't lettin' her go unless I'm ready to."

"So, you mean to tell me if Jada came to you right now and wanted to get back together, you wouldn't leave Cassidy?"

"That ain't fair." He said.

"Why not?" I asked.

"Cuz you know that wouldn't happen." He said.

"I never thought she would be stayin' with you at yo house so it seem like it's more of a chance for it to happen now than ever before." I said.

"I don't wana get into that." He said. "Cassidy the best thing that ever happened to me since Jada."

"Right." I said. "You still holdin' on, waitin' for her to come back. Nicholas they all go off and move on. In yo situation, she was forced to move on so you may have a better chance of getting her back. But my question is, do you want her back?"

"You know I do, Dad." He said. "But she ain't ready to come back so why can't I keep livin' how I'm livin' until she ready."

"In the long run you gon' end up hurtin' Cassidy." I said. "I know that ain't somethin' you wana do."

"I don't." He said. "But I dont wana lose her either."

"Not before Jada's ready, right?" I asked.

"It ain't even like that." He said. "Dad I'm bouta walk into practice. I'll call you later."

He hung up before I could say anything else. I felt bad for my son bein' in that situation. It was terrible when I was stuck there. Nobody should have to go through that. I wasn't gon stop helpin' him with this either. Whether he wanted to hear it or not, he needed to hear somethin' from somebody who experienced it first hand.

Paisley

"I told you I didn't wana do this." I said to him. "But you just had to chase me. I told you this was no good for you. Why don't men just believe me when I warn them?"

I tied his hands to the rails on the headboard of his bed. The money makin' guy from the elevator just would not stop chasin' me. So, I did what I knew best. Strung him along until I found out how I could get his money. At first, I didn't want to get involved with him. He was so cute and sweet. Overall, a really good guy. But he just wouldn't give up. I had no choice but to make him worth my while.

"This ain't even necessary." Devon screamed.
"Shut up." I yelled at him.

I duck taped his mouth closed. I looked through his pockets and took his wallet and all the cash he had in them. Once I made sure he was securely attached to the bed rails, I went to the freezer and took his stash. It was over $50,000 in there. I took every last one of them.

"Stop." He tried to yell through the tape.

His muffled screams might actually get someone else's attention. I had to knock him out. I took my gun and put the barrel over his mouth.

"You say one thing to anybody, and I'll be back." I said to him before I smacked him in the face with my gun.

I put the money in my duffel bag and ran out of the apartment. With the money I had just gotten from him, I could easily find another place. I wasn't worried about runnin' into him after this, 'cuz I knew he would never talk. They never did. I put just enough fear in the men I attacked so that they would never tell a soul. I had even seen a few of them after the incidents and they walked right past me like we had never even met.

That's exactly how I wanted it to go. It was the only way it should be. With all the money I had collected over the years, I coulda been left The Spot. But then what would I do in my spare time? I was so close to havin' enough money to open up my own jewelery store. Really all I needed was two more hits and I would be set. Then I would tell Magic to kiss my ass and set The Spot on fire. If it wasn't for the few friends I made in there I would send the police his way in second. I couldn't do that to my girls though. I wanted to get them all outta there. The ones that wanted to leave. I would have them all come work for me.

I wanted the money to be as good as the money they made at The Spot. That's the main reason I did so many schemes. I coulda been opened the store, but I needed enough to pay them the amount they deserved. I was almost there. Just two more helpless men would put me over the top.

As I got in my car and drove off, my mom called me. I stared at the phone for a minute. After every stunt I pulled, my mother always called me. It was like she knew I was doin' somethin' wrong. I hesitated to answer, but I finally did.

"Hey ma." I said as I answered her call.

"Hey girl." She said. "What you up to?"

"Not much just out shoppin'." I lied. "What's goin' on with you?"

"Same." She said. "Just got home. So, when you gon' come see me? It's been too long. I feel like you just abandoned me."

"Ma you know that ain't true." I said. "I just been busy workin'."

"Paisley, I told you to quit workin' at that club." She said.

"Ma I'm fine." I said. "It's the best way for me to pay my bills right now."

"What do you mean?" She asked. "You are a smart girl I'm sure you can get a regular job. You just too high maintenance and want all these material things you can't afford."

"Ma I already told you I ain't workin' for nobody else." I snapped. "I'm almost done puttin' away money to open my store."

"You still gotta get a business license to even operate it." She said.

"I know that I'm not dumb." I said. "I got it all figured out. Why can't you just trust that?"

"I just worry about you too much." She said. "Especially when I don't hear from you. Maybe I should come stay out there with you for a while. I would feel so much better."

"Sorry Ma, but that ain't happenin'." I said. "I can take care of myself. Just dont worry about me."

"I can't do that, Paisley." She said.

"Okay well at least try to stop doin' it as much." I said. "You gon' stress yoself out over nothin'. You don't need that kinda stress in yo life. Just be glad that I'm outta yo pockets. And sooner or later, I'll be able to take care of you, like you took care of me."

"I'll try." She said. "Paisley, your father is takin' me to court."

"For what?" I asked confused.

"I tried to get back child support to help me out a little bit." She said.

"So, what's wrong with that?" I asked. "He ain't never helped out before, why can't he do it now?"

"Well, he has been helpin' me out." She said. "Since you were born, he's given me money every month, up until your 21st birthday."

"Are you serious?" I asked. "And you been lyin' to me all this time? How much did he give you a month, Ma?"

"Paisley, that don't even matter." She said. "The fact is that he has bank statements and everything to show the deposits."

"How much?" I yelled.

"So now I may have to go to jail." She said. "I'm goin' to get me a lawyer to get me outta this mess."

"How much money Ma?" I yelled again. "Answer me before I hang up this phone."

"$2,500." She said quietly. "But I swear I never used that money for anything that wasn't for you."

"Are you fuckin' serious?" I snapped. "Why would you have me believe he wasn't helpin' at all all this time."

"Paisley givin' money is not bein' a father." She said.

"But at least he did that much." I said. "You probably kept him from seein' me. Is that what it was? He ain't wana be with you so you kept me from him? How could you do that to me? What about me? Didn't I deserve to know him? How selfish can you be?"

"It was for yo own good." She whined. "He was too unstable. I couldn't rely on him to be in yo life and stay in yo life. I ain't wana take that chance of you getting attached to him for him to leave us."

"He already left you." I yelled. "This had nothin' to do with you. It was about me. Your child. And I shoulda been the one to decide if I wanted him in my life or not. Not you."

"You were a kid. You ain't know no better." She said.

"You gotta be kiddin' me." I said. "This a joke right?"

"No it's not baby." She started to cry.

"You deserve everything you get when you go to court." I said. "Don't expect me to be there. How dare you take this man's hard-earned money all my life, and then try to screw him outta more money as if he never helped in the first place? What kinda woman does that to someone she say she love? You said you loved my father! Why do you want to ruin his life?"

"He ruined mine!" She screamed.

"So now you ain't no better than him." I said quietly. "How it feel? Are you satisfied? Did you get what you were lookin' for?"

"It's not like that, Paisley." She whined. "He hurt me so bad."

"People break up all the time, Ma." I said. "So what y'all wasn't posed to be together. Accept it and move on. At least he helped you pay for whatever I needed. And actually wanted to be in my life. How many deadbeat dads you know do that? I can't believe you have tainted my image of this man. You made me hate him. I hated him! For you! All these years I hated him for what he did to us. Come to find out he *has* been doin' for me."

"I raised you by myself." She yelled.

"That was yo decision." I said before I hung up the phone on her.

I couldn't believe what I had just heard from her. She was out of her mind if she thought I was gon' be involved in helpin' her outta this mess. I couldn't be a part of ruinin' my father's life.

Laya

"We have to go home this weekend." I said to Malcolm as he walked up to me.

"What happened?" He asked as his eyes got big.

"My uncle called." I said quietly. "They think they found my mom."

"She alright?" He asked.

"I don't think so." I said. "They found a body, Malcolm."

"Are you serious?" He asked.

"They want me to ID her." I said. "I can't do that. What if it's her?"

"Damn." He said as he hugged me. "I'm sorry baby. Are they sure it's her?"

"Nobody seen the body." I said. "The police just think they have a match."

"They can't check her and see if it match yo mom stuff?" He asked.

"Guess not." I said. "I don't really wana go, Malcolm. I can't see her like that."

"I know it's gon' be hard, babe." He said. "But you gotta go, or you ain't never gon' know. Let's just hope it ain't her."

"What if it is her?" I asked. "Then what I'm gone do?"

"Babe we gon' get through it." He said. "Whether it's her or not, we gon' come through this like we always do. I know we ain't been in this situation before, but we done came close a few times. You know I'ma help you with whatever you need."

"I know." I said quietly. "I just wish I ain't have to deal with this. I'm goin' through a lot with midterms this week. It's just been so much goin' on. Practice and school. Stressin' 'cuz I don't know where she at."

"I know it's a lot for anybody to deal with all at once." He said. "But ain't nothin' gon' stop you from doin' what you need to do to get yo degree. I'ma make sure of that."

"Thanks baby." I smiled at him. "If it ain't her then what do we do?"

"If it ain't her, it's really nothin' else we can do." He said. "Only thing I can think of is to keep doin' what we been doin'. Waitin' for somebody to find her."

"It just seem like it's somethin' else I should be doin'." I said. "Like sittin' back and waitin' for somebody else to find her ain't enough."

"I don't really know what else to tell you baby." He said. "It ain't like you can just up and leave school to go find her. Ain't no tellin' how long that would take."

"Right." I agreed. "I wish the rest of this semester would speed up so we can go home and look for her."

"Even then we only gon' have a few weeks 'cuz of the games." He said. "Hopefully she'll turn up by then. So, you ain't gotta stress about it no more."

"I just need to keep my mind off this stuff right now." I said. "I got two competitions comin' up and I need to make sure everything go good with them."

"I mean if it helps you to focus on somethin' else, I say do it." He said. "But don't get so caught up in keepin' busy, that you can't accept what's really goin' on."

Nina

I was doin' Music Note's hair when my brother Kane's wife Tasha called me.

"Hello." I answered the phone as I continued to finish Music Note's hair.

"Hey Nina." She said. "You got a minute? Somethin' I need to talk to you about."

"Yea what's up?" I asked her as I gave Music Note the comb and brush and gave her the look to leave the room.

"Have you talked to your brother?" She asked.

"Yea yesterday." I said. "What's the problem?"

"He ain't tell you he moved out?" She asked.

"No." I said. "He ain't say nothin' like that. He told me everything was good with y'all and the boys."

"Well the boys are good but we ain't." She said. "He filed for divorce Nina. I don't know what I'm supposed to do."

"What?" I asked surprised. "Why would he do that?"

"Say he just ain't happy no more." She said. "I can't believe after all these years that I stood by his cheatin' ass, he got the nerve to leave me. What did I do to deserve that?"

"You deserve a man you can trust, Tasha." I said. "We all do. Don't get me wrong, I love my brother. He's a great man. But he's one of those men who dont know how to express himself. Especially not to the person he havin' the problem with. That's somethin' he still ain't learned. Unfortunately, you had to suffer because of that. I'm so sorry."

"It ain't yo fault." She said. "I just wish this was as easy for me as it is for him. He just content with bein' without me."

"I don't think it's like that." I said. "I think he just know that you two together ain't workin' no more. So he just wana move on to somethin' that may work for him."

"You think this about another woman?" She asked. "Nina I'm gon' kill that nigga if he leavin' his family for some hoe."

"That ain't what I'm sayin'." I said. "He may just be happier alone. That's what I meant by that. But you know that won't last for long. We both know he gon' find somebody else. That's somethin' you just gon' have to eventually accept. I'm hopin' he give you the time to get over him before he get involved with someone else, but that's somethin' we all just have to wait and see."

"So, I'm just supposed to give up on my marriage?" She asked.

"You can't force a man to stay somewhere he don't wana be." I said. "And why would you want to keep him when you yourself would rather be with somebody else?"

"Nina, I said that years ago when I was mad at him for bein' with other people." She said.

"That don't mean it wasn't true." I said. "I know you ain't happy with him. Y'all been fakin' it for so long, it was only a matter of time before somebody called it quits. I mean yea it's gon' hurt. If it didn't, I would be worried about you. But just know it's somebody else out there that's gon' treat you how you deserve to be treated, if you let him."

"How am I supposed to trust anyone after this?" She asked.

"Girl I went through the same thing with all my drama." I said. "The only man you gon' trust, is gon' be the man you posed to be with. Because we been so hurt, it won't work until we let go. Not the type of let go that's forced, the one that happen before we even realize it. That man, will be the man for you. The one that can make you let your walls down without even seein' what you doin' for him."

"You make it sound so simple." She said quietly.

"It's not." I said. "Nowhere near simple. But I can only talk about it so easily because I been there. It's gon' take a while. Don't think you can rush into somethin' else quick to make you feel better about all this bull shit. That ain't healthy for you or your kids. Now you gotta make decisions for their best interest, and then yours. I mean it kinda sucks, 'cuz it seem like he just out there enjoyin' life while you stressin', but believe me he feelin' it too. He gotta start all over, just like you do."

"Nina, I don't know about this." She said. "I still feel like I should fight for him."

"You gon' be fightin' alone." I said. "It's worth it if y'all both fightin' to make it work, but not when you the only one makin' the effort. If Kane wanted it to work, he would do that. I think he just past tryin' the same shit that ain't workin'. I mean really, what else can y'all do that y'all haven't done?"

"When you put it like that, it really ain't nothin'." She said. "We did counseling. Separation. Tried to work on the things we hate about each other, and we're still here. Hating each other."

"I know y'all dont hate each other." I said.

"Nina, I hate him." She said. "For makin' me this way. Makin' me want to hold on to a man, that don't want to hold on to me. I was never like this before him. I let niggas go in a second."

"This ain't just no nigga, Tasha." I said. "He been yo man for years. Yo husband. The father of yo kids. Nobody expects you to just get over him. You just have to be open to getting over him. You have to want to get over him. It won't work if you dont want it to."

"Can you please just talk to him for me?" She asked. "He listens to you. Maybe you could get him to come home and try again?"

"I have to be honest with you, Tasha." I said. "I don't think y'all need to keep pushin' this. The more you try to pull him back, the more he gon' pull away. He don't want it anymore, and you beggin' him to come home, is only gon' make him so much more sure that movin' on is what's best for him. I have no problem talkin' to my brother. But I can't ask him to do somethin' that I don't think is best for him."

"I didn't ask you for your opinion, Nina." She snapped. "All I asked for is some help."

"I can't help you with somethin' I don't agree on." I said. "You wouldn't do it either, if it was yo brother. I want the best for him. And because I love you like my sister, I want the best for you. Sadly, y'all ain't what's best for each other anymore. I'm sorry to have to put it to you like that, but that's what it is. Now it's time for you to sign the papers. Don't be bitter and fight him in seein' the kids 'cuz then y'all really gon' hate each other. Kane is a great father. Don't take that from him. The boys should not have to pay for his mistakes."

"I just don't know how I can see him take the boys away from here." She said. "Especially if he move on. How am I supposed to be okay with them living out of two different homes?"

"Well if Kane still at the little condo, I'm sure the boys won't be living there." I laughed. "Y'all should just be able to work out him getting the boys every weekend. Or every other weekend. However, you wana do it. But at least let him work somethin' out. This ain't somethin' you can control. It sound messed up, but this time you gotta give in. Let this thing run it's course. Y'all got so much history that if it's really meant for y'all to get back together, it's gon' happen."

"Ain't shit happenin' over here." She said. "If that nigga wana leave me, let 'em leave. I'm done bein' the only fightin' for this. How is that fair to me?"

"It ain't." I said. "Which is why I think it is best for y'all to split up. I would say just take a break but y'all tried that before and it still ain't fix nothin'. If anything, I think it just made y'all more comfortable with bein' apart."

"It kinda prepared me for life after Kane." She said. "That don't mean this somethin' I don't care about, but I had a glimpse of what the single life would be like."

"And how you feel about it?" I asked.

"I hated it." She said. "You don't know how long it's been since I been single. Things have changed so much from how they used to be when we was growin' up. It's so different. I don't even think I would know how to date now."

"I do agree that a lot of things changed since we was growin' up." I said. "But datin' is one thing that ain't. You still gon' be nervous on the first few. You gon' feel like a little kid again. But the good part about that is fallin' in love all over again. And this time, it won't happen until you know it's right. You gon' be too guarded to think about it, and that's when it's gon' mean somethin'."

"My life just ain't what I thought it would be." She said.

"Girl sometimes that's a good thing." I said. "When I was young I just knew I was gon' grow old with Benjamin if he didn't kill me first. Now look what God did. Sent me the man of my dreams, and I ain't even know it 'til it was damn near too late. I don't want that to happen to you. You don't wana miss out on who you supposed to grow old with, bein' stuck with who you think you supposed to grow old with."

"I can't even think about another man, right now." She said. "All I'm worried about is how I'm supposed to tell my boys? How can I support them on my own?"

"Tasha, you know Kane still gon' help you with the boys." I said. "They still his kids."

"I hope so." She said. "He still do for his daughter so I guess he'll do the same with the boys. Everything seem like it just changed overnight. Even though I knew it was comin'. I just didn't wana accept it. I thought it would eventually fix itself."

"Some things do work themselves out." I agreed. "But others just don't. Just look at it this way. At least you got yo babies. Look at the beautiful outcome of this mess. Even though it ain't last like you wanted it too, look at what he gave you. That's how I used to have to make myself feel better about leavin' Benjamin. You would think after how evil that man was to me I wouldn't feel bad about leavin' him, but for a while I felt terrible. I love my Nicholas to pieces. And I will forever be grateful to him for leavin' me with him. I wouldn't change nothin' 'cuz then I wouldn't have my baby. That's just how you gotta look at these situations."

"That is true." She agreed. "Havin' my boys around is what's gon' get me through this."

"Exactly." I agreed. "Just get you some rest. Take it easy for the next few days. You gon' need some time to come through this, but you will Tasha."

"Thanks girl." She said. "Sorry I snapped on you earlier."

"It's fine." I laughed at her. "I know you ain't mad at me."

"I'm glad you understand." She laughed. "I'ma take a nap and call you later."

"Alright." I said. "Bye girl." Before I hung up.

I felt so bad for Tasha and Kane. Divorce was not an easy route. I ain't wish that on nobody.

Malcolm

"Ma you got somethin' else out there?" I asked my mom as she came in the house with two hands full of grocery bags.

"Yea the whole back seat full." She said as she sat the bags down on the kitchen table.

"Alright." I said before I got up and went outside to get the rest of the bags.

Just as I opened the back door of her car I noticed a car slow down in front of my moms driveway. I turned around as they rolled the passenger window down.

"What's up?" She asked. I smiled when I realized it was Jhene.

"Damn Jhene." I smiled at her. "What you been up to?"

"Just workin'." She said. "How you been?"

"Good." I said. "Home for the weekend from school."

"Yea me too." She said. "I finished my nursing degree a few months ago in Atlanta. I'm workin' out there now."

"Aw shit." I smiled. "Look at you getting shit done early."

"Yea I went right after graduation and through both summers." She said. "I just wanted to hurry up and finish it so I could get a job. And luckily I did soon as I got outta school."

"Yea that's really good." I agreed. "I'm proud of you."

"Aw thanks." She smiled. "How everybody else doin'?"

"Good." I said. "Me, Nicholas and Laya at Howard. Jada went to FAMU with Carter. They supposed to be getting married after she graduate."

"Really?" She smiled. "Aw that's so good. I'm proud of all y'all."

"Thanks." I smiled. "Well it was good seein' you. I gotta get these groceries in the house before my mama come back out here."

She laughed. She seemed like she wanted to say more, but she didn't.

"You look really good, Malcolm." She smiled at me.

"So do you." I replied. She looked amazing.

"How long are you in town?" She asked.

"Just for the weekend." I said. "What about you?"

"Same here." She said. "You free later on for dinner?"

"I'm actually supposed to be meetin' up with Laya." I said. "We been back together for a minute."

"I already knew that was comin'." She laughed. "So how bout lunch tomorrow? Is that cool?"

"Yea that's good." I said.

I gave her my phone for her to put her number in it.

"Call me around 12 and let me know where you wana meet." She said as she started her car back up.

"Alright." I said as she started to pull off.

What in the hell was I thinkin'? It was no way Laya would be cool with me havin' lunch with Jhene. Even though our break up was somewhat smooth, Jhene said a lot of disrespectful shit to Laya after we split up. She was constantly startin' shit. First, I thought it was just her friends, but I found out she was involved too. Maybe I could use this lunch to smooth everything over with that issue. All I knew was that I was gon' have a hard time getting Laya to go for this. I wasn't bouta hide it 'cuz she trusted me so it was no reason for that. So, I needed to tell her. I just hoped she was cool with it 'cuz I really did wana catch up with Jhene. Even though we weren't together, she was still a great person. Somewhere down the line I hoped we could still be friends.

I brought all the bags in the house and sat them down on the table.

"Who was that you was talkin' to?" My mom asked me as I sat down on the couch.

"Jhene." I smiled.

"Why you say it like that?" She asked as she sat next to me.

"I ain't say it no specific way." I laughed at her.

"Em hum." She looked at me. "What y'all was talkin' bout?"

"Nothin' really." I said. "She wanted me to go to dinner with her tonight but I'm getting ready to meet up with Laya in a lil' bit."

"You told her that?" She asked.

"Yea." I laughed. "What you mean? I ain't got shit to hide."

"Then what she say?" She asked.

"Asked me to lunch tomorrow." I said.

"Ooooh..." She said. "You gon' go?"

"Yea." I said. "Why not?"

"You know Laya ain't gon' be cool with that." She said. "Especially after the way that girl was actin' after y'all broke up. It was crazy how she felt the need to harass Laya, when you the one broke up with her. She ain't even do nothin' to you. She wasn't even concerned about you."

"Guess she felt like it was Laya fault that me and her broke up." I said.

"And was it?" She asked.

"No." I said. "Jhene know exactly what she did. That shit done and over with, and I definitely ain't tryna get back into it."

Nina

I was sittin' in my office reading over some paper work when my assistant buzzed me.

"Nina, Ms. Tracy Brown is here to see you." She said.
"Okay you can send her in." I said as I replied.
"Hi Mrs. Johnson." Tracy said as she came in my office and sat down.
"Good to see you again, Tracy." I smiled at her as she made herself comfortable.

She took out a tape recorder and sat it on my desk. Then she took out a notepad and pen and looked up at me.

"So where should we begin?" She asked as she smiled.
"Wherever you want to." I said. "Well first, this is a little different for me. I'm used to doin' all my interviews with my husband, Trevor Johnson. He's vice president of the company. When people want a story from me, they usually want to hear somethin' from him too. Is it okay if I invite him?" I texted him before she could respond.

Come in here quick. She's here.

"Well I think it would be best if I just talked to you alone." She said as Trevor walked into my office.

93

I stood up when he came in.

"Tracy this is my husband, Trevor Johnson." I said to her as Trevor shook her hand.

"Nice to meet you." He said as he sat down in the chair next to her. "So, what brings you in today, Ms. Brown?"

"Oh, I just wanted to know how you guys became so successful?" She asked as she smiled at him.

"Well believe me, it didn't happen overnight." He laughed. "My wife and I both have multiple degrees. We put in a lot of hours and hard work to be where we are today."

"He's right." I agreed with him. "I mean it wasn't easy with two kids, but we did it."

"Aw you have kids?" She smiled at me.

"Yup a 19-year-old in college, and an 11-year-old at home." I smiled as I showed her the picture on my desk.

"They are adorable." She said as she looked at the picture. "So what school is your son at? Your alma matter, Trevor?"

"How do you know what school I went to?" He asked her.

"Just research." She answered quickly.

"He's at Howard." I answered. "Playin' basketball and football."

"Just like his dad, huh?" She asked.

"You sure did a lot of research on my husband, Ms. Brown." I said. "You sure you're not here to interview him instead?"

"Oh no I'm sorry." She said. "I didn't mean to offend you."

"You didn't." I smiled at her. "Should we continue this? Or did you wana pick up another day?"

"Oh no right now's fine with me." She answered. "So, let's start." She took out a recorder and looked up at me as she pressed record. "So, Mrs. Johnson, where did you attend school?"

The rest of the interview was a blur. She asked so many great questions, when she wasn't admiring Trevor and his accomplishments. My intuition was right. It never failed me. I knew this whole scheme had somethin' to do with Trevor.

Two hours later she was leaving the office with so much information. Most of the stuff about me, she had just found out. The stuff about Trevor, she already knew.

"That was crazy." He said to me after Tracy left.

"Was it?" I asked as I looked at him suspiciously.

"What you mean?" He asked me.

"How do you know her, Trevor?" I asked him.

"I don't." He said.

"She seemed to know a lot about you." I said.

"Must be a fan." He smiled.

I threw my pen at his forehead.

"Fan my ass." I said. "What the hell was that?"

"She had some good questions though, babe." He laughed.

"Yea the ones she asked me." I said. "When it came to you, it was like she was catchin' up with an old boyfriend or somethin'."

"I ain't never seen that girl before in my life." He said. "I know it sound crazy, but I haven't."

"Well she definitely done seen you somewhere before." I said.

"You the one invited me into this interview." He laughed again.

"Yea 'cuz we always do interviews together." I said.

"No, you wanted to find out what she was really up to." He said. "Now she got you confused."

"Shut up." I said. "I gotta get to the bottom of this."

"And how you plan on doin' that?" He asked. "She freelance so it ain't like you can go to a company or somethin'."

"You still got the number for that PI you used for Benjamin?" She asked.

"He ain't in the business no more." He said.

"How would you know?" I asked.

"I went to his retirement party." He said.

"So that mean you keep in touch with him right?" I asked.

"No." He said. "It just happened close to the time he helped us out. I think you lookin' for trouble. And you need to stay away from it."

"I just don't trust her." I said. "I already knew her showin' up had somethin' to do with you. All she did was confirm my thoughts. But now I need to know how she knows you."

"Why are you wrapped up in this?" He asked. "I ain't even concerned about it."

"Why ain't you?" I asked. "Somethin' you ain't tellin' me?"

"Not at all." He said. "Look if you want, I'll get in touch with my guys from school and see if they remember her. Is that gon' make you feel better?"

"For right now." I said. "Just give 'em her name and see what happen."

"Babe, ain't nobody rememberin' some random girl by her name." He said.

"So how they gon' know if they know her?" I asked.

"Give me the picture." He said.

"What picture?" I asked.

"I know you snuck and took a picture of her when you seen her at the grocery store." He said.

He knew me too well. He was right.

"Fine." I rolled my eyes and sent the picture to his phone.

"Terrible." He shook his head at me. "You need to go home and get this off yo mind. When you get somethin' in yo head, you just can't let it go. This ain't even nothin' for you to be worried about."

"How do you know that?" I asked. "You don't even know the girl."

"I know you makin' somethin' outta nothin'." He said. "She wants somethin'. Whatever it is will come out sooner than later. Just wait for it."

"It's really that simple for you?" I asked.

"It really is babe." He said. "And it should be for you."

"I wish it was." I said.

"With all the work we got comin' up you shouldn't even have time to worry about this girl." He said. "Come on. Let's go have a drink. When we get back, you get back to work, or I'm takin' you home."

"I think I'ma go home anyway afterward." I said.

"Alright." He said. "Let's go."

He stood up and pulled me up out of my chair. He held my hand and led me out of the office.

Laya

"I'm so glad that wasn't my mom." I said to Malcolm as I fixed dinner.

"Me too babe." He said. "Now we just gotta find out where she at. I'm sure she gon' turn up okay."

"I think so too." I said. "I'm just tired of waitin' honestly."

"You just need to keep busy to keep yo mind off it." He said. "I mean I know that ain't gon' be easy, but you know I'll help you."

"Yea I know." I said. "I talked to your mom. She said she comin' to visit next weekend."

"You told her we had a game?" He asked.

"Yea she said she wana see you play anyway." I said.

"Oh alright." He said. "Why she ain't just tell me?"

"Cuz you don't answer the phone." I said.

"Is that from her or you?" He asked.

"Her." I said. "But I agree 100%."

"Shut up. I always answer yo calls." He said.

"I know but I see you ignore the world all the time." I said. "Unless it's Nicholas or Kelly."

"My mama just talk too much now." He said. "She wasn't like that before but ever since I been gone she just been wantin' to talk to me for hours at a time. About nothin'. I just don't have time for that everyday."

"Damn shame." I laughed.

"It's true and you know it." He said. "We both busy. I done seen you have to trick my mama off the phone a million times."

"Whatever." I said. "All I know is, she miss you. So, her and Kelly comin' to see you."

"They comin' to see you too." He said. "Don't be tryna sneak outta this. You approved this visit, so you gon' be right here when they get here. I ain't takin' no excuses either."

"For real?" I whined. "It ain't my fault you act like you too busy all of a sudden."

"Laya you know I'm busy." He said. "You know that better than anybody else."

"I never said you wasn't." I said. "But I'm just as busy as you are, if not more with the tutoring sessions I give twice a week. So, don't pull that busy bull shit. You know that don't work on me."

"Yea I know." He laughed as he read a text message. His facial expression said he was shocked.

"What's wrong?" I asked as I walked over to him.

"Jhene just texted me." He said.

"Really?" I asked. "What she want?"

"She just said what's up." He said. "It just came outta nowhere though."

"I mean you said when y'all went to lunch she ain't seem like she was over you." I said as I sat next to him.

"I know for a fact she ain't." He said.

"Well she probably tryna see how far she can get." I laughed. "I mean you did go to lunch with her. Maybe that's all she needed to think she still had a chance."

"Is that really how females think?" He laughed.

"Only the desperate ones, baby." I laughed with him.

I loved the fact that we were in a place where we could laugh at these hoes together. And he didn't have these hoes laughin' at me. I trusted Malcolm with everything in me.

When he came to me about goin' to lunch with her, I was skeptical at first. Only because I ain't trust her. I ain't like all the drama she started with me after they broke up. But he assured me that he was goin' to set her straight, so I let him do just that.

Clearly the lunch went smooth if she felt like that was her ticket back into his life. Guess she ain't understand that Malcolm was mine. Forever.

Cassidy

"Hey babe." I kissed Nicholas on his cheek and he came up to me.

"What's up." He said as he smiled at me. "Who was that?"

"Who?" I asked as we walked out of the building.

"Whoever you just hugged." He said.

"Oh, that was Josh." I said. "He just gave me the notes from the class I missed last week."

"You was that excited for some notes?" He asked.

"Naw he said he thought he gave 'em to somebody else." I said. "So when he found them, I was excited. What is yo problem?"

"Nothin'." He said. "Just look like a pretty tight hug."

"Nicholas, I have seen you hug girls a lot tighter than that and ain't said a word." I said.

"That's a lie, you sayin' somethin' now." He said.

"Grow up." I said. "Anyways, what you wana eat? I'm starvin'."

"Changing the subject." He said. "Smart move."

"The conversation was over what else you want me to say about it?" I asked.

"Nothin'." He said. "I'm getting ready to go to the gym."

"I thought we was goin' to get somethin' to eat." I said.

"I ain't really hungry." He said.

"But you will be in about 30 minutes when you drop this petty shit." I said.

"Maybe." He said. "I'll see you later." He walked away.

"Wow." I said to myself as I called Laya.

"Hey girl." She answered the phone.

"Hey what you doin'?" I asked.

"Bouta figure out what I'm eatin'." She said. "You wana come?"

"Yea where you at?" I asked.

"Pullin' up in front of you." She said before she hung up.

"Perfect timin'." I said as I got in her car.

"I know." She smiled as she pulled off. "What's wrong with Nicholas. I just seen him lookin' like he had an attitude."

"Mad 'cuz he seen me huggin' Josh." I said. "Claim it was too tight and I was too excited.

"Girl you know these niggas too damn jealous." She laughed.

"And I'm just supposed to accept that?" I asked. "I done seem him huggin' hoes plenty of times, a lil' too tight and I ain't said shit."

"Now see, that's on you." She said. "If Malcolm doin' somethin' I don't like, I call him out on it. They only do what they can get away with. If you don't stop them, they gon' keep pushin' until you do. I mean you would think they know better. Cuz they don't want us doin' that shit to them. But you have to say somethin', or they gon' keep doin' it. And as far as you huggin' niggas, if you don't want him doin' it, you can't do it either. A lil' friendly church hug ain't shit, but I'm sure that ain't what he saw."

"Laya I ain't even mean nothin' by it." I said.

"I know you didn't." She said. "But you can't let them think you do. If you wana hear his mouth about it, then go right ahead and keep doin' what you wana do. But if not, then you just gotta be a lil' more careful. Not even just 'cuz he may be watchin', but it's so many girls on this campus that want yo man and would do anything to get him. If he didn't see you huggin' Josh, somebody would have. And by the time Nicholas woulda asked you about it, it woulda been more than just a hug."

"If he trust me none of that gossip should matter." I said.

"At first it don't." She said. "But the more he keep hearin' small shit, it will matter. It's gon' add up and make him look bad if he don't do nothin' about it. That ain't nothin' you want. Once a nigga feel like you embarassin' him, it's over. It's hard to come back from that. Especially in college. That lil' shit mighta blew over in high school, but here don't nobody let that shit go. Definitely not these hatin' ass hoes. Don't give them a reason to make him entertain them."

"That's bull shit, Laya." I said.

"If you wana date a college athlete, it's shit you can't do like a normal girl can do with her boyfriend. They may not have to worry about the hoes like we do. I know you ain't tryna nag him. And you don't have to. You just gotta find a way to let him know that shit ain't cool. Don't yell. Don't argue. Tell him to stop that shit, and you gon' stop that shit." She said.

"I can't make him do anything." I said. "He a grown man."

"Yo man." She corrected me. "Just let 'em know, either he stop or you don't. He'll listen if he don't want that shit to happen again. It's gotta be equal. Don't get me wrong we do take a lot more dealin' with them. But we should be treated equally."

"It just seem like Malcolm already know that." I said. "And I gotta fight to get Nicholas to understand that."

"Girl only reason Malcolm know is 'cuz I let him know." She said. "If I don't like it, I tell him then. You can't expect these fools to read yo mind. Just like we can't read theirs. You gotta speak up for yourself. But you just gotta handle it the right way or else he ain't gon' be tryna hear it."

"So how do I get him to stop talkin' to Jada?" I asked.

"Now that's a different story." She said.

"Is it possible?" I asked.

"Unfortunately, no." She said. "Not unless he want to."

"What is it about her?" I asked.

"She was his first love, Cassidy." She said. "You gotta understand that. I mean yea they had a crazy relationship, but they're friendship is amazing. I wouldn't give that up either. For nobody."

"So how am I supposed to be okay with that?" I asked. "He already got two other women in his life."

"But he's here sharing his life with you." She said. "Be grateful for that. He wanted you here with him. That should mean somethin' to you."

"It does, but." I stopped.

"But what?" She asked. "Nicholas loves you. And he still loves Jada. But look at where he's at. That should answer all of yo questions."

"Sometimes it do." I said. "Sometimes it just causes more questions. I just don't understand why they gotta see each other everyday."

"They don't." She said. "They a million miles apart."

"FaceTime everyday, Laya." I looked at her.

"Girl that ain't shit." She said. "You gotta stop trippin' about the little shit. He ain't hurtin' nobody. If you trust him, you gotta show him that. Stop tryna be in his face all the time so he can't talk to her."

"He noticed that?" I asked surprised.

"We all noticed it, Cassidy." She said. "All it do is piss him off and make you look bad. What's up with you? You wasn't like this in high school."

"I just thought with him bein' here, and her bein' there, I could have him to myself." I said. "I'm selfish, I shouldn't have to share my man."

"You're not sharing him, Cassidy." She said. "Just let him have 30 minutes a day with his best friend. Is that too much to ask? If you think about it, it really ain't. I mean I know we all busy throughout the day, but the little time he do get alone, he always spendin' it with you."

"If he ain't FaceTimin her." I corrected her.

"Come on now you bein' childish." She said. "At least he do it when you busy so it don't take away from y'all time. Give him some credit. He really tryna make shit work with y'all, and all you doin' is whinin' about the shit he don't do, or the shit you don't like that he do. What about the good shit? Despite all this petty shit, y'all got a good ass relationship. Why you dwelling on the few things you could do without? You can't let that destroy the relationship. He's a great guy. And if you don't stop makin' him feel like he ain't, he will be right back with Jada. Is that what you want?"

"Hell naw." I said.

"Okay then." She said. "You know what you gotta do. Now what you want to eat?"

I had to laugh at her. Laya was the only person who could get me together and then go right back to food. I loved her for that. Even though I met her through Nicholas in high school, she had become like a sister to me in college. It was amazing how far our friendship had come.

Lisa

I had just got home from the grocery store when the phone rung. It was Trevor.

"Hey baby." I answered the phone.

"Hey ma." He said. "What you up to?"

"Not much just got back from the grocery store." She said. "What you doin'?

"Finna pull up." I said. "Open the door."

"What?" I asked as I walked to the door.

I opened it and there he was in my driveway. He got out the driver side and then the passenger door opened and Jamal got out. Jamal went to the back seat and pulled June Bug out of his car seat. They walked up to the porch and my mouth dropped.

"What are y'all doin' here?" I asked as I hugged them.

"Wanted to surprise you." Jamal said as he handed me June Bug.

"Aw don't wake 'em up." I smiled as I rocked June Bug. "I'ma go put 'em in my bed."

"Alright." Trevor said as they sat on the couch.

"Why y'all ain't tell me y'all was comin'?" I asked as I sat down with them. "I coulda fixed a nice dinner. Told yo dad so he could come home early or somethin'."

"You can still do all that." Trevor said. "We just wanted to talk to you before he get home."

"About what?" I asked. "What y'all done got into now?"

"I think we should be askin' you that, Ma." Jamal said. "Who is Valerie Tucker?"

"Didn't yo dad tell you he ain't know who that was?" I asked him.

"I'm askin' you." Jamal said. "Do you know who she is?"

"I don't." I lied. "Is that what you came all the way out here for? To question me? You couldn't'a just called me?"

"I knew you would lie about it." Trevor said.

"Who you talkin' to?" I asked as I shot him a dirty look.

"Ma what is goin' on here?" Jamal asked. "Clearly it's somethin' y'all ain't tellin' us."

"Ain't nothin' to tell." I lied again. "I know y'all ain't come all this way to question me. Who you think you are?"

"We just tryna get to the bottom of this." Trevor said. "Instead of us sneakin' around to find out what it is on our own, we thought the direct approach was better. So, what is it? What's so bad that y'all gotta hide it from us?"

"Jamal." I said. "Trevor. Nothin' is goin' on that y'all need to worry about."

"So what's goin' on that you think we don't need to worry about?" Jamal asked.

"I ain't bouta play these games with y'all." I said. "Y'all are my children, but some parts of me and your fathers lives do not concern y'all."

"So it is somethin', then." Trevor said. "Ma we ain't leavin' here 'til we get answers. This don't make no damn sense."

"Boy I know you done lost yo mind comin' in my house talkin' to me like you ain't got no damn sense." I said as I stood up and looked down at him.

"I ain't mean it like that, Ma." Trevor said.

"I think he just tryna let you know that we serious about whatever it is y'all hidin'." Jamal said.

"Do we come to y'all house if we think y'all hidin' somethin'?" I asked them.

"We don't hide nothin' from y'all." Jamal said. "Everything that go on with us, y'all know about."

"How long did it take me to find out about Trevor's little crazy ass assistant?" I asked.

"I was tryna get it under control so nobody would have to worry about it." Trevor said.

"Did it ever occur to you that maybe me and your father tryna do the same thing?" I asked.

"You could be." Trevor said. "But it ain't necessary. We ain't here to tell y'all what to do. That ain't our job. We just here to find out what it is y'all keepin' from us and why."

"If we decide to keep our business to ourselves, we can do that." I said. "We are both grown adults, who can handle whatever it is we need to. You two are the children, so everything you do is always gon' concern us."

"I understand what you sayin', Ma." Jamal said. "But that don't change the fact that we need to know what it is. We ain't askin' y'all to tell us so we can do somethin' about it. It ain't our business to get involved in whatever mess y'all got y'all selves into. We do deserve to know what it is though."

"And what make you think that?" I asked. "What makes y'all so worthy, to know what goes on in a house y'all no longer live in?"

"Ma we yo kids." Trevor said. "What is so bad, that y'all can't tell us? I mean come on after all the trouble we done got in, what make y'all think we can't handle a little bit of trouble from y'all."

The room fell silent. They were absolutely right. They deserved to know. Joe had convinced me all these years that they really didn't need to know. He had me thinkin' crazy. The same way he was thinkin' when the shit first hit the fan.

I couldn't believe I was here arguin' with my kids about somethin' that concerned them. They had a 24-year-old sister that they never met. They knew nothing about her and she knew nothing about them. How had I fooled myself into thinking it was okay for siblings to not know about each other?

"It's not me." I said quietly after ten minutes of mind wandering.

"What you mean?" Trevor asked.

"I'm not the one who wants to keep this from you." I said. "Which means, I'm not the one who can give this information to you. You guys just have to speak to your dad about this when he gets home."

"And when is that gon' be?" Jamal asked.

"I don't know I think he said he was workin' late." I said as I looked at my watch.

"I'm bouta text him and let 'em know we here so he can come home early." Trevor said.

"Y'all just don't quit." I shook my head at them.

"You really think we would after we came all the way out here?" Jamal asked.

"Guess not." I laughed at them.

My boys were a mess. They were always nosy. I don't know why I thought this was somethin' they wouldn't try to figure out. Guess I just hoped Joe would tell them before it came to this.

This ultimatum they brought to us was ridiculous. I birthed them and here they were callin' the shots. Or attempting to. Today was the day they were gonna find out. I was done hidin' it. I don't care what excuse Joe came up with, he was tellin' these boys the truth. They came all this way. That's the least they deserved.

A few minutes later June Bug came out the room smilin'. He went right over to his daddy and climbed in his lap. It was such a beautiful sight. June Bug looked just like Jamal.

"Hey baby." I smiled at him as he looked at me.

"Hi Grannie." June Bug smiled at me.

"How was yo nap?" I asked him.

"Good." He smiled again.

"Want somethin' to eat?" I asked him.

"Yea." He said.

"Come on." I said as I picked him up and went to the kitchen. I sat him in the chair as I put the groceries up. "What you wana eat June Bug?"

"Macaroni." He said.

"That's gon' take a long time." I said to him.

"Not if you put it in the microwave." He smiled.

"June Bug Grannie don't microwave no macaroni." I said. "How bout peanut butter jelly and milk?"

"Chocolate milk?" He asked.

"Chocolate milk." I smiled. "But it's yo granddad's so don't tell 'em I gave it to you!"

We laughed together as I fixed him a sandwich. He was the most hilarious kid I knew. My babies were funny at his age, but June Bug was a straight up comedian.

Paisley

"Girl this nigga was trippin'." I laughed as I talked to my best friend.

London was my best friend since we were 5. We been inseparable our whole lives. When I left Texas and went to Atlanta she was right there with me. When I left Atlanta and went to Kentucky, she never left my side. From Kentucky we came to Michigan, together. That girl got me through so much bull shit. And I did the same for her.

"Hell naw I don't know why he don't just get the fuck on somewhere." She laughed with me.

"I know." I agreed. "He just don't get it. I can't go back to that shit."

"Right." She said. "So how the new place feel?"

"Girl I love it." I smiled. "When you comin' by to celebrate with me?"

"Sometime this week girl I been workin' my ass off in the office." She said.

"I'm so proud of you for getting yo real estate license girl." I shrieked. "I'm so jealous you got out the club before me."

"Shut up Paisley. You know yo ass shoulda been outta there." She said. "How much closer to yo goal are you?"

"London, I already told you I ain't askin' you for no money." I said.

"You ain't askin' me." She said. "I just gotta nice ass commission from this house I sold and I wana share it with my best friend. Is that too much to ask? You helped me get the license, so why I can't help you get yo dream started?"

"Cuz I didn't help you to get somethin' back from you." I said. "I helped you 'cuz that was right thing to do. You my best friend and if I ain't gon' help you then who will?"

"I know P, but still." She said. "Let me help you. That's what I'm supposed to do."

"Let me think about it, Lo." I said. "In the meantime, let's just focus on makin' my spot feel like home. You wana go furniture shoppin' this weekend?"

"Yea let's do it." She said. "That way we can go back to yo house and celebrate."

"Sound like a plan to me." I said.

"Have you talked to your mom?" She asked.

"Girl naw." I said. "She call me everyday. I ain't answerin' shit."

"You need too before she pop up on you." She said. "You know how she get when she don't hear from you. She been callin' me too and I been coverin' for yo ass like always."

"Lo you ain't gotta cover shit." I said. "I'm a grown ass woman. I told her not to contact me."

"But she always thinkin' somethin' bad done happened to you." She said.

"I respond to her texts just to let her know I'm alive." I said. "Other than that, I ain't really got too much to say."

"So, what about your dad?" She asked. "You gon' try to find him?"

"I thought about it." I said. "Maybe once I get my store and get everything settled. I already found a location I love. I thought about just buildin' a spot, but I kinda wana just find somewhere in a nice location. I already

116

found a few places I like downtown. We can go look at those this weekend too."

"Alright." She said. "So, what you think yo dad gon' say when you find 'em?"

"I have no idea." I said. "I mean it ain't like he don't know about me. He been supportin' me my whole life damn near. I wouldn't even know how to approach him. Like what do I say?"

"Hi daddy." She laughed. "That's what I was thinkin'."

"You a mess for real." I laughed. "I don't even know if I should be approachin' him, Lo. I mean I really don't even know what happened for real. Only thing I'm sure of is that he did help financially."

"Exactly." She said. "Seem like he do actually care since he provided support all that time with no court agreement. Don't get me wrong, I love yo mom and all, but I wouldn't put nothin' past her when it come to somebody doin' her wrong. Especially yo daddy."

"Yea that's true." I agreed. "It's just too much for me to think about right now."

I got up to see who was ringin' my doorbell. I hadn't been in this new condo too long so I ain't know who it could be at my door. The only person who knew I was here was London and she was on my phone.

"Don't let it stress you out." She said.

"Girl let me call you back." I said. "Somebody at my door."

"Who is it?" She asked.

"This fool done found me again." I said as I stared at his face hidden behind a bouquet of flowers.

"Aw shit." She laughed. "Call me as soon as he leave girl. I gotta hear this one."

"Alright." I laughed at her before I hung up the phone. "Explain to me how you just keep findin' my ass."

"I got my ways." He said as he invited himself in. "Finally growin' up huh? Got you a grown up spot now."

"Boy shut up." I laughed at him as I closed the door behind him. "I been grown. You the one still playin' these kiddy ass games."

"P come on now." He whined as he sat the flowers down on the table. "Why we gotta go there everytime I see you? I ain't come all the way over here to argue with you."

"So, what did you come all the way over here for?" I asked. "I seem to remember me askin' you to leave me alone too many times."

"You ain't mean that." He said as he sat on my couch.

"I'm pretty sure I did." I said as I stood over him.

Regardless of how mad he made me I still loved this man. He was so damn fine to me. Every inch of his body made mine weak. The hardest thing I ever had to do was leave him.

To this day he was still a part of me. As much as I tried to fight it, he was the only man I ever thought about. I had to keep away from him as much as possible. I wouldn't be able to fight him off for too much longer. He was my only weakness.

"I brought you somethin'." He smiled as he pulled out an envelope from his pocket.

He went to my refrigerator and pulled out my special occasion champagne I always kept on reserve. He knew me too well. He brought the champagne and glasses back to the living room table. I was now sitting on the couch. I never touched the envelope.

"You ain't read it?" He asked as he filled up two glasses.
"Was I supposed to?" I asked as I wondered what the hell this man could be tryin' to show me.

He took the papers out of the envelope and flipped through some pages. He gave me one of the pages and pointed to the bottom of it. There it was. His name, next to his wife's. His now ex-wife. He was officially divorced. I couldn't believe it. He had to be playin' me. I just knew he made this shit up.

"What the hell is this?" I asked as I threw the paper at him. "You just make up divorce papers and think you just gon' be back in my life or somethin'? You really think I'ma fool huh?"

"You know damn well I ain't make this shit up." He stood up. "Paisley I'm doin' everything I can to show you this where I wana be. What the fuck is yo problem? I'm not stayin' with her no more. We both signed the papers. I'm done with that. It's over. I'm sorry I lied to you about it from the beginning but I just wasn't ready to walk away then."

"So how do I know you ready to walk away now?" I asked quietly. "What's so different now, that you ready to commit to me?"

"I always been committed to you." He said. "We both know that. Just 'cuz I lied about still bein' with somebody, don't mean I wasn't faithful to you. But I realized that I can't lose you 'cuz I don't wana hurt her. We ain't no good for each other and I need to be with somebody that's good for me. That's you. That's why I'm here. Damn near everyday. Calling you every night. Doin' all this shit I ain't did for nobody. And it still ain't good enough? I don't know what else I'm supposed to do."

I didn't have an answer for him. I wanted to jump on top of him and rip all his clothes off, if this was true. I could see myself living a life with him, if this was true. He was the only person I ever felt complete with. He loved everything about me. I never had to lie to him about one thing. He knew all my secrets, so why did he make me one of his?

As much as I wanted to enjoy this moment, as much as I should have enjoyed this moment, I just couldn't take that chance again. He hurt me so bad before. I felt like I would collapse if this came back to be a scheme.

I didn't know how I was supposed to find out if this was actually true. Only thing I could think of was to go directly to the source. But I damn sure wasn't bouta go to his wife, ex wife, whatever she was, and ask her was this shit true. How the hell I look? Goin' to her, askin' were they really done so I could get back with him? Hell naw. One thing Paisley ain't is a fool.

"I think you should leave." I finally said quietly.

"What?" He looked at me as if he didn't hear what I said.

"I think you should leave." I repeated.

"P don't do this." He whined. "Whatever you wana talk about, I'm here. I don't care if it's the same shit you always whine about. I'm just tryna be with you. Why you gotta make this shit so hard?"

"I'm not the one who started this shit off with a fuckin' lie." I snapped. "So, you the one makin' this shit hard. How the fuck you think I'm supposed to trust yo ass after all the lies you told me? Now I'm just supposed to take yo word for it 'cuz you showed me a bull shit piece of paper? Now I'm posed to just jump back on yo team 'cuz you printed up some shit and signed it? The fuck I look like?"

"Babe I'm sorry." He said quietly. "I know it's my fault that we ain't together. I know it's my fault that you can't trust me. But I'm tryna show you that you can now. I can't show you all the changes I made for us, if you ain't givin' me a chance."

"I just can't deal with this right now." I said. "I got a few things I need to take care of early in the mornin', so I need to get some sleep."

"Can we talk about this tomorrow?" He asked.

"I'll let you know." I said as I walked to the door to show him out. He followed me and stopped at the door.

"I ain't givin you up, Paisley." He said as he looked at me. "We both know that. You can fight this shit as much as you want, for as long as you want, but that ain't changin'."

I didn't have anything to say. I just opened the door and watched him leave. But this time it felt different. I felt like I might have been makin' a mistake. My gut was tellin' me that this time was different. I felt like he was finally bein' honest with me, but I had no way to make sure of that. And until I could be 100% sure of what he was sayin', I couldn't give myself to him again.

I walked back to the living room, poured me a glass of champagne, and called London back.

"Lo." I said as she answered the phone. "Let me tell you bout this nigga."

Nina

"So, you still ain't found out what the girl really wanted?" Stacey asked me over the phone. I was polishing my toes while catching up on some gossip with her.

"Girl naw." I said. "Trevor tryna play like he don't know the girl, but I know it's more to that."

"Maybe he just really don't remember her." She said.

"I don't know if that's a good or bad thing." I laughed at her.

"Right." She agreed. "So, did they tell you anything about when they went to they parents house?"

"No and I'm mad about it." I said. "You heard anything?"

"Naw." She said. "All I know is Jamal said they would be back today. I asked him what did he find out and he said nothin'. He said his dad ain't come home that night when he was supposed to tell them what was goin' on."

"What?" I asked surprised. "So, Joe just up and disappeared?"

"Guess so." She said.

"Ain't nobody heard from 'em?" I asked.

"He only talked to Lisa." She said. "And he keep givin' excuses talkin' about a last minute work trip that's gon' last for another week."

"Wow." I said shocked. "I can't believe that. Whatever it is he hidin' gotta be big for him to go through all this. What is Lisa sayin'?"

"She just tryna hang in there." She said. "She say it ain't her business to tell so they need to hear it from him."

"Don't he realize this just makin' him look bad to them?" I asked. "Joe is them boys hero. How he just gon' let them down like that? That ain't a good look for him."

"I know." She said. "I just feel so bad 'cuz Jamal sound so defeated. And it really ain't nothin' I can do to help that's what make it so bad."

"Right." I said. "It's like we wana help as much as we can, but this thing really outta our hands. If he ain't comin' home to face the music when his wife say so, he definitely ain't gon' do it at our demand."

"Exactly." She said. "I don't know what could be so bad, that he gotta keep runnin' away from this? He had to have known whatever it is was gon' come out eventually."

"I'm sure he did." I said. "Clearly he just don't know how to face it. I mean I just wish he would just get it over with. They been so stressed about all the secrets. Trevor just been workin' longer days tryin' not to think about it. But I mean he can't work everyday all day. It's gon' come a time where he just break down if he keep doin' this to himself."

"Same thing for Joe." She said. "Can't run forever. Especially not from yo family."

"I wish Lisa would just tell them." I said. "At least then they'll know."

"She ain't gon' do it." She said. "That's one thing I can say about her. She is loyal to her man. Ain't nothin' wrong with that, but I feel like her kids do need to know."

"She know they do." I said. "That's why she want them to hear it from the horses mouth."

"Em hum." She said.

I looked up when I heard someone come in the door.

"Girl Trevor just walked in." I said as I noticed him. "Let me call you back."

"Alright bye girl." She said before we both hung up.

"Hey babe." I said as I stood up to hug him. "How you feelin'?"

"Tired." Trevor said quietly.

He took off his shoes and lay on the couch.

"What happened?" I asked as I looked at him.

"He say he had to go outta town for work." He looked at me like he ain't believe that either.

"You don't believe 'em?" I had to ask.

"Hell naw." He said. "I mean I ain't gon' chase 'em. We did what we had to do. He actin' like it's the end of the world if we find out he made a mistake. We all human. We all fuck up. Whatever it is ain't gon' change the fact that he still my father. That's why I don't understand why he so embarrassed. As much as me and Jamal messed up, it shouldn't be that hard for him to admit he did too."

"I think it's just his pride." I said as I massaged his shoulders. "I mean y'all look up to him. All y'all life y'all ain't never known him to do no wrong, so he feel like he on a pedestal. And y'all really do keep him there. So how do you come down from a pedestal that yo kids done kept you on they whole lives? I mean you gotta look at it from his point of view too babe."

"I really am tryin' to." He said. "Still, it ain't shit my father could tell me he did that would change what he did for us."

125

"I think that's somethin' you need to tell him." I said. "He just don't wana let y'all down. Think about how y'all felt when y'all messed up and had to admit it to him. You knew he would forgive y'all for it, but you still ain't wana let him down."

"I mean I understand what you sayin'." He said. "I'm just tryna see what the hell is goin' on. It's that simple. But anyways, I'm tired of talkin' bout this. What you been up to since I been gone?"

"Not much." I smiled at him. "Just got done polishing my toes."

"I see that." He laughed. "Where Music Note at?"

"Across the street." I said. "Where she always at. That girl just can't stay home."

"I know." He said. "You talk to Nicholas?"

"Yea." I said. "Say he just started his finals. I can't wait to have him back home."

"You know it ain't gon' be the whole month they outta school." He said.

"I know that Trevor." I said. "I don't care if he here for one day, I'm just ready for my baby to be home."

"I'm sure you are." He said.

Jada

I was sittin' in class when I noticed a few girls behind me whispering and laughin'. I ain't pay 'em no mind cuz it wasn't the first time. I figured they were just talkin' shit about somebody else's business like most girls do.

When class was over I went to talk to my professor about an assignment I had comin' up. A few minutes went by and I left out of the building. I walked outside to see Carter talkin' to the same girls who were just laughin' behind me in class. Then that's when I started to rethink things.

"Hey babe." I said to Carter as I walked up to him.
"What's up." He said to me as he smiled at one of them.

They stood around for a second until the awkwardness became obvious and then walked off after a moment of silence.

"Who was that?" I asked him.
"Nobody." He lied.
"So, what was you talkin' to nobody about?" I asked. "Had to been somethin' if y'all stopped talkin' when I walked up."
"Nothin'." He said. "How was class?"

No, this nigga did not just change the subject on me.

"It was cool." I said. "I could barely hear towards the end over yo lil' girlfriends laughin' behind me. What was so funny that they just had to rush out here and tell you about it?"

"Ain't shit funny, Jada." He snapped.

"So, what's the attitude for?" I asked as I looked at him.

"I don't have an attitude." He said.

"Alright." I said. "Where you park?"

"Down the street." He said as he led me to the parkin' lot.

I looked at my phone when it started to ring. Before I could answer it, it died.

"Bae can I see yo phone my mom just called me." I said.

"Why you ain't answer?" He asked.

"It died." I showed him my phone. He took out his phone and handed it to me. I started dialing my mom's number when a message popped up on his phone from Ce Ce:

Lose the bitch. I need you tonight.

I wanted to throw the phone on the ground and stomp on that shit. I showed him the message on his phone and gave it back to him. He kept walkin' towards the parkin' lot and I started walkin' the opposite way.

"J it ain't what you think." He said quietly as he followed me the other way.

"Don't say shit else to me." I said quietly.

"Where are you goin'?" He asked.

"Get the hell away from me, Carter." I said as I started walkin' faster away from him.

I went to the library and went into the first bathroom I saw. I couldn't even make it to the stall before I started crying my eyes out. I ain't even know who the hell Ce Ce was but somethin' told me it was one of those girls. I couldn't believe they were talkin' and laughin' about me. How did I not know? Why was I so stupid not to see what was goin' on?

I sat in that bathroom and cried so hard. I didn't know what I was supposed to do. I was out here by myself. Away from my family. My close friends. I mean I had friends here, but nobody I wanted to go cryin' too. The only person I wanted to see was Nicholas. But I couldn't because I was a million miles away from him.

Finally, after cryin' so much my eyes were sore, I left out of the bathroom. I plugged up my phone. I found me a hotel room, called a uber and went to the hotel. It was no way in hell I was goin' back to sleep with Carter tonight. I ain't know when I would even be able to look at him again.

Nicholas

I was finally home. And it felt good. Everybody was so happy to come home after the long semester we had. Football and basketball season just seemed so much longer this year than last year. Even my finals were actually challenging this time around. Nothin' I couldn't handle though.

I went to my parents' office to have lunch with them. My dad was in his office, waitin' on my mom as always.

"What's up." I said as I walked into his office.

"Sup man." He said as I sat in his chair. "I don't know what take yo mama so damn long to walk across the hallway."

"She said she had some meetin' at 10." I said as I looked through the window across to her office.

"That meetin' been over." He said as he paged her. "Girl get yo ass over here. Nicholas waitin' on you."

"Here I come." She responded. "Hey baby." She said to me as she came in the office.

"Hey ma." I laughed at her. "What y'all wana eat?"

"It don't matter to me." My dad said.

"I say we just order somethin' and eat it here." My mom said.

"Cool." I said as he pulled out the take out menus.

"So what's been goin' on with you, college man?" My mom asked me after we all placed our orders.

"Too much." I laughed at her. "School and ball keepin' me busy."

"And Cassidy?" She asked.

"Cassidy is Cassidy." I said. "Can't complain."

"Did you forget who you talkin' to?" She asked.

I looked at my dad to see if he had been tellin' her my business. He gave me the look to let me know he wasn't.

"Naw Ma." I laughed. "Everything good with Cassidy."

"Yea okay." She looked at me like she ain't believe me. "You seen Jada?"

"When she came to the school yea." I said.

"What?" She asked. "You ain't tell me that."

"Yes I did." I said. "When she had that competition. Stop actin' like you ain't know."

"Alright." She laughed. "I just missed talkin' to you baby. I don't want you to leave again."

"Ma you said you wasn't gon' do this again." I said. "You know I got games comin' up. I would stay the whole break if I could, but I can't."

"I know." She said quietly.

"Girl quit whinin' and make the best of it while he here." My dad jumped in.

She rolled her eyes at him. These two was too much for me. I did miss them though. But I had business to tend to that just happened to keep me away from my family majority of the year.

Otherwise known as, college life. Regardless of whatever kept me away from them, it still ain't change the fact that I was doin' somethin' for them. It was for me too, but I wanted to keep makin' them proud of me. I had too. It was just somethin' that made me feel good when I made them happy to be my parents. I don't know what it was, but I started to feel like I was really growin' up.

Jamal

Me and Trevor decided to head to the strip club tonight. We had a long work week, felt like we needed to kick back and relax. What better way to do that then to see women shaking they ass. And let's not forget the good ass food they had too.

The night was long as hell. We stayed there til' they closed the doors at 4am. Trevor wanted to see if they could stay open later for us but I told him we ain't need to do that.

"Man I don't know if I'm drunk or what." Trevor said as we left The Spot.
"But did you see that girl Peaches?"
"Yea." I laughed at him 'cuz I already knew what he was about to say.

It was kinda weird, but she looked just like our dad. She wasn't manly, she just looked like a feminine version of him. And for some reason, she was really drawn to us. The whole night she was givin' us free dances and everything.

"Tell me she ain't look like Dad to you." He laughed.
"She did." I laughed with him. "That's crazy. And then she kept givin' us all them free dances. I ain't know what was goin' on."
"Right." He said. "I thought I was trippin' or somethin'."

"Me too." I laughed at him. "Why she put her number in my phone though?"

"Nigga you better delete that shit right now while you remember it." He laughed at me.

"I deleted it right after she walked away." I laughed with him. "I ain't takin' no chances."

We both laughed.

"That shit was just weird as hell." He said. "Why did she look just like him though?"

"Nigga I don't know." I said. "But it was weird as hell. It's crazy though 'cuz it just make you think you seen her somewhere before."

"Hell yea we seen her at the last club we went too." He laughed.

"Shut up fool." I said. "I know that. I mean it just feel like we know her or somethin'."

"That's just 'cuz she look like his twin." He said. "I know what you mean though."

Somethin' about tonight was too crazy. I ain't know what that whole Peaches thing was about. Despite the crazy shit, we still had a good time. With all the bull shit goin' in our lives, we ain't get to go out as much as we used to. I mean it was cool, 'cuz we really were old men now. Not too old, but we were grown ups.

We had wives and kids. Families. Men with families don't hang out in strip clubs all the time. But I was glad to be hangin' out with my little brother. Proud of both of us for bein' successful black fathers and husbands, like our dad was with us. He raised us right. Him and my mom. I knew they were proud of the men we'd become.

Malcolm

Bein' home felt good. I felt like the man around here since I touched back down. Me and Laya had been out every night lookin' for her mom and we finally found her. Sadly, it was at some crack house, but at least she was alive. We took her back to the house, but the next morning she was gone.

Laya didn't take it bad at all though. It was like she was waitin' for it. She was used to it. But she was happy 'cuz at least she knew she wasn't dead. I felt so bad for her though. To be happy for her to just be alive, was crazy. She didn't even wana take her from the crack house, I had to talk her into it. Probably because she already knew she would run right back to where she came from. She knew better than I did. That was only 'cuz she been through it.

I ain't never had to deal with no shit like that before. And she knew her mother better than anybody else so she knew what to expect from her. As long as she was feelin' better about the situation, I was happy. I just ain't want her to be stressed out, messin' up in school, over somethin' that was out of her control.

"Somebody at the door for you." My mom peeked her head in my bedroom door.

It was always somebody interrupting my thoughts. I got out the bed and walked to the living room. It was 1:30 and I had just woke up. I was still in the clothes I slept in and here she was fully dressed like she had been up all day. I couldn't believe Jhene was standin' in my livin' room. I don't know why I ain't see this comin'.

"What's up." I said as I sat down on the couch. She sat next to me.

"Just thought I'd stop by to see if you wanted to get somethin' to eat." She smiled at me.

"How did you even know I was home?" I asked her.

"I mean it is the holiday time." She said. "Lucky guess. So what's up? You hungry or what?"

"I just woke up, Jhene." I said as I yawned. "I ain't really ready to eat yet."

"Now I don't even believe that." She laughed. "Yo stomach growl all through the night."

"Ha." I laughed at her. How did she still remember that shit? "You coulda called me first or somethin'."

"I ain't know if you was gon' be too busy to answer." She said.

"If you thought I wasn't gon' answer, what made you think to just pop up?" I asked. "If I'm too busy to answer, clearly I'm too busy for company."

"It ain't always that simple, Malcolm." She said. "Look I just wanted to hang out with you while we're both in town. Somethin' wrong with that?"

"Naw that's cool." I said. "But you still coulda called me and asked. Then you wouldn'ta had to waste yo time comin' over here."

"So now I'm wastin' my time?" She asked.

"That ain't what I'm sayin', Jhene." I said. "Look what's up man? What is this about? Ever since we had lunch last time I was in town, you been tryna keep in touch with me a little too much. I mean it's cool for us to be friends, but all the I miss you messages, and all that other shit, we ain't doin' that. You know I'm with Laya."

"And?" She asked. "You wasn't thinkin' about my feelings when we was together."

"We ain't bouta get into this again." I said. "If that's what you came over here for, then you really did waste yo time."

"Alright that ain't what I'm here for." She said quietly. "Like I said, I do want us to be friends."

"I mean you say that, but you ain't actin' like that." I said. "Maybe you just need to get yo head together and figure this shit out. Cuz I ain't bouta be havin' you think I'm leading you on or somethin'."

"What is that sposed to mean?" She asked.

"Exactly what I said." I said.

"You mean to tell me you ain't have fun with me last time we went to lunch?" She asked.

"I never said I didn't." I said. "But that don't mean this bouta be a normal thing. Every time we happen to be in town at the same time, we don't have to hang out. You can't still be tryna get back with me after all these years."

She didn't respond.

"Jhene come on." I said. "You shoulda been moved on by now. What did you think was gon' happen?"

She just sat there. I ain't wana hurt her feelings but I ain't know what else to say. I never gave her no reason to think I wanted her back. Never gave her a reason to think she could get me back. Guess she just couldn't let go.

"Are you really happy Malcolm?" She asked lookin' like she couldn't accept the answer she already knew.
"I am Jhene." I said. "It ain't nobody in this world that could get me to leave that girl. It's that simple. I mean I'm sorry shit ain't work out between me and you. But that just wasn't meant to be. I know you gon' meet somebody else but you gotta want too. Stop waitin' around on me. Cuz that shit just ain't gon' happen. Honestly."

I felt like I said too much, but then again, maybe I didn't say enough. She still looked like she was in denial. It was startin' to piss me off. I knew I had to get her out this house or she would sit here and wait for me to change my mind.

"Alright I'm bouta hop in the shower." I said. "Got some moves to make so I can get my day started."
"Okay." She said quietly. "Wana have a drink later?"

"Naw I'ont think so." I said as I stared at her. "I'll call you if I change my mind." I said as I opened the door for her.

She left out lookin' like it was the end of the world. As soon as she pulled out of the driveway, Laya was pullin' up. I ain't think nothin' of it 'til she got out the car lookin' mad as hell. I knew she wasn't trippin' about Jhene. We had a clear understanding that I was not fuckin' with that girl, and she believed me.

"Now I see why you couldn't answer the phone." Laya said as she walked in the house.
"My phone was in the room." I said as I sat on the couch. "I been out here tryna get her to leave for the last 15 minutes. What's up? What's wrong?"

She hesitated. She wanted to say somethin', but she stared at me instead.

"Bae, I just woke up and she was here." I said. "Don't be like that. You can ask my mom."

She knew I wasn't on no bull shit when I told her to ask my mom. My mom covered for me for a lotta shit, but once me and Laya moved in together, she started takin' her side. So if I put my mama in the middle of it, she knew I was tellin' the truth.

"Yea alright." She finally smiled. "I ain't want nothin'."

"What the hell you come over here mad for?" I laughed at her ass.

"What you mean?" She asked. "I don't get no answer from you. Show up and see her leavin' yo house. What I'm sposed to think?"

"I don't give a damn long as it ain't no crazy shit." I said as she followed me back to my room. She sat on the bed as I lay back in it. "What do you want woman? I just wana go back to sleep. You already had me out late every night since we been here. Can't I just have one day to myself?"

"Boy shut up." She said. "Come on I'm hungry. Let's go get somethin' to eat."

"I'm not goin' nowhere." I said to her as I got under the covers. "My mama bouta make me breakfast she just texted me and told me. You wana stay?"

"I guess." She smiled. I pulled her down to get under the covers with me. "I'm not tired I wana get up and get the day started."

"Girl if you don't take yo ass to sleep." I said. "If I'm tired, I know you tired." She stopped fightin' it and dozed off right on my chest.

Jada

Ever since I found out about Carter and Ce Ce I hadn't spoken to him. I stayed at the hotel. He showed up at all the games tryin' to talk to me afterward but I just walked away from him. He was relentless. Especially now that we were both home. My mom was questionin' me about bein' so depressed and why I been ignorin' him. I just told her I needed some alone time and she left it at that.

He called me at least 20 times a day. Sent me at least 50 messages a day. I read them all. Never replied. I ain't even have the energy to entertain his ass.

I had kinda been ignorin' Nicholas too. And he was pissed about it. He had been tryna see me everyday since we got home. I was just makin' excuses.

I was layin' in the bed watchin' TV when my phone rung. It was Nicholas, of course. I really wasn't in themood to answer it, but I did anyway.

"Hello." I said quietly. My voice was still raspy since I hadn't said anything all morning since I woke up.

"I know yo ass ain't still sleep." He said.

"Naw I'm just layin' down." I said.

"Open the door." He said.

145

"Nicholas, I look a mess." I whined. "I ain't even brushed my teeth yet. Can we meet up later or somethin'?"

"Open the door, J." He repeated.

I knew nothin' I said mattered to him. I hung up the phone and went to the front door. I let him in and he followed me back to my room. I got back in the bed. He closed the door and sat in my chair.

"What the hell is goin' on?" He asked. "Yo mom called me talkin' 'bout you been over here moapin' around since you been home. Ain't nobody seen yo ass. You been spinnin' us since we got here. What's wrong with you?"

"Nothin'." I lied. "Just been tryna catch up on some rest. School just been wearin' me out. And we been havin' competitions damn near every weekend. It's a lot."

"Bull shit." He said immediately. "Wana try that again?"

"Not really." I said quietly.

"Let me rephrase that." He said. "Try that one mo' time."

"I just got a lot goin' on right now, Nicholas." I said finally.

"Like what?" He asked.

"Personal problems." I said.

"What kinda personal problems?" He asked. "I know yo ass ain't pregnant."

"No." I yelled. "Why would you say that?"

146

"I don't know what else you could be depressed about." He said. "What he do?"

I got quiet. I ain't know what to say. I knew I needed to tell Nicholas, but I was just so hurt. My eyes started waterin' after the last question. I couldn't hold it in no more. I started cryin' so hard my eyes burned. My whole body started aching. Nicholas got up off the chair and sat on the bed next to me and just held me.

"What happened?" He asked.
"He cheated on me." I cried. "Why would he do that to me?"

He didn't respond. He just held me. I wiped my eyes on his shirt. Immediately I stopped cryin' once I realized who I was cryin' too. The same man I cheated on years ago. If he felt anything like I was feelin' now, I felt so bad.

"I am so sorry, Nicholas." I said as I looked at him. "This is the worst feelin' in the world. I don't know how I could have ever put you through this."
"J don't worry about it." He smiled at me. "I been over that. We been past that. But I know how you feel. It's cool though. You don't need to be with that nigga no way."

I ain't know what to say. He was right. I ain't deserve that. I followed that man to school to make sure we ain't put no unnecessary distance on our relationship and he still cheated on me. He still betrayed me after everything I did for him. He didn't deserve me.

But on the other hand, all I wanted was a second chance after I cheated on Nicholas. I begged him for months to try again. Now here I was getting my ass kicked by karma. The fucked-up part was that I deserved it. I don't know how I thought I could just fuck somebody over like that, and not have it done to me. What the hell was I thinkin'?

"It's my fault." I said. "This just my karma for doin' you wrong."
"You ain't deserve that, Jada." He said. "Don't nobody deserve that shit. I'm sorry you goin' through this and you know I'm here for you. Whatever you need. But you can't sit up in this room all day and expect to feel better about it. I tried that and that shit ain't work."
"Nicholas shut up you did not sit up in yo room cryin' over me for weeks." I laughed at him.
"Alright I ain't cry." He laughed at me. "But I was in my room thinkin' hard for at least a day."
"Aw yea." I smiled. "And what was you thinkin' about?"
"It's crazy 'cuz I wasn't even tryna find a reason to justify it." He said. "I was just mad at myself for still wantin' you."
"You still wanted me after that?" I asked surprised.

I never knew he felt that way. He sure ain't act like it after the fact. His actions really told me the complete opposite.

"I ain't never stopped wantin' you, J." He smiled at me. "But somewhere down the line, I knew I wasn't supposed to be with you at that time. You just wasn't ready and that's cool. Now in his case, I don't know what the problem is. This nigga done proposed and everything, so he should have his shit together."

"You would think so." I laughed at him. "I don't know what it is."

"Me either." He said. "But I ain't bouta let you waste yo whole vacation, feelin' like it's the end of the world. Let's go smoke bumblebee out til' you feel like laughin' again."

"I look a mess." I said. "I can't go nowhere lookin' like this."

"Girl I ain't takin' you nowhere to impress nobody." He laughed as he stood up. "Throw somethin' on and let's go."

I stood up to hug him.

"Thank you." I said as I wrapped my arms around his neck.

"You welcome." He smiled and kissed my cheek. "Now come on. It's time to get high."

Trevor

Nina was still trippin' about this Tracy girl. We hadn't seen the article in any magazine she claimed to be workin on', but I wasn't surprised. I knew that was a lie from the beginning. But I just ain't know what the lie was for. I called up one of my boys from school to see if he knew who this girl was.

"What's up nigga?" Ronnie asked as he answered my call.

"Shit man." I replied. "What's goin' on with you?"

"Same shit." He said. "Just got back home from a few games. Everything goin' good over there?"

"Pretty much." I said. "China and the kids doin' alright?"

"Yea everybody good." He said. "I been sayin' I was gon' get out there to catch up with you and everybody but every free minute I get I'm sleep."

"I know what you mean man." I said. "I ain't playin' but this company keep me runnin' all day and night. Especially now that it's just me and Nina runnin' this office."

"At least you get to set yo own hours." He said. "I'm proud of you man. Came a long way, and you still makin' more money than all of us. How is that possible?"

We both started laughin'.

"Man I can't even get into all that." I laughed at him. "But look some chick showed up a few weeks ago named Tracy. Claiming she doin' a story on me and Nina but it just ain't addin' up."

"What you think she want?" He asked. "Some money or somethin'?"

"We don't know." I said. "But she just seem like she know so much about me."

"Stuff that she could look up and see?" He asked.

"Some of it, but other stuff is kinda like you had to be there type shit. But I just can't remember this girl. I'm bouta send you a picture of her right now to see if you remember her." I said as I sent the picture to his phone.

"She look familiar." He said once he got the picture. "I think she went to school with us."

"At home?" I asked. "Naw I woulda knew that."

"Naw out there." He said. He hesitated for a minute. "I know who she is. You remember the girl you got with right at the beginning of freshman year. The one Carmen thought was stalking you?"

"Damn." I said as I thought about it. "I can't believe that's her. You know I just found out her name. After all these years."

"And what she say her name was?" He asked.

"Tracy." I said. "I ain't know who she was. Damn that's crazy. What she want with me after all this time?"

"I don't know." He said. "Shit might be tryna get with you." He laughed.

"Hell naw." I said. "I got too much goin' on right now to deal with anymore drama. Why she ain't just say how she knew me then?"

"Now that's probably gon' be a problem." He said. "If she actin' like she don't know you when she do, she got somethin' she tryna hide."

"What the hell I got to do with that?" I asked.

"Nigga I don't know." He said. "You need to get in contact with her and let her know you know who the hell she is. Maybe she'll let you know what she want then."

"Boy I'm too damn old to be dealin' with this college bull shit." I said. "It ain't shit I'm doin' for that girl."

"You need to be careful." He said. "She might just be one of them hoes lookin' for a come up. I mean that's what she was in school, so I wouldn't put it past her now."

"What the hell?" I asked. "It's always some shit that wana come back from the past."

"Hell yea." He said. "We ain't even have no crazy college years like most players and we still got hoes comin' from all over tryna get shit from us. Just dont make no damn sense."

"Hell naw." I said. "What happened with Dante and that girl tryna get child support from him?"

"She ain't get shit." He laughed. "You know he ain't been with nobody since he got with Lyric."

"I know." I laughed. "These hoes trippin'."

"That's all they good for." We both started laughin'.

Cassidy

I sat on the toilet for 45 minutes after I saw the results. How in the hell could I possibly be pregnant? I was on birth control faithfully. We used condoms, faithfully. I hadn't been with anyone else since I met Nicholas. It was just not possible for this to happen to me. How could this happen to us? We did everything right. Took all the necessary precautions. And I still get pregnant? What the hell?

It was no way I was havin' a kid right now. I was still a kid my damn self. Nicholas definitely wasn't ready to be a dad. I was nowhere near ready to be a mom. It just wasn't bouta happen. Neither one of us could handle this right now.

I ain't know what to do. I ain't know how I would tell him this without him thinkin' I was with somebody else. Maybe I shouldn't tell 'em. Maybe I should just handle it myself and act like it never happened. I knew I couldn't keep it in forever though. Eventually it would come out. And Nicholas hated secrets.

I called my doctor and made an appointment before I had to go back to school. Now all I had to do was figure out how I was gon' tell him this. It would probably be best if he went to the appointment with me so we could both figure out how this happened. I called him to see if he had anything planned for tomorrow so we could go to the appointment.

"Hey babe." I said as he answered the phone.

"What's up?" Nicholas asked.

"Nothin'." I said. "What you doin'?"

"Shit bouta go smoke with Jada and Malcolm." He said. "What you up to?"

"Nothin' really just woke up." I said. "Nicholas I need to go to the doctor tomorrow and I kinda want you to go with me."

"What's wrong?" He asked.

"I'm like three weeks late." I said. "And I just got a positive result from a pregnancy test."

"What the hell?" He asked. "What you mean? I thought you was still on birth control."

"I am I don't know what happened." I said. "I just wana go and see what the hell is goin' on. I'm hopin' the test was just bad or somethin' 'cuz this don't make no sense."

"Hold on." He said. "This shit ain't addin' up. You on the pill. And we usin' condoms. It's no way in hell you should be pregnant."

"I'm sayin' the same thing." I said. "But I need to go clear this shit up. And I want you to come with me."

"What time is the appointment?" He asked.

"Twelve." I said.

"Alright I'll be there at 11." He said. "Make sure you ready 'cuz you know I ain't gon' be waitin' on yo ass all day."

"I'll be ready crybaby." I laughed at him.

"Alright." He said. "I'll call you later after I leave Malcolm house."

"Okay." I said. "Bye babe." Before we hung up.

I wanted to tell my mama about this, but I wasn't sure if I should before I knew it was right. She didn't need to be stressed out about somethin' that wasn't even true.

This was the last thing I expected for us. Especially with us bein' so careful. Whatever was goin' on with me, I was bouta find out. Cuz I damn sure wasn't bouta be havin' no baby my second year in college. I just wasn't ready to give up my life. Neither one of us was.

Malcolm

"Nigga pour me a damn drink." Nicholas said as he came in my house.

"What's up with you?" I laughed at him. He looked like he was goin' through it.

"I just got off the phone with Cassidy ass and she talkin' 'bout she might be pregnant." He said as he sat down next to Jada.

"Hold on." I said. "Not 'Mr. I Never Go Raw'. I know you ain't got nobody pregnant."

"Man shut the hell up." He said. "I ain't on that shit. She on birth control. We always use condoms. Shit just ain't addin' up."

The room got quiet. It was kinda awkward because we were all here before when Jada got pregnant in high school. Good thing we were all past that, 'cuz shit coulda got ugly then.

"In her defense, the test could be wrong Nicholas." Jada said.

"That's true." Laya agreed. "Or it could just be somethin' 'goin on with her hormones that's givin' her a false positive. It does happen. Trust me."

"I guess so." He said. "We goin' to the doctor tomorrow to clear this shit up. Ain't nobody havin' no damn kids right now."

"Hell naw we ain't got time for that." I had to agree.

I went to the kitchen and brought him the bottle. He opened it up and took three shots.

"Damn slow down." Jada laughed at him as she lit the blunt.

"Shut up." He said. "I'm just goin' across the street. I ain't gotta drive home."

"Damn shame." Laya laughed at him.

"It's always somethin'." He said as he shook his head.

"That's life." I said. "Don't stress about it. Y'all gon' figure it out tomorrow and go from there."

"Try not to let it get to you." Jada said quietly to him. "Just relax." She passed him the blunt.

"So what's goin' on with Music Note?" I asked him. "My mom say Kelly mad at her 'cuz they like the same lil' boy."

"Man I done told her she don't need to be likin' nobody." He said. "She claim she told Kelly she wasn't gon' be his girlfriend. I'm like y'all too damn young to be thinkin' bout that shit anyway."

"Right." I agreed. "I been tellin' Kelly that for too long now. My mama sittin' up here laughin' at it. Talkin' 'bout it's cute and shit. That shit ain't cute. I'll be damned if somebody get Kelly ass pregnant."

"Hell naw." He said. "Ain't nobody goin' for that shit. My mama ain't takin' it seriously neither. They need to be worried about school and ballet. They do so much to stay busy I don't even know how they have time to be fightin' over some lil' boy."

"That's true." I agreed. "We kept busy all the time so that drama shit was minimal for us."

"I know." He said. "I just don't see how you go from fightin' girls together, to not talkin' to yo friend the next day 'cuz y'all like the same lil' boy. They don't even know what likin' somebody mean. And if they do, we gon' have a problem."

"Oh my God." Laya said. "Leave them girls alone. They ain't doin' nothin' wrong. Don't act like y'all wasn't likin' no little girls at they age."

"So what?" I asked. "I know what I was tryna do at that age. And ain't no lil' ass boy bouta try to get my sister to do none of that shit."

"See that's the problem." Jada said. "Y'all can't handle boys bein' the same as y'all was at they age. Y'all real hypocritical."

"I don't give a fuck." Nicholas said. "Music Note ain't allowed to have no boyfriend til' she 18 and graduate high school."

"Now that's crazy." Laya said. "You had girlfriends way before that."

"And I'm responsible." He said. "I don't know how responsible she gon' be. And I'll be damned if I'm just supposed to hope that I taught her enough to make smart decisions. I can't rely on that. I don't know if these boys gon' be able to convince her or not."

"Music Note got her own mind, Nicholas. You know that." Jada said.

"I know a lotta girls who got they own mind and still end up pregnant in high school." He said.

"You're an asshole." Jada laughed at him.

I was glad we could all sit around and laugh about the shit that used to make us uncomfortable. The crew was back in full effect and that shit was cool as hell. Me and Laya hung out with Nicholas and Cassidy on a regular basis, but it was different hangin' out with Jada. It was like it was supposed to be. Even though Cassidy had been around for a while now so it was comfortable with her, Jada just felt like a part of us. Cassidy sometimes seemed like a placeholder.

Nina

"Still ain't heard from yo dad?" I asked Trevor as we lay in bed.

"Nope." He answered. "I don't even ask my mom about him or the situation no more. She just keep apologizin'. I ain't even trippin' on it."

"Yea." I said. "I mean what else can you do? Eventually he gon' have to come around. I don't know how long it's gon' take, but whatever it is must be really bad if he feel like he just can't face it."

"I know." He agreed. We both looked up as the doorbell rung. "Who the hell is that?"

"I don't know." I said. "I'll go see."

I got up, put on my robe and went to the door. I looked threw the peephole to see Tracy standin' on my porch. I opened the door and looked at her.

"Tracy." I said. "What are you doin' here?"

"I'm sorry I know I shoulda called." She said. "I just had a few more questions I thought I could add to my article."

"It's 8 o clock in the morning." I said. "On a Saturday. You couldn't wait until Monday?"

"Well it was kinda just a few ideas that came to my mind." She said. "I wanted to hurry up and act on 'em while they were fresh."

"Tracy I think we can do this Monday morning." I said. "Me and Trevor are both free until 10, if you wana come in at 8."

"I have to go out of town Monday on an assignment." She said. "I won't be back for three weeks. I promise it won't take long, Mrs. Johnson."

As much as I hesitated lettin' her in my house, she was too persistent. Never mind the fact that she shouldn't even know where I lived, but who the hell did she think she was just poppin' up at my house like this. Against my better judgment, I decided to let her in. I opened the screen door and she came in and sat on the couch.

"Babe come out here for a second." I yelled to Trevor. "Tracy's here."
"What?" He yelled back. A few seconds later he came out of the room in sweats and a t shirt. "What's goin' on?"
"Say she need to ask a few more questions." I said as I sat in the chair.
"At 8 in the morning?" He asked as he stood by my chair.
"It won't take long." She smiled at Trevor.
"Look let's cut the bull shit." Trevor said as he looked at her.

I ain't know what he was doin' but I ain't expect that at all. I mean I knew he ain't like people comin' over this early, but this was about somethin' else.

"We both know how we know each other. So what is it that you came here for? You ain't doin' no story on us. We ain't believed that shit since we met you. What are you tryna get from me?" He asked.
"What do you mean?" Tracy asked as she played confused.

"Freshman year at Michigan State." He said. "That's where we met."

I knew this girl had somethin' to do with Trevor. I knew it.

"You must have me confused." She shook her head.

"We too old for these games, Tracy." He said. "Tell me what you want or get the hell out."

"Okay." She said as dropped her head.

"What is it that you want, Tracy?" I had to ask.

"We have a son, Trevor." She said quietly as she looked up at him.

His eyes got huge as my mouth dropped.

"What?" He snapped. "You gotta be fuckin' kiddin' me. You really think I'm fallin' for that shit?"

"He's asked about you everyday since he could talk." She said. "He deserves to know his father."

"Well you need to be lookin' for 'em 'cuz it ain't me." He said.

"Trevor, I been quiet about this for too damn long." She said. "I ain't even trip after you played me for Carmen after we got together."

"We was never together." He said. "You know that. I ain't even know yo name. You was with damn near every nigga on the team. It ain't no tellin' who kid that is."

I could not believe I actually heard him say somethin' like that. It wasn't even in his character to be that disrespectful to a woman. Even if she was wrong, he would never behave like that. Which made me question if this was true or not.

He just wasn't himself after she said it. I ain't know what to think. All I knew was, I had to get this woman out of my house, while I discussed this with my husband.

"Tracy, we'll be in touch with you." I said to her as I stood up to let her out.
"You can't just dismiss me." She said. "We not just gon' go away."
"I don't give a damn what you think gon' happen." He said. "But you ain't getting a dime outta me."

This man was changin' by the minute. It was getting too crazy. She stood up and walked to the door.

"Give us some time to figure some things out." I said to her as I opened the door for her. "I'll call you in a few days."
"Thank you, Nina." She said as she left out the house.

I closed the door and turned around to look at Trevor. I was speechless. When he started talkin' crazy I had so much to say, but now that I looked at him in silence, I felt so bad for him. If this was true, he just became another statistic. The one thing he fought so hard not to be.

"What in the hell was that about?" I asked him as I sat down on the couch.

"I don't even know." He said. "I ain't even get a chance to tell you I remembered where I knew her from."

"So this is true?" I asked him.

"The baby part, no." He said. "But I did sleep with her."

"Trevor, I could care less about who you had sex with in college." I said. "That was way before we even knew each other. But what I do care about is if you have another child that you didn't know about."

"I don't have another child, Nina." He said. "She been with too many niggas to know who the daddy is. Of course, she want it to be me so she can get some money from me. That ain't happenin'."

"Why do you think everybody is after yo money?" I asked as I looked at him confused.

"You mean to tell me you think she ain't?" He asked as he looked at me like I was crazy. "Them hoes only want one thing, Nina. A check. She thought havin' that baby was gon' get her somewhere but I guess that backfired 'cuz now she knockin' at my door. I ain't got shit to do with that. I don't even know why you entertainin' this bull shit."

"What am I supposed to do?" I asked.

"Take my word and leave it at that." He said.

"It ain't that simple." I said. "I know that if you knew about this child you woulda been in his life. But what if she did have yo child and you didn't know about it? If it's any possibility that you could be his father, you need to find out. Regardless of how you feel about her or not. You need to

167

exclude yourself from the rest of the niggas she fucked with in school. Wouldn't you wana know if you had another kid?"

"Nina, I got two kids." He said. "That's all I need. This girl come outta nowhere sayin' she had my kid and you just take that shit?"

"I ain't takin nothin'." I said. "I'm just tryna figure this shit out. Did you use a condom with the girl or not?"

He looked away from me. I knew what that look meant. Even though this was crazy, I wasn't mad at my husband. I just wanted him to make sure that her son, was not his son. And if it was his son, we would deal with it.

It was nothin' in this world that would make me leave this man. We all had skeletons in our closet. He was my best friend. I could never leave him. Especially for somethin' he had no knowledge of.

He looked like he was embarrassed to answer my question. I stood up and walked over to him. I took his face into my hands and lifted it up to meet my eyes.

"Yes or no, Trevor." I said as I looked into his eyes.

"No." He said quietly as he stared at me. I never let go of his face. I kissed him and hugged him. "Babe I know it ain't my kid."

"Can we just make sure?" I asked as I held him. "It ain't gon' hurt nothin' to find out."

"What you mean?" He asked. "If I'm wrong how that's gon' make me look?"

"Like a nigga who ain't know they had a kid." I said. "That ain't nothin' new. I mean I know you ain't never wana be that guy, but things happen baby. At least now you can figure this out and move on from here."

"This shit is crazy." He said. "I ain't tryna mess up my family for this shit."

"Look we ain't goin' nowhere." I said. "But if he's yours, then he is a part of our family. And we can make this shit work. It ain't nothin' for you to worry about. I know this just came outta nowhere, but you know I'm here to get you through this."

"You ain't tryna leave me?" He asked as he leaned back to look at me.

"You know I ain't goin' nowhere." I smiled at him. "This shit was way before me, baby. I can't be mad at that. I mean it's messed up that you missed all these years of his life if he is yours, but I'm sure y'all can figure out a way to make up for loss time."

"I ain't really ready to just change my whole life though." He said. "It's gon' be difficult when it don't have to be."

"How do you know that?" I asked. "You ain't even gave it a chance."

"Look at how she approached us." He said. "All this shit started with lies. Why couldn't she just be up front about her intentions from the beginning. Then I wouldn't be lookin' at her like I can't trust her ass."

"That's true." I agreed. "Maybe she just ain't know how to tell you. Whatever it is, I say we don't worry about it, until we find out if he's yours."

"It ain't that simple." He said. "I just can't believe this shit. I just talked to Ronnie the other day. He the one actually remembered who she was once I sent him the picture of her. I completely forget about her."

"That's fine babe." I laughed at him. "I ain't sayin' I don't believe you. I know you ain't do nothin' to that girl. If that was the case she would really be mad at yo ass. Instead of starin' at you in the office like you were her first crush."

"She was starin' hard." He laughed.

"Hell yea." I laughed with him. "We gon' get to the bottom of all this. But I knew this girl had somethin' to do with you. What I tell you?"

"Shut up." He laughed. "Why you always gotta be right?"

"I don't have to be." I corrected him. "I just am."

"Yea whatever." He said as he wrapped his arms around my waist. "Thanks for getting her outta here."

"Bae, I ain't never seen you talk to no woman like that." I said. "At first I was wonderin' if it was true and you was just mad 'cuz it came out. You just got real rude once she said you was his dad. I was like aw naw let me stop this shit now before it get outta hand."

"I'm glad you seen where it was goin'." He laughed. "I mean I felt it getting bad, but I ain't know what to say to get out the situation calmly. I was just so mad that she was tryna make me seem like I just got some random girl pregnant. That ain't even me."

"I know." I smiled at him and kissed his neck. He squeezed my waist and kissed my cheek. "We done talkin' about this for right now?" I asked as my hands found their way to his pants.

"Em hum." He mumbled as he picked me up and took me back to the bedroom.

At first him talkin' to Tracy kinda caught me off guard, but after the fact, I was kinda turned on by it. I know it was crazy as hell, but I couldn't help how sexy my man was when he was speakin' his mind. Damn he was fine as hell.

Jada

I had just got back to school. It was the first day of class and I was still not stayin' at the house with Carter. The whole time I was at home I kept avoidin' him. Even when he showed up to my mom's house I wouldn't come to the door. I blocked his calls from my phone and deleted all of his text messages as soon as I saw them. I wasn't over what he did to me. I didn't know if I would ever be over it.

I was walkin' out of my hotel room when I saw roses on the windshield of my car. Of course, I knew they were from Carter. I started to just throw them out, but the card with them caught my eye:

> *Just wanted to make you feel better.*
> *-Nicholas*

I couldn't believe these were from Nicholas. That was so adorable of him. It was so cute for him to have them delivered to me. He was always doin' somethin' nice.

I had the biggest smile on my face. In a way, it felt like I was blushin'. I called him on Face Time to thank him.

"You are the sweetest person I know." I smiled at him as he answered my call.

"I see you got the flowers." He smiled at me.

"I did." I said. "You know you ain't have to do that."

"I know." He said. "But I wanted to. That's the smile I was waitin' to see the whole time we was at home. So now that I know you can still smile like that, I feel like I did my part."

"What am I gonna do with you?" I couldn't stop smilin' at him.

"I know you ain't blushin'." He laughed at me.

"No." I lied as I tried to stop smilin'. My cheeks were startin' to hurt from cheesin' so hard.

"I already seen it." He said. "Don't try to hide it now."

"Whatever." I said. "Ain't you posed to be in class anyway?"

"Don't you see me walkin' in the buildin." He said. "Why ain't you in class?"

"I got 30 minutes before mine start." I said. "I'm finna head up to campus now."

"Alright." He said. "You need to hurry up and get outta that hotel. You ain't got no business living out of a suitcase."

"I know Nicholas but I ain't ready to go back to stayin' with him." I said. "I still ain't even talked to him."

"Y'all gon' have to talk eventually." He said. "Whether you wana stay with 'em or not, y'all gotta communicate. Y'all live together. Yo can't be in that hotel forever."

"I just need more time to clear my head." I said as I got in my car. "Is that a problem?"

"Not at all." He said. "But I don't like you stayin' there. You want me to find you somethin' while you figure this shit out?"

"No I can't have you do that." I said.

"If you ain't outta that hotel in the next two weeks, you ain't gon' have a choice." He said. "Don't make me have to come down there and get you a place. Is that really how you want this to go?"

"No." I whined. "Nicholas, you can't rush me to go back to this man. I can't even believe you want me to go back to him."

"You ain't never heard that shit come outta my mouth." He said. "You know where I want you to be. If it was up to me, you would be here livin' with me. But it ain't my decision. I just know you ain't go away to school, to not have a place to stay. Maybe you do need to just get yo own spot for 6 months at least. Even if y'all do work y'all shit out, you may still need some time before you wana live with 'em again."

"Yea." I said. "That do make sense. I don't know let me just think about it for a few days."

"Alright I can do that." He said. "I'm getting ready to walk into class. I'll call you tonight after practice."

"Okay." I smiled at him. "Have a good day. And thanks again."

"You welcome." He blew me a kiss.

I blew him one back before we both hung up the phone. I couldn't believe how close me and Nicholas still were. He was the greatest best friend I ever had.

As soon as I pulled up to school and parked, I saw Carter. He hopped out his car and walked over to mine. At first, I didn't want to get out of the car, but I had to go to class. So, I decided to get out and act like I ain't see him. That didn't work.

"Jada slow down." Carter said as he followed me.

I ignored him. I couldn't even look at him, let alone talk to him. He grabbed my arm and I turned around to give him the look. He knew better than to grab me. He let me go but still kept followin' me.

"Please just talk to me." He whined. I wanted to keep walkin' and act like I ain't hear him but I knew I couldn't avoid him forever.
"What?" I finally turned around and asked him.

His eyes got so big. He was so surprised that I actually acknowledged him.

"I'm so sorry baby." He said. "I know I was trippin' about you and Nicholas and I thought y'all did somethin' while you was out there, so I felt like I needed to get back at you. I mean I know ain't none of this makin' it no better, but I just had to let you know."
"Is that it?" I asked as I looked at him.
"No, can we please just go somewhere and talk about this." He begged.
"I can't let you go. Whatever you want me to do, I'll do it. Just tell me what you need for me to make this right."

"I need you to leave me the hell alone." I said. "Stop textin' my phone. Stop callin' my mama lookin' for me. Leave me alone. I ain't got shit to say to you. And ain't nothin' you can say to me, to fix this shit."

"Jada, you can't just end this." He whined. "Baby I wana marry you. We posed to get married. What about our plans?"

"What about our plans?" I snapped. I had to remember where I was. "You wasn't thinkin' 'bout our plans when you was fuckin' that bitch, was you?"

"J please dont do this." He begged.

"Don't do what?" I asked. "What is it, that you don't want me to do?"

"Can I just get a minute to talk to you?" He asked.

"I been here for more than a minute, Carter." I said. "I gotta go to class."

"Can I see you after that?" He asked.

"For what?" I asked. "Don't you got class or somethin'?"

"I ain't got no classes til' later today." He said. "I'll be outside yo class when you get out. I'm tired of doin' this. It's time for you to come home. I know I fucked up but you gotta let me make it right."

I heard everything he said, but it just wasn't doin' nothin' for me. I ain't know how to respond so I just walked into class. This was the first class of the new semester and I really needed to focus on my work. Carter was just not a priority for me right now.

I was really startin' to consider getting my own place. I ain't want Nicholas to pay for it, but he had a great idea. I would have to figure it out on my own, but at least I could take his advice.

Nicholas

The first few weeks of the semester flew by so fast. My grades were still good as always. And Cassidy was still whinin' as always. It was like she looked for stuff to complain about.

A while ago Laya told me she tried to talk some sense into her. And at first it seemed like it was workin,' but then she just went back to her old naggin' ways. Don't get me wrong. I loved Cassidy. As much as I complained about the shit she complained about, I wasn't leavin her. Not for no petty ass shit like just getting on my nerves. It wasn't nothin' that I couldn't take from her.

The one thing that she knew wasn't changin', was the Jada issue. And because she finally figured out it wasn't changin', she stopped whinin' about it. Sometimes it seemed like she was done tryna keep me from talkin' to Jada, and other times she went back to bein' clingy again.

The whole pregnancy scare thing kinda helped us get closer at first, but then it seemed like it was workin' against us. I had a flashback of the shit with Jada getting pregnant by Will in high school and it really fucked up my head. I had to keep tellin' myself this was different and Cassidy wouldn't do no shit like that to me. I couldn't be too sure 'cuz I knew Jada would never do that to me and she did.

Jada was the first girl I ever trusted besides my mom. And to this day she was the only woman I trusted 100% besides my mom. It was kinda crazy after what she did to me, how I trusted her with my life now. Regardless of what happened between me and her, Jada was one person I couldn't imagine not bein' in my life.

I had just got home from practice and I walked in the room to see Cassidy clothes piled up in my chair. As busy as I was, I kept my place somewhat neat, but I hated clothes layin' around all over the place. Even though they were only in one spot, I just didn't like them bein' out. She knew that. She did it on purpose so she could whine about havin' somewhere to keep her clothes here. She knew I wasn't ready for her to be livin' with me. Slowly but surely she kept inchin' her way to move in with me. I wasn't goin' for it.

That shit just pissed me off. I planned on getting in the shower and then callin' Jada on Face Time. Now I gotta call Cassidy to get this shit together.

"Hey babe." Cassidy said as she answered my call.

"What's up." I said. "Where you at?"

"Just got back to my room." She said. "How was practice?"

"Cool." I said. "I thought I asked you to take these clothes with you when you left."

"Damn I forgot." She said. "You want me to come get 'em now?"

"Naw I'll just bring 'em to yo room in the mornin'." I said.

"What's yo problem?" She asked.

"You know I hate that shit." I said.

"I don't understand what the problem is with me leavin' my clothes at my man house." She said. "Damn you worried yo hoes gon' see another female clothes over there or somethin'?"

"I ain't tryna have shit all over my place." I said.

"It wouldn't be all over if I had somewhere to keep my stuff." She said.

"You do." I said. "In yo room. Where the rest of yo clothes at. What is so hard about that?"

"I don't like feelin' like I'm just somebody hoe who gotta clean up after themselves." She said. "What I look like makin' sure I don't leave a trace at my own nigga house?"

"I don't give a damn about no trace, Cassidy." I said. "I just don't like the clothes bein' left here."

"If you would just let me keep them somewhere there, you wouldn't even know they was there." She said. "Is it too much for me to get a damn drawer?"

"Yes." I said. "That's the first step towards you movin' in and we ain't ready for that."

"I been ready for it." She said. "It's you that's runnin' from it."

"I ain't runnin' from shit." I said. "I'm just not runnin' to it. That shit gon' happen when it's sposed to. As for now, I like bein' on my own. I like havin' my own shit and not bein' obligated to share it with you. I ain't tryna be

181

rude or selfish, but damn can I at least have my own place? You don't see me leavin' shit at yo dorm."

"You never even come to my room." She said. "If we together it's at yo house, or somewhere else."

"Cuz you never in yo room." I said. "You always here."

"Oh that's how you feel?" She asked.

"You know I ain't mean it like that." I said quickly.

"No, I don't know that." She said quietly. "Look I ain't tryna keep havin' this same damn argument. I'm just gon' stop stayin' the night over there, so we won't have this problem."

"That ain't what I want." I said.

"Well I'm tired of caterin' to what you want, when you ain't concerned about what I want." She said. "You could at least meet me halfway, but you can't even do that. It's either yo way or no way at all. Sometimes you just really selfish, Nicholas."

"Stop tryna turn this on me." I said. "I told you from jump when I moved off campus this was not bouta be our spot. You knew what it was."

"Yes, I did." She said. "But somewhere along the line I guess I just thought you would want me to stay there with you."

"Eventually I will." I said. "But I just ain't there right now. Why you in such a rush? We got all the time in the world to live together."

"Whatever, Nicholas." She said. "Is it anything else you wana complain about? Did I not wash the dishes good enough this time?"

"Really?" I asked. "Grow up Cassidy. I ain't say shit about nothin' else and you know it."

"I just wanted to make sure I ain't do nothin' else wrong to upset you." She said.

"Grow the fuck up." I said before I hung up on her ass.

She was really pissin' me off. I wasn't in the mood to deal with her ass today. I called my dad to see what he had to say about it.

"Hello." I said after he answered the phone.

"What's up, man." My dad said. "What you up to?"

"Nothin' just got home from practice." I said. "What y'all doin'?"

"Just finished eatin' dinner." He said.

"Aw yea." I said. "Dad Cassidy is getting on my nerves. She still trippin' about stayin' here and I'm just tired of hearin' it."

"What she do now?" He laughed.

"I come home to her clothes piled up in my chair." I said. "She know I hate that shit. And she do it on purpose so she can whine about havin' somewhere to keep her clothes here."

"Have you talked to her about it?" He asked.

"Too many times." I said. "I'm tired of talkin' about it. I'm tired of hearin' myself say the same shit to her, and hearin' her say the same shit. What don't she understand about me just wantin' to live on my own right now?"

"I don't know, man." He said. "You don't have to be rude about it though, Nicholas."

"I ain't rude." I said. "Only reason I sound rude now is 'cuz I'm fed up. Then she gon' get mad and say she just won't spend the night here since it's that big of a deal. How hard is it to take yo clothes with you when you leave? That shit is the simplest thing I ever heard of, but she make it seem like it's so difficult. She just don't wana do it. She wana see how much she can get away with. And I don't appreciate that. Don't push me. Don't keep tryin' me til' I snap. Then I'ma be exactly where I'm at now. Hangin' up on her ass."

"Calm down." He laughed at me. "You getting all worked up for nothin'. You said what you had to say. So, she made her own decision. If that's the only way she feel like she ain't gon' leave her stuff over there, you have to accept that. I know you want her to sleep there with you, but you can't have yo cake and eat it too. Somethin' gotta give. You can at least compromise with her if you want her to be there every night."

"I don't want her here every night." I said. "Two, three nights a week is enough for me. I'm busy as hell. We both are. We don't have time to entertain each other every night. We know that. We accept that. So why should I have to try that every night just 'cuz she here? No. I'm not. So, I'm cool with her stayin' over a few nights a week. But her not stayin' here at all, that's petty. She doin' that shit just to spite me and I don't appreciate it."

"Well call her on it." He said. "See how long she can go without stayin' over there. And you just wait on her to break first."

"What if that take too long?" I asked him.

"Then you have to be the bigger person and come up with a way for it to work for both of y'all." He said. "Nicholas, I know you. You ain't selfish, but sometimes you get set in yo own ways. So, I know this probably a lot for

Cassidy to deal with. You gotta think about her feelings in all this too. I'm sure she has valid reasons why she leave her stuff there. I know she ain't really just forgettin' all the time."

"I know." I said. "But what I'm sposed to do if I don't agree with her reasons."

"Figure out what you can give up, to give what you want." He said. "But it has to work for her too. Compromising ain't that hard, Nicholas. You just wana control everything 'cuz it's yo spot."

"And what's wrong with that?" I asked. "When she get her own place, then she can make the rules for it. Until then, she gon' have to go by mine if this where she gon' be."

"It's crazy that you actually think you can control this girl." He laughed.

"I ain't tryna control her." I said. "I just want my space. I know that ain't too much to ask. When she want her space, she go to her dorm. Ain't none of my shit there makin' her room look messy. When I wana be by myself, I come home to her shit. It's always here. It ain't been a day that I came home and not seen her stuff here."

"Clearly this is really getting to you." He laughed. "Why is it so important to you to not have anything reminding you of her at yo apartment?"

"It ain't that." I said. "We got pictures together all over the place. That I let her hang up. What I look like hangin' pictures and shit up? She wanted them up, I let her do it. Everybody know we together. And it ain't like no females be here anyway, so I don't have nothin' to hide. I just want my shit, to be my shit, and not have to look at her shit everyday. If she ain't here, she don't see my stuff, but it ain't like that the other way around."

"I mean I get what you sayin'." He said. "Just make sure you wantin' yo space is for the right reasons."

"I ain't havin' this conversation again, Dad." I said.

"Don't tell me what you ain't havin'." He said. "If I wana talk to you about it, I can. I'm not 'cuz once is enough, but still I could bring it up again if I wanted too."

I had to laugh at his old ass. He was crazy.

"I guess." I laughed. "Anyways, what's goin' on there? Music Note still wana quit ballet?"

"Naw." He said. "Now she wana do ballet and tap. She just so confused. First, she wanted to stop ballet and do tap. Now she wana do both. That girl wana be in everything."

"That's a good thing though." I said. "Keep her busy so she ain't got time to be worried bout no lil' boys."

"I know." He agreed.

It was crazy how me and my dad agreed on so much stuff when it came to Music Note. We agreed on stuff about my mama too. But when it came to what was goin' on with me and Cassidy, it's like he just had a different way of seeing things.

I mean I guess it was just because he was in my position, and it didn't play out the way he thought it would. So maybe he just thought the same thing was gon' happen to me. But I already knew where my life was goin'. And I knew who was never leavin' my side. The only thing that was left for me to really do was to sit back and enjoy the show.

Trevor

Ever since the whole thing started with Tracy I was really stressed out. I knew she was with a million guys in college, but it was still a possibility of me bein' the father of her child.

In front of Nina I had to act like it wasn't shit to me, but in reality I did not want another kid. I mean it wasn't like I couldn't support him or help him with anything. The boy was damn near grown now so it ain't like he would need too much from me. But I just wasn't ready to explain that to my family.

Yes, it was common for black men to have kids they didn't know about, but I wasn't that guy. I was never that guy. I know I made the mistake of sleepin' with some random girl without protection, but I never thought that shit would come back to bite me in the ass.

My whole life would change if I was his dad. It was too embarrassing to think about. I was sittin' in my office workin' on a case when Jamal popped up.

"What's up man." I said as he walked in. "What you doin' here?"

"Nina called." He said as he sat in the chair. "Said you been in here lookin' depressed all day."

"Shut up." I laughed at him. "Ain't nobody depressed. I don't know what she called you for. Ain't nothin' wrong with me."

He looked at me like he didn't believe me.

"So, what you workin' on?" He asked.

"Nothin' really." I said.

"You just sittin' there lookin' at the computer?" He asked lookin' at me like I was a fool.

"Alright damn." I said. "It's this Tracy chick."

"Tracy who?" He asked.

"The girl who said she wanted to interview us." I said.

"So y'all found out what she actually wanted, huh?" He asked.

"Yup." I said quietly. "I messed around with her my freshman year. Now she talkin' 'bout she had my son. This shit don't make no damn sense."

"What?" He asked. "Why she wait all this time to tell you he was yours?"

"Man I don't know." I said. "She claim I played her for Carmen, but I wasn't never with that girl. This the first time I ever heard her name so that tell you I ain't even know her."

"Somethin' ain't right about this story." He said.

"That's what I'm sayin'." I said. "I don't know what she think 'bouta happen."

"So, when you take the DNA test?" He asked.

"I didn't." I said.

"What you waitin' on?" He asked. "You know it's yo son?"

"Hell naw." I said. "I just ain't tryna have another kid."

"You ain't havin' another kid." He said. "He already here. Grown as hell. Really you just gon' be makin' up for loss time."

"See that's the problem." He said. "I don't have the time to be doin' all that. I got my own family. My own life. My own shit to take care of. I know it sound selfish but this just ain't a good time for me to be addin' somebody else to the equation."

"Damn." He said. "Now that shit is crazy. Trevor this is outta yo control. You don't even know if the boy gon' want you in his life and you already too busy for 'em? How that sound?"

"Fucked up." I said. "I know. But that's just how I feel."

"You can't avoid that test forever." He said. "The way you actin' it look like you already know the truth. I know it ain't what you wanted, but this shit happen. A lot. You ain't the only one. And you damn sure ain't the last one it could happen to. It's just somethin' you gotta deal with. I don't understand why you runnin' from this shit. At least you in a position to be able to help him if he need somethin'."

"I don't feel like helpin' nobody." I said. "Why is that so wrong?"

"Cuz now you actin' like a kid." He said. "For no damn reason. You made the choice not to use a condom, so now you may have to deal with the consequences. It's that simple Trevor. Why you makin' it so difficult?"

"I know you ain't come down here to yell at me." I said.

"Man I ain't even know none of this was goin' on." He said. "Runnin' away from this shit ain't gon' change it. You actin' like Dad and I can't believe that shit."

As soon as he said I was actin' like our Dad, I knew what my father had done. I couldn't even respond to Jamal's comment 'cuz I was so shocked that I just figured out what my Dad did. I don't know why, but for some reason both of us were scared to face the truth. But Jamal was right. Runnin' from the truth, didn't change it.

Malcolm

I was walking out of my chemistry class when my professor stopped me.

"Malcolm, you got a minute?" Ms. Robinson asked me.

"Yea." I said as I stopped at her desk. "What's goin' on?"

"Well I wanted to talk to you about some private tutoring." She smiled at me.

"For what?" I asked as I looked at her confused.

I know Ms. Robinson was not really tryna get with me.

"Well I noticed a few things in your last paper, that I would like to go over you with." She said.

"Like what?" I asked her.

She was beating around the bush about somethin'. She gave me an A on the last paper so I really didn't know what she wanted me to change.

"It's more of a private issue." She said as she sat on her desk.

She crossed her legs and her skirt slid up to show the majority of her thigh. I tried not to notice but it was so obvious. Ms. Robinson was fine as hell. But I just couldn't do that to Laya. I can't lie she did make me wana take her up on the private lesson though.

"I'ma busy man, Ms. Robinson." I said. "I gotta few minutes now if you wanted me to look at yo comments or somethin'. But when I looked at the paper I ain't see no comments on it. Did you go back over it or somethin'?"

"Why don't you come by my place later on, after practice?" She asked.

"I can't." I said. "I got plans. How bout I come ten minutes before class tomorrow and then we can go over it?"

"I think this issue needs to be discussed off campus." She said.

"I don't really have a lot of free time, Ms. Robinson." I said. "I got class. Practice. Work. A girlfriend. I can fit somethin' in before or after class, but I don't see why we can't meet here."

She smiled at me seductively. Now I knew she wanted me. What in the hell was I gon' do with Ms. Robinson? She was relentless.

She got up off the desk and stood directly in front of me. She kissed my cheek and looked at me. I stood back and looked at her.

"I'm sorry." She said tryin' to play it off. "I didn't mean to offend you."

"It's cool." I smiled at her. "But I gotta go." I said as I left the classroom.

She was really trippin'. It was no way in hell I was messin' up shit with Laya. Even though I felt like I should get a pass 'cuz this was my teacher, she wasn't goin' for that.

I know I ain't do nothin' wrong but I had to tell Laya. Just to cover my ass. In case this shit went on and got outta hand, I needed to let her know right now what Ms. Robinson had goin' on. I called Laya as I was walkin' to my car.

"Hey babe." She said as she answered the phone.

"What's up." I said. "Where you at?"

"Work." She said. "Getting' ready to leave in a minute and go to practice. You just now leavin' class?"

"Yea." I said. "So why Ms. Robinson tryna get with me."

"What?" She asked. "What you mean?"

"She asked me to come to her house for some private tutoring." I laughed as I got in my car.

"Well maybe your work is slippin'." She said.

"She wanted to talk to me about a paper she already gave me an A on." I said. "Ain't nothin' else to improve if she already gave me the highest grade."

"What the hell she on?" She asked finally takin' me seriously.

She was only calm before 'cuz she didn't believe me.

"I don't know." I just kept laughin'.

"So, it's funny?" She asked.

"It was when you was laughin'." I said. "Look it ain't nothin' to trip about. I let her know it wasn't gon' happen."

"I can't believe her." She said. "She always actin' like she wana be my friend. Whole time she tryna get my man, though?"

"Shut up." I said. "Ain't nothin' goin' on so don't worry about It. I just had to let you know 'cuz I thought it was funny."

"I don't see what's so funny but whatever." She said.

"Stop getting mad." I laughed. "I'll see you after practice."

"Alright." She said. "Bye." Before we hung up.

That girl was crazy. Her and Ms. Robinson was crazy. I ain't know what was gon' happen after class tomorrow. Hopefully she ain't try that shit again. Cuz I ain't know how many times I was gon' be able to resist her ass. Especially not with all them short skirts she like to wear. If she kept that up we would definitely have a problem.

Jamal

"Hey sexy." I said to Stacy as I answered her call.

"Hello handsome." She responded. "I miss you. When are you comin' home?"

"I'm actually on my way now." I said. "June Bug sleep?"

"Yup." She said. "How long you think you gon' be?"

"Ten minutes at the most." I smiled. "What you got on?"

She laughed at me then got quiet. I knew she was thinkin' about if she should play along or not.

"Yo t-shirt." She said quietly.

"Anything under that?" I asked.

"Nope." She said.

"Just what I like to hear." I smiled. "Babe I been missin' you like crazy. This new schedule is ridiculous. When I leave you at home, and when you leave I'm there. You sure you really wana keep workin'? I think it might be time for you be a stay at home mom."

"Really?" She asked. "I mean I don't know. June Bug does keep me busy enough to be my full-time job. But I don't know how I'ma feel just stayin' home and not havin' nowhere to go."

"If I promise to have a reason for you to leave the house everyday can you please think about it?" I asked. "I just miss comin' home to you.

Watching you cook dinner. Naked. Half naked. Us layin' around together not havin' shit to do."

"We're parents now Jamal." She said. "So, some of that has to change, ya know. But I do get what you sayin'. We don't have a lot of us time anymore. Maybe we could take a vacation or somethin'. I think we need to get away."

"Hell yea." I said. "Look that shit up now. Let's go this weekend."

She started laughin so loud.

"Who gon' watch June Bug?" She asked.

"I'll see what Nina and Trevor doin' this weekend." I said. "I'm sure they ain't gon' have a problem with it. I'm pullin' up now. Take that t shirt off." I hung up the phone and hopped out of the car.

I went in the house and stared at my beautiful wife. She was amazing. After all these years I was still in love with her. I was more in love with her after she gave me June Bug.

Shit was never easy with us but she never left my side. This was the woman I had been with since high school. I loved the fact that she was still my biggest fan. I picked her up and took her to the bedroom.

I put her on the bed and locked our door. As soon as I started kissin' all over her, somebody rung the doorbell. I ignored it and went back to what I was doin'. Whoever it was started bangin' at the door when we didn't come after the doorbell rung.

"Bae, we gotta get it." She said. "They gon' wake up June Bug."
"Fuck!" I screamed as I got up from on top of her.

I walked to the front door mad as hell. She stayed in the bed and waited for me to get rid of whoever it was. I ain't even look through the peephole. I just had to see who the hell this was bangin' on my door like they ain't have no damn sense. I opened the door and damn near fainted. What the hell was my Dad doin' standin' on my porch.

I ain't even know what to say to him. We just stared at each other for a few minutes. Eventually Stacy came out to see what was goin' on. She looked at us like she was confused. She finally broke the silence.

"Hey Joe." She smiled as she walked up to him. "You comin' in?" She hugged him.
"Yea." He finally spoke.

He came in and sat on the couch. I closed the door and sat in the chair across from him. Stacy sat on the arm of my chair and put her arm around my shoulder. I guess she thought that was supposed to sooth me.

"So..." She said. "This is a nice surprise."

"Yea I needed to get a few things off my chest." He said quietly. "How everybody been?"

"We been really good actually." She said. "June Bug in the back sleep. Everything been goin' good here. What about you? You doin' okay? Look like you been stressin' about somethin'?" She rubbed my back as I stared at him.

"I'm hangin' in there." He said. "Stacy could you give me and Jamal a minute? It's somethin' I need to talk to him about."

"Yea go head." She said.

She gave me the look to let me know to be cool. Sometimes I loved when Stacy gave me the look. Other times I wish she wouldn't treat me like a kid. She knew my dad was trippin'. Once she left the room, the attention was on me.

"So how ya been son?" He asked.

"Cut the small talk." I said. "Who is Valerie?"

"A while ago, I made a mistake." He said. "And that mistake ended up, causing another mistake. Long story short, you and Trevor have a younger sister."

I knew it was some bull shit like that. I couldn't believe he just couldn't tell us. I wasn't even mad that he fucked up. I was mad that he kept this from us all this time.

"How long ago was this?" I asked.

After the shit he just told me I was surprised at how calm I was. It was actually scary how calm I was.

"That's not important, Jamal." He said.

"How long ago, Dad." I repeated myself quietly.

"25 years." He said as he stared at me. "I know I shoulda told y'all then. It shoulda never happened. I never shoulda did that to yo mom."

"So, why did you?" I asked. I had to know how the perfect man, perfect dad, finally fucked up. "I mean let mom tell it you could do no wrong. You acted like you never did anything wrong. I just gotta know how this perfect man, could make a mistake."

"I'm human." He said. "And my biggest mistake was not lettin' y'all see that. Y'all needed to know that it's okay to make mistakes. That's the only way we learn from somethin'. I was so busy tellin' y'all how to be better men than me, I forgot to show y'all how to become a better man. Everybody makes mistakes. Big or small. They happen. It's life. We have no control over that. Instead of me makin' y'all aware of reality, I just raised y'all to not be one of the statistics."

"Whole time you were actually one of the statistics." I said sharply. "Well maybe had we discussed this 25 years ago, your youngest son would know how to deal with the shit he in now. Maybe if we discussed this 25 years ago, I wouldn't be sittin' here starin' at you feelin' sorry for you. Me and Trevor ain't did nothin' but look up to you all our lives. What made you think that you bein' human, would make you any less of a man to us? Any less of a father? If anything that would help us to know that it was okay for us to fuck up. That we didn't disregard everything our perfect father taught us. You didn't even give us a chance to accept this. Now it's just bein' thrown in our face. You ain't even give us a chance to understand you and why you did the shit you did. Why would you think we would judge you? What made you think our perception of you would change?"

"I can't sit here and constantly tell y'all to do the right thing." He said. "Especially by y'all women, when I can't even do right by mine."

"It ain't that you can't." I said. "It's that you didn't. I mean I'm pissed that you would do that to my mama, but you are a man. So, I can understand the temptation. And I know shit ain't always easy with mama. So, I understand. You forget we men too. We know exactly how you was feelin'. You don't think we been there. Now we might have handled the situation differently than you, but don't think we ain't never been there. I don't know what kinda recovery its gon' take for us to look at you the same. Which is fucked up 'cuz it ain't even based on what you did, it's all about how you handled it. We yo kids. We gon' love you regardless. Ain't nothin' you can do to change that. But you can't treat us like we don't deserve the truth."

"I know." He said. "And I'm sorry. I just ain't wana destroy my family. I know I risked losing everything, for nothing. That ain't nothin' I'm proud of. I ain't want y'all to see me that low."

"Dad we all fall." I said. "That ain't what we concerned about. We just want you to shake that shit off and make the best of the situation. I mean

202

that's what you taught us. We ain't expect you to be perfect. You set yoself up for that failure. Not us."

"I just can't believe this happened to me." He said. "I mean I knew what I was out there doin'. I just ain't never think it would go this far."

"Now you really sound like Trevor." I said. "Look Dad, it really ain't nothin' else for me to say. I think you should go on over to Trevor's and talk to him about this. Honestly, he really the one that need to hear this. Me on the other hand, I'm kinda in the middle of somethin' right now. Me and my wife ain't had no alone time in a while, so that's what we workin' on while June Bug sleep."

"Aw well I can take 'em back home with me for the weekend." He smiled. "I know yo mom wana see 'em again."

"Yea that's cool." I said. "We was gon' try to get us a vacation in anyway this weekend. So go on over there and talk to him, and then call me and we can get things set up."

"Alright." He said. "Thanks son. For understanding."

"I wish you had let me do that 25 years ago." I said. "But you welcome old man."

"I'll call you later." He said as he stood up.

"Alright." I said as I walked him to the door.

I opened the door, let him out and closed it quickly before he thought of somethin' else to say. I turned around to see my baby mama standin' in the hallway, naked. With her red heels on.

"I loved the way you handled that baby." She smiled as I walked towards her.

"You gon' love how I handle this." I smiled at her as I led her back to the bedroom. This was long overdue.

Jada

Carter had been tryin' everything possible to get me back. And I had to admit, it was startin' to work. If I didn't start missing him, I felt like I woulda never even entertained what he was sayin'. But I loved him. That never changed. Even though he fucked up, I still loved him.

Ironically, I still wanted to marry him. I felt like he deserved a second chance. When I fucked up with Nicholas I begged him for a second chance. And he could never give it to me. Here I was with somebody beggin' for me to do the same thing I wanted years ago. I had the option to do for somebody else, what another person couldn't do for me. If I didn't give him this shot, I would be just as self-righteous as Nicholas. Actually, I would be a hypocrite.

I'm the one who cheated years ago and expected a second chance. Carter cheated now, and I honestly felt like he should have a chance to make this right. The only question I had in my mind, was could he? What if he did everything possible to get our shit back right and it still wasn't enough for me? What if I was too hurt to be able to leave the mistakes in the past?

Truthfully, I couldn't tell if I would be able to get over it. I ain't know how things would work out with me and Carter in the future. But I did know that I wanted to try and see if we could get back right. I know he made a mistake. I know I might be crazy for forgiving him. But when I was in his shoes, all I wanted was forgiveness. All I wanted was another shot to prove that I wouldn't fuck up again.

So now, I had to give him this shot. After everything we went through, it was the least I could do. Carter had done so much for me since I met him. Things he never had to do. Things I never asked him to do. So I felt like this was the least I could do, for him.

"You ready to come home?" Carter asked me as he stood at my hotel door.

I hadn't been stayin' at the house, but I was allowin' him to see me a few nights a week at my hotel. We were makin' progress. Slowly but surely. I missed him so much it was hard not seeing him everyday. But I felt like if we rushed back into our normal routine, things would never get better.

"I'm not sure yet." I said as I let him in.
"What you mean?" He asked as he sat down. "I thought you said you wanted to come home."
"I mean I do want to." I said. "I just don't want to get there and you think just 'cuz I'm back that you don't have anything to work on."
"I told you that ain't gon' happen." He said. "But you ain't gon' know that if you don't let me show you."

"Carter, I can't go through this again." I said. "This the only fuck up I can take and I need you to know that. Just 'cuz I'm staying does not mean that I'm okay with what you did. I'm tryin' to get past it. That's what it means. I'm tryna get past it 'cuz I love you and I still wana marry you. But I don't want you thinkin' that you got away with it this time so you can keep doin' it. I ain't goin' for that shit."

"Baby I know." He smiled. "Just come home so we can get started on makin' this shit better. We been apart too damn long."

"I know." I had to agree.

It had been months since I even kissed him. He was still so damn sexy to me. This was the longest I had ever stayed mad at him and it wasn't that easy after a while.

"We just need to take this as slow as possible to make sure everything go good this time. I mean, can we do that?" I asked.

"Yes." He said. "We can do whatever you want, baby."

He got up and walked over to me as I sat on the bed. As he approached me my phone started ringing. It was Nicholas. He was callin' me on Face Time. After all this time thinkin' about what I was gon' do with Carter, I hadn't even thought about tellin' Nicholas.

What was he gonna say? I knew he ain't want me to be with Carter, especially after the shit he did, but I I knew he would support whatever decision I made. That ain't mean he had to like it though. I just hoped he ain't cut me off again. The last time he did that I couldn't stand not talkin' to him.

Paisley

I was leavin' out of the spot one night when I noticed somebody in a black Range Rover watchin' me. Every time somebody left alone one of the security guards walked us out. Ray Ray was the biggest one and I made sure he got me to my car safely. I got in the car and rolled my window down to tell him thank you.

"Thanks Ray Ray." I smiled at him.
"No problem, P." He smiled back at me. "Let me know when you make it home.
"I will." I said.

He was always worried about me. Ray Ray was my favorite. If Magic got outta line with any of the girls, Ray Ray put his ass in check. Ray Ray was Magic's younger brother, but he acted like the more mature one.

"Alright." He said as I pulled out the parkin' lot.

When I turned the corner, I noticed the same Range Rover followin' me. Who in the hell was this? I looked in my glove compartment to make sure I still had my gun loaded. I wasn't scared, just had to be prepared. I knew some shit was bouta go down, and I damn sure wasn't runnin' from it.

I kept drivin' my normal speed. Cruisin' down the freeway. Smokin' my nightly after work blunt. The Range Rover never sped up or tried to get on the side of me. So, I turned up my music and forgot they were even there.

When I turned down my street, they went the opposite way. I knew better than that. They were probably goin' around the other way to meet me at my house. Whoever it was, really had somethin' against me. I just couldn't figure out who it was. I done fucked over so many niggas, it could really be anybody in there.
Considering the fact that I always see the niggas after the fact and they don't say nothin' to me, I felt like I was safe from those guys. Maybe somebody just grew some balls.

It was cool with me. I liked a challenge. This was all a game to me. Which is what they all failed to understand. If a nigga wanted to get me, he had to get me while I wasn't lookin' 'cuz I wasn't goin' down without a fight. Bad part for them was, I was always lookin'. Eyes in the back of my head at all times.

I drove past my house and went to one of my spots at the corner, where I could still see my house. The Range Rover pulled up behind my condo with the lights off. Rookie. Who the hell he think he foolin'? I decided to call for back up. I ain't know who was in that car, or how many people they had with 'em.

"Lo." I said as London answered the phone.

"P, what's up?" She asked soundin' worried.

"Shit." I said. "Somebody followed me from The Spot to my house. I'm parked down the street at the corner. They behind my condo with they lights out."

"Alright." She said. "I'm on my way."

I ain't even have to explain shit to her. Lo knew everything I did. She knew at any point in time shit could get real. And I knew she would be there to help me with that shit.

15 minutes later she pulled up and parked her car next to mine. I hopped in the car with her.

"Who you think it is?" She asked as we sat there for a minute.

"Girl I have no idea." I said. We both tucked our guns in the back of our pants.

"You ready?" She asked.

"Hell yea." I said.

She pulled out of the spot and crept down to my condo. The truck was still parked in back tryin' to hide. She parked at the condo in front of mine, and we snuck out of her car. We crept around the back of the truck and then to the front. Once I peeked inside I saw that is was Devon. He was alone. How did this nigga know where I moved to? I ain't like that shit. I could handle myself but I wasn't bouta go through this every night. This wasn't no shit I could just let slide. I had to teach his ass a lesson.

I broke his driver side window with my gun and pointed it straight at his head. Lo broke the passenger side window with hers and aimed at the other side of his head.

"What the fuck you doin' here?" I asked him as he looked terrified.
"I just wanted to see you." He said lookin' scared.
"Bull shit." I said. "It's no reason for you to need to see me. And how the hell you know where I stay anyway?"
"I been watchin' you." He said.

Me and Lo never put our guns down the whole time I talked to him. He just couldn't be trusted.

"You need to get the fuck on and don't come back to my spot." I said.
"Or my job. We ain't got nothin' to talk about."
"Oh I think we do." He said as he pulled his gun out.

Before he got off any shots, me and Lo let 4 go a piece. That nigga never stood a chance. We put his ass in the back of his truck, and I drove his shit downtown. Lo followed me in her car so we could ride back in it.

We set his shit on fire and got rid of him. I got back in her car and we headed back to my house.

"What the fuck was that nigga thinkin'?" Lo asked me as we got in my house.

"I don't even know." I said. "I knew it was gon' be some bull shit. That nigga thought he was gon' get my ass."

"Right." She laughed as we went upstairs to my room.

"I'm bouta hop in the shower." I said.

"I'm goin' in the guest room to do the same." She said as she walked in the guest room.

I got in the shower and sat down on my bench. My shower was the only place I could achieve complete serenity. I loved it. It was so soothing. I sat there in silence and actually thought about what just happened to us. It was fuckin' crazy.

The list of niggas that I robbed was longer than my damn arm. Nobody had every came back for my ass. Never. I guess that had me feelin' untouchable. Even though we got rid of Devon, I didn't like the fact that I had to do that to him. Nobody had ever put me in that position to get rid of they ass. I was glad I could take care of it with somebody I trust with my life, but still I ain't want it to go down like that. I ended up fallin' asleep in the shower. I ain't wake up til' Lo came in the bathroom an hour later.

"P get up." She said as she put on her makeup in the mirror. "Go get in the bed."

"Damn I ain't even know I was sleep." I said. "You bouta go to work?"

"Yup." She said. "Gotta get to the money."

I laughed at her as I turned off the water. I grabbed my robe and put it on before I stepped out.

"Yo hair look so nice, Lo." I said as I sat on the counter watchin' her put on her makeup. "What you do to it?"

"I curled it a few nights ago and slept with rollers." She said. "That's it really."

"Aw okay." I smiled at her.

"You alright?" She asked as she looked at me in the mirror.

"Yea." I said. "You?"

"Yea." She said. "Don't worry about it. That nigga ain't comin' back."

We laughed together.

"Hell naw." I said. "I don't even know why he thought that shit was okay. I ain't never had to deal with no shit like that before."

"Right." She said. "And then he wait all this time to come back and do somethin'. What the hell is that about?"

"Same thing I'm sayin'." I said.

"Well at least we took care of it." She said. "I gotta go, P. I'll call you on my break to check on you."

"Alright." I said as I walked her to the door. "Thanks Lo." I hugged her.

"No problem girl." She smiled at me as she walked out the door.

Once I got back upstairs I heard my phone ringin. I was not in the mood to talk to nobody. I ignored the call and turned my phone off. I climbed in the bed and went back to sleep.

Trevor

I couldn't believe I was right about my dad. But I definitely wasn't expectin' to hear his shit happened over 20 years ago. I couldn't even be mad at him no more. I understood how he could avoid it all this time.

Tracy had been throwin' this baby business around for months now and I was still holdin' off on the DNA test. Nina was startin' to get restless. Tracy was mad too but I ain't give a damn about her. If this shit was true, why would she keep my son away from me all this time?

I had all these different emotions about the situation. One day I wanted him to be mine, the next day I prayed he wasn't. It was really fucked up.

"Hey." I said to Nina as I walked in the house. She was in the livin' room doin' Music Note's hair.
"Hi daddy." Music Note said.

Nina didn't respond. I went back to the bedroom and changed my clothes. When I came back out to the living room, Music Note was gone and Nina was puttin on her shoes.

"Where you goin'?" I asked her.
"Out." She said.

"You got a minute?" I asked.

"Not really." She said as she grabbed her keys.

"Don't be like that." I said.

"Like what?" She asked as she finally looked at me.

She was so cute when she tried to stay mad. I could tell she was ready to give in to me. I don't know why she had to be so stubborn.

"Sit down." I smiled at her as I sat on the couch.

She sat down next to me.

"What?" She asked.

"I ain't tryna have you mad at me right now." I said. "I'm goin' through a lot with this Tracy bull shit, and I just need you to be there for me. Whether you agree with my decisions or not. Why is that impossible?"

"It ain't." She said. "I been here for you. For months. And I'm sorry I feel bad for her that you won't at least take the test. It makes no sense. Especially after all the shit yo dad dealin' with. That should be a sign for you."

"Now see that's different." I said. "My daddy ain't even take the test. My mama set that up." She looked at me like she wanted to do the same.

"Don't get no ideas. Let me find out you sneakin' around and we gon' have a problem."

"The difference between yo parents and us is yo dad was cheatin'." She said. "So yo mom needed to know the truth. All of yo shit happened before me so I don't need to do nothin' to prove somethin' to me. I'm doin' my best to let you get through this at yo own pace but I'm tired of not knowin'. You should be too. It's been goin' on too damn long, for no reason. Cuz you scared? What kinda shit is that? You a grown ass man. Get over that shit and take the damn test."

"It ain't that fuckin' simple." I snapped.

"Who you talkin' to?" She snapped back.

"You think you just bouta sit up here and snap on me and I ain't gon' say shit?" I asked her.

"Whatever, Trevor." She said as she stood up. "I don't need this shit."

"Wait." I jumped up to stop her. "I'm sorry I ain't mean that." I said as I grabbed her.

"Let me go." She said as she looked away.

"Come on let's just finish talkin' about this." I said.

"I ain't got shit else to say." She said.

"Well I do." I said.

"I got somewhere to be." She said.

I let her go and looked at her to see if she was really serious. I knew she wasn't gon' leave like that.

"And where is that?" I asked.

"It don't even matter." She said as she left out of the house.

I couldn't believe she just left in the middle of the conversation. I went to the kitchen and made me a plate when I heard the phone ring. It was my mom. I ain't wana hear it, but I knew if I ain't answer I would have to hear her mouth.

"Hello." I answered as I sat at the table.

"Trevor what is yo problem?" She asked. "Why haven't you taken that test yet?"

"I just got a lot goin' on right now, Ma." I said.

"Boy you ain't got nothin' goin' on but this." She said. "You lettin' this stress you out when you can end all that today. Get it over with so you'll know what to do from there. You can't really be that scared if this boy is yours. It's not gon' be the end of the world. Look at me and yo dad. He did his dirt and I still forgave him. We moved on from that mistake and we've been fine since then. Now it wasn't easy for me to accept him havin' another child with someone else, but I did it. And I know Nina will be just fine handlin' it."

"It ain't her I'm worried about." I said. "I already know she can handle it. It's me. How that make me look? A kid that came outta nowhere and I ain't know nothin' about."

"You're too proud." She said. "Baby I know you're embarrassed. Trust me I know. But somewhere down the line you gotta get off yo high horse and stop thinkin' that you too good to make mistakes. Yo father has put that in y'all head all these years and that ain't reality. We all mess up. And that's where the consequences come in. Now if this boy is yours, you will be dealin' with the consequences. If not, then you thank the Lord and never let nothin' happen like this again. I'm tired of Nina and Jamal callin' me mad at you 'cuz you actin' like a kid. I'm givin' you a week to get in there and take that test, and if not I'm comin' up there to take you to the clinic myself."

"Ma I'ma grown man." I said. "You can't make me take a test."

"You wana bet?" She asked. "Now don't get beside yoself 'cuz we on the phone. You remember who you talkin' to."

"Yes mam." I laughed at her.

She was a mess. I couldn't believe they really called my mama on me.

"Trevor, you are a grown man." She said. "But I need you to act like it. You've always taken responsibility for your actions. What is really goin' on that you can't do that now?"

"Ma I just ain't tryna be another statistic." I said. "That ain't me. The main reason I work so hard is cuz I don't ever want nobody to say he just like everybody else."

"We all know that baby." She said. "Who are you tryna convince? You don't have to prove yoself to nobody. All of your accomplishments do enough of that. Stop worryin' about what other people think and live yo life how you want. Everything you do should not be to prove people wrong."

"I know." I said. "I just ain't see my life turnin' out this way."

"You think I thought I would have a step-daughter that I ain't seen since I gave her mother the DNA? Look at how my life done turned out. It was a mess. But I made the best of it. That's the only way I knew how to deal with it. Nobody life is gon' be perfect. When things start to be too good to be true, they usually are. That's just a warning that somethin' bouta happen. So instead of runnin' from it, be ready for it. Now I know we done taught you that much."

"You have." I said. "But if he is my kid, how y'all gon' explain that to the family?"

"I ain't explainin nothin'." She said. "It ain't my business. Now if he is yours, you can explain that to yo family. Or not. You don't owe anybody anything."

"I mean it's gon' come up at the get togethers and stuff." I said.

"Baby just let go of what other people think." She said. "Or might think. You gon' live a stressful life tryna please everybody. As long as you takin' care of yoself and yo family, none of that other stuff should even matter."

"You make it sound so simple." I said.

"And you make it sound so hard." She said. "The only reason it's hard for you is 'cuz you still fightin. It already happened. You can't change the past. All you can do is learn from it. So, take the test, baby. If not for yourself, do it for me. I hated that I had to sneak and do a test behind yo father's back. Don't push Nina to that level. Things only gon' get worse if she gotta do it on her own."

"Yea you right." I said. "I'ma do it, Ma. I just need to get it over with."

"Thank you, baby." She said.

Nicholas

Cassidy was still stuck in her ways of not sleepin' at my place. Honestly, I was startin' not to care. We were still together. Everything was actually good. She just didn't sleep here anymore. I was too busy to miss it. That sounded bad but it was the truth. Finishin' up with basketball left me more time to work. And that's what I did.

I was workin' in the athletic department at my school. I wanted to own a gym eventually but I actually wanted to know everything that went on behind the scenes. I planned on havin' trainers and physical therapists in there so I wanted to know about that stuff too.

I was workin' with my coach on a project when Jada called me on Face Time.

"What's up?" I smiled at her as I walked away from my coach.

"Hey." She smiled. "You busy?"

"Just workin'." I said. "What you up to?"

"Headed to work." She said. "I just thought I would check up on you. Long time no see."

"Been tryna give you yo space to get shit back right with yo man." I said.

"I appreciate that." She said. "But that don't mean I don't wana see you."

"I guess." I said.

"Are you mad that I decided to go back to him?" She asked.

"I don't agree with it." I said. "But I can't really be mad. If you wana try to make it work, I support you you know that."

"Yea but I just wish it didn't change us." She said.

"Ain't shit changed, J." I said. "You know that."

"Yea whatever." She smiled. "So listen, we decided to move the wedding up."

"What?" I asked her. "You gotta be fuckin' kiddin' me."

"Nicholas don't do that." She said.

"Do what?" I asked. "Gettin' back with the nigga is one thing. But why you tryna rush and marry his ass. You pregnant?"

"No, I'm not pregnant, Nicholas." She said. "I just think that may have been part of our problem. He been ready to get married and I been tryna hold off til' I'm ready. So now we just came to a compromise."

"How the hell that nigga been ready to get married, and he fuckin' other bitches?" I asked. "That sound like a nigga that wana get married?"

"That's fucked up that you would even say some shit like that to me." She said.

"I ain't bouta lie to you." I said. "Listen to yourself. If you can't trust him now, what make you think marryin' him gon' make him faithful? Is that what this is? You think if you marry him he ain't gon' do it again? Jada if the nigga gon' cheat, he gon' do it married or not. A ring ain't gon' stop shit."

"I can't fuckin' believe you." She said as she looked like she wanted to cry.

"I'm not tryna hurt yo feelings J." I said. "I just don't want you to jump up and marry this nigga just to keep him from fuckin' up again. You settin' yourself up to fail if you really think this gon' change somethin'. You expect me to just sit back and let you ruin yo life?"

"You was fine with me marryin' him at first." She said.

"I ain't never been fine with you marryin' any nigga that ain't me." I said. "You know that. I just accepted it 'cuz I ain't have a choice if I wanted us to be cool. But I can't deal with this shit. You really trippin', J. Do yo mama know about this?"

"No." She said.

"Why not?" I asked.

"Cuz I don't wana hear her mouth." She said.

"Exactly 'cuz you know this shit dumb as hell." I said.

"Nicholas, I made up my mind." She said. "You posed to be my best friend. Regardless of what I do, I need to be able to depend on you."

"You can't depend on me to let you make dumb ass decisions to keep a nigga that don't even deserve you." I said.

"Why it gotta be like that?" She asked. "I'm sorry that every nigga ain't perfect like you, Nicholas."

"I never said I was perfect." I said. "You know I ain't perfect. But I damn sure ain't never cheated on you."

"Somethin' you never let me forget." She said.

"Look I gotta get back to work." I said. "I'll talk to you later."

I hung up before she could say somethin' else. I went back to my desk. As soon as I sat down Cassidy walked in. I wasn't in the mood to entertain her ass. Jada had really just pissed me off.

"Hey babe." Cassidy said as she kissed my cheek.

"What's up." I said as I looked at her. "What you up to?"

"Bouta go to my last class then work." She said. "I just wanted to see how yo day was goin'."

"It's alright." I said tryna act normal.

"What's wrong?" She asked.

"Shit." I said. "Just tired." She gave me the look like she knew I was lyin'.

"You gon' stop lyin'?" She asked.

"Babe I got work to do right now." I said. "We can talk about this tonight."

"Okay." She said. "You still comin' to my room?"

"I thought you was comin' over." I said.

"Nicholas, you know we talked about this last night." She whined.

"Alright I'll be over there." I said. "What time you get off?"

"7." She said.

"I'm off at 6 so I'll just stick around campus til' you get off then." I said.

"Okay I'll call you when I get off." She said as she started to walk away.

That went a lot smoother than I expected. Maybe she just ain't wana make a scene in front of my coach. He was the only one in the office that still liked her. Everybody else said she was too loud when she came in. She snapped on me way too many times in front of them so that's really all they knew her for. I kinda felt bad cuz she wasn't just no ghetto ass girl. But she was workin' on getting better at that, so I had to give her that at least.

Lisa

We had just came back from court. Valerie was sentenced to a year and 6 months for perjury. I thought we would see their daughter there, but she didn't show up.

"So how you feelin'?" I asked Joe as we walked in the house.

"I'm alright." He said as he sat down. "I just thought she would be there."

"Me too." I said. "Babe we can find her if you want."

"I do want too." He said. "At first I ain't think I would. But after all these years of Valerie keepin' her away from me, I need to have a relationship with her. She old enough to make her own decisions and I'm hopin' she'll want me in her life."

"I know what you mean." I said. "But you have to be ready for her reaction. We have no idea what Valerie told her about you."

"Right." He said soundin' sad. "I shoulda been tried to get in contact with her. All this time I ain't did nothin' but send money. That ain't shit."

"That's more than a lot of fathers do." I said. "Especially the ones that can't even see they kids."

"Yea I know." He said. "It's just crazy how all this is goin'. What did she need money for so bad, that she had to go through all this? I ain't want her to go to jail. She don't deserve that."

"I agree with that." I said. "But that was out of our hands. She did that to herself."

"Yea." He said. "You talk to Trevor?"

"Yup." I said. "He went and took the DNA test today. He say the results should be back by the end of the week."

"How crazy is that?" He laughed. "Me and him both in this mess."

"Well yo mess is old." I said. "And I just hope this ain't somethin' that's gon' change his life."

"What you mean?" He asked.

"I know it sound bad but I don't want that boy to be his." I said.

"That sounds really bad." He said. "But I understand. He ain't gon' know how to handle it so he definitely don't need that. Let's just pray he catch a break on this one."

"I really hope he do." I said. "So, what you think she like?"

"I don't know." He said. "I wonder if she look like me."

"I'm sure she do." I said. "She came out lookin' just like you so I know it only got worse as she grew up."

"What you mean worse?" He asked. "My good looks ain't nothin' to complain about."

"Yea okay." I laughed at him.

"Thank you." He said. "For everything. You ain't have to deal with this. I appreciate the fact that you did."

"I knew what I had comin' when I decided to take you back." I smiled at him. "As long as you never put me back in that position, we'll be fine."

"Ain't happened since." He said. "And never again.

Malcolm

"What's up?" I asked Nicholas as he walked in my apartment.

"Shit." He said quietly as he sat down.

"Man, what is it now?" I asked. "Yo ass been moapin' around for damn near a month now."

"Man, why the fuck Jada talkin' 'bout movin' up the wedding." He said.

"What?" I asked. "For what?"

"I don't know." He said getting mad all over again. "She on bull shit for real."

"When you find this out?" I asked.

"Bout a month ago." He said.

I laughed at his ass.

"So, I'm guessin' you ain't talked to her since then?" I asked as I shook my head at him.

"Nope." He said. "She been callin' and textin' me but I ain't really got shit to say to her ass."

"That's fucked up." I said. "You think he tryna move the wedding up?"

"Hell yea I know it's him." He said. "Cuz she wasn't even tryna get married til' she graduate. I know she wouldn't just change up now without him tryna change her mind."

"So, what you gon' do?" I asked.

"Man, I'ont know." He said. "What can I do?"

"Gotta do somethin' if you ain't tryna let her go." I said.

"Who said I ain't tryna let her go?" He asked.

"Nigga everybody see that shit." I said. "I don't even know why y'all let this go on this long. It's obvious y'all still wana be together. Y'all just got so comfortable with other people so now y'all ain't tryna hurt them."

"Is it really that obvious?" He asked. "If that's the case then why Cassidy don't see it?"

"She do." I said. "She just wana believe you when you say you don't want Jada. She naive. And you in denial. But y'all need to do somethin' about this 'cuz shit only gon' get worse if you let her marry that nigga."

"If she marry that nigga I ain't gon' have shit else to say to her ass." He said. "Best friend or not, she know she don't need to marry that nigga."

"So what's the plan?" I asked as Laya walked in.

"Hey y'all seen this?" Laya asked as she showed us an envelope. "It just came in the mail today."

I opened it up and saw that it was Jada's wedding invitation. The date was set for two weeks after school ended this summer. She was really goin' through with this.

"What the fuck?" Nicholas said as he looked at the invitation.

"You didn't know?" Laya asked as she walked to the kitchen.

"I mean she told me about it but I ain't think she was serious." He said. "I definitely didn't know it was gon' be this soon."

"Right." Laya said. "That shit just came outta nowhere."

"Hell yea." I agreed.

Laya came over to the couch and sat next to me.

"So, what's the plan?" Laya asked as she looked at Nicholas.

"Man, I can't believe this shit." He said quietly.

"I know it kinda caught you off guard." Laya said to him. "But we need to come up with a plan to stop this shit."

"What you mean?" He asked. "I thought you liked the nigga."

"I do." She smiled. "He's great. But not for her. She know she sposed to be with you. He do too. That's probably why he tryna hurry up and rush this wedding."

"Them getting married ain't gon' stop shit." I said. "People get divorced everyday."

"Like I said before, if she marry that nigga, I ain't got shit to say to her ass." He said. "I ain't bouta be waitin' around for her to see she fuckin' up. If that's the case I might as well marry Cassidy."

"That sounded terrible." Laya laughed. "We all know you ain't doin' that. So, let's just talk some sense into Jada."

"I ain't talked to her since she told me about this shit last month." He said. "And I still ain't ready to."

"That's cool 'cuz I can talk to her for you." She said. "It might sound better comin' from me anyway, you know."

"Yea whatever." He said.

"Nigga you need to do somethin' quick." I said. "Ain't nobody tryna see yo sad ass no more. I know Cassidy been tryna figure you out."

"Man, hell yea." He said. "She won't quit. She pissed me off so bad last night I damn near started to tell her."

"Hell naw." I laughed. "Don't do her like that."

"What you mean?" He asked. "She gotta find out eventually. I ain't bouta stop Jada from marryin' this nigga just for her to be by herself. If I'm stoppin' her she comin' back to me. So, I ain't gon' have no choice but to let Cassidy know."

"Whatever you do, just let her go before you get back with Jada." Laya said. "Cassidy my girl and I ain't tryna see her get hurt like that."

"I'm not tryna hurt her at all." He said. "Main reason I been with her this long. I shoulda been let her ass go that time Jada came out here. That just told me everything I needed to know."

Me and Laya both laughed at that one.

"Like you ain't know you wanted Jada before." I said as we kept laughin' at him.

"Naw I knew since the day Jada came over to tell me about Johnny." He said. "But I ain't know how bad it was til' the last time I seen her."

"This whole situation is fucked up." Laya said. "Now y'all gotta hurt two people who ain't did nothin' to y'all. You and Jada was both lucky to get two really good people after all the bull shit y'all went through. This why I

234

told y'all to just get back together before shit got too serious with other people. Now look where y'all at."

"I know." He said as he gave Laya the look.

"We ain't got a lot of time to fix this shit." She said. "So, you need to stop moapin' and help us figure this thang out."

"Shut up." He said as we laughed at her.

Paisley

Wednesday nights at The Spot were the easiest. No new customers came in at all. The regulars that did come in had specific girls they came to see every week. So that's how we divided them up. It was 7 of us on Wednesday's, and we each had 5 customers a shift. All of the girls had an understanding that if another girl's customer came to you, you would direct him to that girl. The only time you would take somebody else's customer on a Wednesday, was if his usual girl was busy with someone else.

That never really happened. Like I said, Wednesday was the easiest night of the week so everything seemed to always flow smoothly. Never had any drama, or any confusion about who dances for who. Up until now.

"I don't know who she think she rollin' her eyes at." I heard Tonya say to Kay, one of the other dancers.
"You know damn well that's one of her customers." Kay said to Tonya as I walked up to them.

Because I was tryin' not to make a scene, especially on a Wednesday night, I decided to pull Tonya to the side to handle this.

"Let me talk to you for a minute, Tonya." I said to her.

She followed me back to the dressing room.

"What's up?" Tonya asked as she sat down at one of the vanity tables.

"What's up with you dancing for TJ?" I asked as I looked at her.

"One of my customers ain't show up tonight." She said with a straight face. "So, I needed to make up for that loss."

"And you just had to go for one of mine?" I asked.

"Like you really needed him." She smirked.

"That ain't the fuckin' point." I snapped. "That's my money you out there takin'. And you laughin' at that shit? You see me takin' yo customers?"

"Peaches you couldn't take shit of mine if you wanted too." She snapped.

"Bitch you really trippin' now." I yelled. "What the fuck is yo problem? I know we ain't never been cool but at least we ain't been on no bull shit. You actin' like a kid with this petty shit."

"Don't act like you give a damn about what anybody else is doin' in here." She said. "All you think about is Peaches."

"And why not?" I asked. "Y'all just as selfish. What's wrong with that? I ain't come here to make friends, Tonya. I got enough of them. I ain't here for shit but the money. I ain't never told y'all anything else. I don't see what the problem is all of a sudden."

"I can't stand when bitches walk around here like they better than somebody else." She smirked. "We all in here shaking our asses to pay bills. Just 'cuz we might stay in different places and drive different cars, that don't make you better than us."

238

"I ain't never said that shit." I said. "Whatever the hell you on, get the fuck off that shit. It's Wednesday, we don't need that shit tonight. I don't wana have to beat yo ass to end this shit."

"Bitch you ain't on shit." She stood up and got in my face. "You too busy sucking dick outside the club to pay for that condo and that Range Rover."

I smacked her as soon as them words left her mouth.

"You don't know shit." I yelled. "Stop worryin' about me and get yo own shit together. Worry about why one of yo regulars ain't fuckin' with you no more. Clearly it's somethin' you ain't doin right. That same nigga begged me for a dance last Wednesday, and what the fuck I do? Point his ass to you. And you wana hit me with this shit tonight, Tonya?"

"Bitch please." She smacked her lips at me as Kay walked in the dressing room.

"Um Tonya, Jermaine outside waitin' for you." Kay said as she looked at both of us.

"Thanks Kay." Tonya said as she grabbed her bag and left out the room.

"I know that ain't my Jermaine." I said to Kay.

"You know it is." Kay confirmed.

"That bitch dumb as hell." I said. "She think fuckin' my leftovers gon' get her where I am. I work hard just like every other bitch in here. Some days I just might work harder. Ain't shit wrong with that. She just can't accept the fact that she know she was wrong for that shit. It's that simple."

"She know it ain't right." KeKe agreed. "Cuz when one of the girls did that to her a while ago she made a fuckin' scene out on the floor."

"Girl I know I heard about that." I said. "So why she think it's okay for her to do that shit to me. I ain't never did shit to that girl. I mean I know we ain't never liked each other, but it is what it is."

"Right." She said. "I don't know what to tell you, but I'm bouta get outta here. You wana walk out with me?"

"Yea come on." I said.

I threw on my sweats and hoodie and grabbed my bag. We walked out to the parkin' lot.

"You alright?" She asked as we got to our cars. We were parked next to each other but I had an unexpected visitor leaning against my car door waitin' for me.

"Yea." I rolled my eyes. "I'll see you tomorrow." She got in her car and pulled off. "What are you doin' here?" I asked him. "I'm not in the mood to hear this shit tonight."

"I just wanted to see you." He smiled at me. He knew I was a sucker for his smile.

"It's just not a good time for me." I said.

"What's wrong?" He asked as I opened the driver side door. Against my better judgment, I unlocked the doors to let him in on the passenger side. He got in and stared at me. "What happened?"

"Nothin'." I lied. "I just had a long day."

"Tell me about it." He said.

"I don't really feel like talkin'." I said. "Can we do this another time?"

"What is this, Paisley?" He asked. "I'm just here to see you. We ain't gotta say shit."

"You coulda came in if that's really all you wanted to do." I said quietly.

"You know damn well I'm not bouta come see you in there." He snapped.

"So, what's up?" I asked. "What you keep comin' around for when I told you I ain't want nothin' to do with you."

"You ain't mean that." He said. "If you did we wouldn't even be talkin' right now."

"Whatever." I said. "I'm getting ready to head home."

"I left my car at yo house so I can just ride with you." He said.

I rolled my eyes as I started the car. Who in the hell did he think he was assumin' he could ride with me? And why was he parked outside my house like a fuckin' creep? I mean I was all for him provin' me wrong, but I just didn't know if I could trust him.

As I pulled off he grabbed my right hand. I thought he was tryin' to get in between my thighs but he just held my hand the entire ride to my house. In silence. It was weird. He just seemed so happy, and I felt so miserable. I couldn't fall in love with another woman's husband. Not again.

Laya

I had the longest day ever. Classes from 7-5 then work from 5:30-10. When I pulled up to the apartment I expected to see Malcolm's car there but it wasn't. He was probably out with Nicholas somewhere. Didn't bother me 'cuz all I wanted to do was get in the bed. I ain't have the energy to entertain nobody.

I walked in the house and hit the switch to turn on the lights, but nothin' came on. I took my phone out my purse and cut on the flashlight to lead me to the fuse box. I flipped the switch and everything came back on. That was weird, I thought to myself as I walked to the bedroom.

When I opened the bedroom door I damn near fainted. My mother was takin' all of my jewelry out of my jewelry box.

"What the fuck are you doin'?" I yelled at her.

She jumped and turned around to look at me. I had never seen my mother look so bad. She had the biggest bags under her eyes. Her face looked like it hadn't been washed in months. She smelled like fish and gasoline. Her hair was broken off on one side and chopped off on the other side. Her lip was busted and one of her eyes were blacked. She had on a black oversized t shirt with holes in it everywhere. It stopped right where her thigh started. No bottoms on at all. Thong flip flops on her feet.

She was literally a mess. I felt so bad for her for a split second. Then I snapped out of it when I realized she was attempting to steal from me.

"What the hell are you doin' here?" I yelled at her again.

She froze in her stance. Trembling while staring at me with fear in her eyes.

"Hey baby." She tried to get out. Her voice was raspy. Barely above a whisper.
"Don't baby me." I snapped. "Put all my shit back now and explain to me why you in my house tryna take my shit?"

She slowly put back what was in her hand. It was only my diamond earrings and the matching bracelet so I knew she had more on her. She tried to run out of my room but I knocked her out. When she fell on the floor I lifted her shirt to see at least ten more pieces of jewelery stuffed in her bra. I took them all out and put them on my nightstand.

"Wanna try that again?" I asked as I stared at her fraile body on the floor.

She never even tried to hit me back. She was damn near lifeless. As she started to get up, I heard somebody bangin' at my door. She jumped up and ran and hid in the closet.

"Who the hell is that?" I asked as I stared at her.

"Don't answer that." She whispered.

"I'm callin' the police." I said to her as I started to dial 911.

 She jumped out of the closet and snatched my phone out of my hand.

"Don't." She whispered. "They'll take me away."

"Maybe that's what you need." I said. "Do you realize you were just in your daughter's apartment tryna steal her jewelry? And for what? A fix? To pay off a debt? You really need to get yo shit together."

It was so much more I wanted to say to her but I stopped when I heard someone bust through my front door. She jumped back in the closet and I closed and locked my bedroom door. Immediately I called 911 and told them I had an intruder. I ain't want my mom to go away but I ain't know what they was capable of.

I kept the operator on my cell phone and called Malcolm on the house phone. His phone was goin' straight to voice mail so I knew it was dead. Then I called Nicholas. His was goin' to voicemail too. I called Cassidy but she didn't answer. She was probably still at dance practice.

I didn't know what else to do. If I had any issue I always called Malcolm. In situations like this, I guess people would call their parents. Ironically one of my parents is the one who put me in this situation. Who was I supposed to call now?

Jada

The wedding was coming up in a few weeks and I was feelin' sick about not talkin' to Nicholas. He was really ignoring me. And sticking to it. Normally he would not talk to me, but then I'd send him a cute text message and he'd break in no time. I'd sent all the cute text messages I could think of and still no response. He wouldn't answer any of my calls. Definitely didn't answer any of my FaceTime calls either.

Carter's mom planned the whole thing. My mom was too mad to be involved in the planning. She really wanted me to wait until I graduated for us to get married. I couldn't focus on anything that needed to be done.

I was so thankful to have Carter's mom helpin' me with the plans. All I thought about was how upset Nicholas sounded the last time I talked to him. How he sent back my wedding invitation that I sent him. He didn't even open it.

I guess once he saw Malcolm's and Laya's invitation he already knew what to expect. This was supposed to be one of the best times of my life. The most exciting time of my life. It was the exact opposite of that. I was miserable. All because I felt like I lost my best friend, in order to keep my lover.

"Still layin' around moapin'?" Carter asked me as he came in the bedroom.

"Shut up." I said. "I ain't moapin'." I tried to play it off.

"I talked to yo mom." He said as he sat down at the end of the bed.

"You did?" I jumped up and looked at him. "What she say?"

"She said she comin'." He smiled at me.

"For real?" I hugged him tight. "Thank you so much baby."

He laughed at me.

"Now you can stop all this damn whinin'." He said. "I told you everything was gon' work out. I don't know why you always worryin for nothin'."

"Baby I had every reason to worry." I said. "My mom completely stopped talkin' to me. I ain't know how to handle that."

"Well you ain't gotta worry about it no more." He smiled. "Ya man took care of it. Like I told you I would."

"You don't know how much I appreciate it babe." I said as I kissed him. I was finally smiling again.

"Come on, let's go celebrate." He pulled me up out of the bed.

"Let me get dressed." I said as I looked at him.

"Alright hurry up." He said as he left out of the room.

I sat back on the bed and stared at myself in the mirror. I still had a slight smile on my face, but I couldn't help but worry about what I did to my relationship with Nicholas. All I wanted him to do was answer at least one of my calls. I needed to know that we would be okay before I could go any further with Carter. I just couldn't see myself goin' into a whole new journey of my life, without Nicholas bein' there for me to share it with.

Paisley

We finally made it back to my house. The entire ride was silent. I didn't even turn on any music. I was in the worst mood ever. The shit at the club really pissed me off. And I couldn't understand why. Normally I would just correct that shit and keep it pushin'. But that bitch knew better. And she did that shit on purpose. And what the hell was she doin' datin' Jermaine? My ex boyfriend Jermaine. That shit ain't sit well with me at all. One of the niggas I fucked over with one of the bitches I just got into it with. Now I felt like she started that shit with me on purpose. I ain't know what to think. Or where to point the finger. But some shit was bouta hit the fan. I felt it comin'. I ain't know where to turn to figure this shit out.

I know he wanted me to talk to him about all the shit that was goin' on, but I was still so mad about the lies he told me that I wasn't ready to open up to him again.

"You ready to talk?" He asked as I opened my front door. I stopped and turned around to look at him.
"About what?" I asked as I looked at him. "I'm tired of playin' this game with you."
"I'm done with that, Paisley." He said. "I showed you the papers and everything. She already signed 'em. I'm out the house. What else you want me to do?"

"I wanted you to do that shit before I even got involved with you." I snapped. "That's what you told me you did. I wanted that to be the truth. Now it's just too late. I can't trust you. The same shit you did to her, you'a do to me. And I'll be damned if I'ma let that shit happen."

"You know I wouldn't do you like that." He said.

"How I know that?" I asked. "You been with her since high school. She yo kids mom. You still cheated on her. And I know I wasn't the first. Probably not the last either."

I stopped when I noticed I was really hurtin' his feelings. That wasn't my intention at all.

"All I can give you is my word." He said. "I can show you whatever you need me to, to prove shit only gon' get better from here. But I can't show you that if you ain't willin' to take a chance."

"I already took a chance when I let you in." I yelled. "What don't you understand about that? Ain't no man stayed one night at my house but you. You the only nigga I ever answer the phone for. I opened up to you in ways I ain't never opened to nobody else. And the only thing you show me is a lie."

"Baby I can't change the past." He said. "I'm sorry. I just wana make shit right. Just let me come upstairs for a minute. I really ain't tryna talk on yo porch all night."

Everything in me was tellin' me to send him back wherever he came from, but I was so vulnerable tonight. I couldn't put that crazy shit from the club out my head. I knew I could protect myself if it came down to it, but I really just wanted to be held. It was one of those nights when I felt like I needed somebody to just let me get out all my tears. Even if it was the person who brought them.

I turned around and walked in the house. I opened the door for him to come in. He closed the door behind him and locked it. Then he turned around to face me and stood there. I put my arms around his neck and hugged him. I hugged him like I never wanted to let him go. And I knew I didn't. I put up a fight so long tryna convince myself that I ain't want shit to do with him. Truth is I never wanted to do shit without him. He became my best friend when we were together. So, when I let him go, I lost that. I still had Lo, nobody was ever gon' take her away from me.

He wrapped his arms around my waist and pulled me into his chest. I loved his smell. It was still the same. His breath felt so good on my neck. I missed the hell outta this man. I don't know why I had to be so stuck in my own ways sometimes. Nobody ever hurt me like he did. I never gave anyone the chance too. He was it for me. And I was devastated when I found out I wasn't it for him.

I never wanted to be the other woman. And as soon as I found out I was, I cut that shit off. I couldn't do that to another woman willingly. I would never want no woman to do that to me intentionally. Most woman do though. They really don't care about who the man goes home too as long as he's supportin' them, or tellin' them what they want to hear. I'm not that girl.

I don't need a man to sell me no dream. I wana be with somebody who watch me make my dreams come true. Help me if he can, but that's not required. I take care of my damn self. But he made me feel like I didn't have to. That's one of things about him I fell in love with.

"What happened tonight?" He asked as he still held me.
"I really don't wana talk about it." I said quietly still holdin' him. "Can we just lay down?"
"Yea come on." He said not lettin' me go.

I took his hand and led him upstairs to my room. I was so tired I ain't even change into my pajamas. We both got in the bed, completely dressed. I had so many mixed feelings goin' on in my head as he wrapped his arm around my waist in bed. I hadn't felt this in so long and now that I did again, it was no way to be sure if it was right. I mean it felt right, but was it really okay for me to be okay with this? Was it really okay for me to let him back into my life? I couldn't figure out that answer if I tried. I knew nothing was gon' be guaranteed, but I would never find out if I ain't try. I was extremely exhausted but my mind would just not let me rest. He stayed up starin' at me, as I stared at him. I wanted to turn around so we could spoon, but I loved having my face in his chest.

"I want you to meet the boys." He said quietly.

"Huh?" I wasn't sure I heard him correctly.

"You heard me." He laughed.

"I don't know about that." I said quietly.

"Why not?" He asked. "If we gon' be together, they should know about you."

"Who said we gon' be together?" I asked.

"You lettin' me come lay with you say we gon' be together." He said. "Just stop fightin' me. I know this shit ain't happen when you wanted it to, but it did now. Can't we just make the best of it?"

"So now I'm just supposed to settle?" I asked.

"You not settling if I'm who you wana be with." He said. "Some shit just take a lil' more time. I mean I really am sorry I wasn't honest with you from the beginning. But you know you wouldn'ta payed me no attention if you knew I was married."

He was right. That was somethin' I didn't do. Entertaining married men outside of the club was a major no for me. All the men I pretended to date to get their money were single. That was somethin' I made sure of. I was always with them at their place so I knew it was no wife or girlfriend around. So, when it came time for me to really have my own man, I don't know why I didn't double check everything there. It just happened before I even realized it was goin' on.

Laya

The police never came. I ended up hangin' up on the operator once I realized they weren't coming. I found that hard to believe because I was in a nice upper-class neighborhood. My mother was shaking so bad hiding in the closet. I ain't know how to help her. I ain't know how to help myself outta this situation. Whoever was in my apartment, was cleaning everything out of my living room. I'm sure he knew we were hiding in my room, but I guess he was saving us for last. I ain't know what to think. Everything I ever did flashed before my eyes. I was so nervous, but at the same time I felt calm. I wasn't panicking. I couldn't. I had to be dead silent just in case he didn't know we were back here.

I still hadn't heard back from Malcolm or Nicholas. Cassidy never called me back either. I called her 3 more times since the first one. Texted her too sayin' I had an emergency and somebody broke in my house. I couldn't believe she didn't at least call to see if I was okay.

I couldn't worry about that now. I was locked in my room, not knowin' if I would ever see my man again. Not knowin' if I would ever be able to finish school and walk across that stage. I was so mad she put me in this situation. I got this far away from her and her drama and she came all the way out here to fuck my life up again.

I heard them make a few trips in and out of the apartment. I knew they had to be takin' all our shit. Just when it sounded like they got everything, it got quiet for a few minutes. Maybe they wanted to trick us into thinkin' they left. I wasn't goin' for it. I knew they was still out there.

A few minutes later somethin' slammed into my bedroom door. I knew it was them. I had all this time to try to get out through the window, why hadn't I done that? I mean we were on the third floor but I coulda shimmied down the side of the building or somethin'. Sitting here thinkin' about life ain't get me nowhere at all. Now I was faced with this demon. How would I make it out alive? It was only a few minutes before they busted the door down. I was under the bed. I saw his feet go straight to the closet. He dragged my mom out of the closet by the little bit of hair she had left. He slapped her around a few times until she damn near passed out.

Once he pulled out his gun I started crying silently. I felt like I needed to get out from under the bed and save my mother but would she do the same for me? I ain't know if I was supposed to risk my life to find out, but I did it anyway. I got out from under the bed and jumped in front of him. My mother was barely alive. It was nothin' she could do but lay there. I had to protect her. I ain't have a choice. Before I could even attempt to defend her he smacked me down on the floor. I fell right next to her. I could still hear her breathing. I knew she was playin' dead so he would leave her alone.

I lay there quietly. Not wanting to fight anymore. My mouth was full of blood. He figured out that my mom was still alive. He pulled her up by her hair and started to shake her then threw her against the wall. I panicked realizing that I was next to get thrown around.

"Where the fuck is my money?" He yelled at my mother.

"I tried to get you some jewelery til' I could get the rest of it." She said quietly.

"I told yo ass I don't want no fuckin' jewelry." He yelled. "You really think that's gon' cover yo debt?"

"She got a lotta nice shit, Ray." My mom said lookin' at my jewelry box.

I couldn't believe this bitch was really tryna take my shit to pay for some drugs. I knew it all along, but the confirmation hurt like hell. She looked at me and mouthed the word please. I shook my head no at her. She was crazy if she thought I was gon' give her my approval to take my jewelry to pay off her debt.

"I got somethin' else for you." She said desperately.

"I'm tired of that." He snapped. "I told you before. Old ass pussy."

He stopped and looked at me. He picked me up and threw me on the bed. I started kickin' and screamin' as he started to take my clothes off. I was cryin' so hard I could barely see anything. I never stopped fighting him. It was no way in hell I was gon' let him rape me. All of a sudden my mom jumped on his back and pulled him off of me.

"Leave her outta this, Ray." She screamed as he turned around and smacked her. "I'm the one that owe you, so I'll pay."

She crawled over to him and started to unbutton his pants.

"Ma don't do this." I cried to her.

I could not watch her belittle herself like this. I couldn't believe she had really stooped this low. I mean everybody always talked her about doin' shit like that, but I never believed that. How do you believe somethin' like that about yo own mother? The same person who brought you into this world? I mean we were never close, but I still had some type of respect for her.

"Laya shut up." She yelled as she pulled his pants down.

I closed my eyes as I started crying again. I could not watch this. A minute later I heard somebody come in the front door. I ain't know if this guy was workin' with somebody or if the police finally arrived. I prayed it was the police. I opened my eyes to see somethin' better. My man standin' in the bedroom doorway with his gun aimed at the man. He turned around to see Malcolm standin' there. His expression told me that this was not over. He turned back around to look down at my mother on her knees.

"Bye bitch." He said as he smiled and shot her in the face.

Trevor

"So, what it say?" Jamal asked me as I opened the results of the DNA test. "He ain't mine." I said tryin' not to smile. I felt bad bein' happy that the kid wasn't mine. I mean I know it was a good thing, but I just ain't feel like this was somethin' to celebrate.

"Damn." He smiled. "Thank God. You know damn well you couldn't handle it if he was yours."

"Yea I know." I said quietly.

I felt so relieved. I couldn't believe I was actually out of this nightmare.

"Alright so where we goin' to celebrate?" He asked. "We might as well meet the girls while they out. We both need a drink."

"What the hell you need a drink for?" I laughed at him.

"Nigga you and Dad been stressin' me the hell out." He laughed. "Now we just gotta find out about his shit and then we can really celebrate."

"Shut up." I laughed at him.

We left out of his house and went to meet the girls for drinks. When we got to the bar, Nina looked so worried. She knew I got the results. We sat down at the table quietly to try to throw them off. Make 'em think we had some bad news.

"What happened?" Nina finally asked me.

"He ain't mine." I smiled.

I gave her the papers to see for herself. She smiled so hard. It looked like she wanted to cry. She hugged me so tight.

"Oh my God." She finally screamed. "I can't believe this baby. I just knew that boy was gon' be yours."

"I thought he was too." I said. "I was just praying he wasn't. I mean that sound fucked up, but I just ain't tryna have no kids like that. That's some unnecessary drama we just dont need."

"Hell naw." Nina said. "I'm tired of all that shit. Since Nicholas been out the house it's been so much more relaxing. I don't worry so much about 'em. Don't get me wrong you know I love my baby. But with him bein' here, he wasn't doin' shit but secretly getting in trouble."

"What?" Stacey said sarcastically. "Not yo perfect baby. Not King Nicholas."

We all had to laugh at her. Nina treated Nicholas like he was really her King. She loved him like he was and she was not ashamed to show it. She never wanted anybody thinkin' or sayin' anything bad about him. Even if it was the truth. She was so in denial about the shit he got himself into. Damn near naive when somethin' happened to 'em. The lies he told her, she believed everytime.

"Shut up." Nina rolled her eyes at us. "I can say it now that he on the right path. That boy was a mess."

"That ain't nothin' new." Jamal said. "Just be glad he got away from all this bull shit."

"I really am." She smiled.

"Did yo Dad ever find out anything about y'all sister?" Stacey asked us.

"Nope." I answered. "Said he tried to call her. She ain't answer. Left her a message but she ain't called back."

"How he get her number?" Nina asked.

"I don't know." Jamal said. "He ain't say. He said he tryna find out where she stayin' so he can see her."

"Damn." I said. "It's crazy findin' out we got a sister at this age. All these years and we ain't even know."

"I know." Jamal said. "He shoulda been told us this shit. Then at least we coulda grew up with her."

"Well if she in her twenties then y'all woulda been grown when y'all met her anyway." Nina just had to point out the obvious.

"Shut up." Jamal laughed. "You know what I mean. We don't know shit about her. Just like she don't know nothin' about us."

"Probably don't even know y'all exist." Stacey said. "Or even if yo Dad exist. It ain't no tellin' what her mama done told her about him to make her not wana be involved with him."

We spent the rest of the night drinking til' we damn near passed out. We had to take some time to at least sober up to drive home. Nina and I headed to our house as Stacey and Jamal went to theirs.

"So how you feelin'?" Nina asked quietly as we drove home.

I guess she could tell that I was a lil' out of it.

"I'm alright." I said. "Actually, I feel a lot better."
"You don't look like it." She said.
"What you mean?" I asked.
"You look bothered." She said. "And you still look worried."

I didn't know how to respond to that. She knew exactly what I was feelin'.

"You wanted him to be yours?" She asked.
"You know that ain't true." I said.
"Baby it's okay." She said. "I understand. You are way too caring to not give a fuck about somebody. Especially when they could possibly be yo child. As much as you hate to admit it, a small part of you wanted another son. And that's okay. We all have different desires for different reasons. Nobody is takin' that from you. But you gotta be willin' to admit it to yourself. It just wasn't meant to be."
"Yea you right." I smiled at her. She always knew what to say to make shit better. "I mean unless we can pop another one out."

"Now I know you drunk." She laughed at me. "You know damn well I ain't havin' another baby. Music Note is too much for me as it is. I'm just now startin' to let Nicholas have a life of his own without me. I can't get attached to another one then have to give 'em up. Not happenin'."

"What you gon' do when Music Note leave?" I laughed at her.

"She already said we can move with her." She said seriously.

"I ain't followin' my child to school, Nina." I laughed again. "You are really crazy. It's somethin' wrong. I used to think it was just yo obsession with Nicholas, but now I see you obsessed with everything you create."

"Shut up." She laughed. "I made 'em. I can be obsessed with them if I want to."

"Damn shame." I couldn't stop laughin' at her.

Nicholas

"So how she feelin'?" I asked Malcolm about Laya as I passed him the lighter.

"She much better than before." He answered. "After the funeral, she kinda just snapped out of it."

"That's weird." I said. "You would think that would be the worst time for her."

"Naw the whole thing was bad as hell." He said. "For her to have to see her mom killed like that. Shit couldn't get no worse. Guess after the funeral she just felt like it was finally over."

"Damn." I said. "I can't believe that shit. Then both our phones was dead. I know she was mad as hell."

"Hell yea." He said. "I'm just glad I got there when I did. It ain't no tellin' what woulda happened if I showed up after that."

"Man, I ain't even tryna think about that shit." I said.

"What Cassidy say she was doin'?" He asked.

"She claim she left her phone at the girl house they was practicing at." I said.

"What you mean she claim?" He asked. "You don't believe her?"

"Man, I don't know what to believe." I said. "She been lyin' about the dumbest shit lately. Just petty shit for real. Shit she ain't even gotta lie about."

"Damn for real." He said. "What's wrong with her?"

269

"She startin' to get mad that I'm comfortable without her sleepin' here." I said. "She think I got somebody else sleepin' over here."

"How the hell you gon' do that with her leavin' in the middle of the night?" He asked. "What she think you got somebody waitin' outside for her to leave?"

"Right." I said. "She really trippin'. She just mad 'cuz she tried to do somethin' to spite me, and it backfired on her ass."

"So, you really comfortable sleepin' by yoself?" He asked.

"I don't have the time to notice it." I said.

"The time to notice it, or the time to miss her?" He asked.

"What you mean?" I asked.

"Let's be real." He said. "You not busy 24 hours a day. We make time for shit we wana make time for."

"So, you think I don't make time to miss her?" I asked.

"Somewhat." He said. "I think you don't have time to miss her, 'cuz you too busy missin' Jada."

"Nigga I ain't even talked to Jada." I said.

"That's the point." He said. "You so depressed about y'all situation, you ain't had the time to give a damn about you and Cassidy situation."

"Me and Cassidy don't have a situation." I said. "We good. It is what it is. This what's workin' for us."

"Clearly it ain't if she complainin' about it." He said. "Somethin' gotta shake. The wedding comin' up. And I know that shit got you feelin' some type of way."

"I'm good." I said. "I don't know why I gotta keep tellin' y'all that."

270

"You need to keep tellin' yourself that until you believe it." He said. "Cuz we damn sure don't."

"That ain't my problem." I said.

"So why you send the invitation back?" He asked.

"Laya told you that?" I asked.

"Yea." He laughed.

"I ain't need that shit." I said. "I ain't goin'."

"You really ain't gon' go?" He asked. "She would come to yo wedding."

"In my wedding I would be marryin' her." I said. "She wouldn't need no damn invitation."

"Okay so tell her that then." He said. "You been lettin' this shit go on for too damn long. Both of y'all have. It's already bad enough that y'all ain't even go to school together like we planned, but now you gon' let her go off and marry somebody else? I know you ain't really gon' let that shit happen."

"I ain't gotta choice." I said. "She made her decision. What I'm sposed to do, chase her? Hell naw. That ain't even me."

"Man fuck all the bull shit." He said. "Go get the girl. You want her. Everybody see that. I don't even know why Carter goin' through with this shit when he know what it is with y'all."

"Malcolm I'm in a whole other relationship outside of Jada." I said. "What you expect me to do with Cassidy if I go chasin' after Jada?"

"What you mean?" He asked. "You the one said you was gon' have to let her go. You damn near already let her ass go if she ain't sleepin' here no more. Do you ever sleep over there?"

"Hell naw." I said. "I moved off campus for a reason. I ain't signing in shit. I ain't leavin' at no specific time. I'm too damn grown to be sneakin' around."

"Did you decide if you was gon' go home for the summer?" He asked.

"I'ma stay here." I said. "I'm posed to be workin' still through summer school. Thought about takin' some classes to get done earlier. I mean I might as well if I'ma be out here."

"Yea that's what I'm doin'." He said. "Laya wanted to go home before all this bull shit happened. Now I think she wana stay here."

"I would if I ain't really have much to go home to." I said. "Her whole situation fucked up. I feel bad for her."

"Me too." He said. "I'm just tryna make sure I keep shit runnin' smooth for her. We don't need no more drama from nobody else."

"Right." I said. "All this shit just startin' to get old for real. How long did her mama really think she was gon' get away with all the bull shit she pulled?"

"I don't even know." He said. "I'm just mad she had to get Laya involved in that. It ain't no way in hell I would ever let my child see no shit like that."

"Exactly." I agreed. "Her mama been on bull shit since I can remember."

"Yup." He said. "Cassidy posed to be stayin' here for the summer?"

"I think so." I said. "She tryna stay with me so she can get that housing money back. But I ain't goin' for it."

"What?" He asked. "That's half the rent money she can split with you."

"Nigga you know damn well my mama pay my rent." I said. "I don't need her money. I'm just not ready to have nobody in my space all day everyday."

"You keep sayin' that." He said. "I think you just tryna keep her as far away from you as possible while you figure out how to get Jada back."

"Shut the fuck up." I said. "Cassidy my girl. Why would I be tryna keep her away?"

"You tell me." He said. "That's what it look like to me. And I know if I'm thinkin' it, she damn sure thinkin' worse than that."

"She is." I said. "I told you she think I'm cheatin'."

"At least she don't think it's about Jada." He said.

"I'm sure she do." I said. "She just ain't figured out how to put it together yet."

"Damn shame." He said. "You talkin' bout all this shit getting old, but you steady playin' the same game. When you gon' give this shit up?"

"What you talkin' bout?" I asked him.

"You know damn well what I'm talkin about." He said. "Y'all been goin' through this bull shit since Freshman year. Even before you moved off campus. She was always findin' reasons to blame y'all shit on Jada. And you was honestly givin' her shit to be mad about, that always came back to Jada."

"What the fuck is this? A intervention or somethin'?" I laughed at him.

"I'm just sayin'." He said. "This shit is getting old."

"Nigga shut the hell up and smoke this blunt." I said as I passed it to him.

"Get yo shit together." He said as he took it.

"You startin' to sound like my dad." I said.

"Maybe you need to listen." He said. "You my brother so I'm always gon' be real with you. It's time for you to grow up and make shit happen. You can't just sit around waitin' forever."

Paisley

"You still ain't seen Tonya?" Lo asked me as we ate lunch.

"Nope." I said. "And I just don't trust that shit."

"I wouldn't either." She said.

"Jermaine don't have no money to be supportin' her ass." I said. "I damn near cleaned his ass out when I hit 'em. So I know what he workin' with."

"You crazy as hell." She laughed at me. "So what's goin' on with yo man?"

"What man?" I asked. "You know I don't do relationships!"

"So what you call it then?" She asked.

"He tryna get me back." I smiled.

"So you goin' or what?" She smiled knowin' the answer.

"Girl I don't know." I said. "I mean you know how I feel about him. But I'm just too scared for him to be lyin' to me again."

"So go talk to her." She said.

"What?" I asked. "Hell naw. What I look like askin' another woman about my man?"

"Oh so now he yo man." She laughed. "If you ain't tryna do that, only other thing you can do is take his word. Watch what he do, as opposed to what he say."

"That's hard though because even when he was lyin' it seemed so believable. Everything added up. All his moves made sense. He didn't act like a married man. He answered all of my calls and messages. Called me all the time. Slept with me damn near every night. It was too clean for it to

275

have been messy. Then come to find out that shit was more than messy. So now what do I do?"

"You say he showed you the papers right?" She asked.

"Yea but he coulda made that up and signed it himself." I said.

"Show it to yo lawyer and ask him about it." She said. "Maybe he can take a look and tell you if it look legit or not."

"I don't know." I said. "It just seem like I'm doin' too much to try to be happy with him again."

"You don't need to try." She said. "As much as you try to hide it you already happy when he around. Even when you ignorin' his ass you still happy. I gotta give him somethin' for the effort 'cuz after all this time that man ain't gave up. If you was ignorin' my ass like you did him, I woulda been let yo ass go."

"Shut up." I laughed at her. "He ain't goin' nowhere. Even when I tell 'em to he still come around."

"Exactly." She said. "So take that and go with it. He ain't givin' up on you, so I don't think you should give up on him."

"You make it sound so simple." I said.

"Girl you know all the bull shit I had to go through with Isaiah." She said. "I mean yea I left 'em a few times, but I always go back. It ain't nobody else for me but that man. Everybody know that. Ain't nobody gon' be perfect. Especially a man. You just gotta take 'em for what they are. I mean they take us with all our bull shit too."

"Yea I get that." I said. "But how you just stop bein' scared?"

"Stop waitin' for somethin' bad to happen." She said. "You gon' miss out on all the good shit, tryna prepare for the bad. I say try it but keep yo guard up. Just until he can break it down."

"I don't know if I can do that again." I said. "I was all in with him when we first started datin'. I ain't even realize in time to put my guard up. And I loved every minute of it til' the bull shit came. I wana be like that again. Careless."

"Careless works a lot of the time." She said. "The other part of the time, it's really dangerous. Try it however it works for you. But just try it. God forbid if some bull shit happen again you know how to handle it."

"Lo if some shit hit the fan again, I'm blamin' yo ass." I gave her the look.

"Aw whatever." She said. "Now when we gon' double date? You know him and Isaiah still been hangin' out."

"Naw I ain't know that." I said. "Why you ain't tell me?"

"I didn't know til' I told Isaiah you was getting back with him." She said.

"What?" I asked. "How you just gon' assume that I was getting back with him?"

"I know you, P." She said. "You been wantin' that man back since you left his ass. And that's okay. You so worried about how shit make you look you forget lovin' somebody sometimes makes you a fool. But it happens. You ain't the first and damn sure ain't gon' be the last. Look at me. I'm livin' proof that it's okay to love somebody regardless of they mistakes. You know how many times I done fucked up in my relationship. And my man still ain't left me. That's just somethin' you gotta be grateful for."

"I really am tryin' Lo." I said. "I wish I could just let it happen."

"Go over to his house right now and tell 'em you want it to work." She said. "That's all you need to say and he gon' take it from there."

"What?" I asked. "What if she there?"

"If he tryna get you back he know better than to have her over there." She said.

"What if the kids there?" I asked.

"He said he want you meet them, right?" She asked. "So this might be the perfect time."

"And what if it ain't?" I asked.

"Paisley get yo ass over there, now." She said. "Don't make me have to take you over there like you some lil' ass kid."

"I'm grown as hell." I laughed at her. "I don't need you to take me nowhere."

"Alright well go then." She said. "And don't call 'em to tell 'em you comin' over, just go over there."

"Now you really trippin'." I said.

"P just do what I say." She said. "I ain't never stirred you wrong."

"I need a few more shots if I'ma do this crazy shit." I laughed at her.

I had the waiter bring me two more shots and quickly knocked them back.

"You ready?" She asked.

"Guess so." I smiled at her.

Laya

I was finally done feelin' sad about the whole situation. I was very unfortunate to be put in that, but I knew everything happened for a reason. Maybe I needed to see that to get out of my denial stage. I knew my mother was sick, but I never believed all the things people said about her. How could anyone believe that their mother was truly a cracked-out prostitute? She never even had to be that way. She had a great job. House was paid for when her mother left it to her. Car was paid for in cash when she hit the lottery before she got addicted.

Even before the drugs she was addicted to guys that treated her like shit. I don't know what it was that made her think she didn't deserve to be treated with respect. I mean I know I went through my phase of wantin' a bad boy. We all do. But that's all it was, a phase. That's all it's ever supposed to be.

My mother could've led a very healthy and successful life, but instead she gave someone the power to take it away. I couldn't beat myself up about it. I did everything I could for my mother when I could. But I was not about to let her take my jewelry to pay for somethin' she had no business using anyway.

Was I wrong? Should I have let her take the jewelry to keep her life? Was I bein' selfish? The man said he wasn't takin' the jewelry no way.

279

Should I not have called the police and risk them takin' her away? Fuck that. They didn't even show up. Supposedly someone got stabbed at the same time I called so they sent the few officers they had on duty over there. I guess havin' our lives in danger wasn't that important to the police that night. I kinda hoped they did show up. If they locked her up at least she would be able to get clean. Then she woulda been forced to think about her life and why she made the choices she made.

I could sit here for days and think about what shoulda happened, or what coulda happened. But none of that would get me anywhere. I still had a lot of livin' left to do. And I couldn't spend it dwelling on the tragedy I barely made it through. I was goin' into my junior year of college in the fall and I had my best friends wedding coming up in no time. Dealing with the daily stuff was actually fine for me. I felt like I was handling it well.

"So you ready for the big day?" I asked Jada as I talked to her on the phone.
"I guess." She said quietly.
"What you mean?" I asked.
"Girl you know I ain't been involved in none of the plans." She said.
"Why not?" I asked. "His mama took over everything?"
"I asked her too." She said. "I just ain't feel like I could do it. Especially 'cuz my mom wasn't on board at first."
"Is she now?" I asked.

"Not really." She said. "But at least she's talkin' to me. And she said she gon' come."

"Well that's good." I said. "But how do you feel about havin' a wedding where you don't even know what's gon' happen? Did you even pick out a dress?"

"Yea I just got one yesterday." She said. "I had to force myself to go do that."

"I can't believe you waited this long to get one." I said.

"I didn't wait." She said. "I just been puttin' it off."

"I don't understand what the problem is." I said. "You the one said you wanted to move up the date. So is it him that really wanted to?"

"I mean we both agreed on it." She said. "It just didn't give me what I was lookin' for."

"And what was that?" I asked.

"I don't know." She said. "It's one of those things you don't know until you get it. Like you don't know what you need, until it's there. It's hard to explain."

"Sound like you ain't sure if you wana marry this man." I said. "Which is crazy 'cuz you were so sure when you went off to school with him."

"Things change." She said quietly. "I'm a different woman now. And he's a completely different man."

"That's not a bad thing though, is it?" I asked. "I mean we all had to grow up someday. I think y'all just maturing."

"That may be the case." She said. "But for some reason, it seem like the people we are today, just ain't clicking like the people we used to be."

"What is the root of the problem?" I asked. "Have y'all even tried to figure that out?"

"He don't have a problem with me." She said. "I'm the one that got the issue. But I couldn't tell you exactly what the issue is if I tried. It just don't make no sense to me."

"I think you just over thinkin'." I said. "You getting nervous. But I hear that's natural. Don't let yo nerves talk you outta somethin' you know you want."

"I don't know if this what I want anymore." She said. "Girl I'm young. Still in school. I'm not really ready to be a housewife. I mean I could deal with us just stayin' engaged for a lil' bit longer. I don't know what made me think I was ready to do this now. In a way, I kinda wanted to do it for him. I felt like I owed him."

"For what?" I asked. "You don't owe no man, shit. If he can't wait for you, then you don't want him."

"It ain't that simple, Laya." She said.

"It really is, J." I said. "You the only one makin' it complicated."

"Carter really is a great guy." She said quietly.

"You ain't gotta convince me." I said. "I know he great. Maybe it just ain't the right timing for y'all."

"I don't wana break up with him." She said. "I just wana slow shit down for a minute. Everything happened so fast. The engagement. Me goin' to school with 'em. Us livin' together. It feel like it just happened over night."

"The crazy part about that is when everybody was tellin' you that you ain't wana hear it." I said.

"You just had to go there, didn't you?" She laughed.

"I ain't have a choice." I laughed with her. "You know we love you. And we just want the best for you. Sometimes you get so wrapped up in the fast pace shit and don't take time to see what's really goin' on. But that's life. We all do it at some point. Only thing I learned from that is, when everybody sayin' the same thing, believe them. We think we know everything and then we end up bein' wrong when shit hit the fan."

"So true." She said quietly. "I just feel like I'm gon' be provin' everybody right if I don't go through with this."

"You can't marry somebody just to prove everybody wrong." I said. "Don't live yo life based on everybody else opinions. I ain't never knew you to care about what other people think, J. What's up?"

"I'm just so sad." She cried. "I miss Nicholas so much and he won't even talk to me."

"See I knew this was some Nicholas shit." I said. "Girl if yo ass don't stop cryin' and figure out who you wana be with. You posed to be so happy right now and you seem like you miserable."

"I miss my best friend, Laya." She said. "Can you talk to him for me?"

"Hell naw." I said. "You gotta figure out how to get through to him 'cuz you got yoself in this mess. And even if I did talk to Nicholas you know he too damn stubborn to do anything he ain't ready to do."

"Yea he is stubborn." She agreed. "But I really don't know what else to do. He completely cut me off. Like I never even existed. This the longest I ever went without talkin' to him. I haven't seen his face in months. This shit is really killin' me."

"I see that." I laughed at her. "Stop bein' a lil' ass kid and get yo man back. It's that simple."

"Girl I am engaged. This damn wedding is around the corner." She said.

"Fool I know." I said. "Will you be there? Cuz it sure as hell don't sound like you will."

"Shut the hell up." She said. "I can't just back out of it now. It's too close."

"So you just gon' marry him anyway?" I asked. "I'm sure he would rather you break it off now, as opposed to cheatin' on him with Nicholas after y'all married."

"What?" She asked. "You know I ain't never cheated on Carter."

"I never said you did." I said. "But it's bound to happen. The way y'all sad asses been missin' each other."

"Aw he miss me too?" She asked.

"You know damn well he just as miserable as you are." I said. "And Cassidy losin' her mind tryna figure his ass out. She still complain to me damn near everyday. Asking me for advice and shit."

"For real?" She asked surprised. "What you tell her?"

"Girl at first I was tryna be optimistic about the whole situation." I said. "At least to her. Then she just started getting on my nerves so I just told her the truth. Let that nigga go. He ain't actin' like he wana be with her, so why should they stay together?"

"Now I can't believe that shit." She said. "He love Cassidy."

"I know he do." I said. "But he ain't in love with her no more. He always been in love with you. That shit bound to end soon."

"Don't say that." She said. "What is it they arguin' about?"

"He don't want her to move in." I said. "Had her stop leavin' her stuff over there so she tried to get back at him and said she just wasn't gon' sleep over there no more. And he got too comfortable with it so it backfired on her. Now she wana stay here for summer but stay with him to get her housing money back."

"Damn." She said. "I don't know why he just don't let the girl live with 'em."

"Say he ain't ready to have somebody in his space all day everyday." I said. "Which I can understand because once me and Malcolm moved in together it was a major adjustment. I'm used to livin' by myself. You know I had my own place since I was damn near 14. But then when you gotta share yo space with somebody 24/7, it's so different. I was ready for it though. He was too. If Nicholas ain't ready, that ain't somethin' she or anybody else can force on him. He gon' know when he ready."

"If she keep naggin' him about it he definitely ain't gon' be ready no time soon." She said.

"Hell naw." I agreed.

"Somebody need to tell her ass that." She said.

"Girl I have told her." I said. "Too many times to count. I'm done givin' her my good ass advice for her to just do the opposite. Then when I end up being right, she come cryin' to me like 'I shoulda just listened to you in the first place'. And all along I be thinkin' 'damn right.'"

"You crazy as hell." She laughed at me. "So how are you doin' with everything?"

"I'm actually really good." I said.

"I wish you woulda had a public funeral." She said. "You know I wanted to be there for you."

"I know but I just wanted to be alone." I said. "I ain't even tell nobody in my family. It was just me and Malcolm. I ain't know how I was gon' feel and I ain't want nobody to see me like that."

"Girl you know I was at the airport bouta get on the flight and come anyway then Malcolm called me like 'Just let her do it alone'. I figured you had to be goin' through it for him to make me stay away."

"Yea it was kinda rough." I said. "I thought I was doin' good at hiding it, but I guess not if he saw how I was feelin'."

"You know that man know you better than you know yoself." She said. "You can't hide shit from him."

"Hell naw." I agreed. "But overall, I am glad I got to see her again before it all ended. I just wish it ain't have to be like that."

"Right." She said. "Nobody deserve to see no shit like that. I can't believe you holdin' up like you are. Laya you bet not be holdin' all yo emotions in and then explode outta nowhere. You know you can talk to me about it. Cry to me about it. Whatever you need to do. But holdin' that shit in ain't healthy."

"I know, Dr. Phil." I laughed at her ass. "I'm really fine though, J. I know it sound crazy. Shit I'm surprised my damn self. But I don't have any more emotions towards it. I just accepted it as it is. I hate cryin'. That don't help shit. Nothin' I do, can bring her back. And even if I could, I don't think I would want to. She in a better place now. Nobody can hurt her, and she can't hurt me. So maybe that was best for her."

"Oh my God!" She squealed. "You sound so grown up. I can't believe how mature you are now. College really changed you, huh?"

"Girl I guess so." I laughed at her.

Jamal

"Who at the door?" I yelled to Stacey as I put JuneBug in the bed.

She didn't respond so I thought she ain't hear me. I went out to the living room to see my dad standin' in the doorway.

"What you doin' here, old man?" I laughed as I walked over to him.

"Just here on some business." He laughed. "Come take a ride with me."

"Alright." I said. "I'll be back babe." I said to Stacey as I kissed her cheek.

"Okay." She smiled. "Bye Dad. Be careful with him."

"I'll try." My dad laughed as we walked to the car.

"What's up?" I asked as we got in. "Why you ain't call me?"

"It was kinda last minute." He said as we pulled off.

"I know you ain't sneak out here." I laughed at him.

"Shut up." He said. "I found out some stuff about yo sister."

"Huh?" I asked. "What you mean? What kinda stuff?"

"She's living here." He said.

"What?" I asked. "All this time she been in Michigan?"

"Well I don't know about all this time, but I know she here now." He said.

"How you find all this out?" I asked.

"Hired somebody to find her for me." He said. "So that's where I'm getting ready to go now. But I want you and Trevor to come with me."

"You sure about that?" I asked. "Maybe you should meet her first so she can say whatever she wana say to you. I mean we don't wana hit her with too much all at once."

"I'm sure about this." He said. "Y'all her family just as much as I am, and I'm tired of keepin' away from her."

"What mom say about it?" I asked.

"She the one sent me out here." He laughed. "I was nervous at first, but then when I thought about bringin' y'all with me I knew it would be cool."

"Oh so you think we just gon' fix everything?" I laughed at him.

"Y'all can't fix shit if you tried." He laughed at me. "I just want y'all to help me get through this. In case I get over there and shit hit the fan."

"Dad you too old to be lettin' shit hit the fan." I laughed again.

"Shut up fool." He said. "You know what I mean."

"Yea yea." I said. "Well go to the office. Trevor said he was workin' today."

"It's Saturday." He said. "Why he ain't at home?"

"Some campaign they had to have done by Monday." I said. "He ain't wana finish on Monday he want it done by time they get there Monday."

"That boy know he work too damn hard." He laughed.

"Hell yea." I said. "He act like he just can't stop. We be havin' to force him to leave at 5, when they office close at 4."

"I used to be like that." He said. "Before I started havin' to travel all the time. Being gone so much make you wana hurry up and get home."

"Yea that's how I was feelin' after Stacey had JuneBug." I said. "I just cut my schedule down to a few days a week and Stacey just stopped workin' all together. Good thing we had our savings to fall back on. Now that he getting ready to go to preschool we probably both gon' go back to our normal routine."

"Well be glad y'all was in the position to do that." He said. "When we had y'all we was too young to be thinkin' about a savings account. I'm proud of y'all for that."

"Thanks old man." I said.

"What you think Trevor gon' say about all this?" He asked.

"I think he ain't gon' wana do it." I said. "That's why we wait to tell 'em til' we pull out the parkin' lot. Kinda like you tricked me."

"Ain't nobody trick you." He said. "You was comin' regardless. Just like he is. Y'all still my kids I don't care how old y'all get."

"Whatever." I laughed at him.

Paisley

It was raining so hard outside and I could not bring myself to push the button. My dumb ass just had to take London's advice to come see him. I knew better. I knew I shouldn't be doin' this. The rain didn't start til' I pulled up at his complex. When I left from lunch with her the sun was shining and everything. This was a sign that I should not be here openin' myself up to him. I know he thought I opened myself up when he spent the night, but that wasn't the case for me. I had to have been standin' there for 20 minutes getting soaked, when someone came out of the building.

"Oh I'm sorry, did you need to get in?" A man asked me as he held the door open for me.
"Yes. Thank you." I smiled after I hesitated to answer him.

I was so nervous. I ain't know what was bouta happen. All of the worst thoughts ever were goin' through my head. God forbid this actually turn out good. I was feelin' so nauseous. I felt like I would throw up every inch of my crab cakes I just had for lunch. I did my best to hold it all in. I slowly dragged myself to the elevator. The good thing about this walk was that he stayed on the top floor. So I had 15 floors to get my thoughts together.

The elevator went straight up. Nobody even stopped it to get on. It was crazy. This was the busiest building I had ever seen and today it was abandoned. Another sign that I needed to turn my ass around.

I got to the 15th floor and damn near froze. I forced myself off the elevator. I closed my eyes as I stepped in front of his door. I still didn't know what to say. I was hopin' he could read my face and I wouldn't have to say anything at all. As soon as I lifted my hand to knock on the door, he opened it.

"What's up beautiful?" He smiled at me. "What you doin' over this way?"

"How did you know I was here?" I asked as I looked at him.

"I didn't." He said. "I was getting ready to go get my mail. You wana come or just wait in here for me?"

"I think I'll just wait here for you." I smiled at him.

This was the perfect opportunity for me to get a feel for the place. I wasn't the nosy type, but I needed to know this shit was real this time.

"Alright I'll be right back." He said as he came out and I went in.

I closed the door behind me and sat on the couch. Once I was sure that he was on the elevator, I sat my purse down and took a walk around the place. It wasn't messy, but it could've used a good straightening. First sign no woman was livin' here. I went to the bedroom and his closet was full of his clothes, shoes and everything else. No colors or anything decorative in the place at all. Not even in the bathroom. The place just felt like a bachelor pad. Only thing that was missin' was a pole.

I feel like he would've had one if he hadn't met me the way he did. He always seemed tainted by the fact that I was a dancer. After I took a quick view of the place I made my way back to the living room. As he was opening the door, I was sitting on the couch. He gave me the look when he came in.

"Looking for somethin'?" He smiled as he sat his mail on the table.
"Just had to use the bathroom." I smiled at him. He already knew I was lookin' around.
"Yea okay." He laughed as he sat next to me. "So what's on yo mind?"
"Why you think somethin' on my mind?" I asked him.
"Well you came here, so I feel like you got somethin' important to say." He said. "And I can see it on yo face."

I wish you knew what it was, I thought to myself.

"Maybe I just wanted to make sure you was alive." I smiled.
"You coulda called me for that." He said. "I mean I'm glad you here. I planned on comin' over in a lil' bit anyway, but I'll take this anytime."
"I just came from lunch with Lo." I said. "Why you ain't tell me you and Isaiah was still cool?"

"I mean I ain't know I had to." He said. "Why wouldn't we be? Just 'cuz me and you broke up that mean I can't hang out with 'em no more?"

"Naw I ain't say that." I said. "I just didn't know."

"It ain't shit." He said. "You know that's my nigga."

"Guess so." I said.

The awkward silence came into play. I was too nervous to say anything else. I couldn't understand why this man made me feel this way. I felt like I had butterflies. Like I was little kid bouta tell their crush that she liked them. This situation was nowhere near that kid shit. I was a grown woman, tryna make shit work with a grown ass man.

"Lo been givin' you some advice, huh?" He asked as he looked at me.

Thank God he knew where I was goin' with this. Was I that obvious?

"Somethin' like that." I said quietly. "Look I need things to go extremely slow with this if we gon' try again. Don't have me fallin' for you again before I can even realize it. I don't wana be swept up in somethin' and it be too late for me to get out of it."

"I don't want you if you gon' have one foot in, and the other one out the door." He said. "Ain't that what you told me? Well I feel the same way. I know exactly how you was feelin 'cuz now you startin' to put me in that position."

"I'm not married." I snapped.

"And neither am I." He said. "But I was. That don't mean that I can't relate. You dont wana get hurt again and I get that. But we ain't gon' get nowhere if you constantly waiting for me to fuck up again. I can't have you tryna prepare for all the bad shit that you think is gon' happen to you by bein' with me. You gotta take my word and let me show you that I'm not lettin' you go again. Which means that I know what I gotta do to keep you around. I know how to please you. But I'm not gon' do that, if you can't be all in."

"I can be all in." I said. "Just not yet. You have to let me get to that point. I need to see a lot before I can open myself back up to you."

"I can handle that." He said. "So what you tryna say? You want me back or somethin'?"

"Boy please." I laughed. "You the one been harassin' me since I left yo ass last year."

"Aw whatever." He laughed. "You like it. Clearly it brought you over here today."

"Keep thinkin' that'." I smiled. "See where it get you."

"It got me here, so I'll take it." He laughed. "You really tryna do this? Don't be over here bull shittin' me, Paisley."

"I want this to work." I smiled at him. "I care about you too much for it not to."

"I love you too." He smiled at me and kissed me. "Come with me to pick up the kids."

"What?" I asked. "From where?"

"School." He laughed.

"Ain't it too soon for all that?" I asked.

"Not at all." He said. "They gon' be here just as much as you are, if not more. So we need to just get this out the way so everybody can be comfortable with each other."

"But don't you think they gon' go back to they mom and say somethin' to her about me." I said to him.

"I'll just let her know before they do." He laughed. "Come on. Just trust me."

"You sure about this?" I asked. "I ain't tryna make shit worse than it already is."

"Ain't possible." He said as he stood up. "Now let's go."

He pulled me up off the couch. He grabbed my hand and led me out the door. He held my hand the whole way down the elevator. Never let it go until he opened the car door for me. He was always a gentleman with me. Even when shit got heated, he never disrespected me. Nobody ever treated me that way.

In some ways, he was really my first love. I woulda never thought at this age, I would just now really be experiencing a somewhat healthy relationship. Besides the secret wife, it was the healthiest I'd ever been in. Guess that said a lot about the guys I dated in the past.

Malcolm

"You need to learn how to answer the damn phone." Laya yelled at me as she walked in the house.

"Don't come in here with all that noise." I said to her with my face still in the couch.

I had the worst hangover in the world. It was damn near 4 in the afternoon but I had all the blinds closed and lights off. The TV was on with the volume down real low. My phone was on the kitchen table charging so I was not getting up to answer it for nobody.

"Why you in here in the dark?" She asked as she started openin' the blinds.

"That light hurtin' my head." I whined as I closed my eyes.

"Ain't nobody tell yo ass to be out drinkin' all night." She said as she went to the kitchen. She turned my phone on, took it off the charger and brought it to me. "Call yo mama. Now. She been callin' me all mornin' lookin' for you."

"What's wrong?" I asked lookin at her.

"Nothin' she just said she ain't heard from you." She said.

"Man I'm high as hell. Still drunk as fuck." I said. "I ain't finna call her right now. I'll call her later. She don't want nothin'."

"Clearly it's important, if she keep callin' lookin' for you." She said as she sat down next to me on the couch.

"I know it ain't 'cuz she woulda told you to tell me if it was." I said as I put my head on her lap. I closed my eyes and tried to go back to sleep. Then I heard my mama on speakerphone. "You petty as hell." I mumbled as she gave me the phone. "What's up, Ma." I said to my mama on the phone.

"Boy don't make me have to come out there and whoop yo ass since you can't answer my phone calls." She snapped.

"My phone been dead." I said. "It's been on the charger since I got in this mornin' but I forgot to turn it back on. What's goin' on?"

"Yo dad called me lookin' for you today." She said quietly.

"Who?" I asked makin' sure I heard her correctly.

"Marcus called me lookin' for you today." She said.

"For what?" I asked.

I really wasn't interested in anything that nigga had to say, but I felt like I needed to entertain her conversation.

"He wants to see you." She said.

"He must need somethin'." I said.

"Say he don't." She said.

"You seen 'em?" I asked already knowin' the answer.

I been through this before with her. He came back tryna be the good guy long enough to get back in my mama bed and leave us with Kelly. After he ran off with her credit cards we ain't heard from 'em since then. By the time she told me he was lookin' for me, she was already back involved with 'em.

"Why does that matter?" She asked.

"I just asked you a question." I said.

"Well he wants to see you." She said. "You comin' home anytime soon?"

"Ain't plan on it." I said.

"Well we can come out there to see you for a weekend."

"Who is we?" I asked. "I'm workin' a lot this summer, Ma. I really don't have time for this."

"So you don't have time to see your mother, or your sister?" She asked.

"You know I can see y'all at anytime." I said. "But I ain't tryna entertain that nigga."

"That nigga, is still your father, Malcolm." She said.

"I ain't bouta play this game with you again." I said. "When he come around tellin' you what you wana hear, he my father. When that nigga out doin' him, he ain't shit but a sperm donor. Make up yo mind, Ma. Which one is it?"

"Now look here." She said. "I understand you mad about the whole situation. But you will not talk to me like that. Ever. I don't care how grown you think you are. You hear me?"

"I hear you, Ma." I said quietly. "Clearly you don't hear yourself. Listen to how you sound though. You really gon' let this man play you again?"

"What I let that man do, is none of your business." She snapped.

"Like hell it ain't." I snapped. "I'm the one you come cryin' too when shit ain't what you think it is. I'm ten years old and I gotta comfort my mama 'cuz my daddy ain't shit. What you mean it ain't my business? That nigga ain't never did shit for you, or us. I take care of this family. And it ain't my business?"

I was sittin' up now. Mad as hell. Headache and all. She completely blew my high with this bull shit. Eyes wide open I could see Laya lookin' at me shaking her head. I ain't give a fuck right now. My mama was on bull shit and I was lettin' her know. Laya took the phone from me and took my mama off speakerphone. Clearly I said too much 'cuz she was speechless. But we was both too damn old to be sugarcoating shit. I was the only one who kept it real with her. That shit wasn't gon' change just 'cuz he came back around.

"Michelle maybe I should have him call you back once he calm down." Laya said to my mom.
"You tell that nigga don't call me until he ready to apologize." I heard my mom yell into the phone before she hung up.
"Fuck that shit." I said as Laya looked at me.
"What the hell was that Malcolm?" She asked. "I can't believe you just snapped on her like that."
"Laya I ain't no fuckin' kid." I said. "She ain't either. And I'm tired of her actin' like that when this nigga come around. I know it only happened once, but this nigga keep leavin' her. He left after I was born. Came back

and they made Kelly and he left again. With all her fuckin' credit cards. And now he back? What the fuck he want now?"

"Maybe had you not snapped on yo mom like that, you coulda found out what he wanted." She said.

"I don't give a fuck what he want cuz he ain't getting shit from me." I said.

"And if she wasn't so lonely, he wouldn't get shit from her neither."

"You think you should go home to be with them for the summer?" She asked.

"Hell naw." I said. "I can't be her man, Laya. Only thing I would be doin' is holdin' her over til' I leave again. I ain't got no plans of movin' back home once school over. We all know that. So she gon' have to do somethin' else. She got Kelly there. She act like she gotta have a man around or she gon' lose her mind."

"She's lonely Malcolm." She said. "You ain't never felt like that."

"Not at all." I said. "I'ma grown ass man. If I ever felt like that, I knew how to change it. She grown as hell. She could be out there datin' but she choose not too. She just sit around waitin' years for this nigga to come back around. He be there for a damn month. Long enough to get her money and get her pregnant again. Then we ain't gon' see 'em for another 10 years. Kelly ain't even never seen the nigga. How you think that make me feel?"

"I know you mad, babe." She said. "And I ain't sayin' you shouldn't be. But you takin' it out on the wrong person."

"No I'm not." I said. "I'm mad at his ass for bein' a bitch, and I'm mad at her for accepting that. She ain't have to let him back in our life. This time or the last. I mean don't get me wrong I love Kelly and I would never want us to be without her, but he ain't have to take all her money like that. He ain't have to make it harder for us like he did and still not even help us out. What kinda man do that shit? How you call yoself a man but you livin' off yo baby mama? Don't even see yo kids. But you a man though?"

By this time I was standin' up. Pacing around the room. Mad as hell. Laya got up and went to the bedroom. I already knew what she was doin'. She came back out with the grinder and two rellos. I just kept pacing around the room silently as she rolled up two blunts. Guess she knew my mama just blew my high. That was one of my pet peeves. I hated wastin' drugs getting mad at somebody.

The whole point of smokin' was to calm me down. If you took that from me once I smoked, you made shit worse. Laya knew that. Even if she had to find out the hard way. She lit the blunt and handed it to me. I continued to pace around the room.

"You know she want you to apologize." She said as she looked up at me from the couch.
"I don't give a damn what she want right now, Laya." I said. "She need to stop thinkin' about herself and look at what kinda example she settin' for Kelly. She there seein' all this bull shit. She ain't gon' think nothin' of it right now, but when shit hit the fan she gon' be lookin' at her mama for some damn answers. And what the fuck she gon' say then?"

"Guess that's somethin' yo mama gon' have to deal with." She said as she shook her head.

"Naw that's somethin' I'm gon' have to deal with." I said. "I'm the one who fix everything. That's my job. And she don't realize she makin' shit harder on me. She done got so used to me fixing shit when it go wrong that she don't even try to prevent it."

"Babe I really don't think it's as bad as you makin' it out to be." She said quietly.

"Oh I'm sorry were you there?" I asked her sarcastically.

"Look don't give me the attitude." She snapped. "I ain't even tryna hear that shit. I'm just tellin' you from the outside lookin' in, I think you coulda handled that shit a lil' better. I mean I know you mad 'cuz she blew yo high, and you cranky from yo hangover, but that ain't her fault."

"It is 'cuz she coulda just talked to me later once I actually woke up." I snapped. "Instead of forcin' me to wake up to this bull shit. All you had to do was wait for me to call her later. Told you she ain't want shit."

"Wow." She said. "So now it's my fault."

"It's both of y'all." I said. "Just 'cuz my mama call my phone, do not mean I gotta answer right then and there. If I don't answer clearly I'm in the middle of somethin'. So when I call her back, that mean I'm free to talk. You always wana force me to talk to her as soon as I get a minute."

"Nigga yo ass wasn't doin' shit but sittin' around in the dark." She finally snapped.

"Lower yo damn voice." I said to her.

I wasn't bouta be givin' my neighbors nothin' to talk shit about.

"Don't tell me what to do." She said. "You wana put this shit on me when it ain't got nothin' to do with me."

"If it don't concern you, why are you puttin' yoself in it?" I asked quietly. "I never asked you for yo opinion. You just felt like you needed to share it. I ain't ask for yo advice on how to talk to my mama. I know how to talk to her. I know exactly what she need to hear."

"I don't know why you feel you need to make this into a fight with me." She said. "We in this shit together. So of course, I'm gon' give you my opinion. Whether you like it or not. Whether you wana hear it or not. I ain't here to tell you what you wana hear. I'm here to be real with you, just like you wana be with yo mama. Only difference is, I know how to talk to mufuckas. Unlike you, you talk to people like you better than them when they ain't doin' what you want them to do. I brought my opinion to you calmly. The way you shoulda brought yours to yo mama. You don't have to disrespect people to get yo point across. I think my reaction was an instant example of that."

"Man whatever." I said as I lit the other blunt. "I ain't got time for all this bull shit. I'm tired as hell. My head bangin'. And all y'all doin' is makin' it worse." I grabbed my phone and walked out the house.

"Oh okay so now you just gon' leave?" She asked as I walked to the parkin' lot.

"Yup." I said as I got in my car.

As I started it up, she walked back in the house. I was so glad she ain't come out here tryna make a scene. She knew better. She knew I wasn't goin' for that shit. I rolled up another blunt before I pulled off. This shit was really getting to me. I couldn't believe my mama was trippin' over a nigga who ain't never did shit for her. It ain't that much love in the world, to get me to continue to go back to somebody who I always takin' from you.

It ain't even just about the money, he does absolutely nothing for her outside of that. He ain't there for her. She can't turn to him when she stressed out about shit. I'm the one that's there for her. Picking up his slack since I was a kid. After all this shit she let him put us through, I deserve to be able to speak my mind about the situation. I rode around for about an hour before I went back home. I needed a drink but I ain't feel like getting drunk again when I still had a hangover from last night. I felt like I barely even got any sleep when I got in this mornin'.

I got back to the house and prepared myself for Laya's bull shit. When I pulled up, her car was nowhere to be found. I ain't know where she was, but I was relieved that I ain't have to deal with her mouth right now. I went in the house, smoked another blunt, took a few shots of the 1800 I had left in the fridge and passed out.

I woke up the next morning at 8am. I couldn't fall back asleep. I felt like fuckin' death. But at least I got through the night without her bull shit. I looked over to see her knocked out on the other side of me. Normally when we argued she would do some petty shit and sleep on the couch if I was in the bed before her. Guess she wasn't on that last night.

I got up and went to the kitchen to get somethin' for my headache. I went to lay on the couch to try to go back to sleep. I dozed off for about twenty minutes before Laya came out to the living room. Only thing I could think of, was here we go again.

"I know you got somethin' to say to me." She said as she stood over me. "Good mornin' to you too, babe." I smiled at her tryna play it off.

I ain't feel like fightin' with her no more. It was petty as hell for us to really be mad.

"Don't try that bull shit with me, Malcolm." She snapped. "You was really trippin' yesterday."
"Clearly I was upset." I said. "But I am sorry for snappin' on you. You know I ain't mean none of that shit. I was just cranky from that hangover."
"I know you ain't mean that shit you said to me, but what about to yo mom?" She asked as she stared at me.
"I meant all that shit." I said. "And I ain't takin' back a damn thing I said to her either."
"You need to learn how to talk to people." She said. "I don't care if you drunk or high, you ain't just gon' be talkin' to me like you crazy. Or yo

mama. She taught you better than that and don't sit here and act like she didn't."

"Come on with the lecture, bae." I whined as I pulled her on top of me.

"I'm sorry I said that shit to you. Just accept my apology so we can move on from this."

"It ain't that simple." She said.

"You makin' it harder than it gotta be." I said.

"I can't just let you talk to me any type of way and think that shit is okay." She said.

"It's not okay." I said. "I know that. And it ain't gon' happen again. I ain't mean to piss you off. I know you in this shit with me and I ain't havin' it no other way."

"You mean it?" She asked as I wrapped my arms around her.

"You know I do." I said as I kissed her forehead.

"Okay." She said. "I'll accept yo apology, but I do need you to make shit right with yo mom. Now if that mean apologizin', then you gotta do that."

"I'll do everything but that." I said. "I ain't say nothin' I shouldn't have to her. Y'all might not like the way it came out, but I can't keep tryna spare her feelings. That's how we got here in the first place. She ain't takin' shit seriously. She ain't seein' how these decisions affecting her kids. I'm the only one seein' that. I dealt with it firsthand so I know that shit ain't no joke. And it definitely ain't shit I want my sister to experience."

"Baby just try to make it right." She said. "Talk to her calmly. Maybe she'll hear you better that way. Instead of you yellin' at her like she yo child, you should talk to her as her child. That's all I'm sayin'."

"I'm blunt as hell, Laya." I said. "Everybody know that. Ain't shit never gon' change that. Damn sure ain't gon' change when my mama raised me to be this way. She the same way as me. But how you gon' be able to dish it out and can't take it? That shit crazy as hell."

"You heard what I had to say about it." She said. "And that's it. Don't even let it get to you, the way you did. I mean I know you had to go out and calm down, but it shouldn't have this much power over you. To the point where you talkin' to me crazy when I ain't did shit but have yo back like I always do."

"You right." I smiled at her. "I'ma see what I can do to fix this shit."

"Want me to call her?" She laughed.

"Hell naw." I laughed at her. "I'll call her in a few days. Let her ass calm down."

"Terrible." She laughed at me.

Trevor

We had been sittin' outside my sister's house for damn near two hours. This girl was not comin' home.

"You sure you got the right address?" I asked my dad.

"Yea this it." He said.

"Maybe she at work or somethin'." Jamal said.

"Well how much longer we gon' wait?" I asked. "We can't be out here all day like some stalkers."

"I say give it another 30 minutes." My dad said. "If she don't show up by then, we can try again tomorrow."

"What?" I asked. "Yo investigator ain't tell you where she worked at?"

"Said he couldn't find no employers for her." He said.

"That's crazy." Jamal said. "If she livin' in these she gotta be makin' some type of money."

"Shut up." My dad said. "I think this her pullin' up."

We all looked out the window as we saw a white Range Rover pull into her driveway. A girl got out of the car lookin' just like my dad. I looked at him to see his reaction. We all knew that was her. He was froze. It looked like he panicked. He ain't know what to do. Guess he really didn't think this thing all the way through.

"So now what?" I finally broke the silence.

311

"I don't know." He said starin' straight ahead. "I ain't think about all that."
"Man come on." I said as I opened my door.

They both got out the car and followed me to the door. I rang the doorbell and waited for her to answer it.

"Hi." She smiled when she opened the door. "Can I help y'all?"

She looked at my dad and I could tell she knew it was him. She looked like she was bouta pass out.

"Can we come in?" My dad finally asked her.

She looked like she saw a ghost. Guess she ain't think he was alive.

"Yea." She said surprisingly. "Come in." She opened the door for us to come in.

We walked in and she motioned for us to sit down on the couch. Everything was pure white. I felt like I was in heaven' or somethin'. It was no way she had any kids runnin' around in here with all this white I was lookin' at. We sat down as she sat in the chair across from the couch we were on. I looked at Jamal to see if he was starin' at her the same way I was. He was. She was beautiful. But we knew her from somewhere. Just couldn't figure out where from.

"When I got your message, I thought it was a joke." She finally said. "At first my mom told me you were dead. Later on, she ended up tellin' me the truth."

"You know who I am?" My dad asked her.

"Come on." She smiled. "I feel like I'm lookin' in the mirror. Only thing you missin' is the blonde hair."

We all laughed at her. At least she was tryna make us feel comfortable.

"Well then let me introduce these guys." He smiled. "These are your brothers, Jamal and Trevor."

"Hey brothers." She smiled and waved at us.

This girl was goofy. But that ran in our family. She was tryna make the best of the situation. And I appreciated that.

"Have you talked to your mother?" He asked.

"Not since she told me the truth." She said.

"Truth about what?" He asked.

"That you had been givin' her money since I was born." She said. "All my life she let me believe you wasn't doin' shit to help us. Come to find out you were all along. I'm sorry she tried to get more money out of you. I can pay you back for the court costs and all that. I just feel like I owe you. You shouldn't have had to go through that when you been' helpin all along."

"I mean it was unfortunate." He said. "But it's done and over with. You don't owe me anything."

"So how long you been in Michigan?" I asked her.

"About 5 years now." She answered. "Y'all came with 'em for support? That's so nice."

"Actually, he just popped up and told us come on." Jamal laughed. "But it's cool. We wanted to meet you too."

"So y'all stay in Texas too?" She asked.

"Nope." I said. "We both been out here since college."

"Wow." She smiled. "You mean to tell me I been livin' in the same state as both of my brothers all this time and I ain't even know it? How crazy is that?"

"It is really crazy." Jamal said. "Especially 'cuz I live like 5 minutes away from here. And Trevor is only like ten minutes away."

"Damn." She said. "We been in the same area all this time. How did we not run into each other?"

"I feel like we have." I said. "Just don't know where yet."

"I dont know." She said. "I'm normally pretty good with remembering faces."

"So do you have any kids?" My dad asked.

"Nope." She said. "Just me. I couldn't have no babies in all this white stuff right now anyway."

We laughed again together.

"I'm sure you got some questions for me." My dad told her. "I just brought the boys along to meet you. You wana go get somethin' to eat?"

"That would be nice." She smiled.

"You mind if I give the boys my car so they can get back home and I ride with you?" He asked her.

"Yea that's fine." She said. "I can drop you off afterward."

"Alright Dad." I said as he gave me the keys. "Call us later. Glad we got to meet you Ms. Paisley." I hugged her.

"Me too." She said as she hugged Jamal.

"We'll probably come by and see you tomorrow before Dad head back home." Jamal said to her.

"Good." She smiled as we headed to the door. Her and my dad trailed behind us. They got in her truck, and we got in his car.

"You know where we know her from, right?" Jamal asked me as I pulled out of the driveway.

"Naw I still can't figure it out." I said.

"The Spot." He said. "Remember that night we went and it was this girl that looked just like Dad. That's her."

"That ain't her." I laughed.

"That's her." He said. "I don't forget faces."

"What the hell was you doin' lookin' at strippers faces?" I asked.

"It caught me off guard when I seen she looked like him." He said. "Shut up nigga 'cuz you was lookin' at her face too."

"She's gorgeous." I said. "I can't believe she a stripper though."

315

"I can't believe we got a sister that's a stripper." He said. "I think we should let her tell 'em. If she want to. That ain't our business."

"Hell naw it ain't." I said. "I ain't tellin' him shit about that. She don't even have to know that we know."

"Nope." He laughed. "This shit is really crazy. She been livin' here all this time. All this time we coulda been hangin' out with her. Kids gotta auntie and we ain't even know about it."

"Well it's a surprise for everybody." I said. "I'm just glad it's his surprise and not mine. Nigga I woulda lost my mind if I had to explain that shit that I thought happened to me. That shit just ain't me. I don't want nobody thinkin' it's me either."

"We thought it wasn't him either." He said. "And look what happened. Ain't nobody perfect Trevor. I don't know when you gon' accept that."

"Nigga I know that." I said. "That don't mean I wana be like every other nigga."

"Every other nigga ain't like that." He said. "I'm not. And stop tryna make it like you better than somebody 'cuz you ain't. It happened to Dad. That don't make him like every other nigga, do it?"

Damn. He was right. He really had a point there. I was so set on not bein' a stereotype, I ain't realize that my dad was kinda goin' through the same thing. It didn't make him any less of a man in my eyes. I ain't look at him no different. That did not change the fact that he raised me to be a better man than him. I wouldn't trade that for nothin'.

Nicholas

"Did you decide what you gon' do for the summer?" I asked Cassidy as she put the dishes in the dishwasher.

"You already know what I wana do this summer." She said as she sat next to me at the table.

"And you know how I feel about that." I said. "So did you figure somethin' else out?"

"I don't understand what the problem is." She said.

"What is it for you not to understand?" I asked. She was really startin' to piss me off with the same bull shit.

"What is yo problem?" She asked. "I cook for you I clean up after you. And I can't even sleep here?"

"I never said you couldn't sleep here and you know that." I said. "I just don't want you leavin' all yo shit here all over the place."

"It wouldn't be all over the place if I had somewhere to keep it." She said.

"You do." I said. "In yo dresser in yo dorm room. I never asked you to do shit for me."

"You sure as hell don't stop me." She snapped.

"I mean if that's really what you on, then we can fix that shit right now." I said. "I can feed myself. And I have no problem cleaning up after myself. Happy now? You don't have to do shit else for me."

"Nicholas, I don't do shit for you 'cuz I feel like I have to." She said. "I do it 'cuz I want to. That's what you fail to realize. You lookin' at it like I'm doin' you a favor, and I'm lookin' at it as takin' care of my man. That's what I'm supposed to do. And I like to do it for you. But when I'm not getting anything in return, then I start to question where I really stand with you."

"I give you whatever you want, Cassidy." I said. "Why can't I just have this one thing? You don't want for shit. And if you doin' somethin' to get somethin' out of it, then you really don't like doin' that shit like you say you do. You don't help people waitin' for a reward. What kinda selfish ass shit is that?"

"So I'm selfish?" She asked. "You the one that act like you can't share yo space with me. You don't even want to."

"If I'm selfish 'cuz I want my own spot for a while, then I'll be that." I said. "I ain't never told you different. You knew what it was when I moved off campus. You thought if you hung around for a while I would change my mind. That's where you fucked up at. I ain't never gave you the impression that I would change my mind. You saw what you wanted to and ran with it. How is that my fault? You want me to be honest with you. I ain't do what you say and you mad about it. I can't win with yo ass, Cassidy."

"The fact that my feelings are hurt 'cuz you don't really want me around, and you don't give a fuck about it, really pisses me off." She said quietly. "What are we even doin' this for if we ain't goin' nowhere?"

"What you mean?" I asked. "We young as hell. Still in school. We got all our lives to live together. Why it gotta be now or never with this shit? I give yo ass everything you could even think to ask for. Whenever you want it. You mean to tell me it ain't one thing I can say no to? It ain't one thing that I can be okay with wantin' to myself. Sound like you the selfish one, Cassidy."

"Fuck you and everything you sayin' to me." She said as she grabbed her purse and left out the apartment.

I damn sure wasn't goin' after her ass. I was done havin' the same fight. All she did was cry about it, then be over it the next morning. I ain't have the patience to keep dealin' with this bull shit. I started to roll up a blunt as I heard a knock on the door. I knew it was Cassidy. She musta lost her key again. I opened the door without even lookin' through the peephole.

"What the fuck is it now?" I said before I realized it wasn't Cassidy at my door.
"Is this a bad time?" She asked me.
"What you doin' here?" I asked her. I couldn't believe Jada was standin' at my door.
"I needed to see you." She smiled.
"For what?" I asked.

I was still mad at her. And I was mad at Cassidy so Jada was really getting twice the anger.

"You won't return any of my calls." She said. "Or respond to any of my messages. I needed to make sure you were alive."
"I'm alive." I said.

"I needed to make sure you were okay." She said. "Last time I talked to you it ain't sound like you were."

"That was months ago." I said. "I'm good. You came all this way for that? You couldn'ta just asked Malcolm or Laya? Or my mom. I know you still talkin' to her."

"Me and your mom have always been on good terms." She said. "You know that. And I felt like if I really wanted to find out how you were doin', I needed to come see for myself."

"So what's up?" I asked. "You see I'm alive. You see I'm good. What now?"

"I would love to come in." She smiled.

"I don't know if that's a good idea." I said. Her smile quickly faded. "I'm just not in a good mood right now."

"I had a long flight, Nicholas." She said. "It would be nice to at least talk to you. What's botherin' you?"

"I don't really wana talk about it." I said.

"This me you talkin' to." She said. "I know I can help you through it. And I got some things I would like to talk to you about. If you willin' to listen?"

"It's late Jada." I said. "Cassidy just left here. I'm surprised you ain't see her."

"I did." She said. "I pulled up as she was pullin' out."

"Crazy." I laughed.

"At least I got you to smile." She smiled at me.

I opened the door to let her in. She came in and sat on the couch. I lit the blunt and sat down next to her.

"So what's up?" I asked her. "What you wana talk about?"

"You start." She said. "What was the fight about?"

"What fight?" I asked.

"Nicholas, I saw her face when she left here." She said. "Looked like she was ready to kill yo ass."

"Same shit." I said. "She wana stay here and I ain't goin' for it."

"I can't believe y'all still havin' the same argument." She said.

"Me either." I said. "That shit been old. I don't even know why I'm still entertainin' it. It just piss me off. You can do everything for a mufucka and they still ain't satisfied. That girl get everything she ask me for. Some shit she ain't even gotta ask me for. But that ain't enough. She just gotta have the only thing I have to myself. I can't deal with it. Then she say I'm selfish. She the selfish one want everything that I'm doin' to include her. I need somethin' to have to myself. She don't see me takin' over her dorm room. Whatever she want to keep to herself, she do it. And I have no problem with that. I don't understand why I can't get the same from her."

"Well." She smiled. "Clearly you been wantin' to get that off yo chest."

"Shut up." I laughed at her. "She just get on my nerves sometimes for real."

"I know what you mean." She said. "But why do you think you feel so strongly about it?"

"What you mean?" I asked. "I do way too much for that girl, for her to still not be happy. It ain't even about just buyin' her shit. Whenever she wana go out, I'm there. Whatever she want me to do, I'm there. Regardless if I

321

want to or not. I just want her to be happy. I don't want nobody to ever say I ain't try. That's one thing I know I did."

"I know you did." She smiled. "That's just the type of person you are. You give so much so it's only natural for you want somethin' for yourself every once in a while."

"You make it sound so simple." I said. "I wish I could get her to figure that out. Maybe you should talk to her about it."

We both laughed as we continued smokin'.

"I doubt that would go well." She laughed. "She would kill you if she found out you were talkin' to me about y'all problems."

"Hell yea." I had to agree. Cassidy was that type of girl. She ain't even want me and Jada to be as close as we are, let alone talk out our relationship issues. "What's on yo mind?"

"The wedding is in 3 days." She said quietly as she exhaled. "And I been miserable since I told you we were movin' it up."

"What you mean?" I asked. "I thought y'all shit was workin' out."

"It is." She said. "But that just ain't makin' me happy like I thought it would."

"You ain't even gave it a chance." I said.

"I have." She said. "I just feel like if this was really for me, me and you fallin' out would not have this type of effect on me. This the longest I ever went without seein' yo face and I swear it's been killin' me."

"Shut up." I laughed at her. "You know you good without me. Finna get married and have a whole new life with yo man."

"Are you listenin' to me?" She asked me. "I don't think this is a good decision for me. At least right now. I can't share my life with him, when the biggest part of my life is missing."

"If that's really who you wana be with, he should be the biggest part of yo life." I said. "Honestly."

She was speechless for a minute. I sat back and watched her smoke. I loved the way she inhaled. It was just somethin' about her that made it look so sexy. I missed everything about this woman. As mad as I was at her, I was so happy she came to see me. I really needed to be around her. Just for me to feel better about her situation and mine.

"Why you gotta make so much sense?" She asked. "Now you makin' shit seem simple."

"And you just did the same thing with my situation." I said. "Clearly we both makin' it hard for these other people."

"I been thinkin' that for some time now." She said. "I just couldn't put it into words."

"I can't believe you really here." I said. "Even more gorgeous than the last time I seen you."

"Shut up." She blushed.

"How long you in town?" I asked.

"Well I do have a wedding to go to in a few days." She smiled.

"So you stayin' til' then?" I asked.

"I don't know if that's a good idea." She said.

"It's a great idea." I smiled at her. "Anybody know you here?"

"Nope." She said.

"Good." I said. "That mean I can have you to myself."

"And what is that supposed to mean?" She smiled.

"Whatever you want it to." I said sarcastically.

"I can't stay here for 3 days, Nicholas." She said. "What am I supposed to tell him?"

"Nothin'." I said as I took her phone and turned it off. "I'll text your mom and let her know you're okay."

"What about Cassidy?" She asked.

"I'll change the locks tomorrow." I said.

"You can't go through all that." She said. "You know she gon' be mad when she find out."

"I'll just tell her." I said. "Let me handle that. Ain't shit for you to worry about."

"You really gon' go through all that to keep me here?" She smiled.

"Ain't shit I wouldn't do to keep you here." I said. "I thought you knew that by now."

"I mean I really don't know what to think." She said. "What are we doin'? Why didn't we try this years ago? Before we got with other people."

"I guess it took us movin' on, to realize we needed to be together." I said.

"So when did you know?" She asked.

"When you started datin' him." I said. "I played it off cool though."

"Hell yea." She laughed. "I ain't even notice it bothered you til' I told you I was engaged."

"I tried to play that shit off too but I was mad as hell." I laughed. "When did you know?"

"When I came down here with you Freshman year." She said. "It was so hard for me to leave you here. Knowin' that I wasn't comin' back like we planned so many years ago. I felt like I let you down, ya know."

"I don't know why you thought that." I said. "I'm proud of you. You stepped completely out of your comfort zone. Goin' away with just him. Not even the friends you spent yo whole life with. That take a lot to leave people behind that you never imagined life without."

"It really does." She agreed. "That's exactly how I felt. It killed me. I knew then, but I just felt like I was in too deep with Carter. I ain't know how to get out."

"I'm feelin' the same way." I said. "I mean I feel bad 'cuz what me and Cassidy goin' through really ain't big enough to just end it, but I mean I don't see us goin' nowhere. I ain't never seen myself goin' nowhere with nobody but you."

"I don't know what we supposed to do about this Nicholas." She said.

"I say we just keep smokin' til' we figure it out." I said as I gave her the jar.

I handed her a pack of rellos and opened up a pack to roll up myself.

"Sound good to me." She said.

Two hours and 6 blunts later I felt like I had it all figured out. Jada could not stop starin' at me. I caught her so many times and every time I did she laughed and turned away. I picked her up and carried her back to the bedroom. She didn't say anything or even try to stop me. I put her on the bed and turned off the light. I took off everything she had on. I expected her to say somethin' or try to stop me. She was silent. It felt so good just to be around her. I had to take my time with every move.

I felt like we had forever. I put my head on her chest and wrapped my arms around her. I know it was crazy but I just wanted to hold her. I ain't want her to move at all. I just wanted to lay in her for the rest of the night, if not for longer. She ran her fingers up and down my back. This was it for me. It was no way in hell I could let this girl go marry another nigga. She was mine and she was always gon' be mine. That shit wasn't changin' for nobody. The next few hours I spent showing her how much she meant to me. And she showed me exactly how much I meant to her.

Cassidy

I was really at the end of the road with Nicholas. He just didn't want me to live with him and I had no other choice but to accept it. Of course, I could get my own place, but I ain't really wana live alone. I just felt like mailing him his keys back and bein' done with it. I knew that wasn't the right way to go about this, but I just felt like that's what I needed to do. If I saw him again, I knew I wouldn't be able to leave him. I didn't want to leave him. I had to. I didn't know if I was leavin' him to get him to see what he was really missin' out on, or if I was leavin' him to find somebody else that would appreciate me.

My mind was all over the place. Nicholas was so great to me with everything else. He was right. He gave me whatever I asked for. I ain't want for nothin'. Except to live with him. Nobody's perfect so I guess this was his thing I couldn't deal with. But I should be able to deal with it. I should be able to take the good with the bad. He's taken so much from me and never complained. But I'm still naggin' about some shit he told me way before he moved off campus.

He was right I did try to make shit smooth for him so he would change his mind. He knew me too damn well. But somethin' in me just couldn't get past him not wantin' to live with me. Then he ain't even give a damn when I stopped stayin' over there. Never once asked me to stay the night since I stopped sleepin' there. And that shit alone hurt me.

I was just getting ready to call Laya to talk to her about this when I got a message from Nicholas:

Somebody broke in my spot. Getting the locks changed now.

This nigga musta really thought I was stupid. If he wanted his key back, that's all he had to say. And what the fuck did he want his key back for anyway? The argument really ain't even go that far. Or was this his way of sayin' he was done with me. Naw if he was done with me, he wouldn'tve even told me about it.

Instantly I just got even more upset. I called Laya with the quickness. I knew I was getting on her nerves complainin' about Nicholas then never takin' her advice about it, but she was the only female friend I could really trust. Yea I had other friends at school, but I hated people I ain't really trust knowin' my business. Some females here, were just waitin' for me and Nicholas to break up. Even some of the ones that called themselves my friends. It was hard bein' with somebody who everybody knew was goin' somewhere. He hadn't even made it yet and already I felt like they wanted us to fail.

"Hey girl." Laya answered her phone in a better mood than the last time I called her to vent.
"Hey Laya." I said. "What you up to?"

328

"Nothin' just got done cleaning up." She said. "What's up?"

"Girl shit got real last night." I said. "I'm damn near getting ready to mail Nicholas his keys 'cuz I don't even wana see his ass after he pissed me off last night."

"What he do?" She asked.

"Same shit he always do." I said. "He just keep fightin' me on stayin' with him this summer."

"He told you he wasn't ready to have nobody in his space when he first moved, Cassidy." She said. "What made you think that was gon' change?"

"Nicholas gives me everything I ask for, Laya." I said. "I don't never have to go through all this to get what I want. So now all of a sudden, he wana say no and stick to it. And then it's about the most sensitive thing too."

"Why is this so sensitive to you?" She asked. "He just not ready. At least he told you ahead of time, instead of givin' you what you want and you findin' out the hard way later on down the line. You have to respect his honesty. You asked him to be honest with everything and he's doin' that. But ain't shit perfect. It's always gon' be somethin' you don't like in yo relationship. You can't try to change shit up before y'all both ready too."

"Then to make it worse, this nigga just texted me talkin' about somebody broke in his spot, and he getting the locks changed now." I said. "What the fuck is that bull shit?"

"I mean he did call Malcolm this morning sayin' some shit happened." She said soundin' like she was tryna cover for him. "What's wrong with that?"

"I just feel like it was bull shit." I said. "What was the point in tellin' me that?"

"What you mean?" She asked. "You his woman. You got keys to his apartment. Of course, he gon' tell you when shit change ahead of time. Instead of you goin' over there and findin' out on yo own and thinkin' he on some sneaky shit. I think you just mad that you can't get yo way right now so everything he do got you on ten. Let me say this, I been told you to take a break if you couldn't get past this. All you gon' do is ruin what y'all have if you keep naggin' him about this bull shit. I don't know why you continue to do this to yoself. If it's really killin' you like it appears to be, you need to step away from the situation. And don't do it for a reaction 'cuz you won't get it that way. Do it for yourself so you can figure out how to get past someone tellin' you no. This man has got you fuckin' spoiled, and you can't handle not getting your way. That is ridiculous Cassidy."

"I know." I said. "It's just so hard to give him up when he is so good to me."

"You have to think about if you're really bein' good to him." She said. "You're not. I mean I know you do a lot for him too, but you doin' it for a reaction. It's not a genuine feeling of just doin' for yo man. You doin' all this shit to get him to change his mind and want you stay with him and that ain't healthy. He do shit for you because he want to. He don't want his girl out here wantin' for shit. And you don't. Besides this petty shit. We all young as hell. Y'all got yo whole life to live together. What is the rush? Girl it ain't easy. I'm tellin' you right now. I love waking up to Malcolm most of the time, but sometimes I be like I gotta get away from this man. That's the shit you gotta take with the good. But apparently, you not ready to take

330

the bad with the good. Cuz you can't even take him tellin' you no about somethin' that can honestly wait."

"You think it's somebody else?" I asked her.

"Are you fuckin' kiddin' me?" She asked me. "Now you just lookin' for a reason to be mad. Stop this petty shit Cassidy. You know damn well that man don't have time for nobody else. Between class, work and you, when do he have time to entertain' somebody else? I really wana know that."

"Girl a man will find time if he really want to." I said.

"And I truly agree with that, but clearly he don't want to 'cuz he ain't found the time." She said. "You need to know yo man. You need to know what and what not to put past yo man. I don't think you're sure of that yet."

"You are absolutely right." I said. "I been with this man all these years and I really can't separate what he will do, from what he won't. But it ain't always been like that. At one time I was sure he wouldn't do anything to hurt me. Then when I started to see the bond he had with Jada I knew that was somebody I could never compete with."

"Cass, you gotta understand the history they have." She said.

"The history should be just that, history." I said. "You can't keep holdin' on to somebody because of what you had with them. The past needs to stay in the past. Especially when you decide to move on with somebody new. That goes for both of them."

"So you think all of this anger comes from you bein' jealous of what they have?" She asked.

"In a way, yea." I said. "I see how he looks at her. Nicholas has never looked at me that way. Her whole vibe is different when she around him.

Not that she not happy when she around Carter, but it's somethin' about Nicholas that still gives her butterflies. Every time I see them together she smiles with her whole face. Not just her teeth, everything lights up on her face. She don't look like that when Carter come around."

"Wow." She said. "So you really been payin' attention to this shit?"

"It sound crazy I know." I said. "It really ain't even start like that. One day I just noticed his eyes smilin' at her, and ever since then I been catching all this shit. It's crazy as hell."

"I mean if you feel that strongly about it, maybe that's what you need to talk to him about." She said.

"What I'm gon' say to him?" I asked. "Stop lookin at Jada the way you do. Tell her to stop lookin' at you like that? I'ma sound like a fool. Especially when it's somethin' they have no control of. He don't even realize he doin' it. It's like a second nature or somethin'."

"Damn." She said. "I ain't even think of it like that. All this is just makin' me more sure that you need to take a break for a while."

"I think I do too." I said. "I just don't want people thinkin' I'm crazy for walkin' away from a man that would give me the world, all 'cuz I can't live in his. But it's not just about that."

"Girl stop worryin' about what other people think." She said. "They don't know y'all. They dont know y'all relationship. You getting too wrapped up in the image and that ain't what y'all relationship should be based on. You get with somebody because of who they are, not because of how they make you look. And if you don't like who they are or what they doin' no more, then you walk away. People break up everyday. But that don't mean they don't get back together. Look at me and Malcolm. We was so off and on for a long time. Then the last time we broke up girl I really thought it was over. But clearly it was meant to be 'cuz we been together ever since. It took me losin' two men that I cared about, to realize that I wasn't doin' right by nobody but myself. That whole experience changed me."

"So do you think if Johnny was still alive, you woulda got back with Malcolm?" I asked.

"I know I woulda got back with Malcolm." She said. "It probably woulda took a lil' longer for me to get outta that phase with Johnny. It probably woulda took some bad shit to happen, for me to snap outta that. But I know I woulda came back to Malcolm. I always do."

"See that's beautiful." I said. "And I want that shit with Nicholas. I just feel like he already got that with somebody else. He can't have that with two different women."

"That's true." She said. "I mean if it's meant to be, it will. That's somethin' you just can't change. Whether he meant to be with you, or her. That's somethin' he gotta figure out. He not gon' figure that out while y'all goin' through all this nonsense though."

"My point exactly." I said. "So it's time for me to step away. I think I'ma go home for the summer. Just to get away from all this. It'll be easier for me to do this space thing, if I ain't here."

"Are you gon' tell him?" She asked.

"I want to." I said. "But I can't see him. If I do, I know I ain't gon' be able to leave him. And I don't feel like this is a conversation to be had over the phone, so I may not tell him."

"I mean I agree it should be face to face, but if you can't do it that way I think you should at least call him and tell him." She said.

"I do owe him some type of explanation." I said. "I just wana get away from this. It ain't healthy for me so it damn sure ain't healthy for us."

"I'm glad you came to this conclusion." She said. "I mean I don't wana see y'all give up, but I want y'all to be happy. When what y'all doin' ain't workin, it's just time to find a different route. That's all. I don't want you to leave me here by myself this summer, but I guess I can't be selfish."

We both laughed.

"Girl you gon' be fine without me." I said. "I know you gon' be busy workin' anyway."

"Probably." She said. "Just make sure we hang out before you go home. Don't be goin MIA on me without tellin' me. I ain't the one you mad at."

"Shut up." I laughed at her. "You know I wouldn't do you like that. Just do me a favor and don't say anything to Malcolm. At least until I tell Nicholas. I don't want him to hear it before I get the balls to tell him.

"Girl I won't." She laughed at me. "Just call 'em right now and get it over with. You want me to call 'em for you?"

"Shut up Laya." I laughed. "Don't call nobody. I'm bouta do it now."

"Yea okay." She said. "Just make sure you call me back and let me know how it go."

"Okay." I said. "Thanks boo. I'ma call you in a minute."

"Alright girl." She said before she hung up.

I hung up the phone and thought about the next call I was bouta make. I knew I had to do it to get any type of peace this summer. I ain't know how he would react. I was hopin' he would make this as easy as possible. Knowin' him, I knew that wasn't happening. Sometimes he could be so difficult. I stopped thinkin' about the what if's and dialed his number.

"Did you get my message?" He asked when he answered the phone.

"Well good mornin' to you too." I said to correct him.

"My bad good morning." He said. "What's up?"

"Somethin' I wana talk to you about." I said quietly.

"I'm kinda in the middle of somethin' right now." He said. "The lock man still here."

"It won't take long." I said.

"Alright what is it?" He asked.

"We ain't been getting along lately." I said. "Which I'm sure you're aware of. So, I think we need to do each other a favor and take a break before it get too crazy."

"Really?" He asked. "Is that what you wana do?"

"It's not what I wana do." I said. "I wish it was another way we could work it out without doin' this, but I feel like we have to."

"This really what it done came to?" He asked. "Just 'cuz I ain't ready for us to live together?"

"That's not the only reason Nicholas." I said. "We both know it's other issues here. I ain't really tryna get into all of 'em. But I think this for the best. For both of us. Let's just take some time apart and see if this still what we wana do."

"So now you don't know if you wana do this?" He asked. "Wow Cassidy. That's really what you on?"

"I ain't on shit, Nicholas." I said. "I'm just tryna get out of all this drama."

"You the one causing the drama." He said. "Why can't you just get over this shit? You mean to tell me you get everything you want and that still ain't good enough for you?"

"Why are you makin' this difficult?" I asked him.

"This shit posed to be easy?" He asked. "It's that easy for you to leave me?"

"I never said that." I said. "It ain't easy for me. But it's necessary. This ain't how we posed to be. I need to figure out how to accept that you just not ready. And you need to figure out who you wana be with."

"What the hell you talkin' bout?" He asked. "I know who I wana be with."

"Nicholas I'm givin' you this time to clear shit up for yoself." I said. "I know you been feelin' some type of way ever since you found out about Jada movin' up her wedding. If you was sure about bein' with me, that shit wouldn't have even affected you. But it did. And I'm not mad about it. So I'm doin' this for the both of us. If we meant to get back together, we will.

But right now, I need you to take advantage of this time, as much as I'm goin' to."

"Damn." He said. "So that's it? You couldn't even talk to me about this face to face?"

"It's nothin' left to talk about." I said. "I made a decision 'cuz you couldn't do it. That's all it is."

"I made my decision when I decided to be with you." He said. "I don't know what other decision you talkin' about, but I know why I got with you. I guess the fact that I'm still here ain't enough for you. I take yo shit every fuckin' day and still somehow manage to stick it out. You tired of not getting yo way and you ready to fuckin' run. I can't force you to grow up. But if you thought this shit was gon' be easy, then maybe I'm not the person you posed to be with. I do everything I can to keep yo ass happy, but you ain't never gon' be satisfied til' you in my space all day everyday. What the fuck is that about? I ain't gave you no reason not to trust me. No reason for you to be as insecure as you are. But still that shit ain't good enough for you."

"I'm sorry you feel that way." I said. "My bad. I'm sorry if I made you feel that way. But that's just more reasons why we need to take this break. I couldn't do this face to face 'cuz once I saw you I knew I wouldn't be able to go through with it. I know this ain't no phone conversation, but it was either this or me not tell you at all."

"After all this, you really on this bull shit?" He asked. "You wasn't even gon' tell me?"

"I'm goin' home for the summer Nicholas." I said. "I need to get away from you so I can clear my head. You need to do the same thing."

"So that's it?" He asked. "Just tell me you leavin' and ain't shit I can do about it?"

"You'll appreciate this in the long run." I said. "May not seem like it now, but we both will."

"If this what you wana do, I ain't gon' fight you on it." He said. "I mean I thought we could work it out together, but I guess you can't do that."

"Stop tryna put it all on me." I said. "You can't work out yo obsession with Jada while you with me either."

"You can't be fuckin' serious." He said. "I ain't havin' this conversation with you again Cassidy."

"Bye Nicholas." I said before I hung up on him.

He was startin' to piss me off tryna put it all on me. We both had issues we needed to work through. He was just in denial about his shit. I was so mad. All I wanted to do was cry. But that wouldn't change the situation. I called Laya to tell her what happened.

"I did it." I said when she answered her phone.

Malcolm

I hadn't talked to my mom since she called me with that bull shit. She wanted me to apologize but I just wasn't sorry. What I said only hurt her 'cuz she know it's true. It's fucked up that her son gotta be the only adult in this situation. She know better than that. She raised me better than that. So I just couldn't understand how she could constantly put herself down for this nigga that ain't did shit but fuck up her life every time he came around.

"What's up bae." Laya said as she walked in the house with way too many shoppin' bags.
"I sent you out to get some groceries 4 hours ago." I said as I looked at her bags. "And I don't see one grocery bag."
"They in the car." She laughed. "Can you get 'em for me please?"

I shook my head at her as I went out to the car. I brought the groceries in and helped her put everything up.

"So what's all this?" I pointed to her shoppin' bags.
"Boy shut up." She laughed. "I'm grown. You mean to tell me I gotta explain a lil' shoppin' trip?"
"I ain't say explain." I laughed. "I just was wonderin' how you left with a short ass grocery list and came back with all this."

"I had to get a few things." She smiled. "If that's okay with you." She said sarcastically.

"What you get me?" I asked as I looked at the bags to see if I had anything in them.

"Why I always gotta get you somethin' everytime I go shoppin'?" She asked. "Do you get me somethin' everytime you go to the mall?"

"Every time I buy myself somethin' I get you somethin'." I said. "And you know that. So where my stuff at?"

"In that black bag." She laughed at me. "You get on my nerves. Did you talk to yo mom yet?"

"Nope." I said. "Why? She called you?"

"Your dad called me." She said as she sat down at the kitchen table.

"What the fuck?" I snapped. "Who in the hell told her to give him yo number?"

"She gave 'em yours too." She said. "That's not the point though babe. I talked to 'em for a minute and he seemed like he really wanted to talk to you about somethin'."

"You talked to 'em for a minute and already he got you on his side." I laughed. "That nigga good."

"It ain't even like that." She said. "I just think you should hear him out."

"What the fuck do I need to hear from him?" I snapped.

"I thought we talked about this last time." She said quietly. "You ain't mad at me, so don't talk to me like you are. You takin' out yo anger with him, on me. He the one who need to hear everything you sayin'."

"My bad." I said as I corrected myself. "Honestly though, Laya. I'm better off without 'em. I don't need no half ass people in my life. If you ain't gon' be there for me all the time, I don't want you around. You don't want nobody in yo life like that, do you?"

"Well, in my defense, my mother was somewhat like that." She said. "I just had to accept that she was sick. But then there were other times where she knew exactly what she was doin' wrong and she still didn't fix anything. So I let that go. We can't choose our parents babe. We just gotta take them for who they are and accept them anyway. Just like they gotta deal with us, we gotta do the same thing. You may not have to become best friends with 'em, but you can at least hear him out."

"Hear him out and then what?" I asked. "Then you gon' be wantin' me to at least invite 'em out here. Or at least try to get to know him. Once I do the minimum all you gon' do is want more. You and my mama the same damn way with that bull shit. Just to get y'all way. Think you takin' baby steps. I don't want no steps at all."

"I just can't believe you really want nothin' to do with this man." She said.

"Believe it." I said. "Ain't shit he can do for me, that I can't do for myself. We all know that."

"I ain't sayin' you need him to do nothin' for you." She said. "But one of these days, he ain't gon' be around no more. And I don't want you feelin' like you shoulda got to know 'em when you had the chance too."

"I'm not gon' feel anything at all." I said. "Can't miss somethin' you never had. That nigga don't even exist to me so why would I be feelin' some type of way if he stopped existing to the world."

"Damn." She said. "That's really harsh baby."

"It is what it is." I said. "I'm a grown ass man. And I got here from a woman, alone. Fuck I need his ass for now. I done already grew up. Better than his ass did."

"This is ridiculous Malcolm." She said. "You actin' like a kid for real."

"I'm makin' the same decision any grown ass man would make." I said. "I don't entertain bull shit. From nobody. Never have. Never will. Why should I start now?"

"Maybe somethin' changed with him." She said. "Maybe he wana be in yo life for real this time."

"That's fine." I said. "He can want whatever he want. I don't want him in my life. Or Kelly life. Now if my mama wana fuck up her life again by messin' with him, that's on her. I can't be responsible for that. But I damn sure ain't gon' let him do the same thing to Kelly, that he did to me."

"You don't know until you give him a chance." She said.

"You really want me to give him a chance?" I asked. "Knowin' that he just gon' do the same bull shit all over again?"

"You gave me one." She said. "I coulda easily did you wrong like I did before but I didn't. And you wouldn't have found that out if you didn't give me that chance to prove you wrong."

"It's different." I said. "I can't live without you. But I been just fine without him. That ain't somebody that I gotta have in my life. Let alone want. I don't trust niggas like that. Why would I want somebody around me that I don't trust?"

"Malcolm, he took part in bringin' you into this world." She said.

342

"But he didn't take part in keepin' me in this world, now did he?" I asked. "Did he take part in helpin' with anything? My mama did that shit by herself for too damn long. Til' I figured it all out for myself. I'm not bouta give him a chance to reap the benefits that I'm about to come into. Hell naw. He think he slick. Clearly he done heard about me. I ain't dumb. And she dumb as hell if she ain't thought about that."

"You bein' disrespectful again." She said.

"How?" I asked. "I ain't sayin' it to her. I'm just venting to you. Now I gotta watch what I say to you about somebody else? Come on now Laya. I'm too old to not be able to speak my mind. Especially to my woman."

"I guess you right." She said.

"I know I'm right." I laughed.

"Anyways..." She said. "You know Cassidy called me about Nicholas again?"

"Damn that girl just don't quit." I laughed. "What happened now?"

"You ain't talked to him yet?" She asked.

"Naw his phone been goin' to voicemail." I said. "I was gon' go over there later. You wana go with me?"

"Yea we need to." She said. "He ain't really do nothin' else. She just still mad that he don't want her to move in. She broke up with em."

"Hell naw." I laughed. "That girl ain't leavin' him if she tried."

"She did." She laughed. "That's why I'm surprised you ain't heard from 'em. I hope he ain't over there depressed."

"That nigga ain't depressed." I laughed. "He probably on his way to see Jada now that he free."

We both laughed so hard.

"Shut up." She said. "He should be though. Cuz Cassidy serious as hell about this. She say it's just a break but I already know they not gon' get back together. She goin' home for the summer to make it easier on both of them."

"Damn." I said. "That shit is crazy. Was it really that serious for her to leave his ass though?"

"Well from what she told me today, it seemed like it was more than just the livin' situation." She said. "She startin' to realize that he ain't over Jada. I mean I'm sure this ain't just now set in for her, but this the first time I've ever heard her admit that it's a problem for her."

"I don't see what the problem is." I said. "It ain't like he cheatin' on her."

"It still ain't comfortable to be with somebody who still in love with somebody else." She said. "You wouldn't be comfortable with that either."

"Hell naw." I said. "That's why I would just leave they ass. If you ain't over yo ex, you don't need to be movin' on to somebody else. It's that simple. Nicholas ass act like he ain't realize he still wanted that girl. I mean it happens. Once you see yo ex with somebody else you really find out if you over them or not."

"Is that what happened with us?" She smiled at me.

"Not at all." I laughed at her. "The fact that I couldn't hurt you, for her benefit just made me see that I still cared about you. Then when I found out about you datin' somebody else and you ain't even tell me, I knew I had to get yo ass back."

"What?" She laughed. "That don't even make sense."

"It don't have to." I said. "Just know that I wanted you back, and I did what I had to to make it happen."

"Really?" She asked sarcastically.

"Girl shut up and fix me somethin' to eat." I laughed at her ass.

"So demanding today." She laughed before she kissed my cheek.

Paisley

"So what you think about the kids?" He asked me as we waited for our dinner to come.

"I think they're adorable." I smiled at him. "You did a good job. Both of you did."

"Thank you." He smiled. "I'm glad they got to meet you."

"Me too." I smiled.

"So have you talked to your dad?" He asked.

"A little bit here and there since he left." I said. "It just seem crazy for me to be talkin' to him now."

"Why you say that?" He asked.

"I just never thought I would be tryna have a relationship with him." I said. "At first she told me he died. Then later on she told me her version of the truth. But she made him out to be the worst person in the world. Come to find out he been givin' her money every month since I was born. Way more than child support woulda been takin' from him. He been askin' to meet me and see me since I was born but she wouldn't let him 'cuz he wouldn't leave his family for us. What kinda woman keeps her child away from her father cuz he don't wana be with her? That's just so selfish of her. I get mad every time I think about it."

"I see that." He laughed. "I mean I completely understand where you comin' from. That's somethin' I was worried about happenin' with me and my situation once I left. I just been blessed to deal with who I'm dealin' with. She understand that my kids need me. I mean it took her a while to accept that we wasn't gon' be together anymore, but we been through so much it was kinda like she really couldn't do that to me. That's probably the difference with our situation. We been friends for so long. Was yo mom and dad together for a while?"

"From what he say they messed around a few times." I said. "Over the course of two weeks. That was it. Once he found out she was pregnant, he said he stopped everything. And he apologized for that. I can respect somebody who admit they wrongs. At least he tried to make it right when he found out I was his. So they really didn't even know each other. It's crazy to think you gon' make a man leave his family and he don't even know yo ass."

"Yea that is some crazy shit." He laughed. "I'm just glad you ain't lettin' everything she said about him stop you from havin' a relationship with him now. I mean it's fucked up that it took this long for you to meet him, but at least you accepting it."

"It ain't his fault that we don't have a relationship." I said. "And I appreciate the fact now that she's not around to stop him from getting to me, he came around. As soon as he felt he could, he did it. I'm so thankful for that. I ain't sayin' this gon' be the easiest thing for neither one of us, but I definitely am gon' try it."

"That's good to hear." He smiled at me. "So you know the kids gon' be stayin' with me tonight."

"Okay." I said. "What that mean?"

"You said you wasn't comfortable stayin' the night with the kids bein' there." He said.

"I don't have a problem waitin' until they go back to their mom's." I said. "Damn that sound bad."

"Yea it do." He laughed. "But I know what you meant. I do want you to stay the night. We ain't gotta do shit. I just want you to be there. They gon' be knocked out by 9."

"I don't really know about that, just yet." I said.

"The kids already know about you." He said. "My ex already know about you."

"What did you tell her?" I asked. "What did she say?"

"I just told her what it is." He said. "She already knew about you when she found out last year. I just told her we was together. She was mad about it. I mean I know she was hurt 'cuz it look like I left her to be with you, but that wasn't the only reason I had to leave. Shit just wasn't workin' for us. And I know I started all this years ago when I started cheatin'. She never woulda changed had I not kept fuckin' up her head. But I can't change the past. She a whole different person now. It was no way I could get her back to the girl I fell in love with back in school. So I had to move on."

"So what's gon' keep you from doin' to me, what you did to her?" I asked.

"I know that my mistakes can cause me to lose you." He said. "She took me back after everything. She never left. So I took advantage of that. Once you keep fuckin' up and ain't really havin' to face no consequences, you gon' keep doin' the same thing. I fucked up one time with you, and you left me."

"But I'm back." I said. "'So do that mean you gon' take advantage of me?"

"Not at all." He said. "She never left. She never let me just miss her presence. She never made me pay for my mistakes. I ain't have nothin' to fight for 'cuz she was givin' it all to me. For free."

"Damn." I said. "I mean I hear women say shit like that all the time. But I ain't never heard a man admit that shit actually mattered to them."

"I'm bein' real with you." He said. "Ain't shit for me to hide no more. If we gon' do this thing, it's gon' be all or nothin'. I told you that. So of course, I ain't gon' give you no less than that."

"And I appreciate that." I smiled at him.

"So when you gon' stop dancing?" He asked.

"What?" I asked. "I already cut my 5-day week down to 3 days 'cuz of you. And that pay cut has really been missed."

"Whatever you makin' from there, you know I'll take care of it." He said.

"I can't give up my job til' I got everything in order for my jewelry store." I said. "You already know that."

"Speaking of the jewelry store, I got a few friends that wana see your designs." He said. "I set up a meetin' this week for you to show him some of yo work."

"What?" I smiled so hard. "Are you serious?"

"Hell yea." He laughed. "I told you I was gon' help you with it."

"Oh my God thank you so much baby." I jumped up and hugged him.

"No problem." He smiled as I kissed his cheek. "So you got yo stuff together?"

"Yea my portfolio been ready." I said. "Wait a minute, what's the catch?"

"Ain't no catch." He said. "I just want you to have what you want. You want that shop and I'ma do what I gotta do to help you get it."

"This sound too good to be true, babe." I smiled at him, but I knew somethin' else was comin'.

"I want you stop dancing." He said. "Before we go to this meetin'."

"I knew it was somethin' else." I said quietly. "That's not fair. You can't just give me somethin' then take it away if I don't do what you say."

"I'm not takin' nothin' away from you." He said. "We goin' to that meetin', regardless. I just want you to know, that I would appreciate it if you stopped dancing. Like right now. You don't need too. Whatever you need to take care of until you get the shop up and runnin' I can handle. You know I can. Why you can't let me do that? I know you don't wana be in there every night."

"I'm not in there every night thanks to somebody's insecurities." I mumbled.

"What?" He asked like he didn't hear me.

"I already cut back on my income to cater to your ego." I said. "Now I gotta give up all my income and depend on you. What if we don't work out before I get the shop up and runnin'?"

"We gon' work out." He said. "That ain't a question. You just scared to let somebody take care of you. And I don't understand why. I mean I know I fucked up before and you left my ass. But I ain't doin' shit to mess this up again. This it for me. I ain't comfortable with you workin' there. You know that."

"You was comfortable meetin' me there." I said sharply.

351

"I ain't been to a strip club since I met you." He said. "Don't that tell you how I feel about it?"

"Babe I already know how you feel about the situation." I said. "But you can't come back in my life and dictate what I do."

"And I'm not tryin' to." He said. "I'm just sayin' that as a woman in a committed relationship, you shouldn't want everybody seein' parts of you that should only be seen by me."

"I understand that." I said. "But you gotta realize that this is my only source of income until I come up. You can't take that away from me just 'cuz you say you gon' take care of me. I gotta walk away from that when I feel like I'm good and ready. I ain't cut down my days for nobody. This was a big step for me. I came to a compromise for you. Why is that not enough for right now?"

"You right." He said. "I mean I ain't never gon' be comfortable with you bein' there. But I'ma try to wait for you to get this shit together with the shop. Now I really gotta speed this process up."

"Shut up." I laughed at him.

"You found a spot yet?" He asked.

"Hell yea." I smiled. "I been had the perfect spot. You wana see it?"

"Yea I do." He laughed at me. "You gon lease it or what?"

"I'm buyin' it." I smiled at him.

"Damn." He smiled. "For real? You ready for that?"

"If you mean financially... I been ready." I smiled.

"Damn so what's the hold up?" He asked.

"You know I wana get my girls out The Spot and pay them at least what they used to makin'." I said.

"P that's crazy." He said. "You gon' own a jewelry store, and pay yo employees $500 a day?"

"Yes." I said. "That's what's been takin' me so long. I got the money to buy the place. Cover the bills and everything for at least three years. I'm almost at the ¾ mark of havin' the payroll taken care of for two years. So everything for the first two years will be profit. And I know we gon' bring in double that the second year so that way I'll be able to keep payin' them what they deserve."

"This is really crazy, babe." He smiled at me. "I can't believe you really doin' this."

"Me either." I smiled so hard. "I'm so excited to get this shit started, baby. By the end of the month I should have the rest of my payroll. Then I'ma go buy the shop."

"I think you should go buy it in the next two weeks." He said. "Cuz once you have this meetin' everything gon' move real fast after that. It ain't no slowin' down once it start. You ready for all this?"

"I been ready." I smiled.

"So let me give you the rest of the money for the payroll." He smiled.

"I can't do that." I said. "I gotta do this on my own for it to be right. Don't get me wrong I appreciate you tryna help me with this. But I got it."

"I'm just tryna come up with a way for you to stop dancing." He laughed.

"Today! Whatever I gotta do to make this happen, I'ma do it."

"It ain't happenin' today." I smiled at him. "But I love the fact that it means that much to you."

"I been feelin' like this since the day after I met you there." He said. "You know that. I told you everyday we was together."

"So now I gotta hear this everyday again?" I asked.

"Naw." He said. "Just til' the end of the month." He laughed.

"I can't take you seriously." I laughed at his ass. "So what we gon' do about tonight?"

"You stayin' with me and the kids." He said. "I thought we already established that."

"Does she know I'm stayin' the night?" I asked.

"She don't have to know." He said. "I'm grown as hell. I ain't gotta tell her who stayin' at my house. I pay the bills so I decide who stay there."

"I'm just sayin' I don't wana mess up nothin' with you seein' the kids." I said. "I understand this still a new situation for everybody. And I don't wana make things worse."

"I appreciate what you tryna do Paisley, but I want you with me as much as possible." He said. "I don't care who know that. If she got a problem with it, she gon' have to handle it with me. You play a major part in my life so she gon' have to accept you whether she like it or not."

"Babe I ain't tryna force nothin' on her before she ready." I said.

"She ain't never gon' be ready for another woman to be in her kids life." He said. "She ain't never gon' be ready to see me with another woman. That's somethin' I just can't live my life waitin' on."

"Okay." I tried to smile at him.

I felt so bad for jumping into this thing. In a way I wanted to let them sort out all the uncomfortable shit and then I could be with him. But that would be me takin' the easy way out. Maybe it was time for me to meet with his ex.

"What you think about me meetin' with her?" I asked him.

"I think you should." He said. "But I don't know how that's gon' go. I mean I'm sure you gon' be cool, but I don't know how she gon' be."

"I just wana know how she feel about all this." I said. "I dont wana force nothin' on her and make it look like I don't give a fuck about the situation. If it wasn't no kids involved then I would just say whatever, you know. She would get over it. But now I need to make sure that she's okay with me bein' around her kids so soon."

"I know what you mean." He said. "I'll set it up for when I take the kids back home tomorrow. Is that cool with you?"

"Damn that fast?" I laughed.

"Regardless of whenever you meet her, you still stayin' with me tonight." He said. "You ain't getting outta that. So get ready for it."

I had to laugh at him. This man was so amazing. And I was really hopin' I would always feel this way about him. He was everything to me. Even though I had people thinkin' different. I loved every part of him. Even the shit that I hated. I wouldn't have it any other way. Me leavin' him made me realize just how much I cared about him. That it was actually possible for me to let somebody take care of me.

He did it all the time when we were together the first time. The only reason I was so hesitant about it now is because I was too close to getting my business started, to have shit backfire on me now. I wanted to wait this thing out. We jumped into somethin' the last time around. So this time, I felt like I needed to take my time. I know we were movin' fast with me meetin' the kids, and his ex, but if I was gon' be apart of his family like he was tryna get me to be, I needed to get shit cleared up before I signed on for this.

Jada

My phone had been off since I came to Nicholas's apartment. And I had no problem with it. I needed to get away from the world for a few days. So what if it was a few days before my wedding. I needed to get it out of my system if I was really gonna get married. I was fallin' in love with him all over again. So effortlessly. He wasn't doin' anything out of the ordinary to make me fall for him, it was just him being hiself. He fit me like a glove. I couldn't believe it took me this long to come see him. He had the locks changed to keep Cassidy from comin' in. I didn't believe he would go through all that for me, but he was serious about keepin' me here.

I can't say I wish he woulda told her about me 'cuz I ain't know what I wanted him to tell her. I didn't know what we were doin'. As far as I was concerned I was still getting married this weekend. We hadn't even talked about where to go from here. I ain't wana do anything to ruin this moment we were living in. We needed this. And we needed this to go as smoothly as possible.

"Finally up, huh?" Nicholas asked me as he came in the bedroom.

I woke up a little bit when I heard the locksmith come this morning, but I fell back asleep right after that.

"Yea." I smiled as I stretched. "How long I been sleep?"

"It's damn near 3 now." He laughed. "I been up since 11. Had to get the locks changed."

"You ain't have to do that." I smiled at him as he got under the covers with me.

"I wanted to." He said. "We don't need any interruptions."

"I can't believe I slept that long." I said.

"Well you did keep me up all night." He laughed.

"Shut up." I laughed with him. "I needed to relieve some stress from that long flight."

"Yea whatever." He smiled at me. "I'm hungry so I know you are. You wana cook or go get somethin' to eat?"

"How 'bout you cook me somethin'." I said.

"I got some noodles or chicken noodle soup I can make you." He laughed.

"Let's go get somethin'." I shook my head. "Did you talk to my mom?"

"Yea I texted her." He said. "I just told her you were fine and you was with me."

"What she say?" I asked.

"She just sent me back a smiley face." He laughed.

"She is crazy." I said. "You talk to Cassidy?"

"I texted her this morning tellin' her about getting my locks changed." He said. "Then she called me a lil' bit after that sayin' she needed to take a break."

"What?" I asked. "What you mean?"

"She broke up with me." He said quietly.

"Are you serious?" I asked. "Are you okay?"

"I'm cool." He said. "It just came outta nowhere. I mean I know we been arguin' 'cuz I don't want her to move in with me, but I ain't think it was that serious."

"I'm sorry Nicholas." I said. "I shouldn't be here. You should be tryna get her to stay. You gotta fight for her."

"I can't fight for somebody who ain't willin' to do the same for me." He said. "She the one givin' up just 'cuz she can't get her way on one thing. I do way too much for that girl to be so damn ungrateful. I ain't chasin' her. I'm done with that."

"Nicholas you don't mean that." I said. "You just wrapped up in me bein' here right now. I didn't come here to mess nothin' up. I just had to see you."

"I needed to see you." He said. "You ain't mess shit up. We had these issues way before you came here. She ain't wana stick it out and get through it so that ain't somebody that I need to be with."

"I know that's how you feel now, but you don't know how you gon' feel later on." I said.

"I don't wana talk about that." He said. "I'm here with you. So this time is just gon' be about me and you. Come on let's get in the shower so we can get dressed and go."

"What if I ain't got no clothes?" I smiled at him.

"I know you got somethin' in that overnight bag." He laughed at me. "I'm finna go see who at the door."

He left out of the room to see who was knockin'. When I heard the door open, I knew it had to be Malcolm for him to let him in. He'd been ignoring everybody who came to his door yesterday. When I hid from the world, so did he. When he turned my phone off, he turned off his after he texted my mama. Besides him turnin' it back on to text Cassidy this morning, he closed himself off from the world right with me. And I loved him for that alone.

"Malcolm and Laya here." Nicholas said to me when he came back in the room.
"What?" I asked. "I'm naked."

He went in his drawer and gave me some of his shorts and a t shirt to put on. I put them on and followed him out of the room.

"Oh my God!" Laya screamed. "Jada what are you doin' here?" She ran and hugged me.
"It was kinda last minute." I laughed at her as she held on to me.
"Damn what's up, J." Malcolm said as I hugged him. "You ain't let nobody know you was comin' to town?"
"I really didn't plan on it." I said.
"Yea you definitely look like it." Laya said sarcastically.
"So that's why yo phone been goin' to voicemail." Malcolm said to Nicholas. "You coulda just told me that, nigga."

"Man shut up." Nicholas said.

"Girl when did you get here?" Laya asked.

"Last night." I said.

"How long you stayin'?" She asked.

"I don't even know." I said as I looked at Nicholas.

"Well we was finna smoke and go get somethin' to eat." Laya said. "Y'all wana come?"

"We still gotta shower and get dressed." Nicholas said. "But we'll meet y'all somewhere."

"Alright well let's smoke real quick then we'll let y'all get dressed." Malcolm said as he rolled up two blunts.

Strangely I was startin' to feel like we were all back at home. Like we used to be. Even though it wasn't our daily after practice session, it just felt so familiar. I loved it. Not only did I miss Nicholas, but I missed my friends too. We hung out the last time I was here, but that just wasn't enough for me. I felt like I needed a major change in my life. And marriage was not the change I was lookin' for. Only thing that was gon' do was pull me further away from what made me feel good.

We smoked two blunts and laughed our asses off like we used to do in high school. It felt so good to be with the people I had the most fun with. With people that I knew I could trust. Malcolm and Laya left and told us to meet them in 30 minutes or they was comin' back. I knew Laya and I knew they would really come back if we wasn't at least on our way out the door in 30 minutes.

We got in the shower, got dressed and got ready to head out the door. The whole time I kept catching Nicholas starin' at me randomly. He was just so happy. He couldn't stop smilin'. Which seemed weird considering the fact that his girlfriend just broke up with him. You couldn't tell by his vibe though. He seemed like he was complete. Like it was somethin' missin' that he finally got back.

"You cool with this?" He asked me as he held my hand while he drove with his left one.
"Yea." I smiled. "Why wouldn't I be?"
"I mean I know you kinda wanted us to stay to ourselves." He said. "I know you wanted to be alone."
"This is good for me." I said. "I didn't just miss you. I missed them too. I missed us hangin' out. Talkin' shit like we used to do. The whole vibe of havin' everybody together just got me feelin' like I got the greatest life ever."
"Glad I could be a part of that." He smiled.
"I wouldn't have it any other way." I smiled back at him.

Paisley

Today was the day. I was on my way to meet his ex wife. The kids were sleep in the backseat and he had been holdin' my hand since we left his place. I wasn't even nervous, honestly. I was kinda anxious. I wanted to get this over with.

When I told Lo I was goin' to do this she was so proud of me. Said I was really growin' up. But in a way I felt like I was stupid. I mean it wasn't like I was goin' to meet her to ask her anything about him. I just wanted to know that she was okay with me bein' around the kids so quick, so I guess it wasn't that dumb at all. This was probably the smartest decision I made since I got back with him.

We pulled up to the house and got the kids out and carried them in. I followed him to their bedrooms and helped him put them in bed. We went into the living room and sat on the couch, waiting for her. She came out and sat on the chair across from us.

She was beautiful. Long thick black hair. Beautiful golden complexion and an amazing body. Don't get me wrong I still thought I was the best lookin' woman in the world, but she was gorgeous. I can't believe anybody would ever want to leave her. I wasn't even jealous. I was in awe.

"Hello." She said to finally break the silence.

"Tasha, this is Paisley." He introduced me. "My girlfriend."

"Hi." She smiled. "Nice to meet you."

"You too." I smiled back at her.

I felt like my smile was a lot more genuine than her's looked. I could tell this wasn't gon' be easy. But it was necessary.

"So what's up?" She asked.

"Well I asked to meet you just to make sure you were okay with me being around the kids so soon." I said. "I mean I know everything is so new, and y'all really tryna figure out how to make the best of this situation and I ain't wana mess none of that up for him."

"It's nothin' that you can mess up for him, that he hasn't already done himself." She smiled.

"Okay." I said unsure of how to respond to that without it sounding bad.

He looked at her like 'what the hell is wrong with you'. Then he gave me an apologetic look.

"So you don't have a problem with me being around the kids right now?" I asked.

"Clearly I don't have a choice." She smiled.

"No you do have a choice here." I said. "At least with me. I ain't forcin' nothin' on you that ain't ready for."

"I wasn't really ready to meet my husband's mistress, but I guess I had to someday." She smiled again.

"Ex-husband." He said.

"I'm not his mistress." I said. "I ain't know shit about you when we first got together. And when I did find out, I left his ass alone. I came over here to try to be respectful of you being their mother and all, but I don't deserve this attitude."

"Well I don't deserve to have to start my life all over again because the man I was supposed to grow old with decided he ain't want me no more." She said.

"Tasha I'm not here to discuss y'all situation." I said. "Which you are obviously not over yet. I'm just here to make sure you not gon' keep him away from his kids, just because I'm around them. That's it. Whatever else you got to say, that ain't my business."

"It amazes me how you don't take any of the blame in this." She said. "My whole life has been turned upside down, and yet I'm supposed to be cordial to the woman that helped make it happen?"

"I didn't help anything." I said as he cut me off.

"She didn't." He said. "I pursued her. I went after her. She told you she ain't know about you and that's true. None of that is her fault."

"If you wana blame somebody for this, you need to be talkin' to him." I said. "But I feel like y'all shoulda had this conversation before y'all signed the papers."

"We did." He said. "And for the last time Tasha, I'm done talkin' about it. Don't bring her into this."

"You brought her into this when you brought her into my house." She snapped.

"You need to calm yo ass down." He said quietly so he wouldn't wake up the kids. "The least you could do is let her know how you feel about her bein' around the kids. That's the only reason she wanted to meet with you. Don't make this harder than it already is."

"So I'm just supposed to make this easy for y'all?" She asked. "Why should I? You sure as hell ain't make it easy for me. Why am I supposed to do you a favor, and spare the dramatics when clearly you brought her here for a show?"

"You need to take some time and get over this shit." He said. "We been through this too many times. If you can't let this shit go, then maybe we don't need to see each other no more. Is that how you want this to go? Every time I see you you wana talk about what went wrong, and can we still fix it. I'm tired of tellin' you the same thing over and over. We past that stage. I couldn't fix this if I wanted to. And that ain't to hurt you, that's to be real with you."

"To answer your question, Paisley." She stopped. "I don't care for you bein' around my kids at all. But they are also his kids, and if he feels like he wants you around them, then I have to respect that. Regardless of our situation, he's always been a great father and I trust his judgment when it comes to them. He knows who and who not to have around my kids."

"Alright." I said. "We can deal with that."

"I need to talk to you for a minute before you go." She said to him.

"I can't right now, Tasha." He said as he stood up.

I stood up after him and followed him to the door. We got in the car and pulled off.

"I'm sorry about all that." He said as we headed to my house.

"It's fine." I said. "I know how to handle myself."

"I think you did a good job." He laughed.

"I know I did." I laughed with him. "She seems like she ain't over it."

"She ain't." He said. "I don't know if she ever will be. I ain't even tryna see her like that. I ain't never mean to hurt that girl. Shit just got outta control over the years. It all built up and I just couldn't take it no more."

"You ain't gotta explain shit to me, bae." I said. "It all make sense. I just want shit to be cool now. I don't gotta be feelin' some type of way about me bein' around another woman's kids."

"They my kids too." He said.

"I know that." I said. "You know what I mean."

"Yea I guess so." He said. "I really appreciate what you tryna do for me and my kids. It mean a lot that you actually give a damn."

"I mean if we gon' make this work, I gotta look at it from every angle." I said. "I tried to put myself in her shoes, and if I was her, I would want the new girl to check with me first too."

He laughed at me like I was playin'.

"Babe I'm for real." I whined. "Stop laughin'.

"Alright my bad." He stopped laughin' finally. "You right. So what's the plan for tonight?"

"You know I'm workin' tonight." I looked at him.

"What?" He asked. "Can't you call off?"

"I could, but why would I do that?" I asked. "You know I need to keep workin' to finish getting the money for my payroll."

"And you know I told you I would give you the money for the rest of the payroll." He looked at me.

"Bae I ain't tryna talk about this every time I bring up work." I said. "It is what it is. I'ma go make a lil' money, and I'll come over when I get off. Can we just leave it at that?"

"It's really that simple for you?" He asked.

"You don't understand how long I been doin' this." I said. "Whole time I been dancing I been workin' towards the same dream. Don't take that from me."

"I ain't takin' shit from you." He said. "If anything, I wana help you get it as soon as possible. I need to get you outta that club."

"And I will be." I said. "As soon as I finish getting this money. Now if you let me go back to 5 days a week, I can be done in 2 weeks. Is that what you want me to do?"

"Hell naw." He said.

"Well I ain't tryna hear yo mouth about this shit no more so maybe that's what I should do." I said.

"Just hurry up and end that shit, P." He said. "You don't even need to be in there."

"Most of the girls in there don't need to be either." I said. "Which is why I'm takin' them with me when I go. I done already talked to them about it and everything."

"I mean I'm with you regardless." He smiled. "You know that. Let's just make this happen, so I ain't gotta keep sharin' you with these niggas every damn night."

"Ain't nobody getting what I give to you." I kissed him. "You know that."

He smiled as he took in my last statement. I had to say somethin' to make 'em smile through all this bull shit.

Nicholas

"So what's goin' on babe?" My mom asked me as I talked to her on the phone. "Cassidy called me cryin' last night."

"She wasn't cryin'." I laughed at her. "She the one broke up with me."

"She say she feel like you didn't fight for her." She said.

"I been fightin' for Cassidy." I said. "I'm not gon' chase her. If she ready to give up, then I'ma let her. I don't want nobody who can't get through the bull shit with me no way."

"So have you decided if you goin' to the wedding yet?" She asked.

"I'm not sure yet." I smiled at Jada. "But let me call you back. I gotta make a move right quick."

"Yea okay Nicholas." She said. "Don't be getting in no trouble out there, boy."

"I'm not Ma." I said. "I told you I was done with that when I came out here."

"Alright." She said. "I'ma take yo word for it. This time."

"Thanks Ma." I laughed. "I'll call you later."

"Okay love you." She said.

"Love you too, Ma." I said before I hung up.

Jada laughed at me as soon as I got off the phone.

"What you look at me like that for?" She asked.

"My mom was askin' me did I decide if I was goin' to the wedding or not."
I laughed as I told her.

"So did you?" She asked.

"You tell me." I smiled at her.

"I can't even talk about that right now." She looked away.

"I ain't askin' you too." I said. "All I'm tryna do is get high and go to the show with you."

She laughed at me as she rolled up a blunt.

"I can't take you serious." She laughed at me.

"Why not?" I laughed. "I'm for real. We ain't gotta talk about nothin' til' you ready. I ain't tryna ruin our time together, worried about some other shit."

"I really appreciate you for that, babe." She smiled at me. "So I'm tryna get drunk as hell tonight when we leave the show. I wana pass out. You down?"

"Hell yea." I laughed at her.

Jada made me completely forget about the bull shit with Cassidy. I ain't need that stress no way. I feel like she came at the perfect time. Perfect time for me, and definitely the perfect time for her. It was no way in hell I could let her leave again. I ain't give a damn what Cassidy thought. I ain't care if I proved her right or not, I needed to be with Jada. And that was it. I ain't have to explain shit to nobody. I was just waitin' for her to be ready to talk about it so we could figure this shit out.

"Still ain't heard from Cassidy?" She asked me.

"You know I turned my phone off." I said. "I blocked her ass anyway. My mom said she called her last night whinin' 'cuz she think I ain't fight for her."

"Did you?" She asked as she looked at me.

"I been fightin' for her since she started this bull shit." I said. "She gave up on me. What I'm posed to do? Beg her to stay? I can't force nobody to fight for me."

"I know what you mean." She agreed. "But I just don't want you to let her walk away, just 'cuz I'm here takin' all yo attention."

"That ain't the case." I said. "Cassidy ended this shit. And that's all it is to it."

"If she still callin' yo mama about it, maybe she ain't really end it." She said.

"She doin' this for my attention." I said. "She knew my mama would tell me and she thought that would make me give her the attention she lookin' for. But we too old for that shit. She had everything any girl could ask for. And that wasn't enough for her. So I'm gon' take the world I gave her, and give it to somebody else who appreciate it."

"Why is it so cut throat with you?" She asked. "You always been like that."

"I just don't have the patience for bull shit." I said. "Never have. Never will. You know that. I was the same way with you when I found out the shit you did."

"I know." She said. "You just make it seem like it's so simple. You don't take no time and think about it. You don't go back and forth with what you should or shouldn't do."

"When I make up my mind, that's it." I said. "It ain't shit that I do, if I'm unsure about it. I don't make a move, until I know that's the best thing for me. I ain't gotta sit and think about how I'ma feel after I do it. That shit ain't even relevant. Cuz if I'm doin' what I know is best for me, how I feel about it ain't gon' effect anything after that. You gotta look at things in the simplest form. Y'all make them way more complicated then it have to be. Yes, you might love somebody and wana try to make it work, but when you did all you can do, and it still ain't workin', it's no reason to stay around and wait for shit to only get worse."

"Damn." She said. "When you put it like that, it sound so simple."

"Y'all just so worried that shit gon' be bad if y'all walk away from a nigga." I said. "But if walkin' away from that nigga is this best move for y'all, then shit only gon' get better."

"That is so true." She said. "It's still easier said than done when it come down to it."

"For y'all." I laughed. "You just gotta be confident in the decisions you make. We gon' make mistakes. That's life. But you a fool if you keep makin' the same mistakes."

"I think..." She smiled at me. "That you are simply the best thing to ever happen to me. And I mean that shit."

"The blunt getting to you." I laughed at her.

She laughed with me as she passed it to me.

"I'm serious." She tried to give me a straight face but she couldn't stop smilin'.

I hit the blunt a few times, passed it back to her and grabbed her hand. Jada was just now expressin' the same feeling I been feelin' for her since I met her. Even though we went through our bull shit, I ain't never stopped lovin' this girl. I never stopped bein' attracted to this girl. It ain't a day that went by since I met her that she ain't crossed my mind.

Even when me and Cassidy was together, I still thought about her. That was the main reason I made sure we kept in touch when we split up for school. The fact that she was still my best friend after everything we went through meant everything to me. Our relationship became so much better when we weren't forced to be wrapped up in each other. Ironically it led us back to bein' obsessed with each other, but this time, it wasn't forced at all.

Nina

"So how you feelin' about everything?" I asked Trevor as we watched TV.

"What you mean?" He asked.

"Havin' a younger sister." I said. "Not havin' another son. I mean shit just been movin' so fast lately, we ain't really had time to catch up with each other. I feel like we ain't sat up and watched TV in forever."

"I know." He said. "Work been so damn busy. I see you every day in the office, but I really ain't seein' you how I want to."

"I completely agree." I said.

"I mean with everything that's been goin' on, I feel like I been handlin' this shit well." He said. "Everything happen for a reason. So I just gotta look at the Tracy situation as a blessing. As far as us meetin' Paisley, I'm happy about that. It ain't her fault that we ain't know about her. It's crazy how we live so close to each other, and ain't even ran into each other."

"Yea that is crazy." I laughed. "You know Cassidy called me the other night cryin' about Nicholas again."

"Why these girls always callin' you about him?" He laughed.

"Well I'm very much involved in every aspect of my son's life." I said. "I don't see why that's a problem."

"I just don't think you need to be entertainin' this teenage shit." He laughed. "You can't make that boy do anything he don't wana do. So what do they expect to get outta callin' you to complain about him?"

"I mean I don't have a problem talkin' to them about him." I said. "I know him better than any of these little girls."

"But you gotta let him live his own life." He said. "I been tellin' you that for so damn long."

"Listen to me, this the last time I'ma tell you this." I said. "I'ma be involved in whatever my son want me to be involved in."

"Nicholas ain't the one callin' you about all his relationship issues, is he?" He asked.

He had a good point there, but I was still not cuttin' my child loose. That was one thing, that would just never happen.

"That don't matter." I said. "Until he tell me to stop talkin' to these girls, I'ma keep talkin to 'em."

"That ain't never gon' happen 'cuz he don't wana hurt yo feelings." He said.

"What you mean?" I asked. "Did he tell you somethin'?"

"Nicholas talk to me about everything." He said. "Whether he want to or not. I went through the same shit he goin' through now so he gon' hear my advice regardless. But I'm not talkin' to these lil' ass girls about him. That ain't my place. Or yours."

"Whatever." I said. "I can still talk to you about it, can't I?"

"You can talk to me about anything, bae." He laughed.

"Okay, so she call me cryin' the other night talkin' bout she broke up with 'em but she don't think he fought for her." I said. "He act like he was too busy to talk to me about it. What you think he was doin'?"

"I don't know." He covered for him. "Did you ask 'em?"

"You know better than that." I gave him the look. "I'm not just a nosy ass mama."

"Since when?" He asked sarcastically.

"Shut up Trevor." I said. "I gotta get my son life together."

"No you don't." He said. "Let him make his own decisions. He know how to handle himself. He too young to be in a serious relationship anyway. He need to focus on school and football. That's it. All that other shit ain't necessary right now. He got all the time in the world to get him a woman."

"So you want my child to just be out there lonely?" I asked him. "It's bad enough you won't let his mama be near him, but now you want him to be by hiself?"

"You know damn well that ain't what I mean." He said. "I ain't sayin' he can't have no hoes around for his entertainment, but that serious shit, livin' together and shit, all that can wait."

"Ain't nobody livin' with my baby." I said. "That's Cassidy problem to begin with. And he ain't havin' no hoes. That ain't even how I raised him. You know that."

"Calm down." He laughed. "Look we finally getting a chance to catch up after we got rid of all the drama. The last thing I wana spend this time talkin' about is our son's relationship issues."

I hesitated before I responded.

"You right." I smiled at him. "I really didn't even intend on this bein' the topic of our discussion. Actually, I wanted to invite you somewhere."

"Huh?" He laughed. "What you mean? I ain't goin' to Jada wedding with you, I told you that."

"Shut up that ain't what I'm talkin' about." I laughed. "Just come with me." I stood up and slipped on my shoes and jacket.

I pulled him up out of the bed and handed him his jacket.

"Where we goin'?" He asked as he put his shoes on.

Music Note was stayin' the night at Kelly's, so I wanted to take this time and treat my man to somethin' special.

"Just follow me." I said. "That's all you need to know."

He smiled as I led him to the car. We got in and headed to my surprise destination. The whole ride there we talked about everything. It was a really good time spent reminiscing. We just went back to the time we met. And all the crazy stuff we used to do together. All the fun we used to have when we weren't so consumed by work.

I mean yes, we have everything we could want, but that came with the sacrifice of not having a lot of time to just be alone with each other. So tonight was about us, being alone, enjoying each others company. We got to the spot and got out of the car.

"Come on." I said as I led him onto the dock.

I hired someone to take us around the river for a midnight cruise. Everything turned out so beautiful. I had so many candles lit for him all throughout the boat. Not just the bedroom. My man needed to have me everywhere whenever we got the chance, and tonight was one of those nights.

"Damn." He smiled. "You did all this?"

"I had to." I smiled at him. "We needed this. I know we really can't get away like we want to right now. So I thought this would hold us over until we can take a real vacation. We both been so all over the place lately, and I just felt like we needed this time to relax. Turn off our phones and not worry about anybody else but each other, for one night."

"It should be like this every night once we leave the office." He said as he pulled me into him.

"I know." I said. "But since it can't be, let's make it happen now."

I turned off my phone and he turned off his. We put them in my purse and left it at that. We went straight to the bedroom to make more memories to talk about years from now. We had the whole boat to christen, but it just wouldn't be right if we didn't at least get started in the bedroom. I ain't even give a damn about anybody seein' us. The only man that mattered to me tonight, was my husband. And I made sure he knew just that.

Paisley

"I don't know what the fuck is goin' on, Lo." I said to Lo as I walked in her house. "This nigga phone goin' straight to voicemail."

"P it sound like his shit dead." London said. "Why don't you just go over there and make sure he alright?"

"He said he was droppin' somethin' off for the kids a few hours ago." I said. "But for some reason he ain't ask me to go with 'em."

"What you mean?" She asked.

"Lo that man ask me to go everywhere with him." I said. "Sometimes I think it's just to keep me from dancing if it's at night. But today was different."

"Maybe he just ain't want no drama with you and her." She said.

"Naw fuck that." I said. "I ain't stupid. His ass over there fuckin' her. He probably ain't even go to her house. How much you wana bet he got that bitch in his shit right now?"

"Paisley, I highly doubt he fuckin' her." She said. "And I know he ain't got nobody in his spot that you gotta key to."

"Niggas change locks everyday, Lo." I snapped.

"Paisley, calm the fuck down." She said. "You trippin' for nothin'."

I rolled up a blunt to calm me down. That shit still ain't work.

"I can't believe this nigga." I snapped. "I really trusted his ass."

"Why shouldn't you?" She asked. "You trippin' for no reason, Paisley. I'm tellin' you right now. He ain't gave you no reason to doubt him."

"I'm callin' his ass right now." I yelled.

I dialed his number. It rung twice then went to voicemail.

"Now his shit ringin' and he just sent me to voicemail." I yelled. "I gotta go."

"Where you goin'?" She snatched my arm.

"To catch his ass up." I said.

"Don't do it." She said. "You don't wana be that girl. You ain't never been that girl. Don't start that shit now."

"I don't give a fuck. You think you gon' bull shit me, the same way you did her. Fuck that shit. I told his ass from jump I'm not her." I yelled as I grabbed my keys off the counter.

"If I don't hear from yo ass in an hour, I'm comin' to find you." She said to me as I stormed out her house.

I got in my car and sped off to his house. He lived about 15 minutes away from London's house so I had a little bit of time to get my plan together. I knew I was right about this nigga bein' on bull shit. But every bone in my body wanted to be wrong. I just couldn't believe he would do this shit to me. After everything he said to me. All the shit he really had me believing. I smoked another blunt on the way there hopin' that would take away my rage. It seemed like it just heightened it. The whole ride

384

there was a blur to me. I didn't even look at no street signs or nothin', but I made all the right turns to get me to his house. I got there before I even realized what I was doin'.

As soon as I pulled up, I saw his car pull out of the parking lot. Immediately, without even second guessin' myself, I followed him. And it wasn't even a sneaky follow. I wanted that mufucka to know his ass was caught. He merged onto the freeway goin' the complete opposite direction of his ex's house so I knew he was on bull shit. I merged on right behind him and once the lane opened up, I sped up right next to him. I rolled down my passenger window and beeped my horn at his ass. I looked over to his passenger seat to see a woman sittin' there smilin'. He still hadn't even realized I was next to him. I beeped the horn again and swerved a lil' to scare his ass. He finally rolled down his window.

"Paisley what the fuck are you doin'?" He yelled to me.
"Pull the fuck over." I screamed. "Now."

I saw him shaking his head as he slowed down. He pulled over into the shoulder and I did the same. I hopped out the car ready to beat his ass and the bitch he was with. I knew this ain't have shit to do with her though, so I went straight to him.

"What the fuck is this?" I yelled at him. "This why you sendin' me to voicemail?"

"Paisley my phone been dead." He said calmly. "I just put it on the charger bout an hour ago. What is yo problem?"

"What's my problem?" I yelled. "Are you fuckin' kiddin' me? Where did you tell me you was goin' tonight?"

"To drop off some shit the kids left at my house." He said. "I don't know what the problem is with that."

"Did you forget to mention somebody else was goin' with you?" I yelled as I pointed at the girl.

All this time I thought he was fuckin' with his ex, and he had a whole other new bitch.

"Paisley this is my sister, Nina." He said as he introduced her. "Nina, this my woman, Paisley."

"Hi." She smiled at me awkwardly. "Nice to meet you. Wish it coulda been under better circumstances, but I am glad to finally meet you."

"What?" I asked.

Was this shit true?

"Nina wanted to see the kids so she met me at the house to ride with me over there." He said. "I didn't know it was gon' be a problem for you. I woulda told you if I knew that was the case."

Just lookin' at her, I saw the resemblance. I felt like a fuckin' idiot. I was so embarrassed. I ain't even know what to say. He was so calm it scared the hell outta me. When he was mad, he got extremely calm. So this made me paranoid. I ain't know what was bouta happen.

I was on the side of the freeway, makin' a fuckin' scene, for no damn reason. I knew I shoulda listened to Lo. She never steered me wrong. I was speechless. I ain't know what to say. I ran to my car and hopped back in. I sped off and instantly started crying. I knew I really fucked up. I damn near killed him and his sister. What if the kids was in the car? What if her kids was in the car? What the hell was I thinkin'? I never let anybody get me outta my character like that. That shit wasn't even me.

I sped back to London's house and went in still cryin'. I couldn't even talk 'cuz I couldn't stop cryin'. She sat on the couch and I lay down cryin' my eyes out in her lap. She shook her head the whole time 'cuz she already knew I fucked up before I even told her.

Two hours later, I finally stopped cryin'. The only thing that stopped me was the worst headache I ever had.

"What in the hell did you do?" London asked me when I sat up to wipe my face.

I had snot dripping all down my face and not once did I attempt to wipe it as I was cryin'. I didn't try to clean myself up, until I could stop the tears.

"Lo I don't even know where to start." I said. "I wish I had blacked out or somethin', but I feel like I lost my fuckin' mind. How did I let a man get me to become a maniac?"

"That man did not make you react like this." She said. "Whatever insecurities you still have from y'all past, caused this today. How can you move forward with somebody, if you can't get over what they've done? You can't say you forgave him, and still expect the worse from him the first time you can't get in touch with him. All you had to do was wait for him to contact you and I'm sure he would have soon. He's been extremely good at keepin' you in the loop at all times. The one time it was probably just takin' longer than usual, you go and cause a fuckin' scene."

Lo was the only one who could talk to me like that. Cuz she knew me better than anybody else. And she knew I needed her honesty.

"I feel so bad." I whined.

"What did you do, Paisley?" She asked as she stared at me. "And don't lie, 'cuz I have no problem callin' him."

"I went to his house." I said quietly. I couldn't even look at her 'cuz I knew she was bouta smack my ass when I told her the rest. "And I saw him leavin' so I followed him. He got on the freeway, so I did too. I sped up next to him, and damn near side swiped 'em to get his attention. Finally got it and told him to pull over. I snapped when I saw he was with a girl."

"And who was this girl?" She asked like she already knew the answer.

"His sister." I said as I looked away.

"So not only did you embarrass him in front of his sister, but this is the first impression you give her when you finally meet her?" She asked. "I don't understand why you don't just listen to me when I tell you to calm the fuck down. Sometimes you gotta think before you react. All this shit coulda been avoided. You coulda killed him. You coulda killed her. His kids coulda been in the car. Her kids coulda been in the car."

"I know I thought about all that on the way back over here." I cried.

"That's too late to be thinkin' about that shit." She snapped. "Girl we all done snapped on a nigga at least one time. If you ain't never been a fool for a nigga, then you ain't never been in love. But if I'm tellin' you this from experience, you gotta listen to me. A lotta shit you rather find out the hard way. So now you got yoself into some shit, that I can't get you out of. I can't tell you what's gon' happen now. What did he say?"

"He just introduced me to her." I said. "Told me she wanted to see the kids so she was goin' over there with 'em."

"You gotta be fuckin' kiddin' me." She shook her head at me again.
"Somethin' so innocent, you blew all the way outta proportion."

"All he had to do was call me." I said.

"You ain't even give the nigga a chance to." She yelled.

She rolled up and gave me the lighter. She went to the kitchen and came back with two shot glasses and a 5th of Patron.

"If we gon' get through this night, I'ma need a few of these." She said as she poured us both a shot.

An hour later, we were both passed out on the couch. I didn't wake up until I heard her doorbell ring.

"Lo." I shook her to wake her up. "Somebody at yo door."

She woke up and went to see who it was. She opened it and let whoever it was in. After she got up off the couch, I closed my eyes so I couldn't see who it was. Honestly, I really didn't care. I just wanted to go back to sleep and pray for a better day tomorrow.

"How long she been out?" I heard somebody say.
"We both just passed out." London said. "Probably like an hour ago. I'm sorry about tonight. She told me what happened. I tried my hardest to keep her here and make sure she ain't do nothin' stupid."
"It's cool." He said. "I appreciate that though."

I opened my eyes to see my man standin' above me. I couldn't even move. I didn't want to.

"Come on." He said to me.

I was stuck. He noticed that and picked me up. London put my shoes in my purse and followed us out the door. He put me in his car, took my purse from London and got in. I knew shit was bouta get real as soon as he pulled off. I wasn't even ready for this shit tonight.

I fell back asleep on the ride to his house. I woke up once I realized we stopped. He came around to my side, took me out the car, and carried me into his apartment. He put me in his bed with all my clothes on and climbed in the bed next to me.

I ain't know what to think but I felt like this was too damn good to be true. This nigga was not bouta play like that shit ain't happen. I mean don't get me wrong I knew he was a calm ass nigga, but that shit had to get to him. It just had to. And if it didn't, I needed to be on whatever drugs he was on to keep him this cool.

Before I noticed it, I was knocked the fuck out. I woke up the next morning by myself. I panicked for a minute cuz I ain't know where I was at first. I rolled over to see him outside on the balcony smoking. I got up and went to the bathroom. Washed my face and brushed my teeth, then went to face the music. I stood next to him and waited for him to snap on my ass. It never happened.

"How you feelin'?" He asked calmly without even lookin' at me.

"I got the worst headache ever." I whined.

"I'm sure you do." He laughed. "You was passed out when I found you at London house last night."

"What happened last night?" I asked tryna play it off like I ain't remember.

"You really wana go there?" He asked finally lookin' at me.

He passed me the blunt and took a sip of his drink. I felt like it was too damn early to be getting drunk. Then I looked at my watch and realized it was damn near 5pm. I couldn't believe I slept that late.

"My kids coulda been in the car with me, Paisley. You coulda killed us. I know you had to think about that shit." He said quietly.

"On the way there, I didn't think at all." I said. "I ain't even see where I was goin', I just ended up where I needed to be. But once I left and realized I had just lost my mind, I thought about all that. I'm so sorry. I don't even know how to come back from that."

"I don't either." He said as he took the blunt from me.

My heart dropped when he said that. I was hopin' this wouldn't be the end of us, but it looked like it was. I mean if it was me, I don't think I could fuck with somebody who put my life in danger the way I did last night. He had every right to walk away from me. He would be the fool if he didn't.

I had no words for his response. I didn't know if I should, and I felt bad that I didn't. This was the time for me to fight for this relationship, and I just couldn't figure out how. I felt how much I embarrassed him last night. If anything, he was a proud ass man. And I know that shit I pulled last night, really made him look bad.

"If I could take it back, I would." I said quietly.

"Why didn't you just listen to London?" He asked.

"Bae I barely even heard her ass when I was in that moment." I whined. "I can't even tell you what she told me before I went to yo house. I wasn't hearin' shit she was sayin'. My head was just screamin' at me to go find yo ass."

He passed me the blunt and took another sip of his drink.

"I don't even know what I'm supposed to do with yo ass now, Paisley." He said. "How the fuck I look stayin' with you after you just pulled that shit in front of my sister? She done heard so much good shit about you, then finally meet you and this what she see?"

"You right." I said quietly. "I'm not askin' you stay with me. That's selfish on my part. I just want you to try to forgive me. I need you to forgive me, baby."

"I forgave you when I picked yo drunk ass up last night." He said. "I mean I understand why you panicked when you couldn't get in touch with me. But if I'm tellin' you to take my word that I ain't on bull shit with you, and you say you gon' take it, then I believe that shit. That mean that you ain't holdin' none of that shit from the past against me. That mean that you know regardless of you bein' able to reach me or not, I ain't no bull shit with you. I know that ain't gon' be the easiest thing for you to do, seein' how I did my ex, but I don't know how many times I gotta tell you that shit ain't happenin' with me and you. I ain't lettin' it. You not her, and I ain't the same nigga I was when I got with her. I know it's my fault you got these insecurities but I'm doin' my best to take that shit away."

"You are so right." I whined. "You been goin' out yo way to prove this shit to me, and as soon as I get a chance to prove myself to you, I blow that shit. Maybe I'm just not as ready as I thought I was to move past that shit. I mean I wana make this work, but how do I do that without lettin' the past come back and get in my head everytime I can't reach you?"

"Have I given you any reason not to trust me, since we been back together?" He asked me.

"Not at all." I said quickly.

"So why don't you base yo thoughts, off what's been goin' on since we got back together?" He asked. "You need to put that shit from the past, out yo head completely. I know you ain't gon' never forget it but stop reliving it. Stop bringin' it back into what we got goin' on now. We ain't never gon' get nowhere if you still stuck on that shit in the past. We can't move forward if you can't let that go."

"It ain't that simple." I said. "I wish it was, but I can't just turn off my feelings."

"I ain't askin' you to turn 'em off." He said. "But you at least need to learn how to control them. We done been through some shit and I ain't never seen you snap like last night. That wasn't even you out there."

"And that's exactly how I felt." I said. "It wasn't me. I ain't never lost control of myself like that. I ain't never been so careless. Never embarrassed myself like that. I always been too proud to let anybody break me like that."

"I don't know if it's a good thing, or bad thing that I brought you to that point." He said. "But I guess that mean you finally let me in." He laughed.

"How can you laugh at this dumb shit?" I asked him. "This shit is ridiculous."

"It is." He said. "But I can't act like I ain't play a part in pushin' you to this level. You never snapped when you found out the truth last year, so I guess this was just you getting all that out. You been had that shit bottled up all this time, it wasn't gon' come out no other way but wrong. Had you just got it out yo system when it happened, instead of tryna play cool, you probably wouldn'ta been so crazy last night."

"I ain't even think about it like that." I said. "All this time I been tryna figure out why I had so much rage from this petty ass shit, but now it all makes sense to me."

"Paisley I love yo ass." He smiled at me. "Ain't shit you can do to make me stop lovin' yo ass. You know that. Just don't push me away."

"You gotta believe I really ain't tryin' too." I said. "If I'm doin' it, let me know. And I'll do what I can to correct that shit."

"You know I'ma let you know." He turned towards me and stared at me. "You need to apologize to Nina. I don't know how she feelin' about this whole situation. We ain't even talk about it when you left. I was too mad I had to calm my ass down. But you can't have her thinkin' you ain't no good for me."

"So you still think I'm good for you?" I asked smilin' at him.

"Ain't shit better." He smiled. "I'm mad as hell at yo ass still, but ain't shit I can do to change what already happened. I ain't holdin' it against you, but just know I ain't goin' for that bull shit no more. You ain't a kid. Don't throw no fuckin' tantrum like you 5 years old."

"You right." I smiled at him. "Thank you for forgiving me babe." I wrapped my arms around his neck.

"Em hum." He smiled as he put his hands around my waist.

"I promise I'ma fix it." I said still holdin' him.

"I know you will." He said sarcastically. "Next time just listen to Lo. You still got a lil' learning to do."

"Shut up." I laughed. "I'm tryin'. Ain't nobody ever had my emotions so up and down like this."

"Stop actin' crazy." He smiled. "I know you got some sense. Just use it when you start thinkin' too hard about shit."

"I can try that." I smiled as I led him back into the bedroom.

"You gotta trust me when I say I ain't fuckin' up this time." He said.

"I'm tryin' babe." I said as I pushed him onto the bed.

I had some serious makin' up to do. My man was givin' me another chance to prove myself to him, and I needed to show him how much I appreciated that.

Malcolm

"What's up?" I said to my mama as I answered her phone call.

This was the first time I heard from her since our argument. I really wasn't ready to hear her bull shit but I knew I couldn't ignore her forever.

"Shit." She said. "What you been up to?"

"Workin'." I said. "You?"

"Same." She said. "Why you ain't called me?"

"You said don't call you til' I'm ready to apologize." I said. "And I'm not sorry. Time ain't gon' change that."

"I know." She said quietly. "Your father has cancer, Malcolm."

"Really?" I asked sarcastically. "Is that what he told you to get back in yo bed?"

"Boy don't make me beat yo ass." She snapped. "It's true. I took 'em to the doctor and everything."

"How you know he ain't payin' the doctor off?" I asked.

"It's my doctor, Malcolm." She said. "He came to me a while ago when he first started feelin' sick. I took 'em to get some tests done, and that's when they told us."

"Damn." I said not knowin' how else to respond. "That's fucked up."

"That's all you got to say?" She asked.

"What else you want me to say?" I asked.

"You could at least talk to him." She said. "It ain't no tellin' how long he got left."

"What I need to talk to him for?" I asked. "I don't have shit to say to that man."

"That man, is the reason you here today." She snapped.

"No, I'm the reason I'm here today." I said. "Nobody else got me here but me. When you wasn't there 'cuz you was workin' 3 jobs, I raised myself. When he wasn't there 'cuz he just couldn't get it together, I supported my family. For some reason you just keep getting that shit twisted."

"Malcolm I know that he ain't never really been there for you." She said. "But can't you be the bigger person and be there for him? Before it's too late?"

"Its no reason I need to be there for him." I said. "Clearly he already got you on his side."

I hung up on her and turned my phone off. I was done with this bull shit from my mama. She was gettin' on my damn nerves. I was hopin' this conversation was gon' end up good, but I knew it wasn't 'cuz I was still mad at her. I couldn't make shit right until I got over this issue. And I ain't see that happenin' no time soon if she kept feedin' into this nigga bull shit. I pulled up to Laya job and waited for her to come out.

"Hey babe." She said as she got in the car and kissed me.

"What's up." I said. "How was work?"

"Crazy as always." She said. "What's wrong?"

"My mom talkin' bout he got cancer." I said as I pulled off.

"Oh my God." She said. "I'm so sorry baby."

"You ain't gotta apologize to me." I said. "I ain't sorry at all. Selfish niggas get what they deserve. I believe in karma. This just him getting back the bull shit he gave when he shoulda been there for his family."

"Bae, you can not be this fuckin' heartless." She said.

"I'm not heartless." I said. "I just have no sympathy for that nigga."

"Well what about havin' some sympathy for your mom?" She asked.

"Clearly she getting ready to lose the love of her life, and you just actin' like it ain't shit. It may not effect you 'cuz you ain't never really had 'em around to miss him, but that's somebody she spent years of her life with before you came in the picture. She had him there to be able to miss him even though you didn't. So, I can understand how she feelin'. You need to stop bein' so damn selfish and be there for her if you can't be there for him."

"I ain't even think about it like that." I said.

"You never do." She said. "Somebody always gotta point out yo bull shit 'cuz you act like you blind to it."

"Really?" I said sarcastically. "I know when I'm trippin', Laya."

"Clearly you don't this time." She said. "You need to take yo ass home and make sure she okay."

"Don't tell me what I need to do." I said. "I'm grown as hell. I know how to figure this shit out. If she needed me to be there why wouldn't she just say that?"

"She shouldn't have to." She said. "You should know when yo mama goin'
through somethin'. The fact that I know and you actin' like you don't is
fucked up. You just mad 'cuz she give a damn about the nigga. You can't
understand where she comin' from 'cuz you don't know him like she do.
What don't you get about that?"

"I get it, Laya." I said. "Let's just drop it for now."

"Why?" She asked.

"Cuz I don't feel like talkin' about it no more." I said.

"Wow." She said sarcastically.

I didn't even need to reply to her. I said what I needed to say and
that was it. I was in no rush to run home and hold my mama hand while
she cry over a nigga that ain't shit. A nigga that ruined our lives more than
once. Not only did he just up and leave, but he always took our shit to
make us have to start all over again.

It was no way in hell I could feel any type of sympathy for this man,
but clearly she did. Laya was right. He must have been a completely
different guy before my mom got pregnant. If he wasn't I dont see how
they woulda been able to stay together that long before I came into the
picture. But I ain't wana see him. And I knew he was stayin' at the house
'cuz Kelly called and told me. I wasn't in the right frame of mind to see his
ass. I ain't think I ever would be. You can't just let somebody back into yo
life who destroyed it so many times. I would just be playin' the fool like my
mom was if I did that.

I ain't know what I was gon' do about this. I knew what I wanted to do was to just let this shit play out like it always did. But that would make me selfish and I wasn't selfish when it came to my women. Especially my mama. I knew I was gon' have to go home and get this shit straightened out but I knew I couldn't do it before I calmed down.

I couldn't let him get to me when I got there so I needed some time to prepare myself for all the bull shit he was gon' try to hit me with. I had to ignore that shit. It was no way I was lettin' him see how this shit affected me. He wasn't worth the time or the effort but I was mad as hell she was entertaining this nigga and his bull shit again.

Paisley

"Thanks for meetin' me." I said to Nina as she sat down at the table.

After the whole incident with her brother, I needed to clear things up. I ain't want her thinkin' I was just some crazy chick who was trippin' for no reason.

"No problem." She smiled genuinely. "Girl you scared the hell outta me the other night. I ain't even gon' lie."

"I know." I said. "I scared my damn self. I ain't never been in that type of shit before. I mean I know I blew it outta proportion but that just came from him lyin' to me in the past."

"Paisley, I know all about it." She said. "When shit hit the fan with y'all last year, he told me everything. I know exactly how you feel. I was the same way with my ex. That nigga wasn't shit. And every time he was away from me I felt like he was cheatin' on me. Now I don't know if you feel like that, but I been where you at. You wouldn't believe the crazy shit I got into with that fool. But it happens. I'm just thanking God that our kids weren't in the car. That's my only issue. I did the same shit when I was your age. And I never thought about the repercussions if I was wrong, or even if I was right. This shit just finally made me realize how crazy I was when I was doin' the same shit. And I was doin' worse than that. I became somebody I never was with him. All the lies and cheatin', and abuse, turned me into somebody I had never seen. For years I was lost in his mess. Finally, I got out. My brother is nothin' like my ex. But I do believe that all men cheat. We just gotta be lucky enough to meet a man after he already got that outta his system. And if we didn't, then we gotta think about if we the type of women to stay and work through the shit with the man."

"I completely agree with you." I said. "I'm so sorry I put you in that position. I'm sorry I put him in that position. The last thing I wanted to do is embarrass him."

"Girl you ain't embarrass that man." She said. "Lucky for you I been there. And I know all the bull shit he put you through. I'm surprised it took you this long to snap."

"I never wanted it to get like this." I said.

"It's okay." She smiled at me. "Now at least I know you really love his ass." She laughed. "I'm playin'. I knew you loved him just based off what he told me about y'all when y'all first got together. I didn't agree with what he was doin' with not tellin' you or Tasha about each other, but he didn't know how to get outta that situation. At least at that time. And I think he really wanted to make sure it was over with her."

"I can understand that." I said. "I just want you to know that ain't nothin' like that happenin' again. I know what I gotta do to get my head together and I'm workin' on it."

"I admire you acknowledging this after one time." She smiled at me. "I never acknowledged my wrongs until I was with another man that made me realize that shit was not attractive. I was so lost from bein' with my ex I ain't know right from wrong. It's crazy how a lifetime of teaching from your parents, a lifetime of common sense can be completely erased when a nigga take over yo mind. I just thank God that I got outta that place."

"I'm sorry you had to go through all that." I said tryin' to comfort her.

"Girl I'm not." She said. "It made me who I am today. I wouldn't change any of it. Only thing I would take back, is everything my baby saw. He shouldn'ta seen anything but it was some things I couldn't prevent."

"Damn." I said quietly. I ain't know what else to say. "So how is he about all that?"

"He won't talk about it." She said. "Never would. But I know it affects him. I'm just waitin' for the day he explodes and let it all out. Hopefully it'll be him just venting to me about it, instead of it comin' out in anger towards somebody else."

"I hope so too." I smiled. "I am glad I finally got to meet you though."

"Me too." She smiled. "Don't get me wrong, I love Tasha. She's great. But she just wasn't great for my brother anymore. Which kinda came from all the bull shit he put her through but it just wasn't workin' for them. She's the perfect example of tryin' to work through it with the man who ain't got over his cheatin' phase yet. A lot of times it don't work out. Regardless she's still a great mom and I think she's handlin' all of this the best way she know. I heard you went to the house to meet her."

"I did." I smiled. "Um she seemed like she was still upset with everything. Which I completely understand 'cuz this arrangement is still new. To all of us."

"Yea she's definitely still upset." She said. "We talked about me bringin' the kids back and forth 'cuz she really don't need to see him if she tryna get over him, ya know. And then to see him so happy with you, that still hurts. I don't know how long it's gon' take her to get over that, but at least she's workin' through it."

"Definitely." I agreed. "That's one of the main reasons why I wanted to go meet her. I needed to make sure she was cool with me bein' around the kids so fast. I appreciated the fact that she trusted his judgment enough to let him make that call."

"Yea she's been very fair with the kids." She said. "And I gotta say that shit surprised me. Tasha is a very spiteful woman. But when it came to the kids, I guess she knew that wasn't the way to go. I know he happy about that." She laughed.

"I know I am." I said. "I ain't wana force nothin' on her when I knew this shit was already hard enough on her as it is."

"And I appreciate that." She said. "I think he did a great job changin' his mentality for you. He's been so much happier since you came around and I just want it to stay that way."

"Nina, I have every intention of keepin' that man happy as long as he lets me." I smiled. "I'm just so grateful that he was able to forgive me for that scene. If it was the other way around I don't know how quick I would be to let that go. I just get so wrapped up in my pride sometimes. Which sound crazy 'cuz I just threw that to the side the other night but that came outta nowhere. Once I realized I lost myself it was too damn late. I got drunk at my best friend house and passed out."

She started crackin' up.

"Girl I don't blame you." She laughed. "That's some shit you just wana forget about. Wake up the next morning and hope it was all a dream."

"Girl that's exactly what I did." I laughed with her. "I wanted to play it off like I ain't know what he was talkin' about when he was ready to talk about it, but I knew that shit wasn't gon' work."

"Hell naw." She laughed. "He's always been a calm guy. No tolerance for bull shit, but he let you know that calmly. I was the hothead of the family."

"I can't tell now." I laughed.

"Girl I know." She said. "I don't know what happened. I thought I was gon' change once I had my son, but I was still lost dealin' with my ex. When I finally left and got my shit together, it all just clicked for me. I knew I ain't wana take that same drama and bitterness into my next relationship. I met a man who deserved the best of me so I gave him just that. I left all that other shit where it was, in the past. That allowed me to grow up and really be happy with myself. I wasn't happy with myself when I was with my ex so I couldn't remain calm when I needed too. I was angry at everything. So, I couldn't be who I needed to be. But now, it's a whole different story. I let go of all that, and I been happy ever since."

"That is so beautiful." I smiled. "I'm so happy for you."

"Thanks girl." She smiled. "So, when y'all movin' in together? I'm ready for another wedding."

"What?" I laughed. "Girl I'm tryna take this as slow as possible. And she would kill him if he married me that fast."

"Well I mean it's obvious it's gon' happen'." She smiled. "So I'm just gon' wait til' you ready to go pick out the ring."

"Oh my God!" I couldn't stop laughin' at her.

We got along like we knew each other forever. I felt so comfortable with her and I was just getting to know her. I don't know why I ain't get to meet her the first time I was with her brother if he told her about me, but that really ain't matter. At least we were becomin' friends now.

Jada

I knew I couldn't hide out here forever. The wedding was tomorrow and I still didn't know what I was gon' do. I knew what I should do, and what I wanted to do, but somethin' in me was still confused about if I should really make that move.

"Good mornin'." Nicholas said as he brought me breakfast in bed.

He was makin' it so hard for me to leave him. I didn't want to leave him. I knew I wanted to stay here with Nicholas. I had no problem transferring schools and startin' my life over with him. He was my best friend, and the love of my life. But I was engaged to Carter. I told him I would be his wife. How was I supposed to go back on that? Especially the day before the wedding.

I thought comin' here would clear up things for me and make it okay for me to go forward with Carter. All it did was confuse me even more. It showed me what I wanted to do, but it didn't show me what I needed to do. I wanted to just stick to what my mind decided on, like Nicholas said he did, but I couldn't bring myself to hurt Carter. Was I willing to hurt Nicholas, in order to spare Carter's feelings? Did I really want to marry somebody just so I wouldn't hurt them?

There was no doubt in my mind that my future would be amazing with Nicholas. Since Carter cheated on me, I could never see a future with him anymore. I tried so hard to imagine what it would be like bein' married to him, but it just wasn't somethin' I could wrap my head around. Probably because I never saw myself growin' old with him.

Since I met Nicholas I knew I would have his babies. I knew I would be his wife and nobody else's. When Carter proposed I tried to see myself bein' with him the rest of my life. I could never see it. I just hoped that would change throughout the years we were together. It didn't work. And after he cheated that really took away any chance that I could ever imagine myself marryin' him.

My ideal husband was someone who was completely committed to me, and only me. The only person I had ever met who fit that fantasy was Nicholas. He always took care of me. Even when we weren't together, I was still a priority in his life. And I loved his desire to keep me happy. It was obvious just from the way he looked at me.

"Good morning." I smiled and kissed him before I started eatin'. "You ain't eatin' nothin'?"
"Naw I ate while I was cookin'." He smiled. "Alright while I was puttin' yo stuff on a plate."

I laughed at him. That boy couldn't boil water if he tried. But it was fine. I had no problem teaching him how to cook. It was somethin' I felt he needed to learn 'cuz I knew I wasn't gon' be cookin' everyday.

"Em hum." I smiled at him. "We coulda went out to breakfast. Why you ain't wake me up?"

"I tried." He said. "Yo ass was knocked out. I shook you and everything."

"Damn." I laughed. "Musta been a long night."

He started laughin' at me.

"Hell yea." He laughed. "So, what's goin' on for tomorrow? I been tryin' not to talk about it, cuz I ain't wana stress you out, but I think it's time."

"You right." I said. "And I appreciate you givin' me this time. I have no idea what's gon' happen tomorrow. Whatever it is, I owe him the truth."

"Do you really?" He looked at me surprised.

"I mean I know he ain't always been truthful with me, but I can't stoop to his level." I said. "If I did that, I wouldn't be no better than him."

"So what is this?" He asked. "A competition now?"

"Not at all." I said. "I just know that I need to tell him what's been goin' on. For me. So I'ma take a flight out in the morning and meet him at the church."

"So you goin' through with the wedding?" He asked.

"Nicholas, I really don't know." I said. "I don't know if I did everything I could to make this work. How do I know that?"

413

"How you gon' find out before the wedding?" He asked. "Seeing him at the church ain't gon' tell you that."

"That's true." I said. "I just need to show up. At the least. I can't just run away from someone I planned on sharin' my life with."

"You know I can't be there for that." He said quietly. "I mean I wish you the best but after these last few days it's no way in hell I can watch you marry somebody else. And I can't lie and say I ain't mad that you still wana go through with it."

"I'm not tellin' you I still wana go through with it." I said. "But I'm not tellin' you that I'm sure that I don't."

"I can respect that." He said. "I still don't want you to go though."

"I don't either." I said. "But I need to finish what I started. It wouldn't be right, if I didn't."

"Guess I don't have a choice." He forced a smile.

"I love you." I smiled at him. "But right now, you gotta let me do this."

"It ain't gon' be easy, but I guess I can try." He gave me a real smile.

"Come on let's get dressed and go do somethin'." I smiled at him.

"What you wana do?" He asked.

"I wana go bowlin'." I smiled.

"Damn J." He laughed. "We ain't been bowlin' in years."

"I know." I laughed. "That's why I wana go. And call Malcolm and Laya and tell 'em to meet us. We need to get a few sessions in too before I go back tomorrow."

"Ha." He laughed at me. "You gotta be high to go through with it?"

"Somethin' like that." I laughed with him.

"Come on." He smiled as he took the tray out the bed. "Let's get in the shower."

I smiled as he left the room. This man was amazing. I came here and gave him so much hope for us, and now I was possibly gon' marry somebody else tomorrow. What in the hell was I thinkin'? I knew Nicholas was the man I was supposed to marry. So why was I still thinkin' about marryin' Carter? I knew I tried everything I could in our relationship. And I knew it wasn't even in me to try anything else with him. So why was I even goin' back tomorrow? I just felt like I at least owed him the truth. Face to face.

I got up and went into the bathroom to get in the shower with him. He was runnin' me a bath. He had candles lit in the bathroom with the lights off. Rose petals in the tub. First, I thought this was all in his plan to get me to stay, but he had to get them ahead of time to set this all up. I felt like he had this idea in his head before he brought me breakfast. It was so beautiful.

Nicholas never had to try to impress me. Even when he looked a mess, he still made me weak. And he knew that. So, the fact that he was puttin' in all this extra effort when he didn't have too, meant the world to me. I ain't know how in the hell I was gon' get on that plane in the morning. At least not without him next to me.

Malcolm

I ended up goin' home to get all this shit taken care of. As soon as I walked in the house I saw Marcus ass sittin' up on the couch like it was his shit. I wanted to beat his ass as soon as I saw him, but I knew shit would only get worse from here if I did. I walked past him and went to my mom's room. She was in her bed watchin' TV.

"Hey." She smiled as I walked in her room.

"What's up." I said as I sat on the edge of her bed.

"Nothin' much." She said. "What you doin' here? Why you ain't tell me you was comin'?"

"Last minute." I said. "He stayin' here or somethin'?"

"Malcolm, I don't feel like getting into all this with you." She said.

"Well what is he doin' here then?" I asked.

"He's sick." She yelled. "I ain't raise you to be that evil."

"How you expect for me to feel bad for a nigga that ain't never gave a damn about me?" I snapped. "Or Kelly. Even yo ass."

"If you came here to disrespect me again, then take yo ass back where you came from." She said quietly. "I'm not in the mood for all that right now."

"You think I'm in the mood to come home to this?" I asked. "I came home to try to help you feel better, but you doin' this to yourself."

"I'm sorry that I can't just cut off my feelings." She said. "I must be crazy to care about somebody who gave me the best two things in my life. How could I care about the only man I ever loved? It must really be somethin' wrong with me." She said sarcastically.

As much as I hated to admit it, she had a point. I wanted her to hate him just as much as I did, but she just couldn't. She ain't have it in her. It was honestly takin' a lot of energy for me to hate him. I didn't even realize I hated him until he just came back. I thought I could care less about the nigga. But that shit fucked me up. I ain't give a fuck what his excuse was for him not bein' around. It wasn't shit he could say to justify that bull shit.

I ain't even know what to say to my mama. I tried to put myself in her shoes. It wasn't shit Laya could do to me that could make me stop carin' about her. I mean she damn near got me killed, and I still went back to her ass. And I was never leavin' her ass. If I got over that, I guess she could get over all the bull shit he did to her. Especially since he wasn't always this selfish.

"I'm sorry, Ma." I said quietly. "I ain't mean to say all that."
"I know." She said. "Some people, you just have to let back in. Especially when they don't have much time left. I know it's messed up how he wana come back around now, but if I can be here for him when he need somebody, I'ma do it for him. Just like I need you to be here for me when this all said and done, he need me to be there for him and help him through it. I know you just want the best for us, and he honestly ain't it, but

it ain't about us right now. If I treat him how he treated me then I ain't no better than him."

"Yea I see what you mean." I said. "I just want you to be careful. Pay attention this time. If shit don't seem right, then get rid of that nigga. It don't matter if he don't got a lotta time left, that still don't give him the right to take advantage of you."

"I completely agree baby." She smiled at me. "And I'm payin' attention to everything this time. Keepin' all my valuables tucked away." She laughed.

It was good that we could look back and laugh about the bull shit. It still pissed me off, but it was in the past. We couldn't change it.

"That's all I can ask for." I hugged her. "Where Kelly at?"

"Practice." She said. "It's Nina's night to pick them up. She should be here in a little bit."

"Alright." I said. "I'm finna go smoke. I'll be back in a little bit."

"You ain't ask me to smoke." She whined as I stood up.

"Ma you ain't never asked to smoke with me." I laughed. "You must really be goin' through it."

"I really am." She laughed.

"Come on." I shook my head as I pulled her up out the bed. "I'll be in the car."

"Alright." She laughed.

I went out of her room and went straight to the kitchen. I grabbed me a beer and went straight outside.

"Well damn you can't speak to nobody?" Marcus followed me out the house.

"My bad I ain't even see you." I said without turnin' around. I kept walkin' to the car.

"Can I talk to you for a minute?" He asked me as he followed me to the car.

"I'm kinda in the middle of somethin' right now." I said as I got in the car.

"Ain't gon' take long." He said as he walked up to the driver side door.

I looked at him and waited on him to say whatever it was he felt like he had to get off his chest.

"I appreciate you bein' here for ya mama." He said.

"Somebody gotta do it." I looked him dead in his eye.

"I deserve that." He said as he watched my mama come out the house.

"We'll be back." She said to him as she got in the car. I pulled off before he could say somethin' else.

"What was he talkin' about?" She asked.

"Shit." I said.

Paisley

"How was lunch with my sister?" He asked me as I flat ironed my hair.

"It went really good." I smiled. "I feel like I been knowin' her forever."

"She was cool about the whole situation?" He asked.

"Yea." I said. "She said she could relate to everything I was goin' through."

"What you mean?" He asked.

"She's been in my shoes before." I said. "Not technically, but she snapped a few times she said."

"I ain't surprised." He said. "That nigga she was with before was crazy as hell. Beat her ass too many times."

"Damn." I said. "That's fucked up. I'm glad she got outta that situation."

"Yea me too." He said. "And I'm glad you cleared that shit up too. I can't believe yo ass done went crazy on me."

We laughed together.

"It's yo fault." I smiled as I finished my hair. He walked up behind me as I unplugged my flat irons. I looked in the mirror to see him smilin' at me.

"What you smilin' at?"

"Nothin'." He laughed.

"How you think the meetin' went?" I asked.

"Good." He said. "I think it went really good. I wish you would come on so we can go see the place."

"Shut up." I said. "I had to finish my hair. I can't be out in public lookin' a mess."

"Shoulda just wore it curly." He said. "Ain't nobody got all day for you to straighten all that damn hair."

"Clearly you do 'cuz you waited on me to finish it." I said to him as I cleaned up my mess.

"Yea whatever." He said as he went back to the livin' room. "Just throw somethin' on so we can go."

"Don't rush me." I said as I walked into my bedroom. I threw on some clothes and went out to the livin' room. "I thought you was rollin' up."

"You really wana go meet this man high as hell?" He asked lookin at me.

"One blunt ain't gon' have me high as hell, babe." I laughed. "But I don't really wana smell like weed though."

"Right." He said. "We can wait til' we leave there."

He followed me out the door and we got in the car. As soon as I pulled off, my phone rung. I thought it was the realtor callin' me so I answered without even lookin' at it.

"Hello." I said.

"You have a collect call from: Valerie Tucker. An inmate at..." I hung up before the call could go any further. I had nothin' to say to my mother. And I damn sure didn't want hear anything she had to say.

"What happened?" He asked.

"My mom just called me." I said as I put my phone in my purse.

"You ain't even tryna make sure she okay?" He asked.

"Not really." I said. "Clearly she's still alive if she callin' me."

"Damn." He said. "You can't still be that mad at her. You ain't even hear her out. Maybe she had a good reason for keepin' him away from you."

"What reason could justify that?" I asked. "You can't even name one. How would you feel if Tasha kept yo kids away from you?"

"I would be mad as hell." He said. "But that don't mean I would want them to think any differently of her. Yo mom had her own selfish reasons for her to keep him away. You should at least find out if you can relate to those reasons."

"I already know I can't." I said. "Unless a man doin' somethin' to hurt the kids, it's no reason he shouldn't be able to see 'em. He helped make 'em so why can't he be involved in they life? You gon' take his money, but he can't see the kid he helpin' support? What kinda shit is that? Who does that? I mean I couldn't even see 'em once in a while. I'm just now meeting my father. For the first time in the 24 years I been alive, I met my father. How the hell that sound?"

"Fucked up." He said as I pulled up to the store.

"Exactly." I said as we got out the car.

We walked up to the building, got the keys from the realtor, and went inside. It had been months since I came to check on the place. What I didn't tell him was that I put down a deposit on it a while ago, so I knew it wasn't goin' nowhere. I was so close to leavin' The Spot. It felt so good to be standin' in my first jewelry store. I couldn't wait to fill it up with my own designs. Everything in here would be personally designed by me.

"Damn bae." He smiled as he walked around the place. "This a nice ass spot. And you downtown, right in the middle of everything."
"I know." I smiled. "I saw this place a while ago and knew I had to have it. I can't wait to get in here."
"I'm proud of you for makin' this shit happen." He smiled at me. "I mean a lotta people say they wana do shit, and never follow through. But you stuck it out and that's gon' make this shit feel even better once you get it started."
"It already feel good as hell." I couldn't stop smilin'.

I was so happy he liked the place. I felt like I did good pickin' this spot. He was the hardest person to please when it came to business. He wanted everything to be perfect. The fact that he loved my place immediately, without wantin' to fix anything, I felt so proud of myself.

"So..." He pulled me close to him. "I know you don't want me to keep askin' you about leavin The Spot, but this make shit real. Ain't you ready to walk away tonight?"
"I really am babe." I smiled. "I ain't gon' lie. I ain't even tryna go back in there tonight."
"You don't have to." He smiled. "I put the rest of the money you needed for payroll, in the account."

"What?" I asked. "No you didn't." I took my phone out my purse and opened my bank app to check my balance. When I started saving all this money, the only account I opened was specifically for the payroll money. Everything else I kept hidden. I logged on to see that it was way more than I had before. Not only did he put the rest of what I needed, he gave me enough for another year. "I can not believe you did that. I can't take all that money from you, babe."

"You don't have a choice." He said. "I'm not takin' it back. I know you could do this on yo own, and I love the fact that you makin' it happen with or without me. But I felt like I needed to do this for you."

"But you didn't." I smiled at him. "I was so close. All I had to do was finish out this month."

"You know I wanted to get you out The Spot as soon as possible." He said. "So gon' head and let the girls know, this shit gon' be up and runnin' in two weeks. You can give the realtor the money tomorrow and then start getting yo first collection made."

"Baby we ain't even heard back from John after the meetin'." I said. "This goin' kinda fast."

"I told you after the meetin' was over, this shit was gon' pick up." He said. "And ain't no time to slow down. It's a lot that gotta be done in two weeks."

"Oh my God!" I screamed. "This is not really happenin' right now!"

"It is bae." He laughed at me. "Now you gotta call some painters, look at some furniture. Get some lights and shit. You got a lotta shit left to do. You need all the time you can get to make it happen. I couldn't have you stressed out from workin' all night there, to the point where you was rushing getting things done here. So, take all this free time, and figure out exactly what you want in here. Yo sketches are done. All we gotta do is get them made up. So the hard part is over. Now it's just really getting this place ready for business."

I couldn't stop smilin' at him. He was really my superman. Even though I know I made everything happen, it was amazing for him to step in and save me like he did. He always did. I felt like I needed to do all this on my own, but then when he went ahead and helped me anyway, I felt so blessed to be his. He went out of his way to show me how much he cared about me. How much he believed in my dreams. I was fallin' in love with him all over again. Not because he helped me get this shit started, but because he made me feel comfortable with accepting his help.

Cassidy

I finished packin' everything up. My mom offered to come help me drive back home but I needed to be alone. It was a sad end to my sophomore year of college. I never imagined myself without Nicholas. I mean I know we're young, but he was it for me. For a while, I knew I wasn't it for him. A part of me wanted Jada to hurry up and get married so he would let that go. But then I realized he would never be over her. She held the number one spot in his life. And if she decided she wanted that back, he would give it to her, with no hesitation. That was beautiful. To have somebody so in love with you that no matter what you did, or how long it took, you would take them back in a heartbeat.

I wanted to go see Nicholas so bad before I left, but I knew it wouldn't benefit me at all. I'd show up expectin' him to be sad and beg me to stay, and he'd act as if I was botherin' him and wonder what was takin' me so long to leave. Once Nicholas made up his mind about somethin', he stuck to it. That was the hardest thing about him. If you wanted him to do the opposite of what you thought he was gon' do, you had to catch him before he made his decision. Otherwise, it was no getting around it.

I figured I would settle on just callin' him before I left town. I picked up my phone and dialed his number. It went straight to voicemail. My heart dropped. I definitely wasn't expectin' that. Now I felt like I had to go over there. I just couldn't do it though. It wasn't a smart decision for me.

And I decided that I was no longer young and dumb. It was time for me to grow up and make grown up decisions. And that included lettin' go of people, who never really held on to me.

"Hey lady." Laya said as she answered my phone call.

"Hey girl." I said quietly.

"What's wrong?" She asked. "You got everything packed up?"

"Yea." I said. "I just called Nicholas."

"And what happened?" She asked.

"Phone went to voicemail." I said. "Where you at? What's all that noise?"

"Girl I'm at my friend house getting my hair done." She said. "All her friends over here playin' music before they go out."

"Oh okay." I said. "I was getting ready to get on the road and I thought about seein' him before I left."

"You think that's a good idea?" She asked.

"No." I said. "That's why I talked myself out of it. I decided to call instead but couldn't get through."

"Well maybe that's for the best." She said. "You don't need nothin' to go down to make you change yo mind on getting away. Regardless of whether Nicholas chase you or not, you still need to clear yo head. And he do too. You can't go back on somethin' like this when it's so necessary. It's really the best thing for both of y'all right now."

"You are so right." I smiled. "That's why I called you. I knew you would make me feel better about the situation. Have you seen 'em since we broke up?"

"Nope." She said. I felt like she was lyin' but it was no way for me to know.

"Damn he ain't been over there?" I asked.

"Well Malcolm just went home yesterday to check on his mama." She said. "And before that we hadn't heard from 'em."

"Oh okay." I said. "Well maybe he just tryna keep busy or somethin'."

"Yea probably." She said. "Don't be sad goin' home either. This is really good for you. You should be excited!"

"I'm sure I will be once I get home and keep myself busy." I laughed.

"Well I'ma get ready to get outta here before it get too late."

"Okay girl." She said. "Be safe. Call me and check in while you on the road. Love you. Let me know when you make it home."

"Alright I will." I said. "Love you too, Laya."

"Alright bye girl." She said before we both hung up.

It was officially time for me to get outta this place. I would just have to leave without seein' or hearin' from Nicholas. He knew I was goin' home. And if he wanted to see or talk to me, he knew how to get in touch with me. Ever since we broke up, he made no contact with me at all. I hadn't contacted him until today, but I at least felt like he shoulda tried a lil' bit harder. He just gave up when I told him I think we should take a break.

I mean he was a lil' caught off guard, but he didn't fight me on it at all. I guess he really couldn't if I was tellin' him this was my decision. You can't make somebody stay with you, so I guess that's what he was thinkin'.

It didn't matter anymore. I was goin' home to get my mind back right, and I was hopin' he did the same while he was here. A little space never hurt nobody. If anything, I felt like it should help our situation. I just prayed that it wouldn't backfire and push him back into Jada's world.

Malcolm

"Ma, I'm getting ready to head out." I said to my mama.

"Already?" She asked. "You ain't been here no time."

"Yea I know but I gotta flight tomorrow morning from DC to Florida for Jada's wedding." I said.

"What?" She asked. "I thought she was waitin' until she graduated to marry that boy."

"Change of plans." I said.

"Nicholas know about it?" She asked.

"Yep." I said. "I don't know what his plan is, but I'm sure he ain't gon' let that shit happen." We laughed together.

My mom loved gossipin' about my friends. She was terrible when it came to keepin' secrets so I ain't tell her nothin' about Jada sneakin' out there to be with Nicholas this weekend.

"Okay baby well don't stay gone too long this time." She said as she hugged me. "And you keep me posted on that long road trip. I don't want you fallin' asleep or nothin'. Pull over if you gotta use the phone."

"Alright, Ma." I laughed as I walked outta her room. "Tell Kelly I'ma call her in a lil' bit. I tried to wait for her to get home so I could say bye, but that girl too damn busy."

"I know." She laughed. "I barely see her. But I'll tell her. Be careful boy."

"I will." I said as I walked out into the living room.

Marcus was out there ironing his clothes. I guess he was getting ready to go somewhere. Really didn't care where. I picked up my duffel bag and left out the house.

"So that's it, huh?" He asked as he followed me out the house.

This shit was getting old. He acted like he couldn't say nothin' until my back was turned to him. He always wanted to follow me out to the car. I couldn't understand what the point of all that was. I decided to act like I ain't hear him. I needed to hurry up and get on the road and I ain't really have the patience for his bull shit. I got in the car and started it. When I looked up to make sure nobody was comin' down the street, he was leaning in my driver's side window.

"What?" I asked him.
"You ain't hear me?" He asked.
"Naw what you say?" I asked.
"I said I guess that's it." He repeated.
"Oh yea." I said. "Got some shit I gotta take care of."
"So when you comin' back?" He asked.
"I don't know yet." I said.
"Me and yo mom was thinkin' 'bout takin' a trip out there to come see you." He said.
"She got my number." I said.

I switched the gear from park to drive. He moved back from the car and I pulled out of the driveway. Once I got on the freeway I called Laya to let her know I was on my way back.

"Hey bae." She said as she answered my call. "How was it?"

"It went better than I thought it would." I said.

"Did you get a chance to hear him out?" She asked.

"Didn't give 'em that chance." I said. "That ain't what I went there for. You know that."

"I just assumed since you were there you would handle that." She said.

"You assumed wrong." I said. "I don't feel like I hate 'em no more. I actually spoke to 'em. When he said somethin' to me I replied."

"Really Malcolm?" She asked. "You went all the way out there to act like the man don't even exist?"

"He don't exist." I said. "At least not in my world. I don't care if he a part of hers 'cuz I told her what I needed to tell her."

"And what was that?" She asked.

"I just told her to pay attention this time." I said. "Just 'cuz the man might be dying, don't mean you let him take advantage of you. She said she would. Told me she had her valuables tucked away. So I can respect that."

"Wow." She said. "Sound like the trip was somewhat successful. Did you talk to Kelly about him?"

"Yea I talked to her a lil' bit the first night I was there." I said. "She said she don't trust 'em. And I told her she shouldn't. She said she was watchin' him to make sure he ain't do nothin' crazy."

"Oh my God." She laughed. "Y'all are both terrible."

"What you mean?" I laughed. "Somebody gotta look out for her when I ain't there. For the both of 'em. And Kelly understand that. I trust her not to let no bull shit happen either."

"I can't believe how mean y'all bein' to this man." She said.

"Kelly ain't bein' mean." I said. "She at least actin' like she like 'em. She said she doin' that so he can trust her. So she'll know if he tryna scheme or not. Now me, I ain't necessarily bein' mean. Honestly I felt like I was bein' nice when I actually responded to his questions."

"What kinda questions?" She asked.

"Just general questions." I said. "Nothin' major. Just know that I didn't go there to piss him off. But if it happened, I wasn't apologizin' for it."

"Malcolm, I know you ain't start no shit with that man." She said.

"Not at all." I laughed. "I told you it went better than I thought it would. When I walked in and seen him sittin' up on the couch, in the house that I paid off, I wanted to kill that nigga. Instead of beating his ass, I just went straight back to my mama room and she calmed me down a lil' bit. She actually smoked with me too."

"What?" She laughed. "Now I can't believe that."

"Yup." I laughed. "You know she was goin' through somethin' to wana smoke with me. And she asked me herself. No beating around the bush or nothin' just came right out and asked me."

"Damn." She laughed. "I wish I coulda been there for that. How many blunts y'all smoke?"

"4." I laughed.

"Malcolm why you get yo mama that high?" She laughed.

"I was higher than her." I said. "She wanted to keep smokin' but I just couldn't. It wasn't no tellin' where the conversation woulda went if we kept smokin'."

"Yea that woulda been crazy." She laughed. "Well I'm glad it wasn't a complete disaster. I just knew I was gon' have to come bail yo ass outta jail this weekend. But I'm glad you played it smart. You might actually be growin' up a lil' bit babe."

"Shut up." I laughed. "I been grown as hell."

"Yea whatever." She said. "You just now getting on the road?"

"Yea." I said.

"Okay." She said. "I'ma call you in a lil' bit to check on you. Be careful babe. Love you."

"Alright." I said. "Love you too bae." Before we hung up.

Paisley

It was official. I now owned my own jewelry store. I was done workin' at The Spot and all my girls were excited about comin' to work with me. The 'Diamonds by P' sign was finally up and we were ready for business. I had the grand opening coming up this weekend and I was so excited about it. I invited my dad and his wife, and my brothers' and their families to the grand opening. Everybody said they were comin'. I even invited his sister since we hit it off so well. I wanted the night to be full of laughs and good company. I knew that would definitely happen with all the people I invited.

I walked around the store amazed at everything I made happen. Especially so fast. I was so proud of myself. I knew this would happen but it just seemed like it happened over night. I had been workin' and savin' on it for only 2 years. So that really ain't take long at all. I was just glad I was done dancing and my man was done whinin' about it. I was happy to have my own business that would be filled with all of my own designs. And I did it all without goin' to college. I wanted to go to college when I graduated from high school. But the world just took me in a different direction. It was times where I felt like a bum 'cuz I wasn't makin' nothin' happen. But those days were over. I was getting ready to start makin' a very successful life for myself and I couldn't wait to see what it was gon' bring for me and my man.

I went to the back to admire my office. It was beautiful. I painted the walls a bright orange and all of my furniture was white. The room looked amazing to me. I sat in the chair and spun around in it like a lil' kid until I heard someone knockin' on the door. I pulled up the cameras on my computer to see who was standin' out there. It was a delivery man. With flowers. I smiled as I walked to the front door.

"Hello." I smiled at him as I unlocked the door. I didn't want to let him in. "Hi I have a delivery for Paisley Tucker." He said as he handed me the flowers and then a box of chocolates.
"Thank you." I smiled as I signed for it.

I closed the door back and locked it. I put the flowers down and read the card:

> You did it baby!!! I can't tell you how proud I am of you, girl! You did exactly what you said you was gon' do, even sooner than you planned. I can't wait to come celebrate with you! Love you to the moon and back, P.
>
> Love Lo

She was such a good best friend. She always knew how to make me cry. My eyes started to water as I opened the chocolates. They got huge when I realized it was not candy in the holes. She put weed in every single slot. She knew me so well. I took some out and rolled a blunt. As soon as I walked to the back to light it, the flower boy was back. I thought it was kinda weird, but he had more flowers with him. And a whole crew behind him carrying flowers. I ain't know what was goin' on, but if it was more chocolate weed they had with 'em, I would be high all the way til' next month.

I opened the door and let them in. They brought in 50 dozen roses and sat them all out on the counters. It smelled amazing once they left and looked even more beautiful than before. I took out the card to see what she coulda wrote in this one:

> *You the best thing that ever happened to me. I tell you this all the time but I don't think you really understand. I know you in the store tryna take it all in. I'm so proud of you for sticking to this bae. And thank you for lettin' me help you even though you ain't need it. I love you more than anything in this world, Paisley. Hurry up and get to the restaurant 'cuz you always late.*
>
> *Yo man*

Oh my God I really thought all these were from London again. He was the biggest sweetheart I ever met. What in the hell was I gon' do with this man? He made me feel so special and lucky to have him. I had to do everything in my power to make sure he felt the same way.

First, I had to hurry up and get to the restaurant. I was supposed to meet him for lunch like 30 minutes ago. I completely forgot when the first flower boy came. I ran to the back, grabbed my purse, locked up, hopped in the car and lit my blunt.

Laya

"So what you thinkin'?" I asked Nicholas as he sat on the couch. He was waitin' on me and Malcolm to finish getting ready so he could take us to the airport.

"I don't know." Nicholas said. "Why she have to leave again?"

"She gotta make shit right." I said. "You know her. I really wish you would come."

"I can't see that shit, Laya." He said.

"I don't think it's anything for you to worry about." I smiled. "She know exactly what she wana do."

"I do too." He said. "But is she gon' do it, is my question?"'

"That's why you need to come with us." I smiled. "It's another flight in two hours that will get you there right on time. Drop us off. Go home. Put on yo best suit and come get yo woman. You makin' it harder than it gotta be."

"Really?" He asked. "I thought I was makin' this as easy as possible on her."

"You were when she was here." I said. "Now that she out there tryna figure her shit out, you gotta figure yours out too."

"I just don't wana get out there and she go through with it." He said. "That's what I'm worried about."

"As long as you get out there and show her that you still there for her no matter what, I know she ain't gon' go through with it." I smiled at him.

"What the hell y'all talkin about?" Malcolm asked as he came out the bedroom.

"He nervous 'cuz he think Jada gon' marry 'em." I said as he sat down next to me.

"Nigga you know damn well she ain't marryin' that nigga." Malcolm said.

"So you need to just come on and go with us so you can bring her ass back."

"It ain't that simple." Nicholas said.

"It really is." Malcolm said.

"He comin' out on the next flight." I smiled. "He gotta go home and get dressed up for the occasion."

"Don't have me out there waitin' on you, and yo ass don't show up." Malcolm said.

"Shut up." Nicholas laughed. "Come on before y'all miss the flight."

We all hopped in Nicholas' car and headed to the airport.

"Okay hurry up and get dressed so you can get there on time." I smiled at him as we got out the car. "Thanks Nicholas."

"No problem." He said as we walked towards the door.

"Hurry up nigga." Malcolm yelled as we got to the door.

"Alright." Nicholas laughed before he pulled off.

"You think he gon' come?" I asked Malcolm as we checked in.

"Yea." He said. "He'll be there."

Nina

"I'm so glad you made it." Jessica (Jada's mom) said to me as she hugged me.

"Me too." I smiled at her. "Should I be sayin' the same thing about you?"

"Girl come outside with me for a minute." She said as she grabbed my hand. She led me outside the church. "I ain't want nobody to hear our conversation in there."

"You mean Carter's mom?" I smiled.

"Girl I talked to her when I finally decided I was actually gon' show my face here." She said. "You know she planned all this. I told her she know damn well them kids needed to wait. I don't care if they stayed engaged forever. Jada is not gon' be focused on finishing school if she tryna play housewife to that boy."

"That's true." I said. "Have you talked to Jada about it?"

"Too many times." She said. "I wanted to strangle her ass. She just think she know everything."

"They all do." I laughed.

"I just hope she come to her senses before it's too late." She said. "Is Nicholas here?"

"No." I said quietly. "I don't know if he comin'."

"Please get him out here girl." She said. "He the only one who can talk some sense into my child."

"I called him when I got here but his phone was goin' to voicemail." I said.

"I'ma talk to Malcolm and see if he talked to 'em before they left."

"If she was marryin' him I could deal with that." She said. "At least he could keep her head on straight."

"Yea it do seem like they help each other focus." I said. "So she wanted them to move to wedding up?"

"I know she had somethin' to do with it." She said. "But I think he wanted it too. I know Jada ain't really wana do it so soon. Cuz when I asked her why, she ain't have no reason. She couldn't even think of somethin' just to shut me up. She ain't ready for this at all. I don't even think she want this no more."

"I was tryna find her to talk to her." I said. "See how she feelin' about everything."

"Girl she ain't even here yet." She said. "She should be here getting ready."

"Well maybe she getting ready at home." I said.

"Nope." She said. "Everything here. Her dress. Make up artists. Hairdresser. The hair style she wanted is gon' take at least 2 hours with all the hair she got. The wedding start in 4 hours."

"You don't think she just coulda changed her hairstyle?" I asked.

"Not at all." She said. "I been callin' her all morning. And her phone goin' to voicemail."

"Have you seen Carter?" I asked.

"Yea he here." She said. "Nervous as hell cuz ain't nobody seen her."

"Damn." I said. "I can't believe he ain't even talked to her."

"Nope." She said. "This is crazy."

"Come on let's go find Laya and see if she seen her." I said as we walked back in the church.

We went to the room where the bridesmaids were getting dressed and Laya was in there getting her hair done.

"Hey beautiful." I kissed Laya on her cheek.
"Hey Ms. Nina." She smiled at me. "How y'all doin'?"
"I'm worried." Jessica said. "Have you talked to Jada?"
"Um..." She hesitated. "Have you? She should be around here somewhere."

It was obvious Laya was tryna cover for Jada.

"She ain't nowhere to be found." Jessica said. "You ain't heard from her at all?"
"Not lately..." She said still tryin' to cover for her.
"What is lately, Laya?" I asked her.
"Um..." She hesitated again. "Recently."
"You tell her, whenever you talk to her again, that she need to call me." Jessica said. "And that means, in the next 30 minutes if she don't show up."
"Okay." Laya smiled at us.
"I don't know what's goin' on." Jessica said to me as we left out of the room.

"Me either." I said.

"But we damn sure gon' find out." She finished.

Paisley

The night was finally here. My grand opening party was amazing. It was people everywhere. The photographer was getting so many good shots. My dad and his wife were here. My brother's were on their way. His sister was on her way. Lo and Isaiah were here with their friends. So many people came out to celebrate with me. All the girls I took from the club were here. It was a great turn out. The DJ was playin' a great mix of songs. I was on cloud 9, literally. And this time, I didn't even smoke. I grabbed another glass of champagne and headed to the stage.

"Hey everybody." I smiled at the crowd. "I just wanted to thank y'all for comin' out to celebrate with me. This store has been my dream since I was a kid. And tonight it finally came true. I'm so glad I got to share this night with y'all. I hope y'all come back tomorrow and spend all ya money."

Everybody laughed at me. As I was getting ready to wrap up my toast and let people get back to the party, I noticed Tonya walk in. With Jermaine. I knew my eyes got big, but I instantly blocked all distractions. I knew I had to hurry up and finish this so I could get them two outta here.

"Well y'all keep enjoyin' y'all self. It's still an open bar. Champagne is goin' around. Appetizers too. Thanks guys." I smiled before I walked off the stage.

I zipped through the crowd and went straight to my man.

"What's wrong?" He looked at me and instantly knew somethin' wasn't right.

"I gotta major problem." I said quietly. "Stay here for a minute. I'll be right back."

I walked over to Tonya and Jermaine who conveniently made their way to the open bar.

"Who invited you?" I asked Tonya. I had no need to even address Jermaine. I knew she set all this shit up.

"I overheard the girls talkin' about it." She smiled. "Figured you forgot to send me an invitation."

"I didn't forget." I said. "You know I didn't. So let's cut the small talk, and I'll let y'all leave here peacefully."

"Let?" She asked. "Peaches I'm a grown ass woman. Ain't nobody lettin' me do shit. I move on my own."

"My name is Paisley." I smiled. "I left Peaches at The Spot. Same place I thought I left you."

"Funny how a bitch stop dancing and all of a sudden she somebody else." She laughed to Jermaine. He laughed with her.

"I got yo bitch, Tonya." I said. "This the last time I'ma ask you and yo lil' friend here, to leave."

"He got a name." She smiled. "I'm sure you know it pretty well."

"I don't give a damn." I said quietly. "You need to get the hell outta my place. Now!"

"What's goin' on here?" I heard my man ask from behind me.

"I got it bae." I turned around and smiled at him. I turned back around to face Tonya. "We can do this the easy way, or I can have you shown out. The choice is yours."

"Ain't nobody showing me shit." She snapped. "I know how to get outta here my damn self." She slammed her drink down on the bar. She stood up and Jermaine did too.

"Let me show y'all out." He said.

I turned around to him.

"Be cool." I said quietly to him.

"I got it." He smiled at me as he headed towards the door.

Surprisingly, they followed him. Once they were out of the building, he came back over to me.

"What the hell was that about?" He asked.

"Some girl I got into it with at The Spot a while ago." I said.

"So what she come here for?" He asked.

"Same thing I'm tryna figure out." I said. "And she was with my ex."

"What the hell?" He asked. "Somethin' I need to know?"

"You will." I said. "But not right now. I promise I'ma tell you everything when we leave here. I don't want nobody overhearing anything I say."

"Don't have me beatin' no nigga ass." He said.

"Bae I swear it ain't like that." I smiled at him. "Now calm down. And go get another drink to make you feel better." I laughed as he shook his head at me.

"I'll be back." He laughed and walked over to the bar.

I walked over to Lo and pulled her back into my office. I closed the door and made sure I locked it.

"Did you see Tonya come in here with Jermaine?" I whispered.

Even though the door was locked, I ain't know who coulda been out there listenin'.

"Girl yes." She said quietly. "I was watchin' y'all the whole time you was talkin' to em. What the fuck is her problem?"

"I don't know." I said. "But I'm tired of her shit. I wouldn't give a damn if she wasn't with Jermaine. He the problem. Lo I can't deal with this shit. As long as it's been since I was with him, why is he poppin' back up now?"

"P calm down." She said. "Tonight is yo night. We ain't lettin' nobody fuck that up. Now you know you gon' have to tell 'em about everything 'cuz he gon' be involved if some shit go down. We can handle both of 'em, but you still gotta tell him somethin'."

"I know." I said. "I'm tellin 'em when we leave. I just don't know what the hell Jermaine want from me."

"Don't worry about it tonight." She said. "We can go pay 'em a visit tomorrow if you want, but right now, we celebrating 'Diamonds by P'." She smiled at me.

"Okay." I laughed at her.

My best friend was the shit. She knew just what to say to get me back on track. She took my hand and led me back out to the store. I put on my happy face and eventually was right back in my good mood. She was right. This was my night, and I wasn't lettin' nobody take that away from me. Tonya and Jermaine would definitely be handled tomorrow. No more waitin' on they ass to show up. Clearly they wasn't goin' away, so it was time for me to give 'em a reason to.

I was so happy when I saw my brothers finally made it.

"Hi!" I squealed when I saw them.

I hugged them both so tight.

"Hey how are you?" Jamal asked me.

"I am great." I smiled at them.

"Paisley, this is my wife Stacey." Jamal introduced us. "Stacey, this our sister Paisley."

I hugged her.

"This is a really nice place, girl." Stacey said as she smiled. "And a real good turnout."

"Thank you." I smiled at her.

"Paisley I'm sorry my wife Nina couldn't make it." Trevor said. "She outta town for a wedding."

"Aw that's okay." I said. "Will she be back tomorrow to get some shoppin' done?"

"Yea she should." Trevor said.

"What's up y'all?" My man asked. "See y'all met my lady."

"Wait." Trevor said. "Paisley, you datin' Kane?"

"Yea." I smiled. "How y'all know each other?"

"Nina is his sister." Trevor said.

"Aw I just met his sister the other day." I smiled. "We had lunch together."

"Damn." Jamal said. "This world just keep getting smaller."

"Babe these are my brothers." I smiled.

"That's crazy." Kane said.

Everybody laughed so hard when we realized how crazy this situation was. In a way, I felt weird, datin' my step-sister-in-law's brother, but it was no way I was lettin' Kane go. And by the way he looked at me tonight, I knew he felt the same.

"Okay well we gon' get some drinks." Stacey said as she grabbed my hand.

"I can't believe how we all connected." I said to Stacey as we got to the bar.

"I know me either." She said. "It's cool though. Welcome to the crazy family boo."

"Aw thank you." I smiled. "I'm so glad you came."

"Me too." Stacey said as she grabbed a glass of champagne. "So are you gon' be openin' up tomorrow?"

"Yup." I smiled. "Ten o'clock sharp."

"Good 'cuz I see a lot of stuff in here that I need to get before anybody else do." She laughed. "Did you design all this stuff yourself?"

"Every piece in here." I smiled. "I had these designs done for about two years now. I been wantin' to wait til' I could get it all done at once. Buying the place. Paying my girls. Getting my designs made. It all came together really good, and really fast once we got it started."

"That's so good, Paisley." Stacey smiled. "I'm so happy for you."

"Thank you." I smiled. "I think my dad getting ready to leave so I'ma go say bye to him. Y'all keep drinkin' and I'ma be back to check on y'all."

"Alright girl." Stacey said as I walked over towards my dad.

"So what you think about everything?" I asked him. "Anything you like?"

"Everything is really nice, Paisley." He smiled. "I'm really proud of you."

"Aw thank you." I hugged him. "Lisa, you see somethin' you gotta have?"

"A few things." Lisa replied. "We gon' be in town for a few more days so I'm definitely comin' back tomorrow to pick up some things."

"Well I will be here to take care of you." I smiled and hugged her. "Thank y'all for comin' out. I really appreciate it."

"You welcome." Lisa smiled at me. "We gon' get outta here. But I'll be back to see you tomorrow. Maybe around 12. I think I'ma come with Nina if she back."

"Alright." I said. "Well I'm lookin' forward to it."

"Okay." My dad said. "You make sure you be careful getting outta here tonight."

"I will." I smiled at him and kissed his cheek. "Let me know when y'all make it in."

"Alright." He said. "We'll see you later." He said before they headed towards the door.

The party was startin to clear out. I made sure to catch up with everyone before they left. Everybody there told me they would be back tomorrow. I couldn't wait to see who showed up. Once everybody was gone, Kane pulled me back to the office. I was startin' to sober up so I knew he wanted to talk about Tonya and Jermaine. He closed and locked my office door and sat on the edge of my desk.

"You ready to go?" I asked him as I stood in front of him.

He put his arms around my waist and smiled at me.

"What you smilin' at?"

"You." He said. "You look amazing."

"Aw thanks babe." I laughed as I started blushing. He still gave me butterflies.

"I love how you handled everything tonight." He smiled.

"I did better than I thought I would." I laughed.

"I'm so proud of you." He said. "You ain't let nobody take away from yo night. Shit coulda got crazy but you ain't take it there. You really growin' up babe."

"Shut up." I laughed at him. "Thank you for bein' here for me tonight."

"I wouldn't be anywhere else." He smiled. "You made this shit happen and I'm just glad I got to see it. I love yo ambition, P. And I mean that shit."

"Bae are you drunk?" I asked him lookin' in his eyes. He was so drunk. I knew it was somethin' with him just getting all emotional on me.

"I ain't drunk." He laughed as he pulled me into him.

"Babe I smell every type of liquor from the bar, on yo breath." I laughed at him. I held his face in my hands and lifted it up so he could look me in my eye. "What's wrong? Why was you drinkin' so much?"

"Ain't shit wrong." He smiled. "I just wanted to celebrate with you. You was drunk too. I can't get drunk."

"I didn't say that." I laughed at him. "Who drivin' us home?"

"You should be a lil' sober by now." He laughed.

"Oh my God!" I wrapped my arms around his neck. "You are a mess."

"Yea whatever." He laughed as he stared at me.

"You look good tonight, babe." I smiled and stared at him.

He was so handsome. It felt so crazy to be here with him. All to myself. No worries. My man was here to stay. The fact that he wanted to help me with this, and not just do it for me, just showed me that he was really on my team.

"Thank you." He smiled.

I leaned my head back as he kissed my neck. My grip around his neck got tighter as he started hittin' all my spots. He ran his hand up my back and unhooked my bra. He lifted up my skirt. His hands found the way to my breasts anxiously. Next thing I know my man had me all over the room. I was so glad that it wasn't any houses next to the store 'cuz I'm sure everybody on that block woulda heard me.

We damn near fell asleep in the office once we were done. Once we got dressed, we were both completely sober. All I wanted to do was roll a blunt after that work out I just had. And he just couldn't stop smilin' at me. Clearly, I just did everything right.

"Now you know we gotta talk about this shit." He said as we walked out of the office.
"Yea I know." I said quietly as I locked my office door. "It's a lotta shit you don't know about me, babe. I just hope when I tell you this, you don't wana leave me."

"Ain't shit you can say to me to make me leave you." He said. "I don't know how many times I gotta tell you that for you to believe me."

I locked the front door of the store, and we got in the car.

"Long story short, some of the money I saved for the store, was money I took from a few of my exes." I said as we pulled off.
"What?" He looked at me. "Paisley, I don't need all the details 'cuz I ain't tryna be paranoid about us."
"Bae this a completely different thing between you and me." I said. "You gotta know that. I wouldn't be this deep in, if it wasn't."
"I know." He said. "So basically, the guy Tonya showed up with, is somebody you fucked over?"
"Yea." I said.

I was so happy he ain't make me explain everything. I was so embarrassed to tell him anything bad about my life. The last thing I wanted him to think was that our relationship was one of my schemes. Kane was my better half. I could never let that go.

"Alright." He said. "Well let's just go handle it tomorrow."
"What you mean?" I asked.
"This ain't the first time they been on bull shit." He said. "So, we need to go to them and see what is they want."
"Bae, I ain't givin' them a dime." I said. "Especially Tonya ratchet ass."

"We ain't givin' up shit, P." He said. "We just gon' go take care of it. Tell London I got it. She ain't gotta help you with this one. I can take care of this one on my own."

"I'll call Lo off but I'm goin' with you, regardless." I said.

"You really wana do that?" He asked.

"I don't have a choice." I said. "This my mess. So, I gotta make sure it's taken care of."

"Oh so now you don't trust me to handle it?" He smiled.

"Babe you know that ain't it." I said. "I just can't have you doin' nothin' crazy 'cuz of my bull shit."

"Yea okay." He laughed. "That's what I thought."

"Boy shut up." I said. "Why you ain't tell me my brother married to yo sister? Now I feel weird bein' with you."

"How was I supposed to know?" He asked. "You just found out you even had brothers."

"Em hum." I laughed. "What you think of my dad?"

"He cool as hell." He laughed. "I been knowin' Joe for a while though. I met everybody at they wedding. Every time they come in town I see him and Lisa."

"Aw that's good." I smiled. "I can't wait to get the day started tomorrow."

"I know you can't." He smiled. "What time you goin' in?"

"Probably like 8:30 since I gotta straighten up my office, thanks to you." I laughed.

"Don't blame that shit on me." He said. "Yo ass was into that shit too."

"Whatever." I laughed. "But yea I'ma go in at 8:30. Lo said she gon' come in around 9. Then I got the girls comin' in at 9:30."

"Damn." He smiled. "First day runnin' yo own business tomorrow. You nervous?"

"Not at all." I smiled. "I'm anxious as hell. You comin' in with me in the morning?"

"You know I gotta work." He said.

"I thought you was takin' the day off." I whined.

"I ain't say that." He laughed. "I'll be there for lunch though."

"You gon' stay after lunch til' we close?" I asked.

"Paisley, I still gotta work everyday." He laughed at me.

"I know but it's my first day, babe." I whined. "And I really want you to be there!"

"You gon' have Lo and the girls there with you all day, babe." He said.

"I'ma come for lunch and see if I can get the rest of my work done there after that. Is that cool with you?"

"Yes." I smiled and kissed his cheek. "Thank you, baby."

"Yo ass too damn spoiled." He laughed.

"It's all yo fault." I laughed at him as we pulled up at my house.

Jada

"We need to talk." I said to Carter quietly.

I had been lookin' all over for him once I got to the church. The wedding was supposed to start in an hour and I wasn't even dressed. No make up was done and my hair was up in a messy bun.

"Bae I ain't supposed to see you before the wedding." He said. "What's wrong? Why you ain't dressed?"

"Cuz I need to talk to you." I said. "If I'm gon' go through with this, I gotta be honest with you."

"Jada, I already know what you bouta say." He said.

"You do?" I asked confused.

"You been missin' for the last 3 days." He said. "I think I know where you been. You needed to get yo revenge for the shit I did. I can't blame you. I'm just glad you got it out yo system before we got married."

"What?" I asked.

I looked at him like he was on crazy. That statement he just made, made me think he really was.

"We don't need to talk about this, babe." He said. "I get it. It's over. Let's just make it official."

I was speechless. I ain't know what else to say. I felt like I needed to say more, but he really just shut me up. I ain't know how I felt about that. I left out of his room. Went to mine and put on my dress. I stood in the mirror for at least 30 minutes starin' at myself. I looked a mess. And I felt even worse. All I kept thinkin' about was Nicholas. I missed him so much and I just left him hours ago. I heard a knock at the door and hoped it was him. When I turned around I saw my mom and Nicholas' mom come through my door.

"I should slap you for havin' me runnin' around worryin' about you." My mom said as she walked up to me.

"Your dress is beautiful baby." Nicholas' mom Nina smiled at me.

"I know I look a mess." I said quietly.

"Where is yo make up?" My mom asked. "Why yo hair ain't done?"

"I had a rough mornin'." I said.

I took my bun out and brushed my hair. I decided to just wear it straight since I really ain't have time for nothin' else.

"You really gon' go out there lookin' like that?" My mom asked.

"Why not?" I asked as I turned back around to look in the mirror. "Ain't nobody out there for me to impress."

"Yo fiancee is." She said. "This yo wedding day. You should wana look beautiful for yourself if not for yo man."

"You sure you wana do this?" Nina asked.

"Why you say that?" I asked.

"Look at you." Nina said. "You look like it's somewhere else you'd rather be."

"I don't know." I said. "You talked to Nicholas?"

"Not today." Nina said. "Is that what you waitin' on? You need to talk to him first?"

"I don't know." I said. "Can you find Laya and have her come in here. I just need a minute with her."

"Well don't take all day baby." My mom said. "You got a lotta people out here waitin' on you."

"I know." I said. "Thanks for comin', Ma. You too Nina."

"You welcome baby." Nina said. "Don't look so sad. It's yo wedding day."

I sat in the chair once they left out the room. I never took my eyes off the mirror. A few minutes later, Laya walked in.

"What's wrong?" She asked.

She sounded concerned, but she was smiling. She didn't look worried at all.

"What the hell am I doin'?" I asked her as my eyes started to water.

"Aw no don't cry!" She said. "Yo makeup gon'... you don't have no make up on?"

"No." I said as I wiped my eyes.

"J don't do this to yourself." She said as she gave me another tissue. "You really gon' go through with this when it's obvious it ain't what you want?"

"I really don't know Laya." I cried. "I just miss Nicholas so much."

Paisley

My first day at the store was amazing. I made damn near $100,000 in one day. My first day at that. I was so excited. I ain't know what to do with myself. It just sucked that I had to go take care of business once work was over. All I wanted to do was go home and make love to my man. But we had somethin' to tend to.

I called Tonya earlier and told her I was comin' by to clear this shit up when I got off. Told her to make sure Jermaine was there, so I could kill two birds with one stone. We pulled up to her apartment, got out and went to the door. I rung the buzzer and called her. She took forever to open the door. I ain't like that. She finally came to the door with an attitude. We went in and sat down.

"So look, let's get to the point." I said before anybody could start any bull shit ass small talk. "What the fuck do y'all want?"
"Maybe we should talk in private, Paisley." Jermaine smiled at me.
"Jermaine, in case you didn't know, this is my man Kane." I smiled at him.
"It ain't shit you can say to me, that you can't say in front of him. So what is it?"
"Well since you took all my money, I feel like I need a percentage of the store." Jermaine said. "I mean I know some of my money went into getting that shit started."

"Okay." I said. "One, you don't know shit about what it took to get MY store started. Two, it's gon' be a cold day in hell before you get a dime outta me. Yea I fucked you over. My bad. But that's in the past. You wait all this time to try to get somethin' outta me?"

"Jermaine and I were dating before you got to 'em." Tonya said.

"I don't give a fuck." I said.

"Some of that money you took from him, I gave to him to help him re-up." She said. "So therefore, my money was involved too. We both want a fair share of the store, or we go to the police."

"Go to the police and tell them what?" I asked. "I took yo drug money. Y'all can't be serious. I know you ain't wastin' my time with this bull shit."

"We already have our shit in order to go to them and keep us out of it." She said. "The choice is up to you, Peaches."

"I said what I had to say." I said. "I worked my ass off to get that store. Literally. Ain't nobody takin' nothin' from it if I don't feel they deserve it. Y'all sorry asses better get back to ya day job 'cuz I can't help y'all there."

"You sure that's what you wana do?" Jermaine asked as he pulled out his gun.

"She sure." Kane said as he pulled out his.

Jermaine's eyes got big. He seemed really surprised that we came prepared.

"We can just call it even." Jermaine said. "Good luck with everything, Paisley."

"Fuck y'all." I said as we got up and headed out the apartment. We got in the car and pulled off.

Kane took his phone out his pocket and made a phone call.

"Go head and handle that for me." He said once he got an answer.

Two seconds later, he hung up the phone. He grabbed my hand and smiled at me.

"Told you I would take care of it." He said.
"I can't believe you ain't beat his ass when he asked to talk in private." I said. "What kinda bull shit was his ass on?"
"I don't know." He said. "It's taken care of. Don't worry about it."
"Thank you, baby." I smiled and kissed him.

Twenty minutes later as we headed towards his house, we passed a speeding ambulance goin' the direction we just came from. I wondered where they were headed.

Jada

The music started playin' and I damn near fainted. Carter had so much faith in us. Why didn't I have any? My mind was stuck on Nicholas. I couldn't get it to focus on Carter even when I tried. I felt so terrible. Here I was getting ready to marry a man, that I wasn't even in love with anymore. I had been lookin' for that love since he cheated on me. I thought it would come back, but it just never felt the same.

My body was movin' towards him and the minister, but I felt like I wasn't inside of it. I felt like I was floating. Somethin' else was movin' me closer to Carter, 'cuz I was definitely not doin' it on my own.

I finally met him at the alter and the minister started talking. I completely tuned out everything he was saying. All I thought about was the weekend I spent with Nicholas. I couldn't do this to him. I was here lettin' somebody else think I wanted to spend my life with him, when all I wanted to do was wake up to Nicholas every morning. But I felt terrible 'cuz I wasn't really sure if I tried everything to make things work with me and Carter. I snapped back into reality when the minister tapped me.

"Paisley, are you okay?" He asked me.

I hesitated for a minute. I ain't really know how to answer that.

"Yea." Was all I could say.

I looked straight ahead at Carter and knew he was not the man for me. Was it too late for me to change my mind? I couldn't embarrass him in front of his family and friends. Maybe I should just go through with it and get it annulled in the morning. That was much better than humiliating him in front of all these people that came from all over the world. Especially his mother.

"Jada, do you take Carter to be your husband? To have and to hold? In sickness and in health? For richer or poorer? Til death do you part?" I heard the minister ask me.

I didn't want to agree to any of that, but I had to spare him. Before I could lie and say I do, I heard the doors open. It was my man. Nicholas came for me.

"J you can't do this." Nicholas said as he walked towards me. "I can't let you."
"What the fuck?" Carter snapped.

My mom and his mom both looked like they wanted to cry. They were smiling so hard. Carter's mom looked like she wanted to beat my ass.

"We been through too much to let it end like this, baby." Nicholas said as he stood in front of me. "You know that. We all know that."

I was speechless. Again. I wanted to leap into his arms and let him take me away. But how did I do that without hurtin' Carter? I was tired of thinkin' about everybody else's feelings before mine. Today was about me, so I was really gon' make it about me. If I decided to stay with Carter, or leave with Nicholas, it was my decision to make.

"What you gon do, Jada?" Carter asked me after a while of silence.
"J it ain't nobody else for me but you." Nicholas said. "Don't throw that away. We always come back to each other 'cuz we can't let go. It's meant to be. Just stop fightin' it. If this was meant to work with you and him you wouldn't be rushing this damn wedding. Everybody in here know you ain't ready for this. Especially if you ain't marryin' me. Jada, I need you. Come home with me."
"Jada, you have to make a decision." The minister said.

I stared at Nicholas and my heart smiled. I looked to Carter and all I saw was anger. Nicholas had been holdin' my hands since he approached me. I took them out of Carter's and gave it to him without even a second thought.

"I'm sorry." I said to him. "I just can't do this anymore."

471

Courtney Beeman graduated from Central State University in 2013 with a Bachelor's Degree in English Literature. *Let The Chips Fall Where They May* is the final installment of a four-part series. She is also the creator of Built To Last Publishing LLC.

Lightning Source UK Ltd.
Milton Keynes UK
UKHW030617221220
375642UK00005B/136